MAGGIE BF

By

George Donald

Also by George Donald

Billy's Run
Charlie's Promise
A Question of Balance
Natural Justice
Logan
A Ripple of Murder
A Forgotten Murder
The Seed of Fear
The Knicker-knocker
The Cornishman
A Presumption of Murder
A Straight Forward Theft
The Medal
A Decent Wee Man
Charlie's Dilemma
The Second Agenda
Though the Brightest Fell
The ADAT
A Loan with Patsy
A Thread of Murder
Harry's Back
Charlie's Recall
The Broken Woman
Mavisbank Quay

PROLOGUE

Nobody knows what it's like to lose a child unless, God forbid, you have gone through the pain yourself.

I mean, it's soul destroying when the child is taken from you, whether it's your own wean or your grandchild.

No, that's not right.

You don't have to be a parent or a grandparent to feel the loss. Brothers, sisters, aunties, uncles, friends. Anybody who knows a child who's died feels the loss.

You see it's just not right that a child dies before the parent. Not right at all.

And I do know what's it's like because on that day of the funeral I remember that the church was packed out and I didn't even know most of the folk that were there for the wee one's funeral.

Not that I was paying much attention to the faces or what was going on round about me.

No, I was too heartbroken for that.

Anyway…sorry, I need to take a breath here because it's still too raw even to talk about.

So, like I was about to tell you; for me it was my Beth, just six years of age. My lovely wee blonde haired darling, my only grandchild and the apple of my eye as I used to tell her.

That's over four months gone by now and like it or not, you just have to get on with your life, don't you?

The tears, lots of them, they came later and sometimes in quiet moments of reflection, I still grieve.

But I didn't just lose Bethany, to give her her Sunday name; for a good while, over four months as it happens, I lost her mammy too; my daughter Elizabeth.

My only child.

No, sorry, I don't mean that Liz is dead, but when the police found wee Beth's body and broke the news, it was like somebody had thrust a dagger right into her heart for a good bit of her died that day too.

All I recall when they broke the news is staring at the detective as a cold icy hand clutched at my chest and then the sudden inability to breathe.

You see there was just her and me, Liz I mean.

No, sorry, let me explain. Liz was…is married, but that man, that lazy good for nothing Ian Chalmers, he was as much use as a…a…well, I won't say it for using bad language is never my thing. When the police told him about Beth, the bugger just fell apart like a wet paper bag and typical of him he blamed my Liz; of course that only made her worse, not having his support, even if he is a weasel. You'll have guessed I don't like him.

So, like I'm saying, you never really know how you will react when you're told your granddaughter's been murdered, do you?

Not unless it happens to you and if you've got time, here's my story; a wee slice of my life since it happened, since that horrible day.

CHAPTER ONE

I'm already lying awake when the alarm goes off at five-thirty just as it does every working day, Monday to Friday.

Unconsciously I reach over to the side of the bed for my Alex, but he's been gone now these past five years. Why I keep reaching, I just don't know. Habit, I suppose.

It was a heart attack that took Alex, just when he'd turned forty-eight. Up till then he'd been as strong as an ox, never a day's illness in his life and though he liked a beer or three at the weekend, he wasn't what people would refer to as a heavy drinker and he didn't smoke either. Well, saying that, he liked a cigar now and then. They wee thin things that come in the square, tin box, but for the life of me I can't remember their name.

Funny that just a week ago Jessie Cochrane that works with me in the building asked me if I missed him.

Miss him? What a stupid question. Of course I miss him. Every minute in every hour of every day. Alex was the biggest part my life. Well, most of it anyway, until Liz then Beth came along. But no matter how much I loved my daughter and my granddaughter, Alex was the love of my life and God alone knows how I managed to get through what I've suffered since he was taken from me.

I'm smiling when I think of the occasional offer I've had through the recent years, of being invited out for a meal or for a drink, but something inside me has made me refuse, some part of me thinking it would be some kind of betrayal if I was to go out with another man. I know, you're thinking I'm being silly, that maybe I've not yet met the right man, but after my Alex I really doubt that there's anyone like him out there.

Now, I don't want to sound like I'm complaining, for even at forty-nine it's nice to know that I can still turn a man's head and though I do say so myself, I'm not that bad looking a woman for my age. I mean, I won't win any beauty contests, but I think if Butlins still run the glamorous granny competitions I believe I would be in there with a shout for top place. I've only a touch of grey through my shoulder length jet-black hair and I've kept my figure or I should say, as much of it as I can. Of course it helps keeping busy like I do; that and working like a field horse for the company who run us ragged in that big new shiny office block they're contracted to clean and manage.

I turn and glance at the digital clock and realise my daydreaming has kept me a couple of minutes late from getting out of bed.

I'm yawning as I swing my legs from the bed and getting up, pull open the curtains to find it's another dull and overcast October day. Glancing through the window to the street below I see that Willie McPherson who lives in the semi through the wall is slowly backing his car out of the driveway and I watch as he drives away to his work on the buses. As far as I'm aware Willie is a mechanic at the local bus garage and he and his wife Moira are relatively good neighbours. Well, what I really mean is that while we don't exactly mix socially or pop into each other's houses, Willie has been kind to me since Alex died. During the summer he has been keeping the grass down in the front lawn and only a couple of months ago, I returned home to find him up his ladder and cleaning out my gutters. That and when I'm at my cleaning job in the city centre, one or the other will bring my bins in when they've been emptied, though I suspect it is Willie that's doing it. I don't exactly know what age they are even though they've lived through the wall in the adjoining semi for, oh, it must be nigh on five years; in fact if I'm correctly recalling, they moved in just about the time that Alex passed away. I don't know for certain because we never really speak, but I think Moira might have a few years on Willie whom I'm guessing is in his mid forties. Because we don't really see much of each other, I have no idea how she spends her day for I'm almost certain she doesn't have a job and though it's none of my business I don't remember ever seeing any visitors to their house either. I'm not certain, but I don't think she has family up here. What I mean by up here is that Moira is English, though I don't know where about in England she comes from. That said, they seem a nice enough couple though they've no weans; or at least they've never spoke about having any family and I can only imagine she must get pretty lonely during the day. Not that I'd ask about family. I mean, that's too personal a question in my book.

They're the kind of neighbours you know, who you exchange Christmas cards with or stop and speak to when you meet them in the street or when they're maybe out doing their garden. No, let me rephrase that. Stop and speak with Willie because Moira's never been that chatty and on the very few occasions I've tried to engage her in conversation, she turns her head away and stares at her feet. I don't know; maybe she's just very shy though I sometimes get the impression that when she sees me coming out to tend to the garden, she finds an excuse to head back indoors. However, when Beth died I don't recall even exchanging a word with Moira since that time. It used to be that sometimes on a Sunday morning if I was at the window, I'd see her in her Salvation Army uniform heading out, though I don't think Willie's in the Army. And as for Willie, I sometimes think for a man his age he's awfully shy too. Funny though, now that I think about it, I haven't seen Moira attending the church for some time.

Me, I'm Catholic so its St Ninian's for me. The chapel is nice and handy in Baldwin Avenue, just under a mile away and a good brisk walk across the Great Western Road and yes, before you ask, I'm a regular attender though I have to admit me and God had a few cross words when he took my Beth from me. That said, I do take comfort from my faith and the Parish Priest, Father O'Brien, has been a good and supportive friend to me during the last four months.

Getting myself washed and dressed I think about my neighbours here in Clarion Crescent and I have to admit on the whole they have been very supportive since it happened though to be fair, most keep their distance. Not that there's any kind of snobbishness about it. I think that most of them are embarrassed when they see me and don't know what to say, how to talk to me without Beth's murder becoming part of the conversation. The thing is most of us have lived here for nigh on thirty years or more and though just like the McPherson's through the wall, we've all kind of accepted that we all like our own space. That and I think some of the wives might be a wee bit suspicious of me, me being a widow and them thinking I'll be looking for another man.

They couldn't be more wrong.

As it does every single morning since it happened, my gaze is attracted to the park right across the road from my house. In fairness the council do a good job keeping the grass down, the trees trimmed and the thick bushes cut back, but it doesn't prevent me in my minds eye seeing the corner of the white police tent, what they call their forensic tent, sitting just a hundred yards from my window next the huge rhododendron bush where they found my Beth.

Before you ask, a long time ago I gave up shuddering every time I look at it. Still, it doesn't stop me thinking about her, lying in the wee space under the bush where the police dog found her. A couple of months after it happened a man and a woman from the City Council chapped at my door and when I was giving them a coffee, suggested if I wished, the council would cut the bush down. It was a thoughtful offer. They must have wondered if I was a bit hard-hearted when I said the bush hadn't killed my Beth, so I told them, leave it where it is.

I'm sure many of my neighbours must have expected that I would want to move, leave my home since it happened in full view of where I live. The thing is and Liz agrees it would be like leaving Beth behind, kind of abandoning her. I know that's likely very hard to understand, but she loved playing in the park and when I look out onto it, I remember the many good times I had there with her, not the one evening when it happened. No, I'm staying put; at least for the time being.

The park was a popular place for the local weans to play in during the day, but like all the parks throughout the city, the winos and the bampots sometimes moved in at night. Needless to say, it was those types of people who were the police's first suspects.

You probably realised I said *was* a popular place for the weans to play in. These days, since it happened, you never see a child playing in the park without an adult hovering nearby. Understandable, of course.

You know, since they found Beth's body and then packed up their equipment and finished with the cordon around the park, now and then I see people, mostly teenagers, walking around the rhododendron bush, some even using their mobile phones to photograph where it happened.

People can be very sick and thoughtless, can't they?

One evening in the summer when it was still light and just a few weeks after it happened, I even saw a group of kids, couldn't have been more than sixteen or seventeen years of age the lot of them, taking pictures of themselves and making all sorts stupid poses for their pals as they got their photo taken. Though I couldn't be certain, I think they had been drinking because they were very loud and acting stupidly. Fortunately, some of the neighbours are quick on the phone and the police usually turn up and chase them away. On that occasion, though, quite a few of the teenagers ended up in the back of the police van.

One of the local bobbies is PC Cuthbertson. Phil is his first name; though anytime our paths cross I never call him anything other than Constable. He's been working in this area for as many years as I can remember. A big, grey-haired man with a waistline that could do with losing a few pounds, but polite and courteous for all that. I heard he's a right Rangers man and some even said he's anti-Catholic, but when my Beth was found PC Cuthbertson stood at my garden gate and wouldn't let anyone past who wasn't part of the investigation or family; not that I've many family left these days. Anyone else who tried to come to the door got short shrift from him with the exception of Father O'Brien. I remember looking out of my front window, really to see what was going on over in the park, when the Father arrived at the gate. PC Cuthbertson greeted him like an old pal, shaking his hand and they stood for a good five minutes chatting away and shaking their heads before the Father came to the door.

Anti-Catholic indeed.

Did I mention they still haven't caught her killer, that the man who murdered my Beth is still out there?

With a final glance at the park, I turn and head for the bathroom and with a sigh, prepare myself for another week of cleaning. I work a kind of split shift; seven in the morning to nine then back at five-thirty till seven in the evening and the occasional Saturday overtime when the management want one of the large offices gutted or when the decorators have been in and there's a lot of tidying up and cleaning to be done. It's usually only seventeen and a half hours a week, but with the house off paid by the insurance after Alex died and his work pension and the life insurance, I more than get by. Truth be told I don't really need the work, but I know that I need to occupy my time and if I don't do something. I'll just fester away. Though like the rest of the women I'm always moaning and complaining, it's not the worst job in the world and to be fair, the craic has got me through the bad times; Alex's death then Beth's…you know. Some of the lassies I work with are off their heads and the patter? My God, ripe doesn't describe it, particularly when they're talking about their menfolk. That all said, they're a good laugh and once every few months after work on a Friday and usually on a payday, a few of us meet in the Drum and Monkey in St Vincent Street on the corner of Renfield Street for a few drinks or occasionally in the Wetherspoons next to the Hielanman's Umbrella on Argyle Street. Well, I'm usually driving so it's soda water and lime for me, for the fact is, I'm not really a drinker. But like I said, I'm really only there for the craic.

Times cracking on and fifteen minutes later I'm dressed in my working clothes and snatching at the buttered toast and gulping down my first coffee of the day.

If anything, the coffee's my only addiction. Drink pints of it, so I do. Now, I'm not a choirgirl but like I said, the fact is I'm not really a big drinker. One large glass of wine and I'm swaying. I'm what my Liz jokingly calls a cheap date, but I don't smoke and I never or should say, rarely use bad language.

Well, what I mean is I haven't used bad language for a very long time, though God forgive me I was sorely tempted and did on one occasion lose it when those blasted newspaper reporters were at my door and our Liz's door, trying to get us to give them a story. Parasites, the lot of them with no thought or regard for the suffering and pain we were going through.

Thankfully the police liaison woman, Sheila Gardener, was more than fit for them.

I'm in the car now; my wee blue three door Ford Fiesta that I bought second hand when the insurance money came through after Alex died. I'd never really bothered with the driving before that, though I've had my licence for over twenty years, but a couple of months after his death I gave myself a good shake and decided that I wouldn't give in to my grief and with Liz on my arm, went out and bought myself this wee motor. I suppose I could have just kept Alex's old Rover, but like the idiot I am I made the mistake of giving in to Liz's plea and gave the car to her husband, Ian. Of course, the useless sod run it into the ground and six months later he scrapped it. I know he wouldn't have got half of what the car was worth, but that's him all over. Take, take and take again. Liz was embarrassed and at first feart to tell me because she thought I would go nuts, but I just kept my temper and told her that having given him it, the car was Ian's to do with what he wanted.

As for my Fiesta, it's been a great wee runner and only let me down the once, but for the last few months it's been a slow starter and I'm already thinking about trading it in.

I'm about to start the engine when I glance in the rear view mirror and I startle for I could have sworn that Beth was sitting in her booster seat, behind the passenger seat.

You know that nervous sensation you get, that kind of déjà vu feeling? I swallow my surprise and start the engine and I'm on my way to work.

****

At that time of the morning the traffic on the great Western Road isn't too bad, but I prefer the expressway that takes me into the heart of the city. The parking charges start at eight in the morning, but as I finish at nine I'm usually away by ten or quarter past. There's a wee man who is employed to look after the car park that I use on some waste ground down in Carrick Street and he only charges me one pound fifty a day and that includes the evening, so that's where I park and besides, it's just a couple of minutes walk from there to the office block in Wellington Street.

I make it to the staff entrance at the side of the building just as the showery rain starts to get heavier and puling open the heavy fire door, I hear a voice call out, "How was your weekend, Maggie?"

I turn to see one of the other cleaners, Jessie Cochrane, stood at the door to the staff locker room shaking the rain off her brolly, but before I reply I hear another voice.

"What the hell do you think you're doing, Jessie? That water you're dripping off your brolly will cause somebody to slip and break their neck."

I sigh and raise my eyes to heaven, then turn to see Tommy Burton entering the door behind me. Tommy's the building's janitorial supervisor in charge of the maintenance crew and the cleaning staff, about twenty-five of us in total. In his late fifties he can be a right wee nyaff too with his paunchy stomach, pencil moustache and brylcreemed hair.

"Ach, away and bile your heid," Jessie snaps back at him and nods to me that I join her.

Now, I'm not an ignorant woman and I was raised to be polite and courteous just as I raised my own daughter, but sometimes I find it hard to even make eye contact with Tommy who I believe is just a lecherous, bullying man and I stride away without acknowledging him. I've heard it said among the women that he's handy with his hands when he finds one of the cleaners on their own, very touchy feely if you know what I mean, but he only needs to try it on with me once and he'll be walking bow legged for a fortnight.

You'll have guessed I'm not a shrinking violet.

"How was your weekend?" Jessie asks me again as she unlocks the padlock on her locker and fetches out her overall.

"Same old, same old. And yours?" I put mine on too.

She shakes her head and I can see that it's not been good.

"He's on the bevy again. Three weeks he lasted, Maggie. Three fucking weeks and finally, I thought to myself, he's going to make it this time." She lowers her head and is about to continue, but the door opens and two of the other cleaners come into the room, laughing at some story as they greet us with a cheery wave.

"Are you doing anything after the shift this morning?" she asks me with a furtive glance at the other two.

I smile and reply, "Nothing that can't wait. Coffee round the corner in the Wetherspoons when we're finished?"

"That would be grand," Jessie nods and we set off for our floor to start our shift.

****

I change out of my overall and sign the register that I'm leaving the building then nodding and saying cheerio to the other cleaners, find Jessie already outside and waiting for me, anxiously puffing at her umpteenth cigarette of the morning.

"You're sure about this? You've nothing to rush away for?" she rattles on as we walk towards Argyle Street, but before I can answer she continues, "It's just that I need someone to talk to, Maggie and you're my best pal, so you are."

I shake my head that no, I've nothing to rush away for, but feel a little guilty for though I really do like and feel sorry for Jessie, I wouldn't describe her as my best pal. I know it makes me sound a bit standoffish, but the truth is Jessie and I come from completely different backgrounds.

Married to Ernie who at fifty-one is three years her senior and with whom she has five children aged between thirty and eighteen, three of her kids still live at home and of them only her twenty-two-year-old daughter is working. As for the two boys still at home, well, I say boys, but ones twenty-five and the other is twenty-one and if what Jessie says is correct, a pair of good-for-nothings like their father. She's has had a really hard life with her husband for not only is Ernie a waster who hardly worked a day in his life, but he's a gambler and drunkard too and it's not the first time Jessie has turned up at work with a sore face. That and she's confided that both the lads still at home have been in trouble with the police, one for possession of drugs.

As we walk she glances at her mobile phone and mutters, "I've an hour before I need to get to Asda."

I give her a sideways glance. Jessie is holding down three jobs at the minute. Cleaning the office block, then hurrying to her part-time cleaning job in the Maryhill Asda near to where she lives in the flats at Craigbo Place and at the weekends, she cleans the bingo hall in Possilpark. No wonder you're looking so bedraggled, I think to myself.

Her take on it is that it keeps her out of the house and away from her man.

I treat her and me to a latte and I can see she's desperate to sit on the seats outside 'The Sir John Moore' under the overhang where she can have another fag, but it's still raining and I firmly tell her no, I'm not catching my death so she can cough her lungs out.

"So, what happened?"

"Oh," she casts a glance around as if worried she'll be overheard, "you know that pal of his that was taking him to the meeting? The AA meetings?"

"Yes, you told me," I impatiently reply.

"He did go. Well," she shrugs, "at least he went for the last two weeks."

"But?"

She takes a deep breath then slowly lets it out.

"He went to a Lodge meeting last night and come home this morning sometime after one, pissed out of his head."

Maybe I should have mentioned that Jessie's husband Ernie is a member of his local Orange Lodge and while I have nothing against them other than the fact like those bampots who purport to be Catholic and support and sing about the IRA, they strike me as just being hypocrites for as far as I'm concerned, both groups hide behind religion to mask their bigotry. I've even heard it said that the difference between a Lodge member, an IRA supporter and a squeaky wheeled Asda shopping trolley is that the trolley has a mind of its own.

Anyway, though Jessie likes to describe me as her best pal and while I genuinely think she believes that, I'll never get a social invite to her home because in her husband's view, me being a Catholic means I come from the other side of the fence and that makes me the enemy.

"So," I stare at her, "what do you intend doing and before you come out with your excuses for him, Jessie, don't give me that old chestnut about it not being his fault, that it's an illness. We both know you've given him more chances than he deserves."

Okay, so maybe I'm being a bit hard on her and particularly when she needs somebody's shoulder to lean on, but to be honest with you I'm a bit fed up hearing the same story time after time.

"What do you think I should do?" she miserably stares at me.

Now, I'm not a hard-hearted woman though God knows there are times I feel my toes curling with annoyance. So while I really want to shake her and tell her to stand up for herself, I resist temptation and find myself telling her – for the umpteenth time – that she should go to the housing department and get the flat signed over to her then thrown the lazy drunken git out on his ear and if her sons don't get off their backsides, threaten them with being flung out too. *Am* I being too hard on her?

Maybe, but we both know that though she nods in agreement she'll never do it.

I make a point of glancing at my watch and feeling a little guilty, I say, "Look, you're going to be late for your Asda shift. Do you want to walk me down to my car and I'll drop you off?"

"No," she shakes her head, "you're alright, Maggie. I can get the bus in Hope Street that stops right outside the store and they're every ten minutes."

Sliding off her seat she stand upright and shrugs, then says, "It helps to talk to you, even though we both know I'll not do anything about it."

I watch as she clenches her jaw and tears form in her eyes and I can only imagine how trapped she must feel. Standing, I involuntarily give her a hug. That's when almost out of politeness, she asks, "How's your Liz?"

I feel my chest tighten and I force a smile and reply, "Coming along. The doctor told me last week that there's a chance she might get a home visit soon, an overnighter."

"That's great," she gushes and touching me on the arm, adds, "Thanks for the coffee. I'll see you later."

She rushes from the restaurant for her bus and numbly, I sit down and reach for my now cold coffee, knowing that I won't drink it, but needing an excuse to sit for a few minutes to recover myself.

It's not in my nature to lie, but it was easier to fob Jessie off with a story that pleased her rather than tell her that my Liz, my beautiful daughter who I love dearly and who *is* getting a little better wit each passing day, will continue to remain as an adult inpatient at Leverndale Hospital till such times the consultant in charge of her treatment is satisfied that she is no longer a danger to herself.

****

The wee pensioner who looks after the car park for the owner sees me coming and I shuffle over to his hut and apologise for being over my time, but he just gives me a toothless grin and waves me away. I'm guessing the owner, who charges like the Light Infantry for permitting the parking on the waste ground, probably bungs the old guy a couple of pounds for keeping an eye on the cars on the waste ground so it's not really any skin off his nose how long I am overdue. However, in the likelihood it happens again I shove a five-pound note into his hand and tell him to buy himself a pint.

He's that pleased I think I've made a pal for life.

While I'm driving through the rain towards my house I think again of Liz being in the hospital. Maybe at this point I should explain that my Liz was so overcome with grief that two days after the police discovered Beth's body, she took an overdose. Now, before you start thinking that Liz is some kind of drug addict or, what is it they call them again…a junkie, then let me tell you that lassie hardly touched alcohol let alone drugs. No, it was the medication the doctor had prescribed for her that she overdosed on. Valium he'd prescribed for her though I can't remember what the dosage was, only that it was very strong and had to be taken one pill at a time. I recall at the time looking it up on the Internet and discovered it's actually a drug called Diazepam that is designed to produce a calming affect. Calming effect? The poor lassie's daughter was murdered so to be honest I think she had every right to go off her head, to scream and bawl and go mental, don't you?

Calming effect indeed.

Anyway, the long and short of it is that she locked herself in the toilet of the flat she shared with her husband Ian up in Crowhill Street in the Milton and swallowed the whole bottle. Fortunately, Ian's older brother James and his wife Linda were visiting at the time got a wee bit anxious when Liz didn't respond to their knocking then thank the Lord, James put the door in and they found her.

Linda's a nurse so she made up a water and salt drink and made Liz drink it and that forced her to vomit most of the pills back up. Well, the doctor was called and straight away he did that thing to get her into Gartnavel Hospital's psychiatric ward. Sectioned her I think it's called. But a week later she tried to jump out of a second storey window. The doctor got her transferred to Leverndale Hospital over in the south side of the city at Pollok and she's been there since, detained under the Mental Health Act.

Am I worried about her? Of course I am but at least I know she's in a place where she will get help.

They say that time is a great healer. Well, that seems to be true for I visit my daughter every other night or every third night and I'm pleased to say I can see a definite improvement.

Now, you'll be wondering about her husband, Ian.

I never liked him from the day that Liz brought him home. He was twenty-four to her eighteen years and yes, admittedly a good looking young man and a bit of a charmer, but a complete waster if ever there was one. Let me explain. Ian is a man who talks a good game with big ideas about what he wants in life. His only problem is that he expects the good life to land at his feet. Every job the Department of Employment sent him to wasn't good enough for him. Oh no. There was always some excuse and he never lasted more than a couple of weeks or less at any of the jobs that were either in his opinion too poorly paid or beneath his dignity to work at it.

A real live Walter Mitty is Ian Chalmers except that the character of Walter Mitty was a nice guy.

The long and short of it was that though her father and I tried to warn Liz about Ian, she wouldn't listen and within six months of seeing him she was pregnant with Beth. Within a couple of weeks, they were at John Street arranging their civil wedding that later took place in the City Chambers then a small reception in the Carlton Hotel just off George Square.

You'll have guessed who paid for it all.

It was evident within a couple of weeks that Liz realised she had made a huge mistake and ironically, it drew her and I together in a way that had been missing for a couple of years.

As her pregnancy developed, Liz suffered badly from cramps and required more and more time off from her sales job in St Enoch's Centre until finally her company had to let her go. Ian of course was again idle, so a good sum of Alex and my savings went to help out. His parents were both deceased and though he had siblings, years previously they had got wise to his shenanigans and refused to sub him any more money. In fairness, his brother James warned Alex and I about giving him money, but we were more concerned about Liz's welfare and to our regret, we should have listened.

Then our beautiful Bethany was born and to this day I thank God that at least Alex lived long enough to see and to hold his lovely wee granddaughter.

In the years that followed, a good part of our savings went on helping Liz out financially simply because her waster of a husband spent most of their money on stupid things or gambled it away. Believe it or not, do you know that when Alex died, the bugger even had the nerve to ask me if Liz was entitled to half the value of our house?

I often wonder if Ian ever really cared for my daughter. Three weeks before Beth was born, Liz had come to stay with me because in the event she went into early labour, not only did I have a car, but the doctor had recommended bed rest and she knew fine well that she'd never get it at her own place; not with Ian demanding his dinner and having her doing all the housework.

Yes, he's *that* bloody lazy!

When she was admitted from my house to the maternity at the Southern General or the Queen Elizabeth Hospital as it is now, over in Govan, I tried in vain to contact Ian on his mobile phone to let him know his wife was in labour. Could I get him? Could I hell! I ended up phoning his brother James who to his credit, rushed with his wife Linda to the hospital and waited while I was in the labour suite with Liz.

To this day I can't believe Ian missed the birth of his daughter. When he finally showed up at the maternity reception he was drunk and smelling of cheap wine and told us that he had been out celebrating Beth's birth. I think it was only my presence that stopped his brother from taking him round to the back of the building and punching his head in. Can you believe he was that drunk the nursing staff even refused him entry to see the baby?

When Liz was discharged from the hospital, she came to live with me again for a couple of months, but he pleaded with her to return home to the flat. Of course she believed she could change him, that the presence of a baby would turn him into the kind of husband she wanted, but leopards don't really change their spots, do they?

So, that's how it went on; weeks of living with him, arguments, then months of living with me before she went back to him for another two or three weeks.

On that fateful night we lost Beth, she had been living at their flat for several weeks, always willing to make another go of it for the weans sake. I tried at first keeping my mouth shut and letting her rant on and on about him, then I tried to be to be the devils advocate, but no matter what I said Liz always came round to the opinion that he would change.

He never did and I'm convinced never will.

In my book Ian Chalmers will always be a waster, a parasite and a good-for-nothing.

Let me give you another example of what kind of man he really is. Less than a week after Beth's murder and three days following Liz's admission to Leverndale he took off from their flat in Milton and sold or gave away most of the furniture. Of course I didn't know that at the time and only heard about it later when his brother James phoned me to ask if Ian was living at my house.

All I could tell James was that the last time I saw my son-in-law was at Beth's funeral, but to be honest I was too wrapped up in my own grief to pay much attention to him. Needless to say Liz was too unwell to attend and to my knowledge, he has never once visited his wife in hospital.

Anyway, enough about him.

Can you believe that I heard later that at the funeral there were some whispers from a couple of busybodies that I know, local women with too much time on their hands, who spread the malicious rumour that Liz refused to attend the funeral? That and the curiosity from some of my so-called fellow parishioners wondering why the wee one wasn't laid to rest in a Catholic cemetery. Honestly, how can people be so cruel and particularly at a time like that?

As it was, her father Ian had the final say in where Beth was to be laid to rest and she now resides in Langfaulds Cemetery up off the Baljaffray Road. Of course with Liz detained at that time, the decision was his alone and frankly, it's a nice and well-kept cemetery. It was his brother James who later confided to me that Ian didn't really care where Beth went, but James thought as his parents were there, he could and had persuaded Ian to lay Beth in beside them. Though I never met Mister and Missus Chalmers, at least I have the comfort of knowing the wee soul is with family and for that I am eternally grateful for James's thoughtfulness.

As I said earlier, I don't recall much about the ceremony, only that Father O'Brien, God bless and keep him, helped me through it all. For a man well past the age of retirement and that's not a rarity among the priesthood these days, he was everything I needed at the time. Thoughtful and caring.

One of the few memories I have of that day is travelling along Drumchapel Avenue and seeing a policewoman stood there holding back the traffic to allow the cortege to turn into Kinfauns Drive.

There are the four of us in the big funeral car; me, Ian, his brother James and James wife Linda.

As I watched her, the policewoman suddenly stood very erect and saluted the hearse carrying my wee Beth. I can't explain why, but it was that simple, respectful gesture from a young blonde haired lassie that almost broke me and I burst into uncontrollable tears.

Do you know and you won't believe this, but when we pass the policewoman, like I said I'm distraught, Linda's visibly upset, James is pale faced, but Ian?

Ian smirks at the young woman and returns her salute as though he's on some sort of parade.

James was that angry it was only Linda who held him back by tightly grabbing his hand else I think he'd have thrown Ian out of the car.

Honestly, you couldn't make it up.

Thankfully, Linda and James comforted me so by the time we arrived at the cemetery I was a little more composed.

After the ceremony at the grave, James and Linda saw to it that I was taken straight home and do you know what? Other than a cursory nod when he got into the car at the church and no, I didn't see him at the service in St Ninian's, Ian never spoke one word to me throughout the journey nor at the cemetery.

Not one word.

There wasn't any purvey which I know is unusual and especially for a Glasgow funeral, but you have to remember this was the service for a wee six-year-old girl. Yes, it was very well attended from what I saw and recall, but what really annoyed and angered me was that the police had to hold back reporters, all vying with each other to get photos of Ian and me and shouting questions at the detectives, asking if at the time they had any suspects for Beth's murder.

It was awful and I felt…I don't really know how to describe it, but if I were to use a word I'd say I was ashamed. Ashamed that people would react like that at a funeral let alone the funeral of a wee girl.

Funny thing is that on the day and even for a couple of days after the funeral, I couldn't remember much about it. The curious thing is I kept the newspapers and as you can imagine it was front-page news at the time, so I got a lot of information from reading the 'Glasgow News' and the rest of the papers. Maybe it was the reading that prompted my memory because things started coming to back to me after that.

****

That's me arrived home and I backed into my driveway, a skill Alex taught me. He said it's always easier to drive out of a driveway into the road than to back into a road and endanger yourself. Wise man was my Alex.

I switch off the engine and sit and reflect on what happened today with Jessie.

Like I told you, I'm Jessie's best pal rather than her being mine, but I don't really mind. I don't think Jessie has many friends and I'm guessing here, but I'm also certain none that she can unload her troubles to. I only wish she would listen to me and take my advice. I really worry at times that man of hers will eventually put her in the hospital. As I told you, he's handy with his fists, just a bullyboy who can hit women, but likely won't stand up to a man. Course Jessie denies that he's ever hit her but believe you me, I don't need to be a detective to see she's regularly taking a hammering from him.

And as for those weans of hers. Though I've never met any of them, I feel like I know them the way Jessie talks about them and it seems that there's only two out of the five that are worth anything; the lassie that's still at home and working locally and the oldest son who lives with his wife and children in England and works down there in the building trade.

Jessie sometimes has a visit down to see him and always comes back with glowing reports of how well he's doing and that he wants her to travel down there and live with him and his family and how proud of him she is that he got out of the house and didn't turn out like his father.

The other daughter is living with her partner and two kids somewhere in the Gorbals and as far as I know, she has nothing to do with Jessie, but from what Jessie has hinted I suspect it's because there's drink or drugs involved with her and her partner.

The two unemployed wastrels who are also still at home sound like cardboard cut-outs of their father, Ernie.

The younger daughter, Mary, is a success story and holds down a job in Asda and as far as Jessie is concerned, is the only one in the house who does anything for her.

Still, she hasn't got it easy, has Jessie.

The dashboard clock says it's nearly twelve so I get myself out of the car and am just about to lock it when I hear my name called. I turn and there's a man wearing a suit stood at the end of the driveway. He's tall and sturdily built with dark collar length hair that needs cut and is carrying a black leather folder. If this is another PPI thing I'm thinking, but then he asks, "Missus Brogan?"

"Aye, that's me," I stare suspiciously at him and I'm ready to tell him where to go and I don't mean nicely.

"Sorry," he smiles, "I didn't mean to startle you. My name's Detective Sergeant Alan Reid. I wonder if it's convenient to have a word?"

CHAPTER TWO

I'm in the kitchen brewing a pot of tea while the detective is sitting in my front room and my heart is hammering in my chest and I'm wondering if this is going to be good news; that at last they've caught the man who killed my wee Beth.

To be honest I'm surprised how nervous I am and my hands are shaking as I set the tray with my best china cups and saucers, milk and sugar bowls and a plate of digestive.

I take a deep breath then lifting the tray carry it through to the front room where I see the detective is stood looking at the photographs on the sideboard. He turns when I nudge the door open and grimaces like he's been caught being sneaky and says, "Sorry, I hope you don't mind. I was just looking at the photographs."

As if *that's* not obvious I'm thinking, but then I hear myself say, "That's okay."

However, inside I'm shaking like a leaf and my whole body just wants to scream at him, for heaven's sake tell me; why are you here?

I lay the tray down onto the wee glass topped coffee table and nod that he sit down.

So there we are, sat facing each other in the two armchairs on either side of the fireplace and I really have to work hard at keeping my voice steady as I ask him, "Do you want milk or sugar with your tea, Mister Reid?"

"Just milk. The photos," he turns to stare at the three-framed pictures. "Of course I recognise the wee girl is your granddaughter, Bethany, and I presume the young woman is her mother, Elizabeth?"

"Yes, that's right. My daughter Liz is currently in hospital," I'm nodding at him.

"The photo of you and the man. That will be your husband, Mister Brogan?"

"It is. My Alex passed away five years ago. A heart attack," I add and wonder why he needs to know this.

The detective is a man about my own age, maybe a year or two older. For a second I stare at him and see the man he is; maybe four or five inches taller than my five foot seven, with a full head of dark hair that's needing a trim and with a face that looks like he's carried the weight of the world on his shoulders. I'm guessing his wife didn't see him before he went to work this morning for no woman would let her man out of the house wearing an old suit like that, shiny at the elbows and the knees and with a shirt and tie that clearly didn't match.

"Why are you here, Mister Reid?" I finally ask him and I can't help myself because it sounds like I'm barking at him.

He licks at his upper lip before placing his cup back down onto the table and I see him take a breath before he replies, "I've actually been sent by Mister Tarrant, the Detective Chief Inspector who is in charge of your granddaughter's…" he hesitates before he adds, "investigation. Missus Chalmers is unavailable at the minute due to her, eh…"

"Being locked up in Leverndale?" I frostily complete for him.

His shoulders slump and he lets out his breath then slowly, his eyes staring into mine, says, "Look, Missus Brogan, I just joined this Division's CID a couple of weeks ago and though I know about your granddaughter's murder, I was never part of the investigating team." He pauses and I can see that his throat is constricting as he tries to swallow, then continues, "The fact is that the decision has been made to stand down the inquiry until something else crops up…"

"What do you mean stand down the inquiry until something crops up!" I angrily interrupt him.

He raises his hand and replies, "Please, let me explain. The DCI, Mister Tarrant, has made the decision that everything that can be done has been done, but he's no closer to identifying your granddaughter's…"

I raise my own hand and snap, "Bethany. Her name was Bethany. Beth, that's what we called her."

He doesn't immediately respond, but then softly says, "You're right, of course. I apologise. Beth. Anyway, the DCI believes that everything that can be done, every avenue of inquiry has been completed, but we just don't have a suspect for Beth's murder." He shrugs and says, "In the meantime the DCI in consultation with the CID's senior management has decided that with other commitments that face us, we're continuing to monitor the inquiry in the hope that some new evidence or a witness comes forward."

"What does monitor the inquiry mean?" I feel my body shake with rage.

"Well," he slowly drawls, "what it means is that I have been appointed as the detective to oversee the inquiry, ensure that if anything, any new information or whatever is discovered, I will follow it up."

"So in short, the police have given up? Because this man is so difficult to find you're going to forget about what happened?"

"Not at all," he rapidly shakes his head and crosses his hand back and forth. "No murder in Scotland is dropped, Missus Brogan. The inquiry will remain open until such times as the murderer is caught, whether that is tomorrow or in ten years' time or whenever. However, the sad fact is that with the little evidence the police have and the lack of any witnesses, it's always been an uphill struggle for the investigation team."

Our tea has grown cold, but I'm so angry and frustrated that I can hardly take my eyes from him.

"And why can't your boss, DCI Tarrant, why can't he come here and tell me himself? Is he too embarrassed to admit he failed?"

His throat is working overtime and it's then I understand that this man has been given the dirty job to do, the task of telling me that they're done investigating Beth's murder.

I never really took to that fat bugger Martin Tarrant anyway, who appeared to be so optimistic at the start of the inquiry and in my opinion, loved being in front of the television cameras.

Aye, I decide, he definitely dumped the job on this man.

Once more he's slow to respond, but then tells me, "Truth be told I argued that it *is* his job to come here and speak with you, but I'm just a Detective Sergeant, Missus Brogan. He's management so here I am. I'm sorry to have to be the one to break this news," and that's when I hear a little bitterness in his voice, "but for obvious reasons I chose to come here and break the news to you rather than to Elizabeth."

I'm feeling completely deflated at this new development and it's only when the detective reaches into his trouser pocket and brings out a crisply ironed white handkerchief that he hands to me, I realise that I'm crying.

"Thank you" I manage to blurt out and rising from my chair I make my way upstairs to the bathroom to wash my face and to give me a couple of minutes to compose myself.

Drying my face, I stare into the mirror above the sink and see me as I am. My eyes are a little red from crying, but for my age my face is clear skinned with hardly any lines; unaccountably, I find myself smiling when I recall my mother used to tell me that if I have her skin I'll be alright. I'm not what you might call beautiful, certainly not film actress beautiful, but like I said before, I'm pleased to say I've turned a few heads in my time.

Now why the heck am I thinking like this and at a time like this? Taking a deep breath, I shake my head to clear it and return downstairs to the front room and say, "Sorry about that, it's the shock of what you told me."

I've just sat back down when I jump up and say, "Your tea will be cold. I'll put the kettle on again," and before he can argue I've lifted our two cups and I'm out the door and away into the kitchen.

I'm back again a couple of minutes later with fresh tea and lay his cup down onto the saucer.

"I'm guessing that just as I'm not happy about receiving this news, Mister Reid, you're not happy about being the one sent to tell me."

"That's the thing about being a polis, Missus Brogan. We never get to tell people they've won the lottery. It's always the bad news we deliver," he smiles a little sadly at me.

I sip at my tea then ask him, "What exactly does monitoring the inquiry mean for you?"

His eyes widen and he takes a breath, then slowly letting it out as though considering my question, he replies, "Well, like I told you I wasn't part of the investigatory team so the first thing I'll do is sit down when I have the time and read everything that has been filed about the investigation. Who did what, who was interviewed, what lines of inquiry were made, that sort of thing."

"That must by a lot of paperwork," I mused.

"Most of it is on computer CD's, so I can read it at my desk."

"And will that be your only inquiry? I mean you'll not be investigating other things, will you?"

He runs his tongue along his upper lip and shook his head.

"Regretfully, I'll still be on the book, as they say, in that I'll have other criminal inquiries to work on while I'm overseeing Beth's investigation."

"So, Beth's inquiry will be a part-time thing?" I'm back to being frosty.

"It will be given as much time as I can devote to it," he firmly replies. "Remember what I said, Missus Brogan. At the minute, all lines of inquiry have been fully completed. If anything, anything at all crops up, that will become the focus of my full attention."

He laid his cup down onto the saucer and quietly says, "Which brings me to a question I'd like to ask."

"Yes?"

"The computer files, the statements, the Actions," he paused then explained. "That's what we call the lines of inquiry. Actions. Anyway, the Actions give me only so much information, but…" he run his tongue over his upper lip again and I came to realise this is a habit he has, "let me explain. When a witness is interviewed and a statement taken, unless the statement is entirely verbatim…Eh, that means…"

"I know what verbatim means," I nod to him. "It means something like the exact same words used. I read a lot of crime fiction. You know, Ian Rankin and Christopher Brookmyre books?"

He smiles in return and nodding, says, "Yes, well, most statements give an abbreviated version of what a witness saw or did and yes, it probably incudes the facts, but sometimes due to an oversight or perhaps a witness doesn't believe it to be important or not worth mentioning, little things can be missed. Do you follow?"

"Yes, I think I understand. But what is it you want to ask me?"

"One of the few people who were consistently present during the investigation and who likely knows the full story of Beth's disappearance then her being found, is you. What I'd like to ask you and difficult though it might be for you, would you be willing to tell me in your own words exactly what happened that day?"

****

"It was the second last day in June, a Friday," I begin. "Liz had brought the wee one over after school when she got out at three and they were both staying the night with me. Liz and her man Ian were supposed to be going out that night to a birthday party at one of his pal's houses. I remember that Liz wasn't too keen on going because she knew it would just be an excuse for a bevy session for Ian. Liz doesn't drink. No," I shake my head. "That's not quite true. She used to like a wee drink, but when Beth was born she gave it up. Besides, Ian did enough drinking for the two of them."

"I suspect from the way you describe him, you're not that keen on your son-in-law, Missus Brogan," he softly smiles.

"What gave it away," I dryly reply. "If you're asking that I don't like him, Mister Reid, you're absolutely correct. When Ian Chalmers married my lassie he didn't just get himself a wife, he got himself a fulltime cook, cleaner and wage earner to keep him in booze and fags. He's a lazy man, self-centred and…" I stop, catching myself before I go off on one. "All I'll say about Ian is that he's bright enough, but he certainly wasn't the man for my Liz."

"Did he come over that day with his wife and Beth?"

"No," I shake my head. "Suffice to say there's no love lost between us so he's not one for visiting here. Now, where was I?"

"Liz and Beth came over and they intended staying the night."

"Oh, yes. Anyway, you'll have seen the park across the road?"

"I saw it when I drove into the street. It looks quite big."

"Yes, it is and well tended too by the councils parks department. That and the Knightswood Wee Park that's on the other side of Clarion Road. Depending on the weather Liz or I would regularly take the wee one across to let her play in the one or the other of the two parks. Usually during the day there is people walking their dogs or kids playing there, but that day it was overcast and a bit wet, so there weren't too many people around. Liz and Beth got here about half three and while I was putting the kettle on they were in the front room here. I could hear Beth going on and on at her mum to let her go and play in the park and finally Liz said okay, but that Beth was to play just across there," I wave my arm towards the window to the nearby greenery. "From the window here she knew she could keep her eye on the wee one and I heard her tell Beth that she wanted a cup of tea and needed to speak to Grandma."

It still catches in my throat when I remember that day and I'm conscious that I still have his handkerchief and I'm twisting it into knots.

"Anyway, by the time I got back through here from the kitchen, Liz was at the window and I remember her waving to Beth and then," I shrug, "we sat down to have a chat."

"Can I ask you, was the foliage in the park quite dense, it being June?"

"Yes, it was. The bushes are always very thick and the council are forever cutting them back."

"Sorry, I interrupted you there. Go on, please."

"Well, Liz and I chatted and it was a bit of a difficult conversation. You see, she was thinking about leaving her husband *again*," I find myself sighing, "and wanted to know if she and the wee one could come and live with me for a while. Till she got her own place, that is."

"Sorry, I'm interrupting again. Where was Ian Chalmers while this was going on? Did you know?"

"Liz told me that he was in their flat up in Milton watching the horse racing on the telly and as far as I'm aware, the detectives checked that and it proved to be correct."

"Okay, go on."

"As you might imagine, Liz was a bit emotional and I didn't realise how much time had passed when we remembered about Beth being over in the park. That and with the clouds gathering overhead and albeit it was June, it started to get very dull outside. You might remember, we had that couple of weeks of summer storms during that month?"

"Oh, yes, I remember," he nods to me.

"Anyway, I think it was about twenty minutes past five when Liz went to the toilet, so I threw my coat on and rushed across to the park to bring her in."

I can feel my throat tightening again and I'm conscious I'm still twisting the hankie in my hands.

"I couldn't find her then a couple of minutes later Liz had heard me shouting Beth's name and came running across from the house to help me search for her. One of the neighbours up the road, Mister McGregor, was walking his dog Alfie and he helped us look for her, but after ten minutes when it started to get even darker, I started to panic and that's when Mister McGregor used his mobile phone to call the police."

"I can see this is very difficult for you, Missus Brogan. Can I get you a glass of water or something?"

"No," I shake my head, "I'm fine. Anyway, the police, two young men in a panda car, they arrived inside five minutes and when I told them we still couldn't find Beth and what age she was they acted very quickly. By this time Liz was almost hysterical and one of the young officers told me to take her inside the house. Other neighbours had obviously heard the commotion and were coming out of their houses to help look for the wee one. It just seemed like forever before more police cars and vans arrived and when I was at the window I saw that a dog man had come to help in the search. Then two detectives arrived and started to ask Liz and me questions, but to be honest, I was that upset I think I just spoke a lot of rubbish. The next thing I knew there was a doctor here to help Liz because she was going out of her mind with worry."

"Likely the police casualty surgeon summoned by the attending officers," he suggested.

I've stopped speaking because once more, as I have done a hundred times, I'm reliving that evening.

My voice almost whisper, I go on. "I remember looking out of the window towards the park and seeing all the flashing lights from the police torches, then I heard one of the detectives being called to my front door. It's hard to describe, Mister Reid, but I had some kind of instinct, some kind of uncanny suspicion he was being given bad news."

I stop again and take a deep breath.

"He came back into the room here and went straight to Liz. She was sat on the couch there," I nod towards it, "with a young police woman holding her hand. I was too restless to sit down and just paced up and down. The detective who'd came back into the room, he bent down and I remember like it was a minute ago, exactly what he said. He told Liz, 'I'm sorry; it's not good news. They've found your wee girl, Missus Chalmers.' Of course we knew right away what he meant, that Beth was dead."

Again I have to stop and I take another deep breath.

"Please, if this is too hard for you…"

"No, if you're going to be the detective in charge of the inquiry now,

Mister Reid, you need to know everything, but really there's not much more that I can tell you. Liz was sedated and put to bed here upstairs then the next morning, I had to watch the television news to learn that your man, DCI Tarrant, was in charge of the inquiry and do you know, Mister Reid," I can hear my voice rising, "that bugger never came near us for two days? When he did the first thing I asked him was what was he doing to find Beth's murderer and he said, everything possible. What kind of answer is that to a grieving family? Everything possible."

I know I sound bitter, but I can't help keep the scorn from my voice. We sit in silence for a moment then he asks me, "Is that what you think caused your daughter to attempt to take her own life? Overwhelming grief or some feeling of guilt that Beth was out of her sight for that short time?"

I sigh and shaking my head, I reply, "Maybe, but how do you quantify grief, Mister Reid? I don't know your family circumstances, but if you are a parent you'll know that as parents we all make mistakes where our children's safety is concerned and for the most part, we get away with it and vow never to be so stupid again. However, there is the occasional mistake, that one in a million lapse of judgement that costs us dearly. It just so happened that day that Beth was vulnerable and alone when some evil man happened upon her. Another five minutes either way that day, we might not be sitting here having this conversation."

"You're right, of course," he sighs and rubs a hand across his brow. "I have two grown-up daughters and I remember a time when my oldest was just a toddler. She's thirty now," she softly smiles. "She and I were in a Tesco supermarket and I had her by the hand. I let go to reach up and lift something heavy down from a high shelf and when I turned, she was gone. It was just a split second, but my heart froze and I vividly recall the feeling of panic…" he shook his head and blew through pursed lips. "These days, any time I have her laddie, my three-year-old grandson out with me, I have him by the scruff of the neck because trust me," he smiles like any proud grandparent would, "that wee guy is too wily to hold by the hand." He stares down at his feet then raising his head, says, "But while I do understand, Missus Brogan, I can only imagine what you and your daughter experienced that day is too awful for me to even contemplate. The initial feeling of dread you must have experienced when you realised that Beth was missing and then of course…" he leaves the rest unsaid.

I see him hesitate and I know that he wants to ask me something, so I say, "What?"

"It's a difficult question, but unless I was misinformed and mind, I've still to read the full account of the inquiry, but am I correct in saying that Beth was not in any way, eh, interfered with?"

I bristle, though not at him, but at the man who took the life of my granddaughter and then I shake my head and reply, "Your man Tarrant, he told me that when Beth was found by the police dog, it looked like she had been placed under the large rhododendron bush; sort of shoved in was how he described it, but that her clothing was intact. He also said that he believed that the man who killed her must have been disturbed and didn't have time to…you know," I shrug and bite at my lower lip.

"So," his eyes slowly narrow, "Tarrant believes the man was disturbed by someone. Did they ever trace this mysterious individual who disturbed the killer, do you know?"

"Not to my knowledge," I shake my head.

"I understand," he nods and then adds, "Course it could have been anything. A passing car or somebody walking in the park. Anything," he repeats.

I see him glance at his watch as he continues, "I'm taking up too much of your time. Now, before I leave you I'll give you my business card and phone number. If at any time you want to speak to me, it doesn't matter about what and do not think anything you want to ask is silly or unimportant; you just need to give me a call. There's no stupid question, Missus Brogan. The stupidity is not asking it," he smiles. "Now, is there anything you want to ask me before I go?"

He sees me hesitate and says, "What?"

I take a breath and slowly exhale and I wonder how to ask the question that has been bothering me all these long months. Then I say, "Well, when DCI Tarrant told me that Beth hadn't been, you know, interfered with, that it was his opinion; that the man had been disturbed. What I'd like to know, Mister Reid, was Tarrant telling the truth? The reason I ask," it all comes out in a rush, "is that I know that when I'm reading my crime fiction books the man in charge…"

"The Senior Investigating Officer, the SIO?" he interrupts.

"Yes, the SIO. Well, the stories always say the SIO keeps something back, something that only the killer would know. So, will you be able to really find out if he told me the truth?"

He stares at me then gently asks, "What would you gain to know if Beth was interfered with, Missus Brogan? Do you not think it would only add to your pain?"

Of course he's talking sense, but I've given it a lot of thought over time and I reply, "If I know now, it won't hurt me if it comes out as a surprise later, say at a trial."

His eyes widen as he nods and says, "Fair enough. Anything else?"

"Tarrant refused to tell me, but did they find DNA on Beth? Anything that might identify her murderer?"

His brow furrows and I'm thinking that maybe he believes me to be some kind of amateur detective, but let's face it; these days you can't see a news item on television or read about a case in the papers without DNA being mentioned. Finally, his brow creasing, he replies, "I don't know, but I promise you, Missus Brogan, I'll find out the answer to both those questions and get back to you, okay?"

I nod and with a smile I reply, "Thank you. I can't think of anything else at the minute, Mister Reid, but likely when you're away five minutes I'll have a load of further questions."

"That's the way of it," he grins and gets to his feet.

He offers me his hand and says, "Thanks for the tea and biscuits. I'll make a start on the Actions I spoke about and if I have any questions for you, would you mind me giving you a call?"

"Not at all," I assure him.

I see him to the door and watch as he walks down to his car; a CID car I think it is with the two aerials on the roof, one at the front and one at the back.

When he's driven off I wonder if Mister Reid will find anything in the computer files he spoke about and nice man that he seems to be, but I'm still blazing angry with the pompous bugger Tarrant not visiting me himself.

CHAPTER THREE

It's my custom when I'm rising early for my work to have a wee break midday where I have a light lunch, then sit back in my favourite chair for an hour or so with my Kindle. Sometimes I find myself dozing off for fifteen or twenty minutes, but never longer than half an hour. After Beth's death and as you might imagine, my sleep pattern went to buggery and it took me several months to get back to normal. Now most nights I'm in bed for no later than ten-thirty, weekends too.

Yes, you've got it in one. I've no social life and even the close friends I have make less frequent phone calls now. Like the neighbours, I believe they just don't know what to say to me that won't sound condescending or patronising.

Because I'm back at work for starting the second shift at five-thirty, I usually have a light dinner prepared for me getting home in the evenings and that's normally anytime after eight, depending on the traffic. I don't usually take the car in the summer months because the traffic is too heavy, so I've taken to catching the bus for the late shift and usually jump onto the 6A bus to and from work that I catch on Great Western Road at Paladin Avenue. The bus takes me into Sauchiehall Street and it's a short walk to the office from there. Not tonight though because I'll be taking the car, for when I finish work I'm heading straight across the city to visit Liz at Leverndale Hospital. I can't say I've always looked forward to the visits, but in the recent months it has got a lot easier now that I see some improvement in her.

In the beginning, you see, the visits to see Liz were more than difficult, a lot of that being because she was very sedated…or in layman terms, doped up with God knows what. I have to admit the doctor treating her, John Francis, Liz's consultant who is a psychiatrist, is a very nice and approachable man in his mid sixties and who I think looks a little like William Hartnell, who if you're old enough will recall was the man who was the first Doctor Who. He explained Liz's condition to me like doctors always do; using medical terminology that to be frank I hardly understood, but again in layman's terms here's what he said.

He told me that because she had already been in a highly emotional state just before Beth's death when she had been worrying about leaving her husband, what her and her daughter's future was to be, then the devastating shock of Beth's murder and her overwhelming feeling of guilt that she was to blame by not being there for her daughter, had combined to quite literally send her over the edge. Over the edge is my interpretation, not his because Doctor Francis used a fancy technical term that I can't remember. However, what I did understand was him telling me that patience with her and plenty of rest, along with medication that will be reduced as her mind improves, are the best healers. He also assured me that though Liz's recovery would take some time he was absolutely certain that though she would never completely get over Beth's death, counselling and care would help Liz regain her sense of normality.

In short he had every confidence she would be able to re-join society.

Of course my first question was the likelihood of her again attempting suicide, but he fell back on that old adage that time will tell. Then I asked how long she would need to remain sectioned at Leverndale. He told me that her case was reviewed monthly and that he foresaw her being discharged well before the end of the year then with a gentle smile had teasingly added, "If not sooner."

Now, that's given me some hope.

Needless to say as the months passed it seems to me the doctor was right for I do see a dramatic change in Liz. She no longer wears the face of the haunted young woman who was admitted over four months ago and weekly, her medication is being reduced to the point that she now takes just two tablets; one in the morning to calm her nerves and a second tablet at night to help her sleep. She's also permitted to roam the grounds alone, though any time she leaves the hospital to maybe do some shopping or to the café down on the Paisley Road West, she's usually accompanied by a care worker.

"It is not that I no longer trust her to self-harm, it's just that it's the rules," Doctor Francis had assured me.

One of the things that worried me for some time is that having been closeted in the hospital for all those months, she might become a wee bit institutionalised, like she might be afraid to leave the place and face the world outside.

However, the last time I visited her on Saturday afternoon, we took a walk together in the hospital's secure grounds and though it was raining a bit, I have to admit I enjoyed the wee bit of freedom with her. And do you know it was the first time I sensed a frustration in

Liz. It was the things she said, the words she used; a feeling that she was desperate to get out of there and try to get her life back on track. Now, if that's not a step forward, what is?
****
I have no notion of falling asleep until the thud of my Kindle hitting the carpet startles me.

The clock on the mantelpiece tells me it's half past two so I get up out of my chair and after using the loo, head into the kitchen and spend fifteen minutes making a pot of vegetable soup for my dinner this evening. As it simmers away, I prepare a couple of sandwiches for Liz, tuna mayonnaise on brown seeded bread and that done, put them in the fridge for the time being. Later I'll transfer them to a cool bag and they can sit in the boot of my car while I'm at work. It's just a wee thing, but I know that she likes a nibble at night with her cup of tea and it also makes me feel as though I'm doing something for her.

I glance at the kitchen clock and sigh. I really can't be bothered going into work tonight, but if I don't I'll feel guilty for I'm certain that Jessie will be looking for me and likely with an update about what's going on in her world. Poor Jessie. No matter what advice I give her we both know that she'll never get out of that never-ending circle of stress and worry.

Before I know it, it's almost time to get myself ready to leave and by the time I've packed up Liz's sandwiches, turned off the cooker and fetched my coat from the hall cupboard, I'm running a couple of minutes late.

Once I'm in my car I start the engine and slowly move along my driveway to the gate, but then I pause and glance along the road to ensure there's no traffic coming and as I'm looking along the road, again the memories come flooding back.

Did I tell you about my own near breakdown? About two days after they found Beth's body?

Let me explain that.

When the man in charge, DCI Tarrant, came to see me and Liz at the house he told us that he did not believe the murder was random and was convinced that the man who killed Beth had to be someone living locally. Maybe not in the street, he had added, but certainly somebody who frequented or knew the area. Whether or not the killer had taken advantage of Beth being on her own…and of course that comment set my Liz off, didn't it…or whether the killer had previously seen or knew Beth, Tarrant wasn't sure or if he was, he wouldn't tell us.

When he spoke with us and even though Tarrant was aware of Liz's fragile state at the time, he didn't even have the courtesy to be gentle with his comments? No, he just ploughed ahead in his gruff voice as though he were lecturing his detectives.

I should say by that time the police had appointed what they call a family liaison officer to be with us, a policewoman called Sheila Gardener.

Sheila sat with us when Tarrant was spouting off and I remember how red her face got because it was clearly evident she wasn't only embarrassed by his attitude, but angry too. The thing is though that Sheila was just a constable while he was a Detective Chief Inspector, so it's not as if she could have jumped up off the couch and said, 'Hey, hang on a minute. You're being a complete arse, sir,' if you'll pardon my French.

It was only after he left and in fairness to her, Sheila tried to apologise for his behaviour and she told us that Tarrant was a dinosaur, that detectives of his rank didn't usually act like that and that he was right out of order.

However, what he said stuck with me and from that time and for weeks after it, to me every man who I knew lived locally and who crossed my path was suspicious and I wondered, is he the killer?

By the time several weeks had passed I was a nervous wreck, what with Liz being sectioned and the police getting nowhere in their search for the murderer.

I used to watch the detectives going about their business up and down the Crescent, knocking on doors and taking statements. The worst thing was that the neighbours began to shun me too, not because they were angry with me or anything like that, but I think they were all a bit embarrassed and didn't want to impose on my grief. The only ones who came near or anything like it was, curiously, Willie McPherson. He came to the door a couple of times that first week with plastic containers of soup and sandwiches he said Moira had made, but though I can't explain it I'm positive the soup and the sandwiches were store bought. Anyway that aside, Willie would come to the door and mutter how sorry he was, that if I needed him or Moira for anything, anything at all. And he kept reminding me that he'd get the bins and I wasn't to bother about them.

Then there were the sympathy cards that came through the door; some posted and others dropped through the letterbox. Hurtfully, not every card was sympathetic to our loss. There were two really nasty, handwritten and of course unsigned cards, one that accused Liz and me of killing Beth and the other that said we deserved what we got for not keeping our eye on the wean. I never let Liz see these cards but gave them to Sheila and she told me there were spiteful folk out there with twisted minds, trolls she called them, that like to take advantage of people's grief and enjoy causing distress. Sheila took the cards away, but said it was unlikely that she'd be able to find out who sent them.

Did I mention the flowers?

You know that routine folk have got into these days, placing flowers at the spot where somebody's died, like road accidents and places like that?

Time was flowers were handed in to the bereaved house, but the day after they found Beth a mountain of flowers began to pile up in the park across the road. Of course the television vans and the reporters were eager to interview people who knew Beth or lived in the Crescent. As it happened crowds of people turned up that neither knew my granddaughter nor lived here and gave out all sorts of rubbish just so they could get on the telly. I recall watching the STV news and this middle aged woman with tears tripping her and who I'd never in my life seen before was telling the reporter she was a close neighbour and knew Beth growing up here. Why the reporter never mentioned Beth didn't actually live here, but grew up in the Milton I just don't know, but what it is they say about reporters? They never let the truth get in the way of a good story?

Making my way along the road I'm glancing at the houses as I pass them and my imagination is working overtime. Could the killer be living here after all? Is it one of the men living in these houses near me who murdered my wee angel?

Then of course the rumours started.

Word soon got round that Liz had been sectioned. Don't ask me how it happened though I suspect it was a loose-tongued police officer telling one of my neighbours. The next thing I'm being told by Sheila is that the 'Glasgow News' was running a story that the mother of the dead child, who has mental health issues, is being interviewed about the murder.

My God, if Liz hadn't already been locked up in Leverndale that certainly would have sent her off her head, reading that the police suspected her of Beth's murder.

Of course Sheila tried to play it down to me, telling me it was nonsense, that neither Liz nor I were suspects; however, do you know that bugger Tarrant sent two of his detectives to re-interview me and they actually asked me if Liz was really in the house when Beth was alone across the road in the park?

I'm still fizzing and needless to say, when I complained about their questioning nothing was done about it other than me being told it was…*procedure.*

I'm driving with my mind in automatic and before I know it I'm approaching the car park in Carrick Street. I'm not surprised to see it's the old man who is still sitting there in the wee rundown shed. He gives me a wave and points to a spot that's near to the shed.

I get out of the car and winking, he tugs at his bunnet as he tells me, "You just leave it there, hen, no charge. I'm here for another half an hour and it gets dark round here, so just be careful when you get back, eh? There's a lot of funny characters kicking about at the minute."

Thanking him, I lock the car and make my way through the drizzly rain to the office.

I'm a couple of minutes early and changing into my tabard when the door opens, but it's not Jessie, which is strange for to be fair to her, she's never late.

A couple of minutes later I'm heading for the fourth floor where I work when getting out of the lift I meet the supervisor, Tommy Burton, who says, "You'll need to manage the fourth floor on your own tonight, Maggie. Jessie's daughter phoned in to say she's had a wee accident and won't be in. Leaves me bloody shorthanded again," he shook his head and moaned.

"An accident? Did the lassie say what happened?"

"Ah, no, I never asked."

I can feel my temper rising and my face flushing when I retort, "One of your staff has had an accident, Tommy, and you never thought to ask what happened to her, how serious it is or if she's okay!"

His face turns red as he blusters, "I never thought. I'd other things on my mind. I mean," he gulps, "I've three other women off at the minute so I'm trying to cope with…"

But I've raised my hand to shut him up and I storm off because I can't abide listening to his whining.

****

All through my shift I'm wondering what's happened to Jessie and promise myself that before I visit Liz I'll try to get Jessie on her mobile.

I'm bloody angry with Tommy Burton, yet I know that he's under pressure too and likely I also know what other things he had on his mind. Me and the rest of the cleaning staff as well as the janitorial staff like Tommy are employed by a small subcontractor and in the cutthroat world of commerce, if another company and particularly one of the larger cleaning companies can offer the building factors a cheaper contract, then Tommy and the rest of us are out on our ear. Like I said earlier, it wouldn't be the end of the world for me for I have other means, but for Tommy and Jessie and some of the others it would be catastrophic trying to find work at this time of the year and especially with Christmas just a couple of months away.

Yet that doesn't excuse 'touch-feely' Tommy's stupidity. I mean, how hard would it have been to ask what happened to poor Jessie.

I'm so preoccupied with what might have happened to her the time passes quickly and mopping the floor of the last inner office, I realise it's a couple of minutes before seven o'clock. Returning my pail and mop to the large walk-in cupboard in the corridor, I hurry downstairs and arrive at the locker room just as the rest of the women are collecting their things.

Tommy Burton is waiting at the door for me and I can see he's abashed.

"Just wanted a quick word before you left, Maggie," he nods that I follow him out of earshot of the rest of the staff. Of course women being women, the usual ribald comments and laughs follow us along the corridor.

He stops and glancing over my shoulder to ensure we can't be heard, he says, "I phoned Jessie's mobile, the number that's on the contact list I have and it was her daughter, Mary, who answered the phone. She says that her mother fell and hurt her face and was too embarrassed to come into work, but should be back in a couple of days. Are you thinking what I'm thinking?"

He's staring at me and like me, he knows that's not the truth, that more than likely Jessie's man has given her another bleaching because after all, it's not the first time she has come to work with a sore face or a black eye. And of course, he's right. Mark my words; if Jessie had a pound for every time she has supposedly fallen and hurt her face, she'd have a right few quid in her purse.

Now I'm in a bit of a quandary. Should I go and visit Liz like I've planned or just brazen it and visit Jessie at her house. Course if I do that and see her sore face she'll have to admit that her husband is abusing her and I just know her pride will be hurt. Not that it's ever happened to me, but it must be an awful thing to admit that your husband is hitting you.

"Thanks, Tommy," I drily nod at him, but he reaches out to stop me turning away and when I'm about to angrily shake his hand off, he quickly withdraws it and defensively raising his hands, says, "Look, I know you and I don't really get on, Maggie, but don't you go doing something stupid here." He wipes the back of his hand across his mouth as though he's nervous about warning me, and then continues in a low voice, "Jessie's a grown woman. If she needs help with her man she's better off going to the polis. I know you, you'll want to go up there and set about him, but you'll only get yourself into bother, okay?"

I can't help but slowly smile and I ask, "You think I'll go to her house and batter him or something?"

"Aye," he vigorously nods, "I do."

Suddenly he's taking a deep breath and his voice lowers when he says, "I've seen a right change in you since you lost your wee granddaughter, Maggie. We all have. There was a time when you were quiet, did your job and kept your head down. But now," he's shaking his head. "Now you're like a woman on a mission. Christ, me and some of the lads are feart to speak to you these days and worried what to say because you'll snap our heads off."

I'm taken aback and stunned and I can only stare at him, too surprised to respond.

"You take on board what I'm saying, Maggie? You'll not do anything daft?"

I find my voice and ask, "Are you worried it might reflect back on you, Tommy, that the management might get to hear about me doing something rash and you'll lose your job?"

"No, Maggie," he suddenly grins widely, "I'm more worried that you'll get yourself the jail and I'll be another cleaner down."

I can't argue with that and grinning at him I lightly punch him on the chest and then head back towards my locker. By now the rest of the women have gone and I've made up my mind.

I'll visit Liz at the hospital then maybe take a wee drive up to see how Jessie's doing.

Just a short, social call you understand…from her best pal.

CHAPTER FOUR

The drive from the car park to Crookston Road where the hospital is located takes just over ten minutes longer than the usual twenty minutes. It's not just because the traffic on the M8 is slow due to the drizzling rain, but more to do with the idiotic rubberneckers slowing to watch the police dealing with a three car pile-up, though from the number of people wandering about I don't think there's any real injuries.

Turning off the motorway at the Hillington junction, I make my way towards Crookston Road and I recall that years ago when I was a child, Leverndale Hospital was known throughout Glasgow as the loony bin, where all the mad people were sent. However, driving through the gates to the main building it's nothing like you might imagine.

When I first realised Liz was being detained here I was naturally horrified, but at my first meeting with Doctor Francis I have to say he completely changed my view of the place. Of course, I'm not a medical person or more correctly, I'm no longer a medical person, so he explained it as simply as possible that the in-patients are in the hospital for a variety of reasons ranging from conditions like depression and suicidal tendencies to extreme ADHD issues. Of course there is a multitude of conditions related to mental health, far too many to be simply explained, but I have to say the compassion and empathy shown to Liz since she has been in the care of Doctor

Francis and the nursing staff is exemplary. Well, it must be for even I can see that my girl's getting a whole lot better.

I make my way through to the Balmore Ward, but before I get there I bump into Colin Paterson, who greets me like an old friend.

Colin is a Staff Nurse on the ward and very likeable. He's kind of taken Liz under his wing and I know that every time I visit she manages somehow to include his name in the conversation. He's a couple of years older than my Liz, maybe four or five years actually, stocky build and thinning brown hair, but there's no denying he's a very nice young man.

"See you've got the teatime snacks, Missus B," he nods to the cool bag in my hand.

"Tuna and mayonnaise, her favourite," I smile at him.

"Is that right? My favourite too. I just might be popping by when the tea trolley passes," he grins and heads off in the opposite direction.

I walk on and in the day room beside the ward I find Liz watching television with another couple of patients. She doesn't immediately see me and I stare at my lovely daughter. Fair hair to her shoulders and a figure most women would kill for, Liz inherited her clear skin from me and even now I wonder how the hell she ended up with a man like Ian Chalmers when so many far more suitable young men chased after her. Still, there's no rhyme or reason to attraction, is there?

"Mum!" she turns and grins and getting out of her chair throws her arms around my neck to give me a hug.

Aye, there's no doubt about it. She's definitely on the mend.

We take a couple of chairs at the back of the dayroom and though it was only a couple of days since we saw each other, there's still a lot of news to impart.

Liz starts by telling me that just that day, Doctor Francis decided she no longer requires to take her morning tablet and suggested too that if she's up for it, she could also forego the evening tablet that helps her sleep and he'd see her in the morning to find out how she slept. Liz is excited for like me she realises that this could be the first step to her being fully discharged.

"And there's something else too," she frowns, "but first, what's your news, Mum? Anything happening in your world?"

She senses my hesitation and her brow knits as she stares into my eyes and says, "What?"

As calmly as I can I tell her about the visit from the policeman, Detective Sergeant Reid, and the decision by the police to put Beth's inquiry on what is effectively a back burner.

"Bastards!" she snaps as I reach for her hand. However, if I worried this was going to cause her to relapse, I am pleased to be mistaken for she surprises me when she says, "I don't suppose we can expect the police to devote all the officers they had working on the case for much longer. I mean, angry as I am at them for pulling the plug," she shrugs, "I suppose it's inevitable that if as that man Tarrant says the police don't have the resources and probably the money to continue their investigation…" she left the rest unsaid, her face contorting as though she's uncertain whether to be relieved or saddened by my news.

I won't admit that I was shocked, but it came to me in a sudden flash of clarity.

Over four months later and unlike me, Liz has moved on, has seemingly accepted closure; Beth is dead and that really there is nothing more that she can do other than to remember her little girl.

Me?

I'm forcing a smile because I want Liz to know that I'm happy, happy that my lovely daughter is getting back to the place she should be.

But me?

Inside my stomach is doing somersaults because God forgive me, but I'm not letting my anger and fury go.

Not until the man who killed my Beth is found and jailed.

****

We're interrupted by Colin Paterson who's pulling the tea trolley into the room and winking at us both, serves the other patients with their cuppas and digestive biscuits first before pulling the trolley over to where we're sitting.

"Heard a rumour there might be a sandwich available here so thought I'd do the tea run tonight," he has a quick look around him before dragging a chair across to join us.

I'm smiling as I open the cool bag and take out the plastic bag with the sandwiches, then hand them one each.

"You're a star, Missus B," he grins at me before wolfing it down.

"So, you've heard the good news about our favourite patient here," he turns to stare at Liz.

Liz has the good grace to blush and while I'm thinking that Liz definitely likes him, I'm also wondering if Colin's attention is more professional than romantic. Then I find myself hoping that he really likes my Liz, that he's not just doing his job, because I'm worrying that if she wears her heart on her sleeve and gets a knockback and vulnerable as she is, it could set her recovery back and she might be in here even longer.

He's not aware I'm staring at him and then I think, oh my God! What if he's married!

What a tizzy I'm getting into as I try to manoeuvre myself to catch a glimpse of his left hand, just as Liz asks me, "Are you okay, Mum? You're looking a wee bit pale there."

I startle and can feel my face getting red and stutter, "Oh, I'm fine. Honest."

I decided to brazen it and ask him, "So, what do you get up to on your days off, Colin?"

"Me?" his brow creases as though he's thinking hard then replies, "Bit of fishing, tidying the house, catching up with washing; all the domestic stuff, you know? Oh, and catching up with my favourite shows that I miss when I'm on shift. Game of Thrones, for example. Do you watch it yourself, Missus B?"

Is that an attempt to deflect me, I'm wondering, but press on with, "Nobody to do your washing and ironing for you, then?"

"Not unless you're volunteering," he grins.

He's shaking his head and I don't have to look to feel that Liz is glaring at me as he continues, "No, not yet. But I'm still looking." There's a definite innuendo there, so I decide it might not be prudent to carry on and brightly smiling, I turn to Liz and tell her, "Father O'Brien sends his best. Asked me if you wouldn't mind him coming over and giving you a visit one afternoon."

I don't miss the sharp glance between them and don't have time to take a suspicious breath, but it's Colin who replies, "She was wanting to keep it a secret for the minute, but there's a likelihood that Liz might be going home before the end of the week."

I'm speechless and a little overwhelmed and I can feel myself well up with tears. I bite at my lower lip to stop the flood as Liz reaches across to take my hand.

"I wanted to surprise you, Mum. You okay?"

I can only nod and take a deep breathy that I slowly let out as Colin

says, "Of course, it's up to Doc Francis and there's one stipulation."
"That is?" I narrow my eyes.
"Weekly counselling as an outpatient, but the good news is when she comes back for the counselling, I get to see her," he blushes.
Liz playfully punches him on the shoulder and like a big wean he pretends it hurt, but the playacting between them confirms what I was already coming to suspect.
There was more going on between this pair than simple patient and nurse and for some reason, I felt a warm glow; something I hadn't felt since…well, since God knows when.
"Right," Colin suddenly stood up and grabbed at the tea trolley.
"I've other patients to attend to, Missus Chalmers." With a nod to me, he wheels the trolley away, whistling cheerfully as he leaves the room.
"I think he likes you," I whisper to her, which is about as perceptive as noticing it's dark outside.
"You think so?" her face reddens.
"Do you like him, sweetheart?"
"Aye, Mum, I do. He's been very kind to me and he knows the state I was in when I got here, so it's not as if I can hide anything from him."
"Isn't there some kind of code of ethics, though? Him being a nurse and you being a patient?"
"I think that's more to do with doctors and patients, Mum," she gives me a reproving frown, "but you're right. He said that as much as he'd like to see me, he'll wait till I was discharged and then he'll ask me out. Do you mind?"
I'm a little surprised that she needs my approval, but realise she desperately wants me to like him. Then I ask, "Why would I mind, Liz? All I want is for you to get well and for your happiness, you know that."
I watch as she visibly relaxes, then she says, "It's just that you being a strong Catholic and, well, legally and in the eyes of God…"
"The eyes of the church," I correct her because I know what's coming next.
"Okay, in the eyes of the *church*, I'm still married to Ian. If I was to start going out with Colin," she shrugs.
"You think that I'd be angry or annoyed with you?"
I'm shaking my head as though to confirm her foolishness at

thinking such a thing then open my arms and she rises from her chair to give me a cuddle.

"Listen, hen, I don't always disagree with the Big Man upstairs, but there are some things that He and I do agree about and that's the right for someone to be happy, regardless what Canon Law might say."

I'm staring into her bright blue eyes and for a brief second I see Alex's eyes, then I continue. "If making you well and more importantly, making you happy means living outside the rules of the church, then that's okay by me. Besides, I pray enough for the two of us, don't I?"

She's smiling happily then as if something has just come to mind, she gushes, "That other thing I wanted to tell you. Wait here," and hurries out of the room.

She's gone but a minute and returns with a large, opened brown envelope that she hands to me.

"This was delivered to me this morning."

I reach in and withdraw several typed A4 pages and first glancing at the papers, stare curiously at her.

"Don't bother reading it all, I'll explain what's in it. It's from Ian's solicitor," she shrugs again and to my surprise, smiles widely. "He wants a divorce on the ground I'm a raving nutter who is out to get him."

****

Its half an hour later when Liz walks me to the door of the Ward. Now that she's on the mend and on the cusp of being discharged, there's really nothing to stop her walking me to my car, but it's raining hard and I insist she stay indoors because I don't want her catching her death of cold.

After hugging her goodnight, I'm in the motor and driving through the gates onto Crookston Road. The dashboard clock says it's ten minutes after nine, but I've already made up my mind; I'm just going to visit Jessie for ten minutes and see that she's okay.

Or that's what I tell myself.

As I head down Sandwood Road and onto Hillington Road to join the M8, my mind is playing over and over what Liz told me is in the lawyer's letter.

Basically, the way Liz explained it, it seems that Ian is blaming Liz for the loss of their daughter, citing that having care and custody of

Beth, her poor parenting skills led to their daughter being abandoned in a dark and hostile environment that resulted in her murder.

How nasty is that, eh?

The letter also indicated that as Liz was now a Sectioned Patient of the State and therefore due to her current unstable mental state, Ian believed Liz to be untrustworthy and if she were ever to be released to continue their marriage might leave him open and vulnerable to physical violence from her.

Shocked and outraged, I had been about to let go a few expletives, something I never do, but Liz only grinned and said, "Look at it this way, Mum. I fight this divorce and stay married to him or I speak to a lawyer to get his allegations changed and agree to the divorce. Of course, it might mean that at the end of the day I'm the bad guy in this, but it would also mean that I'm free of him."

When did my lassie become so smart? I stare at her in wonder, then a thought had struck me and I'd asked, "Have you already spoken with someone about this?"

"I showed the letter to Colin. His brother's wife works in a law office and he says he'll ask her what she knows about divorce law. He said he'd go with me to any meeting if I get a lawyer of my own."

She's staring nervously at me and I know why. She's worried I'll be upset that she never asked me to accompany her.

"That sound like a good idea," I hear myself saying, though if I'm honest, yes; I'd like to be the one to accompany her when she visits a lawyer, but I suppose if there is going to be something between her and Colin Paterson then maybe it's time I stood back and let her have her head.

I'm turning onto the M8 and the Satnav on my mobile phone is telling me that I should use the Clyde Tunnel. Marvellous things, these mobile phones, aren't they?

Anyway, it's getting really dark and the rain doesn't help any, what with the wipers going back and forth. Very distracting it is and particularly as I'm beginning to feel this wasn't one of my best ideas.

Thank heavens for the Satnav for without it I'd be really lost because I don't know the Summerston area that well.

At last it directs me to Craigbo Place and I turn into some council flats that are ground floor and two storeys high. There's a burned out van parked beside the brick built enclosure that holds the bins and a couple of other cars parked there that cause me to think the area isn't that affluent. Not all the street lighting is working, but there's enough light to permit me to see that across the car park on the opposite building, rusting scaffolding is clamped to the outside building where the roughcast has fallen off and looks like it's been there for years. I get the impression that after the council gave up on the area, so did the tenants. But then I notice that some of the flats have replacement windows that seems to me to be privately owned homes, so perhaps then some of the residents do care about the place.

I peer through the windscreen at the entrance to the close at number four and my stomach is doing somersaults because again, I'm wondering what the heck made me think visiting Jessie was going to do her any good.

I sit for a minute and that's when I notice the gang of teenagers; well, I say gang, but there is maybe about four or five of them who are standing in the dimly lit foyer out of the rain and staring out through the glass in the door at me. Then I'm thinking; what number constitutes a gang?

Heavens, the funny things that you think about when you're nervous. Before I know it suddenly I'm pulling the key out of the ignition and getting out of the car, I hurry across the road through the rain towards the entrance. When I get there I pull open the door and the wee buggers are all staring at me.

My heart's in my mouth and my throat is as dry as a bone. One of the group, a young lad no more than fifteen wearing a dark coloured hooded top with the hood up, is stood in the middle of the entrance blocking my way.

What is it about teenagers and wearing their hoods up when they're indoors or under cover?

Now, don't ask me where it comes from, but I sound as though I'm a cast member of 'Taggart' when I stare him down and hear my voice rasp, "You got a problem, wee man?"

A young girl beside him giggles as sullenly, he moves to one side and I step past him, half expecting a big knife to be thrust into my back.

My legs are fair shaking, but I don't even look behind me, just walk towards the first door, but neither of the ground flat doors is Jessie's house.

My legs still shaking, I make my way up the cold stairs to the first landing and the first door I come to bears the name 'Cochrane' on a highly polished brass plate. That's got to be Jessie's flat, I'm thinking. If nothing else she's a cleaner through and through.

Taking a deep breath and still not convinced I'm doing the right thing, I knock on the door that's fractionally opened within seconds by a young lassie who I rightly guess is Jessie's twenty-two-year-old daughter Mary, though from the height and stout build of her she must take after her father because she's nothing like her slightly built mother. Her shoulder length fair hair is damp and she's wearing her work uniform so I'm guessing she's just arrived home after her shift at the Asda store in Maryhill.

Mary stares curiously at me, but before I can say who I am, I hear Jessie behind her asking, "Who the devil is knocking on the door at this time of night?"

Jessie whose wearing a faded blue coloured cotton dressing gown with her hair pulled back into a tight ponytail, pulls the door fully open and her eyes open in surprise. Well, one eye anyway, because the other one is black and blue and swollen shut.

"Maggie! What the hell are you doing here at this time of the night? Is something wrong, hen? Are you okay?"

I have an immediate sense of guilt, for this woman who believes me to be her best friend and who quite obviously has taken another beating from her husband, is more concerned with my welfare than her own.

I swallow with difficulty and reply, "I'm fine, Jessie. I'm just back from the hospital visiting Liz and thought I'd pop up to see how you're doing."

Before she can respond, I hear a mans voice call out, "Who the fuck is that at the door, Jessie! I'm watching the telly. Tell them to get to hell."

Both she and Mary nervously glance behind them then in a lowered voice, Jessie says, "This is maybe not a good time for a visit, hen. I'm sorry, but we're a wee bit busy, you understand."

Did I tell you I read a lot of crime fiction? That and I'm a big fan of 'Still Game?'

Well, it's the sight of Jessie's eye that sets me off and you'll never in a million years believe me when I tell you what I did next. In fact, I can hardly believe it myself, idiot that I am.

I will never, ever understand where I got the idea or the determination, but the next thing I know is that I'm moving past Jessie and Mary like a woman possessed and aware that the two of them are staring at me like I'm demented because there's me marching down the hallway to where I can hear the television blaring and I'm pushing open the door into what is the front room. An unshaven and fat, balding man who from her description of him is Jessie's husband Ernie, is sitting in an armchair facing the blaring television. He's wearing a vest and tracksuit bottoms, but no socks or shoes and is holding a can of Tenants lager in his fist. A younger, skinny man dressed in a bright yellow tracksuit and looking like an overripe banana, presumably Jessie's son I'm thinking, is lounging on the couch. The two of them stare curiously at me, but I'm looking for the remote control and see it sitting on the arm of the armchair. I grab it and, well, everybody knows the red button is the on off switch, isn't it?

By now my dander is up and I throw the remote into Ernie's lap and tell him, "You, ya fat git! You've hit my pal for the last time! Call yourself a man, ya coward! Well, your wife might not be reporting you to the polis, but under the terms of Common Law then as a citizen I can act on her behalf and I'm leaving here to head down to Maryhill police station to have them send two constables up here to arrest you! And you *do* know that domestic assault means a night in the jail and an appearance tomorrow morning at the Sheriff Court where likely you will be detained in custody till time of trial!"

Well, it's all hokum of course, but he doesn't know it. Besides, I've run out of steam and my heart is beating that fast in my chest I'm almost sure that the rest of them can hear it.

Nobody says a word, they just all stare wide-eyed at me, but then Ernie slowly says, "Who the fuck *are* you?"

"Me?" I've got my breath back and I bend down till my face is just a foot from his and glaring at him, I hiss, "I'm the woman that's going to get you the jail!"

My eyes are boring into his and it's like that old game you played when you were weans; do you remember? The 'who's going to blink first' game?

Thankfully, he does, then he turns to her and his face contorted, mumbles, "Jessie?"

Right on cue, God bless and keep her, she replies, "It's just like she says, Ernie. She wants to get you the jail. I've tried to talk her out of it," she glibly lies, "but she'll not hear of it. She's determined to get you done for hitting me, so she is."

His head swivels on his shoulders as a couple of times he looks at us in turn.

"I'm sorry, hen, it was the drink," he blusters, his face reddening and turns to stare almost beseechingly at me, but I'm just stood there trying my best not to panic and throw up. Then he turns to Jessie's and whines, "You know I didn't really mean it, hen."

"For fucks sake, Da, what are you listening to her for?" the skinny son gets off the couch and takes a step towards me, his face red and angry and his fists bunching, but to my surprise and definitely to my relief, Jessie's daughter Mary steps between us and pushing him back down onto the couch, she sneers, "You going to be a big man, Billy, and hit a woman too? Why don't you try and hit me, ya bandy-legged wee shite, ya!"

The tension in the room cracks up to almost breaking point, but then Jessie grabs me by the arm and pulls me to the door as she loudly says, "Stay there, Ernie, I'll try to talk her out of it."

Pulling me into the hallway, she slams the door behind her and starts to push me to the front door.

"Are you out of your mind, ya halfwit!" she whispers to me. "Where did you get all that stuff about acting for me and getting the polis up her to arrest my man?"

Did I mention my legs are shaking? That and I'm thinking I should have gone for a pee before I left the hospital.

"I'm sorry, Jessie, but when I saw what he's done to you," I'm nodding at her eye.

"Aye, that's all well and good, Maggie, but I'm not wanting the polis calling at my door. I'm already the talk of the neighbourhood," she mutters as she leads me onto the stair landing.

I suddenly feel the need to shiver, but it's nothing to do with the chill in the close.

"I made it up, about getting the police I mean," I tell her and I'm feeling a bit sheepish as I make my confession.

She's staring blankly at me, then to my astonishment she begins to giggle.

"You made it up! Bloody hell, Maggie, I don't know about Ernie, but you had me convinced! Did you see his face when you burst in and switched off the football? And when you threatened him with the cops? My God, that was worth getting a black eye," she's now got a hand across her mouth to stifle her laughter and begins to grunt like a pig on steroids.

I find I'm laughing too, though to be honest I think mine is delayed hysteria. Then the door opens and Mary, looking at us like we've gone off our heads, steps out into the landing and pulls the front door closed behind her.

"He's in there talking to Billy about what might happen to him if you get the polis," she directs her comment to me, then her brow creases as she asks, "Will you get the polis to him, missus? Not like he doesn't deserve it," she sighs, her arms crossed and it's evident she's no time for her father.

I'm about to explain that I was bluffing, but Jessie is way ahead of me and raising one hand, says, "Not tonight, hen. I've talked her out of it, but if your father ever lifts his hand to me again…" she shrugs. Yet no matter how confident Jessie might sound I think we both know that all I've maybe done is won her a wee bit of a respite for men like her bullying husband just don't change, do they?

"Are they wondering at work why I'm off," she asks and I can see the shame in her face.

As gently as I dare, I reply, "They can wonder all they want, Jessie. Your business is your business, hen, so…"

But I get no further for Mary, her eyes widening as though a light has been turned on, butts in with, "Maggie! That's who you are! You're my mammy's pal from her work, the woman whose wee granddaughter was killed, is that right?"

If ever there was a conversation killer, this is it. I simply nod and turning back to Jessie, suggest she use Arnica gel on her eye before I tell her that if she needs anything, she's just to give me a phone and hurriedly I give her my mobile number.

It's only when I'm heading back down the stairs and find the teenagers gone from the foyer and the rain stopped that I realise how frightened I really was.

****

On the drive all the way home, I'm still reeling from my cheek in facing up to Jessie's husband and it's only when I reach Knightswood that I start smiling. But then I'm thinking I'm lucky he didn't see through my bluff or it might have been me that had a black eye this time. That said though, I'm not his wife. I'd have been straight down to the police station and had him charged.

Believe it or not I've been home a good thirty minutes and had a bowl of soup before I see that the wee red light is blinking on my phone's answer machine and my heart nearly stops. It's the first thing I think of; is something happened to Liz?

It's an old machine and when I press the button and the tape stops whirring around, I hear a man mutter: *"Bloody machines."* Then as if he realises he's now being recorded, he says, *"Oh, Missus Brogan? It's, eh, five minutes past six and...sorry, its DS Reid, Alan Reid calling. I'm still at the office going through the investigation files. Sorry, I've just remembered that you said you work split shifts so likely I'll be away home when you get in. The thing is, I was wondering if you'll be home tomorrow about midday? There's a couple of points I'd like to clarify with you, if you don't mind. If that time doesn't suit you can call me at the office and we can arrange a mutually agreeable time. The office number is on the card I left you. Eh, right, thank you. Bye."*

Now, I'm wondering, what exactly is it that he wants clarified?

CHAPTER FIVE

When the alarm goes off at five-thirty I've already been awake a good hour because to be honest my mind was in a whirl thinking about how stupid I had been last night. I mean, imagine me going to Jessie's house and acting like that actor guy Rambo. Just as well I got away with it and I'm not sporting a sore face like my wee pal. Of course getting up for my work at that time is just like what everyone else does, it's a routine. However, because of my sleepless night I'm feeling a bit lethargic this morning and it even crosses my mind to phone in sick. But doesn't everybody at some time use that excuse?

Anyway, I don't and after a quick breakfast of my usual toast and coffee I'm washed and dressed and out of the door.

In the car I stop at the end of the driveway and see Willie from next door just arriving home from his work. I give him a wave, but either he doesn't see me, which is likely, or he's ignoring me, which is unlikely. Like I told you, he's an awfully shy man is Willie.

His wife Moira is a fulltime housewife, I think. I say I think because to be frank I've never had a long enough conversation with her to ask her if she's working or not. You probably think that's pretty odd, us having been neighbours for over five years, but they're that quiet so they are. In fact, I don't think it's just me; I can't recall ever seeing them mixing socially with any of the neighbours.

Listen to me; you'd think by the way I'm talking I was the life and soul of the Crescent but far from it. Like I said before, it's a quiet area and folk keep themselves to themselves. Most of the houses in the Crescent are what the council used to call four in a block, but what the estate agents call quarter villas; however, I'm in one of the few two bedroomed semi-detached houses, though years ago we extended at the back to give us a good sized dining kitchen that's bright and airy and like Alex predicated, added value to the property.

As for the neighbours in the Crescent, that's not to say there wasn't a lot of kindness shown during that initial period after Beth's body was found. Some of them put genuine sympathy cards through the door and some even arranged for Father O'Brien to say special masses for Beth thought I gather not everyone who arranged the masses were Catholic. One incident always comes to mind.

The reporters from the papers who went round the doors to try and get information about Beth made the mistake of calling on old Sammy who lives five doors along. A widower, Sammy must be nearly eighty now and I once heard it said he was a committed Communist who worked in the shipyards, but he's a feisty old guy and when the reporters turned up at his door he had a hosepipe ready and waiting. Called them parasites and doused the lot of them and when they complained to the police about their clothes and camera equipment getting soaked, it was PC Phil Cuthbertson who arrived and told them that if they hadn't been harassing the residents it wouldn't have happened.

The memory still brings a smile to my face and I admit it surprised me when Father O'Brien let it slip that Sammy was one of the neighbours who had called upon him to arrange a Mass for Beth. Bless the old bugger.

Driving along I glance up and I'm pleased to see for a change it's a bright October day and I'm into work sharp.

Tommy Burton is waiting for me and I can see he's relieved that I'm there.

"What, did you think I was going to get myself arrested?" I ask him.

"I just never know with you, hen," he shakes his head and walks off.

I head for the changing room and almost immediately I'm aware of the conversation dying to a whisper as I enter the locker room and realise I've been getting talked about.

Honest, I can't have been in the room a minute when I'm called by my name and as usual, it's big Eileen McNulty with her arms crossed who asks me, "Heard Jessie's man gave her another doing, Maggie. Is that right?"

Now, let me describe Eileen to you. About my age and height, so that makes her five feet seven, her hair has been dyed blonde so many times its like crinkly straw. She's easily seven or eight stone overweight and with a face that would stop a bus, she looks like a woman searching for somewhere to have a stroke or a heart attack. Don't let me forget to mention she's an aversion to personal hygiene too. She's the barrack room lawyer of the cleaning staff with a voice that could shatter glass. I once heard she's also been suspected to be light-fingered and suffice to say if money goes missing from a purse, Eileen's usually the first name that comes to everybody's mind.

Now, you'll be wondering why Tommy Burton and the rest of the supervisors don't find an excuse to get shot of her? Well, the word is that Eileen has something on Tommy or as one of the cleaners once put it, she has him by the short and curlies. What that something is I haven't a clue, but given his reputation for wandering hands, I can hazard a guess.

Most of the women, though they'd never admit to it, are scared of her but guess what; I'm not one of them.

I don't even turn around to look at her when I reply, "Who told you that, Eileen?"

"I just heard, on the grapevine, you know?"

"No, I don't really know," I drily reply. "What grapevine is that, Eileen?"

I still don't look at her, but fetching my tabard out from the locker and slipping it on I'm aware of the silence in the room as the rest of the staff watch me.

"Just what's being said," I can hear the sneer in her voice.

"And who's saying it, Eileen."

"So, it's true?"

I turn slowly to face her and there's just an arms length between us and for some reason I have this unaccustomed but irresistible urge to take her by her dyed hair and bash her head off the lockers.

Now don't get me wrong here, I'm not a woman who would even think about getting engaged in a physical fight or anything like that, but sometimes, just like everybody else, I get that urge, you know? However, I surprise myself with my restraint as I calmly reply, "What's true? That you're standing here blethering about one of your colleagues? That you're a nosey two-faced cow with such a sad life that you think by delving into another woman's private life it will make you feel better about yourself?"

I watch her face redden as her mouth falls open and I see her hands clench into fists, but I'm not finished.

"So tell me…" but then I stop and wave a hand about the room. "No, tell us all, Eileen. What exactly do *you* get out of it, gossiping about Jessie Cochrane and her life?"

She grits her teeth and I get the feeling she's about to go for me, but big as she is I'm ready for her and the thing is, I can see it in her eyes that she knows it.

Unaware of the tension in the room, Tommy Burton steamrolls through the door, clapping his hands as if that's going to make us react faster.

"Come on now, ladies, let's get your arses out there."

It's the perfect opportunity for Eileen to turn about to save face and leave without answering me.

Nobody says anything, but I don't miss the hesitant smiles and approving looks that I get as we're all hustled out of the room by Tommy to our cleaning floors.

****

Now don't be thinking I'm any kind of hero standing up to Eileen McNulty. Far from it. Catching the lift to the fourth floor, my knees are knocking again and I can feel a sweat breaking out under my arms. Yet, and please don't ask me to explain it, I'm grinning like an idiot. Okay, I'll admit it, I'm a wee bit proud of myself for standing up for my pal Jessie when nobody else would and yes, it made Eileen look foolish in the eyes of the other women; women who frightened of her will be more than happy to see her taken down a peg or two.

When the lift stops I head for the corridor cupboards and fetch out my cleaning materials.

My first job is emptying the bins into large plastic sacks and leaving them by the lift to be collected by the male janitors who take them out to the big bins at the rear of the building, then, it's down to the dusting, hoovering and mopping the laminated floors.

Without Jessie to help it's going to be a busy time for me and I've just filled my fourth bag with rubbish and making my way to the lift when the doors open and to my disbelief, who steps out but Eileen McNulty.

Of course my heart misses a beat and I'm thinking she's followed me up here for what I'm guessing is another round, but this time with fists, when to my surprise she averts her eyes and sullenly says, "Tommy told me I've to give you a hand with Jessie being off on the pat and mick."

Before I can reply, she sniffs and continues, "And before you ask, it wasn't my idea, okay?"

Me? I'm only happy that I'm not rolling about the corridor with the fat tub of lard and nodding, I tell her, "I've emptied the bins. If you want to make a start in the offices down that end," I nod behind her, "I'll do the ones this side of the lift, okay?"

"Fair enough," she mutters and off she rolls with her bucket and mop.

Much as I'd like to continue to tell you she's a waste of space, I have to admit that nobody can criticise her work ethos and I'm thinking maybe that's the real reason that Tommy Burton doesn't get rid of her, because she is such a good worker.

That said I still consider her to be a horrible bitch.

Before I know it the first of the office staff begin to arrive for work and of course, me being cleaning staff, none of them give me a blind bit of notice for after all, why would they?

No, that's not quite true. There are a couple of the older women, one or two of the younger ones and one or two of the older men who will regularly give me a nod or say hello, but most of the younger people are so far up their own backside with inflated egos of their job status that they must think it's beneath them to acknowledge the women wearing the tabards. I mean, who notices the women in the pinnies pushing the mop buckets unless they're wanting to moan about the toilets not being cleaned or their bins not being emptied.

As for me, I learned a long time ago when I was nursing that no matter the occupation, every job brings its own dignity so I simply ignore the stuck-up chins as I myself am ignored.

Before you ask, yes, I was once and admittedly briefly a qualified Enrolled Nurse working in the Royal Infirmary in the Medical Ward, but when I had my Liz, Alex and I decided that I would be a full time housewife and though the loss of my income meant tightening our belts a bit, I've never regretted my time with her. You see Liz was to be our only child for during the labour at the Rottenrow Maternity Hospital there was a complication. I developed a uterine rupture due to the retention of the afterbirth, which caused haemorrhaging and resulted in me having a hysterectomy. There was always a lingering doubt in my mind whether this was entirely necessary, but in those days nobody really questioned the decisions of doctors. Poor Alex was just so grateful to have me and Liz survive the birth that I don't think it ever occurred to him that maybe the hysterectomy might not have been necessary. Anyway, suffice to say that was the end of any further childbearing for me and hard though it was for both Alex and me to accept at the time, I give thanks every day for my Liz.

It's nearly nine o'clock and I'm just about to enter the cupboard to stow away my cleaning stuff when I see Eileen pushing her wheeled bucket towards me. Courteous person that I am, I stop to hold the door open for her but just as she reaches me a young woman, a teenage girl really that I recognise as one of the office staff, hurries after Eileen calling out to her, "Excuse me."

Whether Eileen hears her or just ignores her, I'm not certain, but the lassie, who can't have been more than eighteen or nineteen, is red faced and calls out louder, "Excuse me! Hey you! I'm speaking to you!"

Eileen briefly glances at me and I see her eyes flash, then pokerfaced turns to the lassie and pretending surprise, asks, "Are you speaking to me?"

"Yes, you, the cleaning person," the lassie haughtily waves her forefinger at Eileen and with a put on posh voice and apparently full of her own self-importance, says, "There's no toilet rolls in the downstairs ladies."

Eileen McNulty or not, I find I'm suddenly angry at the rudeness of the lassie and I'm biting at my lower lip because the corridor is now full of staff heading into their offices and you know that feeling you get when you know that something is going to happen?

To be fair to her, Eileen doesn't lose her temper or anything, but her face is the picture of innocence when very politely and loud enough for everybody passing by to hear, she says to the lassie, "We've two types of toilet rolls, miss. Do you want the normal tissues because you need to wipe yourself after having a pee or the quilted type for your morning shite?"

Well, if the floor could have opened up that poor lassie would have fallen through to the basement. Her face turns crimson and to loud laughter, she stomps off.

Turning away, Eileen winks at me then mutters in a low voice, "I'll cleaning person her, the cheeky wee cow."

I can't stop myself from grinning and for that one moment, that one brief instance; Eileen is forgiven being a bitch.

****

It's when I'm driving home that I think about what happened last night at Jessie's house and what happened this morning with Eileen McNulty and Tommy Burton's comments come to mind.

I'll say it again for you have to understand I'm not a confrontational person, not at all. Yet within the space of twenty-fours hours I've challenged a man who likely could have beaten me to death if he hadn't been such a coward and a woman twice my size who if she got me in a clinch, could have asphyxiated me with her underarm body odour.

What the devil is wrong with me?

It's not a midlife crisis. Heaven knows, I've had more than my fair share of that during the last four and a bit months. So, what's causing this behaviour, I ask myself?

I'm resolved that I need to speak to someone about it and decide if he's free this afternoon, I'll go and visit Father O'Brien; see what he thinks is wrong with me.

When I arrive home I'm about to turn to reverse into my driveway, but see my neighbour, Peter McGregor with his wee dog Alfie on the lead, just about to cross the entrance and wave him on. Peter skips across the driveway entrance and stops on the pavement on the other side and it's apparent he wants a word with me.

Locking the car I walk to the entrance of the driveway and say, "Morning, Peter, how are you?"

He's a fine looking big man, is Peter, and about my age and I've always thought of him as a Pierce Brosnan lookalike. He's married to Wilma, who's a hairdresser and who always dresses very glamorously. Peter is a lecturer at Glasgow Kelvin College, the former Stow College and father to their two sons who are up and away, both now married with their own families.

"Fine, Maggie, fine," he smiles at me with his dark hair that is just touched with grey, tanned face and a perfect set of white teeth and I can see why he's turned many a woman's head in his day.

"Not working today then?"

"No," he shakes his head. "I've some days lying and thought I'd take a couple off, recharge the old batteries so to speak, you know?"

I'm sensing that he's a little nervous and as I reach down to pet Alfie, he asks me, "So, what are you doing these days? Socially I mean?"

"Socially?"

His face reddens a little and clearing his throat, he licks nervously at his lips when he adds, "I mean, getting out much? It's just that I thought, if you were up for it, maybe you and I…"

In that instant I recognise where this is going, but I'm not wanting to embarrass him any further and glancing up at him I interrupt with a forced cheeriness into my voice as I lie, "Yes, family and friends have been very thoughtful, Peter. What about you and Wilma? Still a happily married couple?"

"Eh, oh, yes, of course," he blushes.

"Well, that was an early rise for me this morning," I tell him, "So I'll away in and get some housework done. Bye for now and tell Wilma you were speaking to me and that I said hello. I must pop by some time and have a cuppa with her."

Let me just say at this point I've no idea why I suggest that for I've never in my life popped by to have a cup of tea with his wife, never even been inside their house, but my rebuff and veiled warning is clear and unequivocal and he abruptly replies, "Yes, of course."

Then giving me a backhanded wave, he yanks at Alfie's lead and pulls the protesting wee dog along the road.

I'm smiling humourlessly as I walk to my front door, though I don't know whether to be flattered at Peter's clumsy attempt to ask me out or be angry at him for being a married man who's trying to chat me up and cheat on his wife.

In the house I stop and glance into the mirror in the hallway and though I know I've said it before, I'm aware I'm not a bad looking woman for my age, but here and now, let me tell you this; Alex was my husband for twenty-three years and though he's been dead these past five years, I haven't looked at or been with another man in that time.

So I wonder, what is it with men who suppose that because a woman is divorced or widowed they feel the need to step in and provide some sexual comfort?

As for me, okay, I admit that I can still admire a handsome man, but it's like window-shopping, isn't it? You can look, but you don't need to buy.

The other thing about widowhood is yes; at times I do get lonely. I admit to missing the companionship of a man, the companionship I shared with Alex. Someone to hold, to talk to, to lie in bed with and be close to. To laugh with, to share a meal and a glass of wine with. Someone in the evening when I'm tired to fetch me a cuppa or rub my weary feet. Simple things like someone to go to the movies or to a show at the Pavilion or the Kings Theatre.

Yes, I still have a few girl friends and it's all right saying I can do some of these things with my pals, but it's just not the same. I mean with Alex there was someone to hold my hand in the dark at the pictures or at the theatre or just even sitting in an evening at home, having a cuddle while watching the television.

Then there's lovemaking. Do I miss the sex you'll be wondering? Of course I do.

****

I'm conscious that the detective, DS Reid, is calling by at midday and decide that I'll have a cuppa and a digestive, but wait till he's gone to have lunch. I'm hoping whatever he wants to tell me or find out won't take that long for I like a sit down and to close my eyes before I get ready for the evening shift. I won't be visiting Liz this evening; it'll be straight home after work and a catch up with Poldark and NCIS on the telly.

I've over an hour before DS Reid arrives so I take the opportunity to do a bit of ironing and while I'm humming along to ABBA on Smooth Radio, before I know it the doorbell's ringing.

Bugger, I think and hurriedly sweep the clothes I've ironed into the basket with the rest of the stuff I've not got round to, unplug then lift the iron into the kitchen and folding the table, jam it into the hall cupboard as the doorbell rings again.

He must see my car in the driveway and that I'm in, I'm angrily thinking, so why does he persist in ringing the bloody bell again? Patting at my hair, I pull open the front door and see him stepping down off the steps as though he's leaving, but he turns and smiling, says, "Sorry, I thought maybe you'd popped out or something."

I can't keep the sarcasm from my voice when I nod at my motor and retort, "And I thought you were supposed to be a detective. Is the car not a clue?"

His eyes widen and then narrow as he replies with a soft smile, "Having a bad day, Missus Brogan?"

It's not what he says, it's the way he says it that makes it sound like a gentle rebuke and I flush before I apologise with, "Sorry, that was uncalled for. Please," I step to one side, "come in."

He steps up the two stairs and past me into the hallway and I nod that he goes through to the front room. I follow him and see that he's waiting to be invited to sit down and I indicate the chair where he sat before.

I see he's wearing the same suit, but a different shirt and if the collar is anything to go by, it's not been ironed either. I'm about to remark that five minutes earlier I could have done it for him, but hold my tongue because it would sound like sarcasm, then ask, "Your message said you wanted to clarify some points, Mister Reid? How can I help?"

Now, you might wonder why I'm not enthusiastic about him visiting, but I've already reasoned that if his visit was to impart some new information, like a break in the investigation, it would be his boss DCI Tennant who would be calling to brag about it, not the man who looks like a middle-aged, burned out Detective Sergeant who has had my granddaughter's murder dumped in his lap.

Honestly, I'm not usually so inhospitable, but I'm keen to get this done for I haven't had anything to eat since my slice of toast this morning and the digestive biscuit over an hour ago. That and the aroma from the pot of soup on the cooker that is wafting through the house smells delicious, though I say so myself.

Before he replies I see his nose twitch, then noticing me watching him, he smiles again as though he's caught sniffing the air and says, "Ah, yes, right. I've made a start on the investigation files. Everything has been downloaded onto computer CD's that contain all the statements and the Action's that I spoke of yesterday. Now, in response to your questions yesterday, Missus Brogan, I went straight to the post-mortem report and I can tell you that DCI Tarrant told you the truth; it seems the killer was disturbed before he could complete what he probably intended. Quite categorically, your granddaughter was not in any way sexually interfered with."

A sudden feeling of relief washes over me and I realise my hands are so tightly clasped in my lap that my fingers are hurting.

"As for your second question regarding the DNA. Regretfully, it's assessed the killer wore gloves and I'm trusting you to keep this to yourself," he grimaces. "It was assessed by the pathologist at the time of the post mortem that the killer placed his hand across her nose and mouth that caused her to suffocate. I'm sorry to be so blunt," he frowned, "but I'd rather be upfront with you than give you some kind of half-truth."

"Thank you," I hear myself whisper.

He obviously recognises that this information has caused me to be a little upset and waits for a moment or so to permit me to compose myself, and then he says, "One of the first statements I read was your own statement, Missus Brogan."

He fumbled with the catch of the leather folder he carried and took out some stapled sheets of paper. "I've printed out your statement that I have here," he waved the paper at me. "Do you recall the statement you gave?"

"Yes, well, most of it, I think. Why do you ask? Is there something wrong with it?"

"No, not all," he vigorously shakes his head. "Here, have a read of it just to refresh your memory," then hands it to me."

I'm a quick reader and scan the two typed sheets and when I'm done, I hand them back to him.

"So again," I'm realise I'm feeling a bit defensive here, "is there something wrong with my statement?"

"It's not that, but your statement was taken on the evening your granddaughter was killed, Missus Brogan. In fact, if the time the statement was taken is correct, it was just a few hours after her…" he stopped and staring at me, must have remembered my previous annoyance, because then he continues, "Sorry. Just a few hours after *Beth's* body was discovered."

"I'm not sure I know what you mean," I slowly drawl because truthfully, I don't really understand.

He suddenly leans forward as though he's about to divulge a great secret and slowly says, "Missus Brogan, at that time this statement was taken," he pokes a finger at the pages, "you had just learned of your granddaughter's murder. I can only imagine the grief you must have felt at the time. Your daughter Elizabeth is distraught, probably hysterical too and you're in your own state of distress at the awful news and the barest details are taken from you to complete this?" he flicks a hand against the sheets. "A page and a half of you trying to describe a wee girl's life?"

He's not gnashing teeth angry, but I can see he's clearly annoyed as he continues, "In the days that followed the discovery of Beth's body, did anyone from the inquiry, any of the investigating officers come back to you for further details about what happened? I mean, did *anyone* go over your original statement with you or did you give a second statement because to be frank," he's slowly shaking his head, "I can't find one."

I'm a bit taken aback and can only shake my own head, but then I find my voice and I tell him, "They, the police I mean, they had a policewoman stay with us for most of each day. A woman called Constable Sheila Gardener who told me she is a Family Liaison Officer. Sheila is very nice and kept me informed about what was happening, but no, I don't remember her going over my statement with me. Sheila has kept in touch with me," I tell him. "In fact, I'm having a coffee with her tomorrow morning in the city centre when I finish my work. Should I tell her about this, the police winding down the investigation?"

"There's no reason why not," he replies, "because I'm sure word will have got round the station by now anyway."

He sits back on the couch and stares thoughtfully at me then to my complete embarrassment, my stomach rumbles.

He dips his head and pretends to read the paperwork in his hand, but I can see he's trying not to laugh and I'm blushing when I say, "Sorry. It's just that I've not had anything since breakfast and to be honest, I could probably eat a monkey dipped in fat."

"My fault," he raises a hand, "I should have known better than to call at lunchtime. Please, if you need to eat something, go ahead and don't mind me."

And why shouldn't I, I'm thinking, because after all this *is* my house. I start to rise from my chair when on impulse; I ask him, "Have you had your lunch?"

His eyes betray his surprise when he replies, "No, I was intending grabbing a sandwich later."

"How about a bowl of soup, then? It's homemade."

His face lights up and when he broadly smiles, it definitely takes years off him.

"That would be grand, yes please."

In the kitchen I quickly set two places and microwave enough soup for us both, then cut up a crusty loaf and setting it between us, call him through while I set the kettle to boil for tea.

"Please," I indicate with my hand, "sit yourself down."

"This is awfully kind of you," he smiles as I place the soup down in front of him. I watch him take a sip then he says, "It's a been a while since I've had a good bowl of tasty, homemade soup."

I'm tempted to ask if his wife or partner cooks, but I don't want to seem nosey so just smile at the compliment.

We sit with both of us slurping away at the soup when the kettle clicking off breaks our silence.

"Would you prefer tea or coffee?" I ask him as I begin to rise from my chair.

"Tea would be fine," he nods, then adds, "but please, finish your soup first."

I sit back down and stifling a nervous laugh I wryly realise that for the first time since Alex died, I'm having lunch with a man.

Then it occurs to me how to find out something about Mister Reid, so I ask, "You said you had daughters and grandchildren?"
I don't say anymore, just wait for him to take my cue.
"Ah, yes, two girls and just the one grandchild, a boy. Fiona, she's thirty, the oldest. She's married and has Finn aged three. Bryony is twenty-seven and single. Well, she's seeing somebody, but I'm uncertain how serious it might be," and he grimaces.
"I'm guessing that you don't approve," I give him a slight grin.
"I'm probably just being judgemental because he's a painter and I don't mean decorator. I mean, who makes money these days painting pictures?"
I shrug and reply, "Maybe if she's happy that's all she needs."
He looks at me as though I'm mad then sighs and says, "I can't argue with that one, Missus Brogan. Money, status and influence don't make you happy, but it's not his occupation that annoys me. No, not annoy, I should say bothers me. It's his, well, I think it's his attitude more than anything."
I'm sensing there's more to that statement than he's letting on and he still hasn't mentioned a wife or partner. I'm reluctant to push it and get up to make the tea.
"Your statement says you were widowed five years ago," he says from behind me. "It can't have been easy being on your own and dealing with the loss of Beth and your daughter being admitted to the hospital so soon after it happened."
I remember he takes just milk and while I'm pouring a spot into both mugs, I respond, "Liz was twenty-one when Alex died and already out of the house living with her husband, Ian Chalmers. That said, the relationship with Liz and Ian was," I pause, searching for the right word and settle for, "…difficult. Neither Alex nor I approved of Ian and I still don't. He's treated Liz very badly throughout their relationship, but I'm pleased to say that it will soon come to an end."
"How so?"
I pour the tea and turning, lay the mugs down onto the table.
I can't help but smile as I tell him, "Liz is to be discharged from the hospital and probably by the end of the week. Ian consistently failed to support or even visit her while she was in there and only yesterday she learned that he intends divorcing her."
"Wait," he seems surprised, "I was unaware that your daughter, Liz, was still in the hospital." His brow wrinkles when he asks, "She's

been there for over four months? Oh, that kind of puts paid to me re-interviewing her, then."

As I sit down, for some reason I find I can hardly speak, that I'm suddenly overcome by emotion and can only nod. To my embarrassment, my eyes fill with tears and hurriedly getting to my feet, I manage to mumble, "Excuse me," and flee to the bathroom upstairs.

I take the opportunity to pee then washing my hands and face; I stare moodily at my reflection in the mirror.

What the heck got into me, I'm wondering, making a fool of myself in front of a complete stranger. I can only think that the confrontations with Jessie's husband and big Eileen McNulty and the news that the police are giving up investigating Beth's murder has all combined to shatter my nerves.

I brush back my hair and taking a deep breath, I head back downstairs.

I walk into the kitchen and about to apologise for my dashing out, but I'm surprised to see him stood at the kitchen drying off the second of the two soup bowls.

"You washed up?"

"Well, you did treat me to lunch so it's the least I could do," he grins at me.

"I'm sorry, you must think me a right idiot."

"What?" he flaps the dishtowel then drapes it across the back of a chair, "Because you obviously care and worry about your daughter's welfare, Missus Brogan?" I watch his face as he purses his lips, before he adds, "Look, when I arrived yesterday with the news that the police are standing down the investigation, I don't think I realised just how much it must affect you. Officially I have to stand by DCI Tarrant's decision. Unofficially," he shrugs, "I think he's making a dreadful mistake. Yes," he nods, "I'm guessing that he's had official backing from the senior management who likely are more conscious of the cost of keeping a team working full time on the investigation than the impact Tarrant's decision has on the victim's family. Oh," his voice drips with sarcasm when he continues, "and far from me being the one who thinks the public would be outraged if they knew that it was a financial decision to wind down the investigation."

He stares keenly at me then says, "But then the media would have to learn about it, wouldn't they?"

My eyes narrow as I consider his suggestion and I say, "So, if I contacted the papers and told them about the police's decision, they might run a story about it and it could change Tarrant's mind?"

He stares at me for a few seconds then with a wide smile, replies, "Now, how did you come up with that idea, Missus Brogan, about contacting the media?"

I return his smile and say, "I fancy another cup of tea, Mister Reid. Now, what else do you want to discuss about my statement?"

****

We've sat now for a good hour and I'm mentally drained for he's asked so many question about the night Beth was killed, about Liz's relationship with Ian and with me, about my relationship with Ian as well as my relationship with my neighbours and who if any of them showed any particular interest in Beth. He's quizzed me about any regular or casual callers to the house who might have known or interacted with Beth and finally, any suspicions I had or have about anyone in particular.

I've watched as he made multiple notes on several sheets of paper and of course it occurs to me why these questions were not previously asked of me.

At last he seems satisfied that he's got enough and I watch as he shoves the papers into his leather folder and zips it closed.

"I'm conscious you work a split shift, Missus Brogan, so maybe we'll call it a day for now, eh?"

I turn to glance at the clock and to my surprise it's almost four o'clock and I briefly wonder where the time went.

"Have you got what you want," I nod at the folder.

"For now," he smiles as he stands up, "but if I learn you're putting on another pot of that delicious homemade soup, I might have some more questions to ask."

"Oh, thanks for washing up. You must be quite domesticated," I smile back at him as he turns towards the door.

"Aye, well living alone, I've learned to keep on top of things. Well, most things," he offers me a grin."

"Oh, you're not married then?" I blurt out then mentally kick myself for being so nosey.

He opens the door and stepping out into the hallway, replies, "I was for a number of years, but it didn't work out."

"Oh, I'm sorry," I instinctively reply, though why *I'm* sorry God knows. I mean his failed marriage is nothing to do with me, is it? An awkward silence falls between us, but then as he pulls open the front door he brightly says, "If nothing else, I've two smashing daughters to show for the marriage so I don't see it as a complete disaster. Right then," he turns to me as he steps out onto the door. "You'll likely see me in the street darting back and forth over the next couple of days because I intend re-interviewing some of your neighbours. I'll ask that any of them you happen to speak to, don't mention I'll be calling. Is that okay?"

"Of course," I reply and watch as he turns to walk down the driveway to his CID car.

I close the door and glance at my wristwatch and realise I don't have time before I leave for work, but tomorrow morning when I get home, I think I'll be looking for the phone number of the news desk for the 'Glasgow News.'

CHAPTER SIX

Wednesday morning dawns bright and thankfully dry, so if the weather broadcast is correct, it should be a rain free day, if a little windy. That prompts me to get up a little early and get a washing done that I manage to hang out on the line before I leave for work. Jessie still hasn't turned up and I'm guessing she wants her eye to die down a little before she makes an appearance. To my relief I get no more than a cursory nod from Eileen McNulty and while I don't expect she's forgotten or forgiven me standing up to her, for the minute there's a tacit truce between us.

I get through the morning without any problem, the only thing of interest is the young woman who Eileen ridiculed yesterday passed me by a couple of time with her face turned away and her eyes still showing that she's blazing mad. That will be the cleaning staff off the Christmas card list then, I think to myself.

I've brought a change of clothes with me for when I'm done and before I leave the building I nip into the ladies' loo and change from my jeans and old sweater into a blouse and skirt and pair of sling back heels. That done I undo my ponytail and brush my hair before applying some war paint and with a final glance in the mirror and my works clothes and trainers stuffed into my oversized shoulder bag, that's me ready to go and meet Sheila Gardener, the policewoman.

When I parked earlier this morning I warned my wee pal at the car park that I might be a bit late getting back to the car, but he just tipped his bunnet at me and said, "Don't you worry about that, Missus. I'll look after your motor for you and you just come back when you're ready."

That will be worth a fiver in the old guy's pocket when I collect it later and that's a damn sight cheaper than the more central car parks.
****

I've arranged to meet Sheila at ten in Café Nero in Frasers on Buchanan Street and when I get there I find that she's waiting for me and already grabbed a table by the small window that looks out onto the precinct. On the four or five occasions we've previously met, we take turns buying and it is Sheila's turn today so after a quick hug, she's away to the counter and returns with two large lattes and two plates with what she assures me is low calorie cakes.

Aye, right.

Sheila is forty-five, a good looking woman about my height with auburn hair to her shoulders who has been a policewoman for twenty-five years and worked in the Maryhill area for most of that time. She's married with a son at Glasgow Uni and a daughter studying for her Highers. Her husband is a uniformed Inspector who works in the Motherwell area and though I've not met him, the way she talks about him causes me to think they're happily married.

I know that she lives out in the Carnbroe area that is somewhere in North Lanarkshire, but I've not been invited to visit and I wouldn't ask. If the truth be told, while I like Sheila and had we met under any other circumstances, I think we might have become good friends, but the tragedy of losing Beth is the reason we met and that will always be an unspoken elephant in the room.

We start off with pleasantries: I ask about her family and how they're doing and then she asks how Liz is getting on? I tell her the good news about Liz being discharged by the end of the week and I'm pleased that she seems genuinely happy for me. Before I can help myself I'm telling her about the nurse Colin Paterson and my suspicions that Liz has become increasingly fond of him.

"About time that lassie had a bit of good luck," she sighs, then seeing my face, says, "What?"

I tell her about my reservations, that maybe Liz has mistaken Colin's attention to her as personal rather than professional.

"Do you not think, Maggie, that maybe you're just being an overprotective mother? Not that it's a bad thing," she hastily holds up her hand to quell my protest, "but knowing what Liz has gone through and not just since Beth died, but the years before with that clown of a husband of her…"

You'll have guessed Sheila has met Ian Chalmers,

"…then perhaps you might consider taking a step back and letting Liz have her head. If it turns out that she gets hurt again, well, you're still her mum and you'll be there for her. If on the other hand it turns out this guy really *does* like her…"

She leaves the rest unsaid as I shrug. When I then tell her about Ian Chalmers lawyers letter to Liz, she mutters, "Bastard!" then grins as she apologises.

I can see that she's got it on her mind and is keen to know and so I take a bite of my cake to give her the opportunity to ask me, then almost warily she says, "You'll have been told that the CID have pulled the plug on Beth's investigation?"

I'm nodding as I return my plate with the cake to the table and swallow, dusting some crumbs off my skirt as I do so before I reply, "I had a visit on Monday from a Detective Sergeant Reid who broke the news. Do you know him?"

"No," she shakes her head. "I heard there's a new DS joined the Maryhill CID, but I don't know anything about him."

"Anyway, DS Reid said he had been sent by DCI Tarrant and inferred it was because the lazy bugger was too busy to come himself."

"Aye, that Tarrant's a piece of work," she shook her head. "Word in the office is that the senior management weren't too happy about him winding down the investigation…"

"So just over four months giving up on investigating a child's murder isn't normal?" I quickly butt in.

"I'm no expert, Maggie, but I wouldn't think so, no. Look," she stares at me, "I'm not trying to justify Tarrant's decision, but these days with the cuts in budget and the pressures on managers, officers of Tarrant's rank are between a rock and a hard place. In the face of public and local government pressure, with dwindling numbers of officers and even less resources they're given targets to achieve and told to get results no matter what. That and some of the bad press the senior management have gotten in the last couple of years. Yes," she raised a hand as if to quell my interruption, "I know the newspapers say that recruitment is up blah, blah, blah, but figures can be manipulated, can't they? I mean, on my shift on paper there are, let me think," her forehead wrinkles as she mentally counts them off, "sixteen constables to cover the Maryhill beats. However, lose two to sickness or injury, lose another couple to courses, lose two more to office duties then a couple more off the street because they're catching up with paperwork or doing reports for the Procurator Fiscal and we've also got a young probationer who is off on maternity leave. So you're left with what," she uses her fingers to count them off, and her voice drips with sarcasm when she adds, "Aye, it looks good on paper, but it's seven cops doing the work of sixteen. Now, for talking's sake, let's say it's a Friday night and four cops are involved in a disturbance and arrest three neds. That ties them up in the office doing the paperwork, etcetera. That leaves three of us *now* doing the work of sixteen." She pauses then continues and almost apologetically says, "While I don't agree with Tarrant I can only imagine that he's been told by someone higher up who likely will deny ever saying it, that if his crime figures do not increase because he's seconding detectives to a murder investigation with no probability of a detection, then it's his career and promotion on the line. So what are his choices? Keep sending detectives out looking for clues or evidence where there is none or wrap up the investigation in the meantime in the forlorn hope something pops up at a later date? Or as he has done, put this guy Reid onto the case with a watching brief and use his CID to investigate detectable crime that will increase his arrest statistics."

"I do understand, Sheila," I slowly reply and to my embarrassment again, I feel tears pricking at my eyes, "but to be honest I don't care about the pressures that Tarrant or any police officer is under. All I want is someone to tell me that my wee Beth's murder will not be forgotten."

She reaches across the table and tightly holds my hand.

"No murder in Scotland is forgotten, Maggie. Something will turn up and we'll get the man that did it. Now, why don't you nip to the ladies' and wash your face and I'll get us another couple of lattes?"

I do as she suggests and five minutes later, feeling better, I return to the table where I see Sheila's head bent as she pores over her mobile phone and I can see that she's worried.

I slowly sit back down as she raises a finger that she'll just be a minute, and then closing her phone says, "Sorry, that was a text in from my Inspector. There's a wean gone missing from the high flats at Kelso Street over in the Yoker area. I'm supposed to be off duty, but I'm on call as a Family Liaison Officer, I'll need to go, Maggie. Sorry," she shrugs as she stands up and grabs at her handbag from the back of her chair."

"The wean, is it a boy or a girl," I gasp.

"I don't know. All the text says is a four year old child."

But then she stops and placing a comforting hand on my shoulder, says, "Look, Maggie, don't be getting your hopes up over somebody else's missing wean. That will only drive you nuts," then as if realising the enormity of her expression, she reddens and says, "Sorry, I didn't mean…"

But I've already got my hand raised and telling her, "Don't be silly. Now go and if you get the chance, give me a phone, okay?"

"Will do," she nods and I watch as she hurries from the cafe.

In my heart I'm hoping that the child, the boy or the girl will be found safe and well, yet I'm also hating myself for a dark part of my soul wishes the child to be dead to permit the police to associate the child's murder with that of Beth and force them to reopen her investigation.

****

As soon as I'm returned to the car park and bunged the wee man his fiver, I'm in my car and switching on the radio in time to catch the twelve o'clock news.

The first item is another bloody Brexit story, but then the reporter relates that Police are seeking public assistance in Yoker in the west of the city to locate a missing four-year-old girl who was last seen playing in the foyer of the high rise flats in Kelso Street. The reporter describes the wee girl and what she is wearing, but does not name her and I'm wondering why? Then it strikes me that if someone has taken the wee girl and hears her name on the radio it would make it so much easier for him to…God!

Still sat in the car, I'm conscious the old man is watching me from his hut and decide that before he comes over to ask if I'm alright, I'll drive off, giving him a wave as the car trundles across the waste ground to the exit and out onto the tarmacadam road. Turning right, I drive towards the Broomielaw, but before the junction I slam on the brakes and stall the engine because quite literally, my tears are blinding me.

I don't know why, but maybe it's the news about the missing wee girl bringing it all back to me for before I know it I'm hunched across the steering wheel and sobbing like a baby.

You know something, these days I'm like that old song from the fifties, the one that my mother used to sing whenever there was a family party. Back in the day when I was a child growing up in Drumchapel, family parties in Glasgow were always on a Friday night, which was payday for the working man. I remember when I was very young we'd all gather in the one house and the men would bring the drink. On occasion the neighbours in the close would be invited to join in and when the party was in full swing the singing would commence. Everybody had their own favourite song and nobody else was allowed to sing someone else's song. 'Cry Me A River,' was my mother's song. Sometimes, though not too often these days, I'll hear Julie London singing it on the radio and it brings back all those happy memories.

I take a breath and don't know how long I've been sitting here, but I know I'm havering and if nothing else, thinking about those days has been a bit therapeutic because now I'm all cried out.

Curiously, I'm feeling a wee bit better too.

I grab a handkerchief from my handbag and wipe my eyes and snotty nose and take a deep breath. When I'm ready I restart the engine and head home.

The guilt I feel about wishing the missing child dead is overwhelming and it's when I'm passing through Anniesland Cross that I decide that I won't go straight home, that I'll drive to St Ninian's and see if Father O'Brien is at his house.

I stop at the lights on the junction of Great Western Road and Baldwin Avenue and I'm so distracted that when I go to make my right turn, I almost collide with a motorcyclist travelling through the green light on his side of the road and brake so hard I bang my breasts on the steering wheel and later that night I find I've actually bruised myself. Of course the motorcyclist must have got a fright too, but he didn't stop though I can imagine what he must have been calling me.

Shaken, I kangaroo across the junction and with some relief, drive into the church car park where I see Father O'Brien's old Renault estate car parked outside the church house.

Knocking the door, it's his elderly Irish housekeeper, Katie Doherty, who opens it and seeing my face, she says, "Jesus, Mary and Joseph. What's wrong Margaret, you're as white as a sheet," then ushers me through the door into the small reception room.

Margaret is what we Weegies call my Sunday name for to family and friends for as long as I recall I've always been Maggie, so it's strange to hear it being used.

She guides me to a chair and then leaving the room I hear her calling out, "Father! Father O'Brien! Will you get yourself down here this minute, now!"

Katie comes back into the room and in a quiet voice, says, "You stay here the now, my darling, and I'll fetch you a nice cup of tea. Father will be with you shortly."

Left alone, I'm crying and fetching my handkerchief out from my handbag when Father O'Brien, his mop of unruly grey hair and thick white moustache uncombed and dressed in an old blue collarless shirt, faded brown corduroy trousers with open toed sandals on his feet, enters the room. Every time I look at Father I can't help but compare him to the big Glasgow actor, the white haired guy, James Cosmo.

"Maggie," he greets me and staring curiously at me, says, "What's happened, dear? Is it Elizabeth?"

I can't trust myself to speak and can only shake my head and watch as he sits in the old, but comfortable chair across from me.

Then during the next five minutes, it all comes out and seemingly without me taking a breath.

I tell him about my moments of rage with Jessie's husband Ernie and Eileen McNulty and even the threat I made against my neighbour Peter McGregor about telling his wife, when he made the pass at me.

I'm about to tell him more when the door opens and Katie shuffles in carrying a tray with two mugs of tea and a plate of biscuits that she wordlessly deposits on the small table between the Father and I before she leaves, gently closing the door behind her.

"I know she's the soul of discretion, that woman," he loudly says and nods at the door, "but there's no need to tempt her with gossip that might find it's way through the door now, is there?"

I almost burst into laughter as I hear the shuffle of feet in the hallway outside.

He turns to me and sighing, says, "You were saying, Maggie?"

I know it sounds silly, but that little bit of humour on his part seems to have settled me down and stifling the tears, I tell him about learning of the missing wee girl and the horrible thoughts I had.

He leans forward to pour the tea into the mugs and when he points to the sugar bowl, I manage to croak, "Milk only, thanks."

I watch as he spoons two large sugars into his tea, then his eyes are almost twinkling when he says, "You'd think with Type Two Diabetes I should know better," then milks both mugs before handing me one.

"So," he slowly stirs his tea, "you think you're a really bad person then?"

"Aren't I?" I sniff.

"Well," he drawls, "I've never thought of you as an individual who will succumb to bullies, Maggie, and standing up to both those individuals seems to confirm that. However, from what you're telling me it might be prudent if you're going to face down a bully like your friends' husband and this large woman at work to carry a big stick in your handbag."

Now this isn't the advice I expected and I'm staring open-mouthed at him as he widely grins.

"The bible tells us to turn the other cheek, but you and I both know that's a lot of tosh when you're acting in defence of someone else."

He raises a hand and continues, "I know that you're wondering where this courage is coming from, but do you know that I believe you to be a very strong young woman, Maggie? Think about it. What you have been through would break most men and women. But you? You continue to carry the burden of knowing the man who murdered your beloved granddaughter, God love and keep her in His arms," he makes the sign of the cross, "still walks among us and not only do you fight the heartache that must knock every single night at your door, but you have the added responsibility of caring for dear

Elizabeth who is so grief-stricken she has spent all that time in hospital. And you a widow too with no one to share your sorrow. No, Maggie," he shakes his head, "I'm only surprised that during the last four months you haven't taken a big stick and beaten to death every man who crosses your path."

"And what about my thoughts for this poor, missing child, Father? Can you possibly excuse or explain that?"

He stares sorrowfully at me and I see him take a breath before he replies in a soft voice, "I know in the last four months you've not had your troubles to seek," he slowly tells me, "and sometimes, Maggie, you have to accept that you are human with human feelings and human emotions. What I'm trying to say is in your heart you don't wish that wee girl any harm for it seems to me it's not the wee girl you're angry with, it's the police who you feel have let you down, isn't it?"

I don't respond, but I know he's correct. Of course I want the girl to be found safe and well and don't want another family to suffer as Liz and me have suffered.

"I'm an idiot, aren't I?"

"No, Maggie, you're not an idiot. You're a lonely woman with too much time to think things through and nobody to share those thoughts with. Unless," he stares keenly at me. "Alex has been gone these what, four or five years now?"

"Five years last June."

"You're a fine looking young woman, Maggie. Has no man knocked at your door in the recent past?"

"Father," I find myself blushing, "I wouldn't have taken you for a matchmaker."

"Ah, well now," he grins, "I might be an old celibate priest, but I do like to hear about romance now and again. Sure, isn't 'Casablanca' with Humphrey Bogart and that beautiful Ingrid Bergman my favourite movie and is it not the most romantic film ever? And besides," there's a definite twinkle in his eye now as he leans forward and with a stubby finger taps the side of his nose, "I was a young man before I was a priest," he softly tells me.

I think it's time to go, but I'm so pleased that I called in to see Father because speaking to him has certainly cleared my head and lifted my spirits a bit.

I get to my feet as he pushes himself up from his chair and hearing him wince, I offer him a hand.

"It's the arthritis," he says, declining my help. Then his eyes narrow as he adds, "Either that or too much altar wine."

I'm laughing and feeling much better as he escorts me to the front door.

"Oh, I forgot," I turn and tell him about Liz's pending discharge at the end of the week.

"Now that's fairly cheered me up," he smiles, then asks, "And her young man, the nurse? He'll be fairly pleased too, eh?"

Straight away he can see from my face he believes he's spoken out of turn and his face flushes as he says, "Sorry, Maggie, but even an old man like me can see that every time I visit Liz, that young nurse is there or thereabouts and for what it's worth, he seems to be a nice young fellow."

"Well, time will tell, Father," I brightly reply and waving him cheerio I ignore the tightening feeling in my gut.

****

On the way home and a lot calmer now, I consider DS Reid's suggestion that I inform the newspapers about the police winding down Beth's investigation, but decide to wait for the outcome about this missing child, tragic though it is for the wean and the family.

Still hating what I'm thinking it seems to me that if the worst comes to the very worst it might just turn out that the police will reopen Beth's investigation of their own volition.

I'm reversing into my driveway when I spot my neighbour Wilma McGregor marching along the road towards my house. That's right, not walking but quite literally marching.

Switching off the engine I stroll to the end of the driveway to await her and my hands clasped in front of me, I have a sneaking suspicion this isn't a social call.

"You, ya fucking harlot!" she screams at me.

To say I'm taken aback doesn't cut it, but I stand my ground and raising both hands in defence, as coolly as I can I tell her, "Perhaps you might want to calm down, Wilma, and before you start the name-calling, tell me exactly what your husband has told you."

Her face is beetroot and her body shaking and her fists are clenched too, but it's her eyes that give her away for she's ready for tears.

I see her throat working overtime as she's gulping, trying to draw air in and as gently as I can, I say, "You've known me for some years, Wilma. I'm not a woman that messes around with men, so can we please discuss this inside," I turn and nod at my house, "rather than have the whole neighbourhood listening to us?"

I'm very tense and I realise I'm taking a chance here because there's every likelihood she'll jump on my back as I turn away, but I force myself to turn from her and walk to the front door and opening it, stand there and wait for her. Thankfully, she follows me into the house and I resist sighing with relief as I close the door behind her. She's staring at me as I say, "Why don't we go into the kitchen and you can tell me what Peter's told you because I can assure you, he's not told you the truth."

I'm about to make my way through to the kitchen but stop when Wilma bursts into tears, her hands over her eyes as she sobs uncontrollably.

I'm conscious that I've to leave for work in a couple of hours, but there's no way I can avoid this situation so placing an arm around Wilma's shoulders I lead her into the kitchen and sit her down before I turn and switch on the kettle.

While she sobs I prepare two mugs and then go upstairs to the bathroom and fetch a hand towel that I give to her. It takes a good four or five minutes before she composes herself by which time I've the tea prepared and poured.

"Can I wash my face," she asks and I nod towards the door.

Minutes later she's back and resumes her seat, her eyes red and watery. As I've said before, she's in her early forties and a really attractive woman is Wilma, though could probably afford to lose a few pounds. Sorry, that's me being bitchy when the last thing the poor woman needs is criticism about her figure.

"I'm sorry, Maggie, it's just…" she bites at her lower lip.

I place her mug and the milk jug in front of her and sit down opposite and patiently wait for her explanation.

Inwardly I'm wryly thinking, I started out an emotional wreck after hearing about the missing wee girl and now here I am, trying to comfort another emotional wreck. Who'd guess, eh?

She takes a deep breath then slowly exhales and says, "He told me that yesterday, you asked him into your house and that he had to walk away because you wanted to start an affair."

I resist the urge to smile at Peter's bloody cheek and realise he is protecting himself and likely worried sick that I might indeed drop a hint to Wilma about his pathetic attempt at infidelity. Now, I don't know Wilma *that* well, but I had a sudden intuitive sense that her behaviour seems out of character with what I know to be her normal, easy-going nature and so I take a wild guess and ask her, "This isn't the first time he's made excuses for his behaviour with women, is it Wilma?"

My stomach is again in a knot as she quickly glances at me then her shoulders droop and shaking her head, she quietly replies, "No."

I'm relieved that Wilma has made her own decision and that I don't need to defend myself, for now I can see it in her eyes she accepts that the bad guy is her husband, not me.

She stares at the table as her fingers trace the pattern on the mug then her voice now brittle, she says, "You're not the first he's tried it on with, Maggie, though why the *fuck* I keep believing his pathetic lies I don't know. I'm just a stupid, idiotic…"

"Perhaps it's because you want to believe him, Wilma," I hastily interrupt. "Perhaps it's because we women don't like the thought of our life partner cheating on us with other women," I tell her as I wonder how the heck did I come up with that wee jewel of wisdom? I mean, it's not as if my Alex ever cheated on me. Of that I'm absolutely certain.

She sniffs and wipes her nose on the hand towel then realising what she's doing, tries to apologetically smile as she says, "Sorry."

"Don't worry," I tell her, "it can go straight into the wash. Go on."

"He says he attracts the attention of women because he's a handsome man. I mean, he is, isn't he?" she looks at me, her head cocked to one side as if for confirmation.

Aye, and modest with it I'm thinking, but decide a little diplomacy is called for and so I respond, "He is, Wilma, but he's someone else's husband and that makes him out of bounds for most women."

"But not all," she bitterly snaps back then adds, "and particularly the young and impressionable ones. His students I mean and that's why I thought it strange when he said a woman of your age tried it on with him."

A woman of my age indeed!

Cheeky sod, I'm thinking, but this is not the time to get into another spat over her husband and oh, when she refers to his students, I think

I mentioned Peter is a college lecturer.

I pretend surprise and reply, "But surely his students are too young for a man Peter's age?"

"Don't kid yourself," she manages to scoff and scowl at the same time. "The younger the better as far as he's concerned." Then she makes quotation marks with her forefingers and continues, "I've lost count of the number of times he's had to stay late at the college to give extra tuition or at least that's what *he* calls it," she almost spits the words out.

There's a bell ringing in my head and my eyes narrow when I slowly ask, "How young is young, Wilma?"

"Oh, I've had sixteen and seventeen-year-olds phoning the house at all times of the night, sometimes drunk and sometimes giggling, all asking to speak with Mister *fucking* McGregor," she's again close to angry tears, then lifting her head to stare at me, her lips are quivering as she says, "Sorry, Maggie, it just seemed that, well, when he said that you, you know…"

I didn't really know, but to save her any further embarrassment I nod and slowly get to my feet for as far as I'm concerned, that is her cue to leave and go and deal with his betrayal and her matrimonial problems, for I sure as hell don't want to get involved.

Haven't I enough issues going on in my own life?

In fairness she takes the hint and gets to her feet and holding the hand towel, says, "I'll get this washed for you," but I shake my head and taking it from her, reply, "No need. It can go in with the next wash tomorrow morning."

I see her to the door, she all the time apologising for her behaviour and I close the door as she makes her way down the driveway.

With my back to the door, I sigh with relief then begin to smile for I'm wondering what it might be like in the next hour to be a fly on the wall of the McGregor household.

But then I again wonder.

Just how young *is* young, for Peter McGregor?

CHAPTER SEVEN

Work is the usual routine and when I'm in the locker room getting out of my tabard I find that I've a message from Liz on my answer phone.

You can't imagine the difference in that's lassie's voice since she's been told she is to be discharged and my heart races when she tells me, "Hi mum, it's me. There's no need to visit tonight or tomorrow night because Doctor Francis has confirmed Friday and can you pick me up around midday? Oh," she adds, "and can we get dinner or something in to celebrate? Love you."

I listen to the message again and feel like bursting into song and telling everybody, but the other cleaners are more interested in talking about their soaps than hearing about my good news, so I get my stuff together and with a nod to the ones I get on with, make my way out into the rain.

Walking to my car I pass quite a few people for the thing about Glasgow is no matter the day or the weather there's always somebody out to have a good time.

In fact, I'm so pleased to hear Liz's news I promise myself a wee glass of Chardonnay when I get home.

That's something you should know about me. I've already said I'm not really much of a drinker though I do like the occasional glass of vino, but strictly never more than two. That said, I'm not one for keeping drink in the house and though Alex liked a couple or three cans of Tenants at the weekend, he wasn't really a pub man.

When I turn into Carrick Street it's deserted and a wee bit creepy at that time of the night because the old man has locked up his hut and is gone. My car is one of only a half dozen that remain parked on the waste ground. I get in and the first thing I do is lock the doors before driving off. I'm not timid, but neither am I stupid.

On the drive home my head is full of nonsense as I reflect on my day and I think of Wilma McGregor and her wayward husband Peter and I find I'm shaking my head. I'm glad I didn't overreact when she challenged me because it might have got really nasty. Funny, I've known the couple since they moved into the Crescent and that's what, nearly seventeen or eighteen years? Certainly their younger boy was still at the local primary when they arrived, but for the life of me I'd always thought them to be a happily married couple. Just goes to show you never know what goes on behind closed doors, do you?

Then with a start I wonder if the wee girl has been found. It's not yet eight o'clock and likely I'll be home before the Smooth radio news broadcast comes on.

As it happens I arrive a couple of minutes before eight and find I'm rushing through the door to switch on the radio in the kitchen. As you might guess the first item is about the wee girl who is reportedly still missing. According to the police the search that will include local volunteers will continue throughout the night and briefly I wonder if I should go along and offer my help, but then I decide not to.

Why, you might wonder and particularly as I've been through this grief myself and know how it will be affecting the parents.

Well, two reasons.

One is that I'm not a local person and don't know the Yoker area at all. The other reason is the police might not be happy to see me there for if a reporter recognises me it might lead to awkward questions; me being the grandmother of a murder girl whose killer has yet to be caught.

No, I'll hear the news on the radio or the late night news on the telly and besides, I remember; Sheila promised that she'd phone me.

There's still enough soup in the fridge for me so I set a tray with a bowl as the soup heats in the microwave and prepare myself some sandwiches of corn beef and beetroot. You might think I live on snack foods, but when I get in from work I'm usually too tired to prepare a full meal.

Before I know it I'm watching the STV news that comes on after the News at Ten and still the wee girl hasn't been found.

That's when the doorbell rings.

Now, I don't get late night visitors and so I'm a little anxious and first peek through the front room curtains, but it's very dark and still raining and the doorbell goes again and causes me to jump.

I switch on the hall light and call loudly through the door, "Who is it?"

"Maggie, it's me. Sheila."

I open the door and she's stood there, her auburn hair plastered to her face and looking really pale. I usher her into the hallway and take her sodden jacket from her then lead her through to the kitchen as she keeps apologising for coming at this time of the night while I'm talking over her and telling her not to be silly, it's not problem.

In the kitchen I make her sit down while I stick the kettle on and but for the fact she's got to drive home and her being a policewoman, I'd have fetched the Macallan from the back of the larder that belonged to Alex and has been there for about ten years following a Christmas party.

I turn to ask her what's happened, but she beats me to it and says, "It's bad news, Maggie. They've found the wee girl.

****

Five minutes later we're sitting in front of the gas fire that I've switched on because Sheila was shivering, though I suspect it's more from shock than the cold.

"The news didn't say she'd been found," I tell Sheila, who replies, "No. They've kept it back for the minute, but likely it will be out by the morning when the reporters see the Scene of Crime vehicles in the area. I don't know how they missed her the first time," she shakes her head, "but they went back over the search area again and found her body hidden under a piece of wriggly tin."

I can feel my body going cold, but I don't say anything, I just sit quietly and listen.

Sheila isn't looking at me; she's staring at the fire as she speaks with both hands curled round the mug of coffee. She tells me that the wee girl, her name was Kylie Murdoch, had often been permitted by her mother to play in the foyer of the high rise flats where they live on the first floor and where a concierge is on duty in a glass enclosed office in the foyer area. However, while Kylie was playing with her doll and pram, the female concierge nipped to the toilet at the back of the office and when she returned didn't immediately notice Kylie was gone.

"Of course the poor woman is going off her head," Sheila says, "and blaming herself for the wee one being taken."

She sips at her coffee and takes a breath that she slowly lets out.

"The local cops were called once the concierge realised the wee girl hadn't gone upstairs to the flat and they were there sharpish. I have to say when it's a child gone missing it's all hands on deck and in fairness to the polis, though I can be their biggest critic," she attempts a smile, "they were right on the ball within minutes of the call coming in."

She turns to me and continues, "When I got the call while we were in Frasers, the wee girl had been missing for forty-five minutes and

believe me, Maggie, that's a lifetime for the family as you well
know. Anyway," she shrugged, "all the attending cops and some
local people from the flats that know…" she stopped and takes a
breath, "I mean knew the wee girl, spread out with the flats being the
centre of the circle, to look for her. I don't know if you know that
area at all?"

I shake my head.

"The railway line passes under a bridge that runs over the top of
Kelso Street about two hundred yards from the flats and there's a
Lidl's and a pub on the opposite side of the bridge. Some of the
cops, I don't know who, did a quick check of the area around the
bridge, but didn't find anything. The thing is," I could almost hear
her teeth grating and I'm thinking if she squeezes that mug any
harder it will shatter, "because of the bloody Health and Safety
regulations, some stupid bastard of a supervisor, some fucking *jobs
worth* sergeant, told the cops not to go down onto the line, that
they'd to wait for the British Transport cops to arrive because it's the
BT cops who are trained for that sort of thing. Well, the cops did as
they were told and didn't go down the embankment, not at first
anyway. It was later when they were going over the area again that
one of the cops said fuck it…" she stops aware I don't use or like
bad language and says, "Sorry, Maggie," but seeing how upset she
is, I think right now her language is acceptable and wave her
apology away.

"Anyway, the cop squeezed himself through a gap in the metal
railings by the side of the bridge and went down the embankment to
check underneath the bridge; that's where he found her."

She took a sip of her coffee and I realise it's just to take a couple of
seconds to compose herself, then says, "I know you wouldn't
normally allow it in the house and I wouldn't normally ask, but do
you mind if I have a fag?"

I don't like cigarette smoke, but under the circumstances I'm hardly
likely to refuse so I say, "No, of course I don't mind."

I take her mug from her and my heart pounding, go through to the
kitchen to refill it and fetch a saucer for her to use as an ashtray.

When I return to the front room, Sheila is hunched over, her knees
tightly drawn together and drawing deeply on her cigarette.

"Obviously there will need to be a post mortem, but one of the CID
told me she's been strangled and…" she hesitated and turned to me,

tears welling in her eyes and biting at her lower lip, "you know, interfered with."

I don't even try to respond for I know I will not be able to speak.

"I was with that callous bastard Tarrant when he broke the news to the mother. Jesus Christ, you'd think she was to blame, the way he spoke to her! Asking if it was usual for her daughter to be left alone in the foyer and other stupid fucking questions like that when the poor lassie was beside herself with grief! The heartless bastard!" she snarls.

Of course, I'm ignoring Sheila's use of expletives for I'm thinking the way she's feeling she needs to express her anger.

At last I find my voice and I ask, "Is there a husband or a partner?"

"No," she's shaking her head. "The mum, Isobel Murdoch is her name, is a single mother and Kylie was her only child. As far as I know the boyfriend buggered off when she fell pregnant. Nice clean and tidy wee flat, I have to say," she absentmindedly remarks.

I can only imagine how heartbroken the young woman must be, but dreadful as the whole story is and hating myself for being so selfish, I need to know.

"Is anyone arrested?"

"No, not yet," she shakes her head then as though reading my thoughts, adds, "There's nothing at the minute to connect the killing to Beth, but we both know, Maggie, that when we get the bastard he'll be interviewed about her murder too."

To be honest, I'm numb at the terrible death of the wee girl and silently sit back in my chair as the quiet moments pass.

Sheila takes a deep breath and quietly says, "I know I'd said I'd phone you, but I thought it better that you hear it from me. Nothing's been mentioned yet about linking Beth and Kylie's murders, but I'm certain you'll get a visit sometime tomorrow and probably the papers will be back at your door too. I thought you'd need a heads up."

She's staring curiously at me then asks, "Are you okay, hen?"

I smile for I'm grateful at Sheila's thoughtfulness for considering my feelings when she herself is so obviously upset and I nod before asking, "I take it you're to be the liaison for the mother and the family?"

She sighs and taps ash from her cigarette onto the saucer before replying, "Actually, no. The powers that be have decided that the new guy who's on the Divisional list needs to get some experience, so he's been given the job. Can't say I'm unhappy," she wryly smiles at me, then lowers her eyes to stare at the hearth.

"Truth be told it's a harrowing task comforting the family of a murder victim and don't be annoyed, but I'm still reeling from Beth's death."

My eyes open wide with surprise for I'd always imagined that being a professional police office, Sheila had been able to detach herself from the emotional side of her job and her revelation stuns me as I respond, "I'm sorry, I never realised just how much it must have affected you too."

She slowly nods and continues to softly smile.

I watch as she stubs out her cigarette on the ashtray and gets to her feet, uncertain what to do with the ashtray, but I reach out and take it from her and tell her, "I'll get rid of it."

In the kitchen I throw the butt into the bin and fetch her coat from behind the chair.

I walk her to the door and ask, "Will you be okay to drive? I mean if you need to stay here it's not a problem. I've got Liz's room ready."

"No," she shakes her head, "I'll be fine." She stares out in to the blackness of the night and I'm conscious that the rain has stopped, the air smells fresh. In the distance I can hear the wail of a siren, but whether it's the police or an ambulance I can't tell.

"I'm supposed to be off tomorrow, Maggie, but if you promise me that you won't tell anyone where you're getting your information, I'll give Joe Clarke," she stops and explains, "he's the new liaison guy that will be on the wee girl's murder. I'll give him a call and find out what's happening and then I'll let you know, okay?"

I promise her that I'll not say a word to anyone then watch as she gets into her car and drives off. I don't know how long I stand there with the door open, smelling the grass and just listening to the sounds of the night, then I yawn, but my mind is still racing with what Sheila has told me. I close the door and decide to go to bed though I know that it will be several hours before I'll get to sleep; if I ever will.

****

Unusually, it's the alarm that wakes me and my eyes feel like someone has take them from my head and rolled them in grit before returning them to their sockets.

It's a struggle to get out of bed, but I've already made up my mind that I'm going to work. No, it's not because I'm dedicated or worried about losing a mornings pay. I just want my daily routine to continue and don't want to become obsessed with the child's murder; I don't want to raise my hopes that it's the same man who killed Beth and that this time the police will catch him.

Half dazed, I struggle to the bathroom, make my toilet, wash and dress and am downstairs switching on the radio in plenty of time for the six-o'clock news. Though it's in my nature to eat something before I go to work, this morning I satisfy myself with just a strong mug of coffee and with my back to the worktop, I stand and wait patiently for the news to begin.

I'm hardly breathing as the first item starts and the reporter announces the discovery of the child's body, but as the item continues there's nothing about an arrest.

It's early days yet, I tell myself and finishing my coffee, unplug my mobile phone from the charger to find there's a text message in and I see it arrived just after midnight.

It's from Liz.

Mum, don't know if you heard about a wee girl killed in Yoker. It's on the news on the radio. Doctor Francis turned up late last night and spoke to me about it, call me in the morning, xxxx.

I briefly wonder if I should visit Liz rather than phone, but then remember Sheila telling me that I might get a visit from the police so instead make a mental note to remind myself to phone her when I get home from work. Her text worries me a wee bit and I'm thinking if she obsesses about this murder it might bring back all the pain and hurt of losing Beth.

I have a final glance round the kitchen then grabbing my phone and handbag; collect my jacket on the way out of the door. I'm making my way to the car when I see my neighbour Willie McPherson slowly driving by as he prepares to turn into his driveway. I'm just about to raise a hand to wave good morning, but his head it turned away and I choose to believe he didn't see me.

Opening the car door, I glance up at the cloudy sky. It's nippy, but bright and thankfully the rain has finally stopped.

When I arrive at work the first thing I notice is that some of the other cleaners tightly smile or nod, but there's a definite subdued silence in the locker room. Curiously, it's Eileen McNulty who sidles up to me and as I tense, she quietly says, "You heard about the wee lassie over in Yoker?"

I turn to stare her in the eye. I nod and I'm thinking she looks embarrassed as she continues, "Well, me and the lassies were thinking that, eh, given the circumstances and that, what with your granddaughter being killed, you might want to take a couple of days off. Well, only if you want to, that is. Anyway," she huffs, "me and the lassies will cover for you so that bugger Tommy Burton doesn't know. Just leave your time card with us and we'll see your floor gets done, okay?"

I'm stunned, actually stunned and staring at her I'm aware my jaw is dropping.

I don't know how long, maybe it's seconds or minutes pass before I'm glancing round the locker room to see everyone's watching me, waiting for my reaction.

I gulp and letting out my breath, I hear myself say, "Look, Eileen," I stare at the faces and add, "girls. I'm grateful for the offer. Really, I am, but the best thing for me right now is to be working, keeping myself occupied." Now, don't ask me where this next bit comes from, but I then add, "Among my pals."

It takes a few seconds, but when that wee gem sets in there's smiles all round and before I know it I'm in the centre of a huddle with the women all trying to pat my back, squeeze my arms and just lay a comforting hand upon me as though I'm needing their sympathy.

Strangest of all is big Eileen reaching for my hand and loudly saying, "Come on girls, give her a bit of room here, eh?"

"What's going on here? Why are you lot not out on your floors?"

Tommy Burton's voice booms out from the door, then seeing me in the centre of the throng, he takes a step back as though ready to run when Eileen calls out, "Can you not see we're giving Maggie some condolence here, ya ignorant bastard!"

"But it's not her wee…" he's about to retort, then thinks better of it and simply turns about and leaves.

Frankly, I don't need this kind of attention and I'm still a bit shocked that it's Eileen who's seemingly organised the women for this wee sympathy meeting, but that's just like the Glasgow folk, isn't it?

They're either warm or cold, but never tepid and as I've heard said before, everybody in Glasgow is your pal until such times you fall out with them.

I'm vaguely aware of thanking everyone for their concern and Eileen telling me that if I need anything I've just to ask, but I can't help wondering if she's doing this to gain some favour or regain her status among the women.

Course that's me all over, isn't it? Missus Cynicism.

I get through the morning, but my mind is on Sheila's visit the night before and her warning that the police will likely come to the house. Will it be DCI Tarrant I wonder and if it is, what will he have to tell me?

More importantly, will I be capable of holding my tongue and not give him the roasting I think he deserves?

Nine o'clock arrives and I'm itching for the minutes to pass to let me get downstairs and away. Before long I'm back in the car and unconsciously racing along Great Western Road. It's when I see a police car travelling on the opposite lane I glance at my speedometer and realise I'm doing almost fifty miles an hour.

Of course I slow right down and I'm a little shaken because normally I'm not one to speed.

At last I arrive home and I'm in the house with the kettle boiling when the phone goes.

It's Linda, Liz's sister-in-law who is married to James, Ian's brother. You already know that I'm fond of Linda and her man because they know exactly what Ian's like and have also been good to my Liz and treated her well; that and she undoubtedly saved my Liz's life when she took that overdose.

"Maggie," she greets me, "you're not too busy for a minutes chat?"

"No, of course not, Linda. How are you and James getting on?"

Linda and her husband have kept in touch during the months since we lost Beth and though they don't phone every week, a fortnight will not go by without one of them giving me a call to inquire about Liz and I also now that on occasion, they've visited her too. They haven't yet been blessed with children and I know how much they loved their niece and often had Beth staying with them overnight at weekends.

We exchange pleasantries and when she asks about Liz, I'm happy to tell her about Liz being discharged on Friday. As I expect, Linda is genuinely pleased for me.

However, I'm hearing a wee edge to her voice and eventually she tells me that Ian told James he intends divorcing Liz.

"I already know. He's had his letter sent to Liz at the hospital," I tell her. "In short, he says he's blaming her for Beth's death."

"Bastard!" I hear her mutter before she says, "Sorry, Maggie. I tell you, Liz is better of without him. Even James says that."

Touchingly, she asks me how I'm coping and admits she was a bit worried when she heard about the death of the wee girl in Yoker and how it might bring it all back to me, the pain of losing Beth.

"God knows how you must be feeling, Maggie," she says, " I know I had a right good cry to myself."

There's a bit of an awkward pause then she says, "Have you heard that Ian's got himself a girlfriend?"

My eyes narrow as I ask, "What's the story there, then?"

"It was James that heard about it from somebody at his work who knows Ian. Then just last week James bumped into them in the city centre strolling along arm in arm. He says she seems a nice enough lassie, but you know what's he like about tattoos," she softly laughs, "and he says she's covered in them. Likely doesn't know what she's letting herself in for tying up with that lazy, two-timing sod. His mate at work told James she's a barmaid and works in a pub in Saracen. I've not met her and frankly, no harm to the lassie but I don't want to meet her either. Anyway, Ian told James he's living with her in her flat in Southdeen Road and James thinks that's somewhere in Garscadden. When he met them the lassie let it slip she's got a couple of kids, too."

We chat for another five minutes or so then I realise she's calling from her Ward for she quickly tells me, "I'll need to go. That's the Sister heading towards the office. Speak soon and give Liz my love. Bye."

I've just hung up the phone when the doorbell goes and I know it in my bones it's the police. I hurry through to the hallway, take a deep breath to prepare myself, glance at my hair in the hall mirror and pull open the door.

I don't know why, but I'm disappointed because it's not Tarrant; it's DS Reid.

"Come in," I stand to one side.

I see that this morning he's looking a wee bit tidier and his shirt is ironed. That and his shoes have been shined. Now, don't be asking me why I'm noticing these wee things, because I can't even explain it myself. I just do.

I direct him through to the front room and ask if he'd prefer tea or coffee.

"A coffee. Just with milk, please," then as I turn away, I'm a wee bit taken aback because he plonks himself down as if making himself at home. Not that I'm really minding, you understand. Just a wee curious thing I'm noticing.

When I'm giving him his mug and sitting with mine, he asks, "You'll have heard the news about the murder of the child in Yoker?"

"I did and to be honest, I was kind of expecting you to call. Sorry, when I say you, I mean the CID and thought it might be DCI Tarrant himself. Is that why you're here?"

"Well, yes. I wanted to see how you were."

I'm a bit surprised by his reply and ask him, "Are you not here to tell me that it might be the same man who killed my Beth?"

"Is that what you think, Missus Brogan? That it's the same man?"

I'm confused and reply, "I just thought that there might be a…what do you call it?"

"A link with Beth's murder?"

He shakes his head and I can feel my heart sink as he continues, "At the minute the murder of the wee girl is being treated as a separate investigation. There's yet nothing to suggest that it might be the same man. That said," he sighs, "when we catch him we'll interview him about Beth's murder, but please," he shakes his head, "don't get your hopes up that it's the same killer."

"But it's possible it *is* the same man?"

He parts his hands and slowly shaking his head, replies, "Anything is possible, but obviously I can't answer that question because at the minute inquiries are still on going."

He sees I'm about to interrupt and quickly continues, "It's not that I won't or don't want to answer your question, Missus Brogan, it's just that I don't know. Nobody knows yet. Not until we find this man. When we do find him and interview him, like I told you we'll be better placed to confirm if he has any knowledge of Beth's murder."

We sit in silence for a moment. I'm disappointed at what he's telling me, especially after Sheila's visit. How could I fail to get my hopes up and of course I can't mention that Sheila was here and what she told me?

Then he surprises me by asking, "How is your daughter, Elizabeth?"
My eyes narrow when I tightly ask, "What do you mean? For you
interviewing her, is that what you mean?"

"No, not yet, not till she's ready. No, what I mean is it's out there
now in the media about the wee girl in Yoker. She must have heard
about it and it will prey on her mind as it is obviously preying on
yours, that it might be the same man. Will she be able to deal with it,
do you think?"

I feel myself relax for I've already had the same thought and share
with him that Liz is due to be discharged tomorrow and yes, I tell
him, I'm confident she'll be able to handle it.

"That's good," he nods. "That poor young woman has gone through
enough," and oddly I realise I'm touched by his apparent concern for
her.

"Are you on the investigation team, Mister Reid?"

"Ah, no, I'm not," he frowns.

I'm not only curious I'm puzzled too and ask, "Why not?"

Now, maybe that's a wee bit cheeky of me, but that's me all over,
letting my mouth run away from me.

"Eh, it's a bit of a long story, Missus Brogan, but the easy answer is
that as far as the CID is concerned, I'm not the flavour of the month.
In fact, you could say I was posted to this Division as a kind of
punishment for, ah, an incident that occurred where I used to work."

Now my curiosity is really killing me and I'm just about to ask what
that was when my I hear my mobile phone ringing from the kitchen
worktop.

"Excuse me," I tell him and hurry though to find it's Jessie Cochrane
calling me.

"Jessie," I breathlessly greet her.

"Maggie. I've seen the news on the television, Are you all right,
hen?"

I find myself smiling. I've never realised just how many people have
me in their thoughts and so I reply, "I'm fine, Jessie, just fine. Look,
I have the police in the front room at the minute. Can I call you
back?"

"Eh, aye, of course. Oh, and Maggie?" her voice drops to a whisper.
"Things are going okay with me the now. Right, then. I'll call you
later. Bye," she hangs up.

When I return to the front room, he says, "I hope I'm not keeping you back from anything. Like I said, I just wanted to check you were okay."

I smile and about to tell him I'm okay when I remember and sitting back down, I slowly say, "I had a wee incident yesterday, Mister Reid, with one of my neighbours. Do you have time to listen?"

****

Ten minutes have passed and he hasn't spoken, just listened to me rambling on, but then asks me, "This man, Peter McGregor. I seem to recall his name on the witness list so there must have been a statement taken from him."

I'm nodding when I tell him, "Peter was walking his dog when we started to look for Beth. He's the person who phoned for the police when we couldn't find her."

"Ah, yes, now I remember reading that in the synopsis of the investigation," his eyes narrow. "And after his ah, failed attempt to chat *you* up, his wife challenged you about you chatting *him* up, is that right?"

I can see it in his eyes that he's teasing me, so I give him a scornful look.

He continues, but I just know he wants to grin.

"So, she then confided in you that he's a bit of a philanderer?"

I choke back a laugh and he pretends to scowl and says, "What?"

"Philanderer? Is that the modern police jargon, Mister Reid," my hand covers over my mouth I snigger like a braying donkey.

Before I know it we're both laughing and I'm wiping tears from my eyes.

"Phew, I think I needed that," I smile at him, then shaking my head at the nonsense of it, I mock him again with, "Philanderer."

"Call me old fashioned," he grins, "but isn't that the best word to describe McGregor?"

"It probably is though I suspect his wife Wilma might have added a few choice words of her own," I agree with a smile and a nod.

"So," his voice serious now, "when his wife told you he prefers them, them being females we'll assume, that he prefers them the younger the better, you're obviously thinking he might be a suspect for Beth's murder?"

"I really don't know," I shrug, "but on that evening he was out alone with his dog in the area so I suppose unless the police completely, what is the term again that you use?"

"Eliminated him from the inquiry."

"Yes, well, if the police eliminated him from the inquiry, he won't be will he; but did they?"

"I don't know the answer to that, but I do know there must be a statement if he's on the witness list though I can't recall the content. As soon as I'm back in the office I'll check that out and I'll also make some discreet inquiry about Mister McGregor."

My face must have registered my concern for he held up a hand and added, "Don't worry, Missus Brogan. I will be discreet and my inquiry about him won't get back to you."

He gets to his feet and I stand too and walk with him to the door. When I open it, he turns to me and almost as if he's embarrassed to mention it, as if he's being too personal, he says, "I'm pleased for you that your daughter is being discharged on Friday."

"Thank you."

"Now," he huffs and again is all official, "if I can trust you to keep whatever I tell you in confidence, I assume you'd like me to call back again and let you know how the investigation is going and whether it will impact on Beth's inquiry?"

"Yes, of course," I eagerly reply, then add, "Thank you."

"Right then, I'll either phone to make sure you're in or pop by tomorrow. Is that okay with you?"

"It is," I agree and then with a cheery wave he makes his way down the driveway.

CHAPTER EIGHT

When he's gone and even though it doesn't really need it, I go upstairs and give Liz's bedroom a right good going over; hoovering the carpet that's already spick and span, dust where there's nothing to dust, wipe down the window that's already sparkling and pull the bedspread taut where there isn't a crease. I stand back and staring at the room make a mental note to remind myself to buy a bunch of flowers for the dressing table in the corner.

Downstairs I tidy the front room though like upstairs, there's nothing to really tidy and in the kitchen, wash up the two mugs.

My curiosity is killing me and I wonder what it was that caused DS Reid's transfer to Maryhill from…then realise he didn't actually say from where. Well, whatever it was it must have been something bad. I startle and I remember Liz's text to call her and reaching for my mobile, dial her number.

"Mum, are you okay?" she gasps.

"Yes, darling. Why?"

"Oh, it's just when I heard on the news about the, you know, the wee girl in Yoker, I thought…" she stops and my chest feels tight that even dealing with her own grief my daughter should be so worried about me.

I swallow with difficulty and manage to say, "Look, I'm okay. I'm more concerned about you when you heard the news. How are you?"

"Who, me? No, I'm okay, mum. Really. Doctor Francis popped in this morning to check on me and he's still happy for me to be discharged tomorrow. On that point," my eyes narrow because I just know I'm about to be told something I don't want to hear, "would you mind if Colin brings me home? He's off tomorrow and, well, he said he'd like to."

I tightly close my eyes because to be really honest and I'll admit it; I'm miffed and disappointed that it's not me collecting my wee girl from the hospital. But in that heartbeat I know I've an important decision to make and that saying the wrong thing might create a barrier between us, so taking a deep breath, I hear myself reply, "No, that's fine, love. What time do you think you'll be here?"

"Are you sure that you're really okay with it, mum?"

"Aye, of course. I wouldn't say unless I was, would I?" I try hard to keep the edge from my voice and ask again, "So, what time will you be arriving?"

"Eh, well, Doctor Francis says that since I've been here for a while, there's a fair bit of documentation to go through and he wants to give me a full medical before I leave, so I should be fully discharged by midday. And Mum?"

"Yes?"

"As from this evening, my medication is down to one tablet in the evening, then Doctor Francis says depending on how I sleep at night, he'll review that medication at my first outpatient appointment."

I'm genuinely pleased at that wee titbit and tell her, "That's good news, sweetheart. Right, it's about twenty or twenty-five minutes to get here so I should see you about, say, twelve-thirty?"

"Half twelve then, mum. I'm looking forward to coming home," her voice drops almost to a whisper and I realise that's she about to cry.

"And I can't wait for you to get home, darling," I'm close to tears myself. So, what if it is Colin bringing her home? The main thing is that she *is* coming home. "I'll have a pot of soup made and your friend can have lunch too," I hear myself saying.

That bucks her up and I can hear the relief in her voice when she says, "I love you, mum."

"I love you too, Elizabeth," I reply and end the call.

I stand still for a few seconds trying to remember the last time I called her Elizabeth.

I take another minute to gather my thoughts at the young nurse Colin bringing her home and I wonder, perhaps whatever is between them is more serious than I first imagined.

I check the cupboard to see what vegetables I have in and realise I'll need to do a shopping if I'm going to get that pot of soup made.

Grabbing a pen and a piece of paper, I start to make a note of what I'll need and decide if I'm going to Asda, I might as well go ahead and do a full shop.

I smile as I write. It's what Alex used to call the idiot list because on the odd occasion he nipped to the shops for me, I never trusted him to remember everything and would insist he write it down. That said he always came back with something missing or the wrong thing.

I glance at the clock and decide to do the shopping before I go to work rather than that the back of nine when I know the last thing I'll want to do is traipse around a supermarket.

As I'm checking the cupboards for what I need, my thoughts turn to Colin Paterson. On the few occasions I've met him and always with Liz there, he's been polite and courteous and I can't say he hasn't.

However, it worries me that regardless of Doctor Francis believing she's fit to be discharged, I know she's still vulnerable and she only knows Colin from her time in the hospital.

I mean, what else does she know about him, I wonder? What has he told her of himself?

A cold chill grips me and even though I know that Liz would never forgive me for prying, I decide to make a phone call.

I obtain the switchboard number from my mobile phone, but use the landline to call the hospital and ask to be put through to Doctor Francis' secretary.

When she answers, I tell her it's Margaret Brogan, Elizabeth Brogan's mother and ask if I can speak to him.

"He's out in the wards right now, Missus Brogan. Is it urgent or can I get him to call you when he's back in the office?"

I agree to a return call and giving her my house number, inwardly pray I'm doing the right thing.

While I'm waiting I open a can of beans and toast some bread for my lunch. Big eater me, eh?

Just less than twenty minutes later, Doctor Francis calls back. Cheerily, he says, "Is this an invite to the welcome home party?"

I smile, but then reply, "Actually, Liz is being brought home by Colin Paterson, Doctor. That's the reason I phoned you." Suddenly, my mouth is very dry, but I press on. "I'm wondering if it's the usual practice for a nurse to bring a patient home or am I reading into something else? A relationship perhaps?"

He doesn't immediately respond, but then says, "Of course the NHS and the General Nursing Council would completely disapprove of any kind of personal relationship that occurred between a nurse and a patient; however, when Elizabeth is discharged she is no longer a patient and, well, I'd be lying if I didn't admit that I'm aware that the two of them have bonded during her time here. Developed a relationship, if you will, though I hasten to add it certainly is not to my knowledge intimate, if you follow me. That I would most certainly disapprove of and if I suspected there is or was a relationship of that nature while Elizabeth is a patient under my care, I absolutely assure you I would take immediate action not only to discipline young Colin, but report the circumstances to the relevant authorities."

He pauses and I'm about to speak, but before I do he asks, "Do *you* suspect some kind of improper relationship has occurred, Missus Brogan?"

"Well, no, but we both know the difficulties Liz has had with the murder of her daughter and now with her husband divorcing her, I'm worried that in her vulnerable mental state she might be taken advantage of." I then pause and ask, "Am I being too protective, Doctor?"

"Not at all," he hastens to assure me, "but if I might speak freely?"

"Please do."

"I've known Colin Paterson for almost ten years and in that time I've never known him to be anything but professional. I believe him to be a fine young man and a very good mental health nurse and in fact though Colin is unaware of this, I'm considering recommending him for a promotion to Charge Nurse. As we are both aware we are undoubtedly discussing a personal issue, Missus Brogan, I will be grateful if you might keep that information to yourself."

"Of course."

"You know I spoke with Elizabeth yesterday when it was reported in the news about the child being murdered in Yoker?"

"She did text me about you speaking with her, yes."

"I was concerned that the news might have disturbed her," he stops and then almost to himself, he says, "My God, who wouldn't be disturbed at that kind of news. However," I hear him take a breath, "I was relieved that while she was naturally upset and wondering if the murder was related to her own daughter, I do not believe that it has in any way set back her recovery. Her reaction to the news reassured me that my decision to discharge her is the correct one when I learned that Elizabeth was more concerned with the affect the murder would have on you, Missus Brogan. In short, if I might describe it in such terms, her shock at the murder had been as an observer rather than paralleling her reaction as the relative of a similar victim. Now, that itself is a great stride forward. Have I explained it thoroughly?"

Now, I'm not stupid and I don't take offence at him speaking to me as though I am daft, but Doctor Francis does tend to run off with fancy words at times, so I reply, "Yes, thank you, Doctor. However, my concern was her relationship with Colin Paterson and in short, you don't see a problem there? That the young man's…" I search for the word, but he interrupts with, "You worry that his fondness for your daughter is genuine, Missus Brogan?"

"Yes," I sigh and though I'm on the phone, I feel that I've been caught out and find that I'm blushing.

I can almost hear him smiling as he replies, "I can see the attraction Colin has for Elizabeth, Missus Brogan for even an old duffer like me can see that Elizabeth is a striking looking young woman and if I may be bold, definitely her mother's daughter."

The old bugger! Now he's flirting with me!

Before I can answer, he says, "Well, I suspect that the real reason for your phone call is to ask me if you believe that after Elizabeth is discharged, will Colin Paterson be a suitable suitor for her? Well, if she was my daughter, Missus Brogan, I would have no concern on that account. Now, is there anything else?"

"No, thank you, Doctor, you've been most helpful and…" I decide to come clean, "you've answered my questions about Colin."

"Well, as long as you're now comfortable with him continuing to see Elizabeth, that's good news. Goodbye, Missus Brogan."

I hang up and find that I'm smiling, but with relief rather than at his compliment.

Well, maybe just a little of that too.

****

I set off a good hour early for the Maryhill Asda superstore that I normally use for what I call my big shopping, because I've gotten used to where everything is and I can whizz round the aisles and be out in less than half an hour. Course that depends how busy the tills are.

I'm at the vegetable aisle when I hear my name called and turning, see a young staff member waving as she walks towards me. I'm a little taken aback, but then realise its Jessie's daughter, Mary.

"Thought it was you," she grins at me.

"How's your mum?" I ask her.

Her voice lowers a little as she glances around and then replies, "Her eye's a lot better. She's been using that Arnica gel that you suggested and the bruising has fairly went down. She's talking about starting back at work on Monday. Did she not phone you?"

"Yes, she did, but I had the police in at the time and I didn't really get to chat."

"Oh, the polis. Was that about your wee granddaughter and that new murder?"

"Yes," I tightly smile.

"Sorry," she looks a bit chasten and then surprises me when she reaches out to rub gently at my arm. "I'm guessing it must still be very raw for you, Maggie."

"How are things at home," I change the subject.

Mary leans a little closer and excitedly says, "Well, here's a bit of news for you. I've been on the council housing list since I turned eighteen and you know what? Because I'm in employment and I'm good for the rent, they've offered me a two-bedroom flat in Killearn Street in Possilpark. It's on the first floor and it's right nice, so it is. Modern too. I'm getting the keys next Monday morning and you'll never guess? My Ma is moving in with me."

I'm surprised and find myself smiling, then ask, "What does your dad think about that?"

"Him? He's not getting told and neither are my brothers and I'm not giving them the address either. No, my Ma and me have had enough of them three. They can fend for themselves, the shiftless, lazy bastards, the three of them."

"Good for you," I grin at her. "That's a big move for the two of you."

"Oh, aye," she sniffs and brow knitting, nods before she continues, "We've no furniture yet, but the British Heart Foundation have a second hand furniture store down on Dumbarton Road and there's some right good stuff in there, so there is. I'm going down there today after my shift to order a few things. My Ma and me have agreed that we'll split the rent and the living costs and that way it will help me save up for a mortgage because I really want to get my own place, you know?"

She peers at me then says, "You might not appreciate it, Maggie, but when you arrived that night and gave the old bastard what for, you helped make her mind up for her, so you did. Thanks for that. Maybe you can take a wee turn up and visit us after we've moved in, eh? Maybe come for your dinner?"

I'm a little humbled at what she tells me and, yes, maybe a little pleased with myself too before I reply, "Of course I will."

She's about to move off, but stops and surprises me when she asks, "How's your daughter doing? Ma told me that she's still in the hospital, but might be getting out soon?"

"Oh, Liz?" I smile and though I promised myself I'd not divulge it too soon, I can't help the feeling of pleasure I get in sharing my good news, so tell her, "She's being discharged on Friday, fit and well."

"That's brilliant, so it is. You'll be well chuffed, eh?"

"It is, yes, so likely she'll be looking for a job, Mary, if you hear of anything, I'll be very grateful."

Now even as I'm saying it, I'm thinking that's bang out of order. The lassie was just being polite and here's me trying to solicit work for my Liz. But then again you'll barter your soul with the devil if it's for your weans, won't you?

However, she replies, "I'll keep my ears open. Right, onwards and upwards," she grins, then before she goes, leans in again and in a low voice says, "Take the vegetables from the back of the pile. That's where all the fresh stuff get restocked, okay?"

"Okay," I grin at her as she winks then walks off to assist an elderly man.

Funny, but meeting Mary and hearing that she and Jessie are getting away from her abusive father has cheered me a little and suddenly the shopping isn't as tedious as it might have been.

****

My cleaning shift is just another day at the office, as they say, and by knocking off time I'm ready for him. I'm getting a fair number of nods from the other women and even big Eileen says hello, so it seems that our wee spat is a thing of the past.

Just as I'm leaving, I'm cornered by Tommy Burton who tells me, "I've had a phone call from Jessie. She says she'll be back for Mondays early shift."

"Oh, right," I pretend I didn't know and thanking him, head out the door.

Walking towards Carrick Street, the rain starts to come on then almost at the same time my mobile phone rings.

I duck into a doorway and fetching it from my handbag, I say, "Hello?"

"Maggie, it's Sheila, Can you talk?"

Keen as I am to speak with her, I tell her that I'm on my way home and I'm in a part of Argyle Street where I don't want to be hanging about and can I phone her when I'm in the house?

She agrees and a couple of minutes later I'm in the car and on my way home.

I've missed the nine o'clock news on the car radio, but even with the radio playing music, I'm only half listening because I'm eager to hear what Sheila has learned.

When I arrive home the rain is coming down full pelt and though it's just a the few yards from the boot of the car to the door, I regret not wearing my rain jacket because I'm soaked by the time I get the four bags of shopping indoors.

First thing I do is pack away the shopping then switching on the kettle, I fetch a towel to wrap round my hair and then nip upstairs to run a bath.

While that's running I make myself a coffee and with my mobile phone, return to the bathroom and strip off.

Minutes later I'm grinning like an idiot as I sink into the steaming hot bath and then I phone Sheila.

"It's me," I say when she answers.

She doesn't bother with niceties, but gets straight into and says, "I spoke with Joe Clarke, the guy I told you about who's the liaison for the wee girl's murder." She stops to take a breath then reminds me that I can't disclose where I heard this or even that I know, for she tells me, "They've found DNA on the wee girl."

"DNA? Does that mean the wee girl was…"

She hurriedly interrupts and says, "You don't need to hear details, Maggie. Believe me. You *really* don't need to know."

My mind is ticking faster than a drunks blood pressure, but a little confused I reply, "But surely when I was told Beth wasn't interfered with, they wouldn't have found DNA on her, so how can they compare…"

I stop, a sudden panic clutching at my throat as I almost scream out, "Are you suggesting that what they told me wasn't true! That Beth was…"

"No, Maggie! Listen to me!" she sharply interrupts. "Beth was *not* sexually assaulted! I'm telling you the truth! Do you hear me! Don't even think that!"

I'm breathing so fast I think I'm having palpitations, but force myself to be calm and take a deep breath before I ask, "But how does the DNA they found on the wee girl help prove it's the same man who killed Beth if there is nothing to compare it with?"

"I'm not talking about a comparison," she replies. "Finding the DNA means that it dramatically increases the chance of finding the wee girls killer. And when they find her killer, it will give the investigation team the opportunity to interview him about Beth. Do you see?"

I do see. Now. I force myself to be calm then ask, "How is the wee girls mother?"

I say wee girl because you know something? I can hardly bring myself to even say the poor child's name, God bless and keep her. "Joe says she's been heavily sedated. Apparently her parents are being very supportive and keep this to yourself. Mister Murdoch, her father has made it known he's lodging an official complaint about the way DCI Tarrant spoke to his daughter."

I'm a bit suspicious when I ask, "How did he hear about that?"

"I know what you're thinking, but truthfully, it wasn't me. What Joe told me is that a couple of detectives were present in the room and were disgusted by Tarrant's attitude. Joe said they've both told the father how he treated his daughter and are prepared to speak up, too. He also says when I return to duty on Monday, it's likely I'll be asked to provide a statement about what Tarrant said. "

I know it's wrong, but I take a perverse pleasure in hearing that rude and insensitive man might be taken to task for his awful attitude.

"Have they arrested anyone yet?" I ask, but I'm already guessing the answer.

"No, not yet, but the DNA will be tested and they should get a quick result, certainly within the next day or so if not earlier. What the investigation team will do is research all known sex offenders in the area and they'll be the first comparison. Then if they don't get a hit, they'll widen the net and begin taking voluntary samples from the residents in the flats and surrounding houses. Don't worry, Maggie. The success rate for DNA arrests is extremely high. We'll get the bastard. Sorry," she tails off.

I smile for like I told you and though I don't like bad language, I'm not a prude and yes, I have been known in times of stress to use the occasional expletive, though it's not something I admit outside of the confessional box.

"By the way, your man Alan Reid?"

She caught me by surprise before I realise she's talking about DS Reid.

"I spoke with my Bert. You remember he's an Inspector in Coatbridge?"

"Yes."

"Well, it seems that there's a wee story about why Mister Reid was moved into a city division. Nothing official like, but apparently it's well known in the Lanarkshire area."

Tittle-tattle was never my thing, but I'm a woman so it's part of my genetic makeup to hear gossip or so I tell myself.

"Go on."

"Sorry, I should have asked. Have you time for this?"

"Of course," I impatiently reply, particularly as I'm now going to hear something about DS Reid.

"Anyway, it seems he worked in the Airdrie office and was literally weeks away from being promoted; however, as Bert tells it there was a murder in Park Street in the Whinhill area of Airdrie. Do you know Airdrie at all?"

"No," I quickly reply, keen to hear the story.

"It seems this young woman and her boyfriend lived in a lower cottage flat, you know, like the four in a block type houses where you are. About seven or eight weeks ago, the couple had an argument and the lassie went for a bath. She got out of the bath and wrapped herself in a towel, but the boyfriend, who was drunk and is known locally as a right violent bugger, pulled the towel off her and threatened her with a big knife and when she turned to run away, he stabbed her in the back. Bert says the boyfriend later claimed he didn't mean to hit her with the knife, just meant to frighten her, but the blade pierced her heart and she fell down dead."

"My God," I whisper for I'm shocked by the story.

"Bert says Alan Reid was the DS on duty so he went with the Detective Inspector, Bert told me the guys name but I can't remember it. When they got to the locus; you know, the crime scene? Anyway, apparently the lassie was lying face down." She pauses and I'm wondering if the connection's broken, but then she says, "Again according to Bert, the lassie was apparently a strikingly good looking young woman and the DI has supposedly said he wanted her turned over so he could have a good look at her."

"You mean," I'm almost too shocked to ask, "in a perverted way?"

"Aye, Maggie, in a perverted way," she brittlely replies and I can hear the disgust in her voice.

I shudder at the very thought of it.

"Cut a long story short, it seems that Alan Reid lost it and hooked the DI; I mean, he punched him and broke his jaw."

"Oh," I mumble.

"The long and short of it is that one of the cops in the room was a young female and her neighbour is a Baptist, an older cop who my

Bert knows and says is a good guy. Anyway, they put their heads above the parapet and complained to their Inspector about what the DI said. Can you imagine what the papers would have made of that wee gem? So, the long and short of it is that management cut a deal and rather than arrest and charge Reid for the assault, particularly as it occurred in a room among other polis and where a murder victim was lying, the high heid yins thought it prudent first to suspend Reid then move him to another Division. Needless to say his pending promotion was cancelled and the DI warned that if he dared complain he'd be brought up on discipline charges by the rubber heels; you know, the Professional Standards Unit. Of course, that kind of charge would mean his dismissal from the service and his pension floating down the proverbial Suwannee River."

"And the boyfriend?"

"In the Ruchazie Hotel awaiting trial for the murder."

"So, DS Reid did the honourable thing and was punished for it?"

"You know better than most, Maggie, that life's not always fair and besides, he did break a mans jaw."

"Yet that man, that pervert, is still a policeman?"

"Regretfully, yes, but Bert's heard he won't ever conduct another murder inquiry and his career is going nowhere. There's talk when he gets back to work of him being bounced out of the CID and back to uniform."

"Sounds like the Detective Inspector deserved what happened to him," I snap back.

"Couldn't agree more," Sheila softly laughs, then adds, "Anyway, I've got Joe primed up so if there's any further information, Maggie, I'll phone you and again, let's keep it between us."

When's she rung off, I lie soaking for another ten minutes and wonder about DS Reid.

CHAPTER NINE

Friday dawns bright and sunny, but remember it's October so it's still warm jackets and scarves for most folk.

I'm up a good fifteen minutes before the alarm is due to activate and downstairs to the kitchen where the barley has been soaking all night. The first thing I do is switch on the slow cooker and add the ham hock from the fridge. Midday can't come fast enough for me and by the time Liz and…I take a slow breath…when Liz and with what sounds like it's her new man get here, the soup in the cooker will be ready.

I have my toast and coffee and with a quick glance round the front room to ensure everything is spick and span for her arrival, I'm almost out of the door before I remember to pin the 'Welcome Home' banner of the door of the front room.

Yes, I suppose I could have done that when I got in from work, but what's wrong with being prepared?

At work and in my excitement, I let it slip to one of the women that Liz is coming home and before I know it, there's congratulations from them all. Tommy Burton gets to hear and just about five minutes to eight, he arrives at the fourth floor with big Eileen and her pal, wee toothless Janey in tow and tells me, "Heard the good news, hen. The lassies here will finish up for you, so you get yourself away home. Don't worry, I'll see to your time card."

"Aye, away and get yourself ready for the homecoming party," Eileen grins.

"And don't forget us if there's any Prosecco left," toothless Janey smiles at me.

Well, there's a first I'm thinking and about to say, it's okay, I'm all prepared, but instead hear myself simply respond, "Thank you."

I'm embarrassed and like a buffoon continue to mumble my thanks and after stowing my mop and bucket away, head downstairs to the locker room.

I'm lifting my jacket from the locker when Tommy appears behind me to hold it open for me to slip on and in a low voice, he says, "Listen, Maggie, with your lassie coming home there's no need to come back today, so I'll not expect to see you till Monday, okay hen?"

Heavens, people surprise you when you least expect it, don't they?

I have a lump in my throat and can only nod my thanks and as I pass him by and don't ask me why, I reach out and give him a quick hug. He's that surprised he just stares wide-eyed and tight-lipped nods as I make my way to the door.

As I'm heading for the lift, I hear Tommy jokingly call after me, "And don't think this will be a regular thing, either. Can't have you lot take advantage of my good nature."

When I arrive at the car park the wee man is surprised to see me so early and worriedly calls out, "They sack you, hen?"

"No," I grin at him, "they've given me a wee flyer."

"Aye, well, you must have deserved it," he waves as I drive out the exit.

It's the first time that I can recall driving through traffic at that time of the morning going out of the city and I'm surprised how heavy it is.

However, after I turn into Clarion Crescent and just as I'm slowing to reverse into my driveway and even though it's still early, I see my neighbour Moira McPherson walking past the entrance with a plastic Cooperative shopping bag in her hand. I stop to let her pass and raise my hand to wave, but she keeps her head down and to my surprise, ignores me.

Aye, there's absolutely no doubt about it, she completely ignores me.

Now, I'm that taken aback I just sit in the car and watch her walk away then turn into her own driveway. I'm in a mind to get out and shout did you not see me, but the last thing I want is another confrontation and especially with another neighbour.

The incident leaves me a wee bit confused and I shake my head and slowly reversing my car, wonder what the devil I've done to offend her?

Should I give her the benefit of the doubt, that she was so engrossed in her own thoughts she just didn't see me? I shake my head and recall what my mother used to say; there's nothing queerer than folk.

Unusually for that time of the morning, the postman's been and there are some leaflets and a brown envelope behind the door with Liz's name on it.

While she has been in the hospital, Liz has trusted me to open any mail that might arrive for her and either deal with it or bring it to the ward for her attention. Walking through to the kitchen I stuff the leaflets into the recycle bin and tear open the envelope.

Reading the typed letter, my blood runs cold with anger and I'm snarling at the insensitivity of the bloody Education Department who are threatening court action against Elizabeth Chalmers who they complain has consistently failed to send her daughter, Bethany Margaret Chalmers, to school since August this year. There's a squiggle for a signature, but the name 'Eleanor O'Donnell' is printed beneath. Tears are nipping at my eyes and my anger knows no bounds.

All I can do is thank God I opened the letter and not Liz.

It's not yet nine o'clock so there seems little point in now phoning the contact number printed at the top of the letter. To calm myself I make a coffee, set the table for three, check the soup in the slow cooker and all the while prepare in my head what I'm going to say to whoever answers that bloody number.

At last the clock turns to nine and I'm on the handset straight away dialling the number on the letter. Frustratingly, the number turns out to be one of these menu numbers were it takes forever to get through to the right department.

At last I press button eight, but to my annoyance I'm through to another menu and this time it's another button.

Finally, I get through to a real person, Chloe, who sounds about twelve years of age and cheerfully asks me who I want to speak with. I tell her Eleanor O'Donnell and she transfers me through to an extension that rings for a good minute before this plummy, crisp voice of a woman who I'm guessing sounds in her twenties, says, "Missus O'Donnell speaking."

If you're like me and have lived in Glasgow all your life, you'll recognise when someone is assuming a posh accent and this woman is definitely one of that type of aspiring snob.

"Good morning. My name is Missus Brogan. I'm responding to a letter you sent to my daughter, Elizabeth Chalmers, about my granddaughter, Bethany Chalmers."

"Is Missus Chalmers there? I'm afraid I can only speak to her about her daughter. Data Protection forbids me from speaking to anyone else about her child," she tells me.

I force myself to be calm and reply, "My daughter is currently detained in hospital and if you have checked the school record for Beth, you will be aware I have authority to deal with any issue regarding my granddaughter."

I'm not lying because when at the time she was working, Liz had informed the school that it would often be me who dropped off or collected Beth from her school as well as attending meetings with her teacher.

You'll have guessed there was no point in Liz asking her husband to do anything that involved his daughter.

There's a distinct pause that leads me to believe the woman has not checked the school record and at last she says, "Very well," in a voice that sounds as though she's doing me a favour.

Then she says, "What is the child's full name?"

I grit my teeth and reply, "Bethany Margaret Chalmers."

"And her date of birth?"

No please or thank you in fact, no civility at all.

By now I'm really angry and I snap back, "Why do you need these details and why have you sent this letter asking about Beth failing to attend school?"

"Clearly the child's record indicates she has failed to attend school since the term started in August, Missus Brogan, and *I* would like to know why?"

I pause before replying, "And does your record indicate that my granddaughter, Bethany, the little girl you keep referring to as the child, was unable to attend school in August because she was murdered in July? Or is it that your record has not been updated with the fact she is now dead?"

Now, you would expect that any person with some kind of compassion would say, 'I'm sorry' or 'I regret...' or at least offer some form of sympathy, but all the woman calmly says is, "I don't have any information on the school record about this. Why weren't we informed?"

I'm stunned at her reaction to the worst kind of news that anyone with a sense of dignity could hear, so I'm snarling when I reply, "God forgive me for saying this, but if you should ever have the misfortunate to lose a child then I hope for your sake you do not have to deal with a cold and heartless bitch like yourself. Good day, Missus O'Donnell!"

Then I slam the phone down so hard my hand goes numb.

Honestly, using language like that is just not me and I can't ever recall speaking on the phone to anyone like that. It's just not in my nature. But I'm so angry at the woman's attitude I'm shaking with rage and stomp up and down the front room, looking for something to kick.

After a couple of minutes, I drink a glass of water and force myself to calm myself to down and tell myself I won't let the phone call ruin my day because after all, I'm getting my daughter back home, aren't I?

****

The house is spotless and I decide as I'm a couple of hours ahead of my schedule, I'll have a bath and pick out something nice to wear; particularly as Liz is bringing home what sounds like her new man. Upstairs while the bath is running, I delve into my wardrobe and pull out a couple or five dresses that I hold against my body in front of the full-length mirror. I'm a neat size ten though depending on the make and let's face it, not all dressmakers stick to the same size rule, I sometimes find a size twelve fits a little more comfortably.

I'm aware it's not really summer, but finally I choose a black coloured floral short sleeve midi-A line dress with a square neckline by Floryday that I haven't worn for, my brow creases as I try to recall. Heavens, I'm smiling, it must be at least three years. I'm worried that it might not fit, but when I take off my jeans and top and try it on, it does. If anything, I might have lost a couple of pounds since I last wore it. At the bottom of the wardrobe I find a pair of Loaki gold twist strap sandals that haven't seen the light of day for at least two years, but as I've only worn them a couple of time they're like brand new and will do nicely to complement the dress. I stand back and look through the dresses hanging in the wardrobe and the shoes and sandals in the racks at the bottom and I shake my head. Since Beth died I don't think I've worn anything but jeans for work and everyday wear, though for Mass on Sunday I usually pull on a pair of trousers.

I'm pleased with my choice though, then head into the bathroom and soak for twenty minutes.

I'm vigorously rubbing myself dry when I glance in the bathroom mirror and decide I might even apply a little make-up.

I brush my hair then for the first time since Beth died, fetch my cosmetic bag from the cupboard under the sink. Minutes later I stand back and critically examine myself. Well, I might be forty-nine, but I'm happy with the result, though my hair does need a bit of a trim. In the bedroom the dress fits perfectly and I'm well pleased with what I see in the mirror.

I'm downstairs just twenty minutes when the front doorbell rings.

I'm frowning a bit because I'm not expecting any visitors, and then brighten when I think maybe Liz got discharged a bit early.

When I open the door I don't quite get the shock of my life, but I am more than annoyed to find its Ian Chalmers.

I can't imagine why but he looks surprised to see me too, then I remember I'm done up to the nines as he grins and says, "Looking good, Maggie. Going to a party?"

I'm almost speechless, but not quite.

I can't help the loathing in my voice when I ask him, "What do you want, Ian?"

"Want? Well, I'd like to see my wife. Is she here?"

"You know very well Liz is in the hospital and has been for over four months," my voice is as deadpan as my face. "Shall I give you the address so you can find it?"

"No need to be like that, Maggie," he continues to grin at me. "I'm only here to work out the terms of a settlement. I mean, Liz has probably told you about us getting a divorce."

"No, Ian, she told me about *you* wanting to divorce her, not a mutual agreement. She also told me that you are accusing her of poor parenting skills that led to her daughter's death and her being, what was it your lawyer inferred? Oh, yes a raving looney or something like that."

He opens his hands wide and with an almost theatrical sigh says, "Can I please come in and discuss this rather we than argue about it on your doorstep?"

"Discuss what exactly, Ian?"

He doesn't even have the good grace to look shamefaced when he replies, "Well, I'm wondering about a settlement fee when we get divorced."

Of course I'm puzzled and I ask, "What the hell are you on about, a settlement fee?"

His eyes narrow as he peers at me and he says, "Did Liz not claim for some kind of criminal compensation when Beth got killed? Or what about the newspapers? Did she not think that she could have got one of them women's magazines to pay good money for that kind of story?" Then he slowly grins as he continues, "She did, didn't she? She got some kind of pay off, didn't she? Come on, Maggie, all I want is my fair share. I'll even get my lawyer to drop the thing about poor parenting skills, eh?"

I'm speechless, truly speechless as I stare at him and my legs are shaking so much I reach out to hold onto the metal handrail of the steps.

I'm so engrossed in listening and staring at him I don't see the figure approaching up the driveway and only become aware when he says, "Good morning, Missus Brogan. I hope I'm not disturbing you."

I glance from him to see DS Reid stood behind him as Ian turns to stare curiously at the detective who stands a good three or four inches taller than him.

I still can't find my voice and it must seem to DS Reid that something is wrong for he then politely asks Ian, "And you are?"

"Who the hell wants to know?" Ian arrogantly replies.

"The police want to know, so again, what's your name, pal?"

"How do I know you're a police office?" he turns to face DS Reid.

I watch as the tall detective slowly draws a small black wallet from his jacket pocket and opening it, almost shoves it into Ian's face as he says, "Now, for the last time before you *really* annoy me. What's you name…*pal*!"

Ian has his back to me, but I hear him stutter, "Ian Chalmers. I'm Maggie's son-in-law."

I find my voice and though my throat is dry and my voice quivering, I manage to snarl, "Soon to be ex-son-in-law."

DS Reid glances at me over Ian's shoulder and his voice calm and level, politely asks me, "Do you want this man off your property, Missus Brogan?"

"Please," I vigorously nod.

That's enough for him because he takes a couple of steps to one side and waving a thumb over his shoulder, says, "Git."

Ian turns his head towards me and I see his face his pale, but he tries one last shot and sneers at me, "This isn't finished, Maggie."

I see DS Reid take a step towards him, but I shake my head and then see him halt as Ian quickly makes his way down the driveway to the pavement, then walks to the pavement and turning right, makes his way along Clarion Crescent.

I watch in silence till he's out of sight then realise I'm holding the handrail so tightly I can see the white of my knuckles.

DS Reid takes a step towards me before he asks, "Are you okay?"

"Yes," I manage to croak, then add, "I will be. Thank you."

To my surprise, he smiles widely and tells me, "Eh, you look, well, very nice," then he grins and nodding, says again, "Yes, very nice indeed."

Personally I think I look really good, but I'll take very nice if that's on offer.

****

Well, I'm hardly likely to turn away a man who has come to my rescue, am I, and invite DS Reid in. Besides, there must be a reason for his visit.

"Hope you don't mind me popping by without phoning first, Missus Brogan, but I thought I'd give you a wee update," he says as he follows me into the house and I see him take a subtle sniff of the air. I'm calmer now and trying not to blush at his obvious admiring glance, but then he smacks a hand at his brow and says, "Liz. She's coming home today. Sorry," he begins to rise from his chair, "I clean forgot. Look, I'll get out of your way and maybe…"

"Don't be silly," I wave him back from the front room door. "She's not being discharged till midday so it will be another hour and a half or more before she gets here. Tea or coffee?"

He opts for coffee and to my surprise, follows me into the kitchen and watches while I fill the kettle and prepare two mugs. The smell of the soup causes even my mouth to water and I hide a grin when again I catch him sniffing the air.

"So, that was Beth's father?" he says.

"That was him," I wearily reply.

"I've not yet had the opportunity to interview him. After that little episode outside your front door, I'm sure when I do it will prove to be interesting," he smiles, then continues, "Can I ask what that argument was about?"

I tell him about the delivery of the divorce papers to Liz, the allegation Ian is making about her care of Beth and her mental health and his cheap shot at trying to get money out of me.

"And he's got a cheek," I add, "considering that I've been told he's living with another woman right now."

"Oh? Do you know who and where?"

"Eh, no," I frown. "Only that she's a barmaid with a couple of children. I *was* told the address, but I can't remember it. I think Garscadden was mentioned."

He smiles and stroking at his chin, says, "When your daughter engages a lawyer to act for her, it might be worth mentioning that. Unless I'm mistaken, adultery is still grounds for divorce in Scotland. Why don't you let me collect a business card for you from a lawyer pal of mine and if you and Liz are happy to speak with him, I could maybe put in a word for you."

I hadn't given much thought to Liz needing a lawyer and I smile as I reply, "Yes, please. So, you're suggesting Liz could divorce *him* for adultery?"

"I'm no expert in civil law, but it seems to me if what you've been told is true, she might have a case, yes. And this attempt to get money from you, is that his style?"

I tell him about the time when Alex died and how Ian wanted to know if Liz was entitled to half the value of the house. I'm surprised to see his face tighten and his eyes narrow and I'm guessing he doesn't think much of Ian Chalmers.

He stares curiously at me before he raises both hands in defence and asks, "I take it none of the magazines or newspapers have tried to contact you for a story?"

"I have one word for those kind of magazines," I frown. "Trash, the lot of them."

I shake my head in disgust at the very thought someone would sell a story about the death of their child, then ask him, "You said you had some sort of update for me?"

"Ah, yes, the reason I'm calling is to tell you some evidence was discovered on the wee girl that was murdered, Kylie Murdoch. Evidence that might give us a clue to who her killer might be."

I know he's talking about DNA, but I can't let him know that because it would reveal that Sheila Gardener has already disclosed that information; something she might get into trouble for.

"Now, the evidence in itself doesn't directly tie the girl's murder in with the murder of Beth, but if we arrest the wee girl's killer it's a starter for ten in that we can interview him about Beth's murder. Do you see?"

"I do," I'm nodding, and then ask, "I take it DCI Tarrant still refuses to link both murders?"

He takes a few seconds to respond, then nodding, replies, "He's apparently convinced the murders are not linked."

"And what do you think, Mister Reid?"

He stares at me then a slow smile lights up his face when he says, "You can call me Alan, if you like."

Before I can respond he clears his throat, and then continues, "I wouldn't rule out a link. To be honest though, while the CID teaches us that there is no such thing as coincidence, it is possible that Tarrant just might be correct. The murder of Beth and the murder of the wee girl Murdoch could be two completely separate issues. The problem I have with Tarrant's decision is that without evidence to the contrary, I would *not* rule out a link. What I mean is when we catch the Murdoch girls killer, if he is proven categorically not to be Beth's killer then it confirms Tarrants decision. However, until such time he is caught, I think I'd hedge my bet and look at both murders together or at least continue to make inquiry to see if there is any kind of link between the murders."

"You sound very confident this man who killed the wee girl will be caught, Mister…Alan," I correct myself and smile.

"I think the odds are on the police side, Missus Brogan."

"Maggie. Please call me Maggie."

"Maggie," he says with a nod and to be honest, I like the way he says it.

Now I'm really blushing so to hide my embarrassment, I turn away and pour the boiling water into the two mugs.

Handing him his mug, I turn and holding mine in both hands, lean with my back to the worktop.

"I had an interesting phone call with a colleague this morning," he begins.

My eyes narrow with interest as he continues. "Sheila Gardener, the liaison officer who it turns out is pretty fond of you."

"Yes, Sheila and I get on well," I reply and there seems little point in denying it.

"Yes, that came across during the call. It's been my experience that sometimes liaison officers and the families of victims they counsel can become quite close," he's staring curiously at me. I take a sip of my coffee to hide my confusion and wonder, what exactly is he getting at? Does he know Sheila's been telling me things?

I decide to ask, "What caused you to phone Sheila?"

He shrugs and replies, "To ask about you. You and Liz."

My eyes widen as I ask, "Me and Liz? What did you want to know that you couldn't ask me yourself?"

He's clearly uncomfortable and setting his mug down onto the table behind him, he places his hands in his trouser pockets. He continues to stare at me and I just know it's something I'm not going to like. Then he tells me.

"You have to understand, Maggie, written statements can only tell me so much. I needed to know what kind of relationship you had with your granddaughter and your daughter and what kind of relationship Beth had with her mother."

Maybe I'm not thinking straight, maybe I've just not picked up on what's he's insinuating, but then as clear and as sharp as a knife being plunged into my heart, I understand.

I feel my blood run cold as I stare back into his eyes and finding my voice, I manage to speak.

"You think that either Liz or I would have harmed…could have killed Beth?"

He continues to stare at me then replies, "Until we find who did kill Beth, everyone is…was a suspect, but I know now it wasn't you or your daughter. I'm sorry, but I had to find out for sure."

For the second time within an hour, my legs are shaking and I feel faint, so much so I feel the colour drain from my face. I lurch towards a chair and feel myself falling, but he catches me and helps me to sit down.

"I'm sorry," he repeats, "but I had to know for certain."

I turn to see him down on one knee as his hand continues to hold my arm and his arm is around my waist. Then, as if he suddenly realises he's being inappropriate, he withdraws his hand and arm and regaining his feet, backs off a step.

Remember those palpitations? Well, I'm having them again and my heart is beating like a drum in my chest.

He draws a glass of water and places it on the table in front of me before he says, "I don't get to ask the nice questions, Maggie. When I read your statement and your daughter's statement, it was clear that nobody had considered you to be suspects. The sad fact is that when there's an unsolved murder in a family the CID always look for the suspect from the inside out, starting with the spouse, then family members. It's the way we do things or at least the way it *should* have been done," he awkwardly shrugs.

I raise my head to stare at him and ask, "All this time, those visits you made to me, you thought I might have killed Beth or my Liz might have killed her daughter?"

"No," he slowly shakes his head and calmly replies, "not all the time and to be honest, I didn't believe you capable of it, but I had to ask. It's my job."

"And that's why you phoned Sheila? To ask about me and Liz, if I we were capable of hurting Beth?"

"Yes."

I feel a cold rage and my teeth gritted, my voice no more than a whisper, I hear myself say, "Get Out! Get out of my house! Go!"

He doesn't reply, but his head nodding in acknowledgment, he leaves and seconds later, I hear the front door close.

I continue to sit at the table, a feeling of numbness creeping across me as I stare blankly at nothing.

CHAPTER TEN

By midday I've calmed down, had a wee angry cry to myself, washed my face, reapplied my makeup and I'm ready for the arrival of Liz and Colin Paterson.

The phone rings and its Sheila Gardener who tells me, "Alan Reid phoned this morning, Maggie. He wanted to know if you and Liz were at any time suspected of," she pauses, "hurting Beth."

"I know. He called by here and told me about phoning you." I shake my head and add, "The bloody cheek of the man."

There's a definite hesitation in her voice when she replies, "I know you don't want to hear this, Maggie, but he was only doing his job."

I'm not angry at Sheila because I know when he spoke to her she defended Liz and me, but I'm very angry at Reid and I respond, "Do you know he was being really nice to me before he hit me with those questions? Getting underneath my defences then wham, did you and her mother ever hurt Beth?"

"Is that what he asked you, if you'd hurt Beth?"

"Well, in so many words," I huffily snap. "He told me he asked you about our relationship with her, but that's what he meant, isn't it?"

She doesn't immediately reply and I continue, "I mean, that *is* what he meant, isn't it?"

"I suppose so, but he's not Martin Tarrant, Maggie. From what I've heard about Alan Reid, he's a good guy and he's very well thought of at his job. I'm sure it can't have been easy for him admitting he'd asked about you and Liz."

I don't answer, but think about what she said then I ask, "Why weren't Liz and I asked those questions when they first found Beth?"

"You know I don't know the answer to that question, Maggie. What I can tell you is that part of my training as a liaison officer is not only to counsel the victim's family and act as the go-between them and the investigation team, but as a police officer I'm also obliged to monitor the family's reaction to the death and the ensuing investigation and report any suspicions I might have that any of the family are complicit in the death or have knowledge of the circumstances of the victim's death. You do understand that, don't you, Maggie?"

"Well, yes, I suppose so," though I had never really given it any thought, that Sheila would be not only acting as our go-between with the police, but would also need to consider Liz and I might be suspects.

"The thing is, almost immediately it was pretty clear to me to tell that neither you nor Liz had anything to do with Beth's murder."

"Then if you told Alan Reid that," I defensively ask, "Why did he have to tell me he had to ask that question?"

I hear her sigh and she says, "Probably because nobody *had* asked it. Look, put it this way. If…" she stops. "I mean *when* we catch the man who killed Beth and if it goes to trial, some smartarse lawyer might learn the police never asked you if you did it or if Liz had anything to do with Beth's death, so to deflect the jury's interest in his client the lawyer might put those questions to that plonker Tarrant while he's in the witness box. Can you imagine if he were asked that in a witness box; did you consider the mother and grandmother as suspects? Obviously he's going to reply he didn't. Then he'll be asked, if everyone was a suspect why then not the mother and grandmother?"

I'm trying to take in what Sheila's saying, but then after a pause she says, "I know what you're thinking, but a good lawyer will use any means at his disposal to cast a shadow of doubt upon the accused's guilt and sowing the seed of doubt in a jury's minds might include casting you and Liz as suspects for Beths murder. The last thing you want is the murderer getting off with a Not Proven or even a Not Guilty verdict, isn't it? Do you see what I'm getting at?"

Even though I now accept Sheila's explanation, I'm still a little irritated with Alan Reid and now I'm feeling a little annoyed at myself too, for being so offhanded with him. Then I remember I'm on the phone and reply, "I see what you mean."

"Did you give him a hard time when he asked you about Beth's death?"

I suppress a grin and tell her, "I ordered him out of the house."

"You never did!"

"I did," I'm giggling now, but it's more to do with my embarrassment than humour. "Do you think I was a bit hard on him, then?"

"Well, like I told you he was just doing his job. Don't worry about it, though, he's a grown man, I'm sure he'll get over it and I'll bet it's not the first time he's been thrown out of someone's house. Besides, Maggie, it's not in your nature to be rude and I'm certain he'll understand that you were taken aback and probably just reacted as anyone would."

"I hope so," I hear myself reply.

I hear her laugh and then she asks, "What did you mean, he was being really nice to you?"

"What?"

"You said he was being really nice to you."

"Oh," I find I'm blushing. "With Liz coming home I put on a dress and some makeup and well, he told me I looked very nice."

"He said you looked nice!" she's laughing now, then adds, "Do you think he fancies you?"

"Don't be ridiculous, Sheila," I laugh with her, but I'm a little uncomfortable at her suggestion, then add, "He's a married man, for God's sake."

"Oh, who told you that? Did he tell you that?"

"Well, no, but he did say he's got two daughters and a grandson. He did tell me that much."

"Hmm, that's not what I heard, him being married I mean. Let me get back to you on that one," she says, but then I hear the sound of tyres on the stone chips in the driveway and glancing out the window, see a small white car edge up the driveway to stop a couple of feet behind mine. As I move towards the window, I see Liz sitting in the passenger seat and she's waving furiously at me through the windscreen.

"Oh, I need to go, hen," I tell Sheila. "That's Liz just arrived."

"Good luck," she hurriedly replies. "I'll give you a phone if I hear anything else from Martin Clarke. Bye," and she's gone.

I rush to open the door and you know that old saying, the picture of health? Well, fortunately the rain has stayed away for as she steps from the car that's exactly how I will describe my Liz. She looks radiant; her shoulder length fair hair swept back into a ponytail, her face needing no makeup for her skin is clear and fresh. She's wearing a white blouse and light coloured pink cardigan that's unbuttoned, a short, dark grey pencil skirt, black leather knee high boots and looks far younger than her twenty-six years.

"Mum!" she rushes forward to give me a hug as behind her, Colin Paterson fetches her cabin luggage case from the boot of the Nissan Micra and approaching the door where we're still stood embracing, shyly says, "Hello, Missus B. Hope you don't mind that it's me that brought Liz home."

I'm thinking that Doctor Francis has maybe had a wee word of caution with him, but I'm too delighted to think of anything else other than my girl's back home where she should be.

"Come away in, the two of you," I happily tell them and after Colin deposits the case at the bottom of the stairs, I usher them both into the front room.

It doesn't escape my notice that Liz grabs at Colin's hand and quite literally drags him down to sit beside her on the couch as she stares at me, as if challenging me to say anything about them holding hands. He's blushing as I stare from one to the other, but I only sigh and with a smile on my face, say, "Are you ready for some lunch?"
****

I'm about to seat them at the kitchen table when Colin says, "Oh, sorry, I've left something in the car." He returns a minute later with a large bouquet of flowers that he hands to me and says, "Thanks for having me for lunch, Missus B."

I'm a bit surprised, but I don't think there's any guile in the gift. The flowers are from Marks and Spencer and include half dozen sunflowers, my favourite, so he's obviously been tipped off by Liz.

They're lovely, so must have cost him a few quid and to be honest, I'm pleased at his thoughtfulness and involuntarily give him a peck on the cheek as a thank you. I turn to place them on the worktop and catch Liz's eye and I can see she's glad I'm being so hospitable.

I'm at the worktop cutting up the crusty bread when Liz tells me, "I'm thinking of looking for a job right away, mum."

"Do you not think you should give yourself a wee bit of space, love?" I turn to face her. "I mean you've been in the hospital for over four months. Why not take a week or so to yourself, get out and catch up with your friends."

"Friends?" her face clouds over. "Do you know that apart from you, Linda and James and Father O'Brien, the only friends who visited me were Debbie and Laura? As for my other so-called friends," she makes quotation marks in the air with her forefingers, "they were either too embarrassed to visit me in a mental hospital or just couldn't care less about me being in there."

I see Colin reach across and stroke at her hand to calm her and she reacts by placing her free hand on top of his.

"Anyway," she turns to me, "I spoke with Doctor Francis about it and Colin agrees with him that getting a job and back into the world will do me more good than moping about here."

Well, I'm hardly likely to argue with medical advice am I, so I sigh and tell her, "Whatever you decide, hen, you know you have my full support."

"Thanks, mum," and springs from her chair to give me another crushing hug.

I mean, it's not as if I'm going to say no, is it and besides; maybe it will do her a world of good.

It's idle chitchat through the meal that includes Colin telling me he still lives with his parents and that one of his younger sisters is married while the other lives with her partner. Liz asks if I'm still going to work that afternoon and I say no, that I'm taking the late shift off. I don't bother explaining that I've been given it off because she's so pleased I'm staying at home.

I've also made the decision not to mention the letter from the Education Department. As far as I'm concerned that's dealt with nor will I tell her about Ian's visit. No, there's time enough for that and probably when we get round to discussing getting her a lawyer to fight his divorce allegations.

The thought of getting her a lawyer brings to mind DS Reid…Alan's offer, and I wish I hadn't been so hard on the man.

You have to understand when Alex was alive it would have been his job to speak to any boyfriend of Liz's, but with him gone that now falls to me.

So, when she excuses herself to go to the loo and it's just Colin and me sitting having our coffee, I take the plunge and ask him, "Are you serious about my daughter?"

His eyes open wide in surprise and sitting back in his chair, he takes a deep breath before he replies, "I am Missus B. Is that okay with you?"

"Will you be good to her?"

His face flushes and nodding, he says, "I've never met anyone like her. To be honest," his face goes even redder, "I've never been that confident around women, Missus B. Aye, I've had a couple of girlfriends, but nothing that's lasted longer than a few months. Liz," he shrugs, "well, she's definitely different."

"And do you think she might feel the same way about you, Colin? To be frank, I'm worried that after everything thats happened she's very vulnerable right now. That and you're a few years older and don't forget too, she's still a married woman."

Well, in the eyes of the law anyway, I tell myself.

"Firstly, I'm thirty-one, Missus B, and secondly, I know how vulnerable she is and what she's been through, but honestly," he raises his hands defensively, "I will never do anything to hurt her and after a while if she doesn't feel the same way about me; well, I'll back off. You have my word."

I'm staring thoughtfully at him when the kitchen door opens and Liz comes in. Glancing suspiciously at us both, she asks, "What?"

****

I'm washing the dishes and tidying up and while the rain is staying off and the sun is even peeking out from behind the clouds, Liz and Colin have taken a walk. I have to admit she'd surprised me when she bravely said, "I want to show him the park, mum, where it happened. Doctor Francis says I should face my fears." Her face is pale, but I see a determination in her eyes that I've not seen for a long time and I can only nod and agree when she takes a sunflower from the bunch that Colin brought.

Okay, I admit when they left and were walking down the driveway I hid behind the front room curtain and peeked out to watch them and though I can't explain it, I was so relieved that Colin had her by the hand as they crossed the road to enter the park. I watched as they walked straight to the rhododendron bush and stood for a wee while, their hands still clasped together. I saw Liz bend down and lay the sunflower on the ground then when she stood back up, they walked further into the park and out of my sight.

I'm not kidding when I tell you that that seeing her bravely do that brought a tear to my eye and I felt so drained that I had to sit for a couple of minutes to compose myself.

They were gone for over an hour, but during that time I took a phone call from Jessie Cochrane who said, "I hear you met my Mary in Asda and she told you about the flat."

There was a definite excitement in Jessie's voice and when I told her I was looking forward to visiting her in the flat, she replied, "Why not come up for your dinner one night?"

"Seems like a plan," I had agreed, then I told her my own good news about Liz coming home.

"Oh, my, that's great, hen," she gushed and my throat tightened at the obvious sincerity of her reply. I wish I could be as good a friend to Jessie as she obviously is to me.

"I take it your man still hasn't a clue you're leaving?"

"No, and I'm not telling him neither," she had sniffed, before adding, "Him nor the boys. I've put enough years in looking after they buggers, Maggie, and I'm sick to the bone running after them like a skivvy, so I am. Cooking and cleaning for them when they'll not lift a hand to help, but oh aye," she bitterly complained, "they're there on my payday looking for a hand-out. Well, from now on they can fend for themselves. I'm done with them."

There was something about her voice that caused me to think that maybe, just maybe this time, Jessie was resolute and means what she says.

I certainly hope so.

Assuring me that she'd be back to work on Monday she rung off. I didn't bother telling her about my confrontation with big Eileen or Tommy Burton giving me most of the day off for Liz coming home. That could wait till later.

When at last Liz and Colin returned to the house, they were running up the driveway to escape the sudden squall that arrived. Laughing as they burst through the front door, I'm ready with a couple of bath towels and while they rub themselves dry, I tell Liz to nip upstairs to change into something dry. Seeing Colin's shirt, pullover and his jeans is soaked through, I say, "My husband was a bit bigger than you, son, but wait here and I'll see if there's anything in the cupboard that might fit."

You might think it strange that I kept some of Alex old clothes, but though I gave most away to the local Cancer Research shop, I did keep a couple of polo shirts and tracksuit bottoms that were too old for the charity to sell, convincing myself they might come in handy for me when I got round to working in the garden.

Needless to say, I never did use them and stupidly I'm too sentimental just to toss them into the bin where really they should have gone, they lay folded in a cardboard box in the cupboard at the top of the stairs.

I find a decent enough top and a pair of bottoms and calling him upstairs, send him into my room to get changed.

"Bring down the wet things and I'll hang them around the radiators," I tell him.

Minutes later Liz joins me in the front room and in a low voice, says, "Thanks, mum, for being so nice to Colin."

"Am I not usually nice?" I tease her.

She grins and replies, "You know what I mean. Do you like him?"

Now, an honest answer would have been, 'Yes I like him, but is he right for you?' However, knowing it's really important to her, what I simply say is, "Yes, love. I like him."

I'm not fibbing for really, I do like Colin. He seems a nice and steady young man, but again it haunts me; is Liz ready for a relationship? I suppose time will tell, but I just don't want my lassie getting hurt again.

When Colin comes downstairs, I choke back a laugh while Liz can't help herself and bursts out giggling. Like I said Alex was a big man, but his polo shirt dwarfs Colin who sheepishly grinning back at us, I see has rolled the bottom of the tracksuit trousers up a couple of times too.

"They'll do till I get home," he tells me. "Thanks, Missus B."

The afternoon draws to a close with the rain thundering down now and while Liz fetches out one of my old photo albums and they pore over it, I'm in the kitchen and about to prepare dinner.

Of course I didn't think Colin would be staying so long and I've just slipped on my apron when he pops his head in the door and says, "If you don't mind me hanging on, Missus B, I was wondering if I could phone a chippy in for the three of us? On me, course. Fish suppers okay with you?"

I can't recall the last time I had shop fish suppers and smiling, fetch the local chip shops menu from the kitchen drawer and tell him that would be grand.

"Right then," he flushes with pleasure, "I'll get it done."
****

I've thirty minutes before the STV news starts at six because I'm keen to see what the headlines are, if there's any breakthrough in the wee girl Murdoch's murder.

I'm still wearing my apron and setting the table when Liz comes into the kitchen and frowning, says, "Mum, there's a man at the door."

Puzzled, I ask her, "What's he wanting?"

"I don't know. I saw the shadow behind the glass and he was just about to put something through the door. Says he didn't mean to disturb us, but I told him to hang on in case it was someone you knew."

I hurry through to the hallway and the front door is still ajar. The rain is pelting it down and stood in the doorway is DS Reid wearing one of those full-length Australian oilskin coats and a dark grey bunnet.

Liz stands behind me and I'm honestly taken aback because frankly I didn't expect to see him again and certainly not today.

Before I say anything, he apologises and says, "Sorry, Missus Brogan. I didn't want to disturb you. I know your daughter has just arrived home, but I wanted to drop this off. I was going to push it through the letterbox," he grimaces, "but I was caught."

He hands me a business card and with the briefest of glances at Liz, adds, "It's for that issue we spoke about earlier today?"

Of course I know exactly what it is, his lawyer friend's card.

I'm staring at him and seeing his coat is all wet as well as feeling a little guilty about the way I treated him, I reply, "Please come in, Mister Reid."

Oh, you'll have noticed we're back to the formal titles again.

"No, really, I'm soaking wet," he says and holding up his hands is about to turn away, but I interrupt and standing no nonsense, tell him, "And if you've taken the trouble to drop this off, that's as good a reason for me to offer you something hot to drink. Please, come in. I insist."

When he steps through the door, Liz gives me a curious glance before taking his wet coat and bunnet and then nips upstairs to hang them to drip over the bath while I lead him into the front room.

Colin is stood in front of the fireplace with the menu in one hand and his mobile phone in the other, then seeing us, is clearly perplexed and says, "I've just ordered the food. Should I have got another supper?"

"No, you're fine son," I tell him and as Liz returns to the room, I introduce her then nod to him and say, "And this is her friend, Colin Paterson."

Is it a bit early to introduce him as her boyfriend? I think so and seeing her frowning, decide I'll deal with that when the two of us are alone.

"This is Detective Sergeant Reid. Mister Reid," I explain, "is the detective who is now dealing with Beth's murder."

Liz's confusion shows in her face and she mutters, "But I thought it was the detective called Tarrant who was…?"

"It's a long story, hen," I sigh, "but in the meantime Mister Reid…" I glance at him and soften. "Alan, is our contact with the police. Please, Alan, sit down."

I place the business card on the mantelpiece because that's a conversation for later, then politely ask, "Coffee or tea?"

He's clearly ill at ease, but nods, "Tea will be fine, thanks. Just milk."

"I'll help you," Liz makes eye contact with me and follows me into the kitchen.

She shuts the door behind her and her eyes flashing with anger, hisses, "When were you going to tell me about this, mum? I thought it was a senior detective who was dealing with Beth's investigation, not a bloody sergeant!"

I stare at her and forcing myself to be calm, reply in even voice, "You've been home just a few hours, Elizabeth and with a man I hardly know. At which point during those few hours were we supposed to sit down and discuss your daughter's murder and what's being happening since you were confined to hospital?"

She stares at me, both shocked by the use of her Sunday name as well as the tone of my voice that lets her know I'm *really* not in the mood for an argument.

I see her wilt in front of me and I reach out to take her in my arms and soothingly whisper in her ear, "When we're alone, I'll tell you everything, but right now isn't the time, okay?"

She raises her head from my shoulder and I see her eyes glistening with unshed tears before she asks, "Everything?"

"Everything," I reassuringly nod.

I hold her for another minute, then tell her, "You organise the tea and that will give you the chance to wash your face. I'll go out and make polite conversation," I tightly smile at her.

"Okay," she sniffs and I know she'll be fine.

Colin is explaining his job as a mental health nurse, but stops when I re-enter the room.

"I was just telling Alan how I met Liz," he smiles, blissfully unaware of what was going on in the kitchen, but Alan, who is sat in an armchair, is more astute and asks me, "Is she okay?"

Colin's eyes dart to him, suddenly aware something might be amiss, but before he can ask, I sit down in the opposite armchair and say, "Just a bit taken aback at what's happening in the investigation. I'll explain it all to her later."

I glance at my wristwatch and see it's just gone five minutes to six and I continue, "Would you think it awfully rude of me if I switch on the six o'clock news?"

Alan nods and replies, "Actually I'd be keen to watch it too. I'm told there is to be a press briefing about the wee girl Murdoch's murder. Would you mind if I watch it with you?"

I know is sounds a bit macabre us wanting to watch the news about the wee girls murder, but you have to remember that whatever they discover in that investigation might impact on Beth's investigation.

I dart back to the kitchen and switch on the oven because Sods Law is that the chip suppers will arrive during the news and sure enough, minutes later the doorbell goes as the news begins.

Colin volunteers to get the door and while he takes the suppers through to the kitchen, Liz, Alan and I are glued to the screen.

As you would expect, the wee girl's murder is the main headline and when John McKay the anchor man passes across to the reporter Mike Edwards who is stood in front of a brown brick and weather beaten building, Alan murmurs, "That's the Maryhill office."

Sure enough there's DCI Tarrant stood outside the entrance and curiously is ignoring the glass overhang at the door, preferring to face the cameras in the rain as he gives his media briefing. A dark haired woman wearing a dark business suit and fawn coloured raincoat is stood beside him holding a large umbrella over him to protect him from the deluge as he begins,

"Yesterday evening the body of a four-year-old girl now identified as Kylie Murdoch, was discovered beneath a railway bridge that runs under Kelso Street in the Yoker area of the city. Kylie had earlier been reported missing from the foyer area of the flats where she resided with her mother. Subsequent to a post mortem examination the death is now being treated as murder. Inquiries are continuing but as yet there has been no arrest; however, I am confident that with the assistance of the public the killer of this young girl will be found."

"Short and sweet and no big words which suggests that somebody must have written it for him," Alan mutters and leaves me in no doubt that he does not like Tarrant.

At this point, but off camera, the assembled reporters start to hurl questions at Tarrant and though we can't make out what's being shouted at him he holds up a hand and bluntly replies to a question,

"Not yet, not unless some credible evidence arises that suggests otherwise, I am not linking it to the murder of Bethany Chalmers. However, when the killer is found he will as a matter of course be interviewed about the murder of Bethany Chalmers."

Kneeling by my armchair, I feel Liz's hand reach for mine and squeeze my fingers tightly.

Colin steps out from the kitchen, but remains silent for he can see we're engrossed in the news bulletin. However, I can hear the kettle boiling and realise he must have switched it on again.

Other questions are asked of Tarrant, but he only replies to one when he says, *"Yes, I can confirm that there was evidence found on Kylie's body."*

As he turns away, the harassed woman holding the brolly calls out, *"That's all for today, ladies and gentlemen,"* and turns to quickly follow Tarrant who is already at the doors of Maryhill office.

I turn to stare when I hear Alan quietly mutter, "Jesus Christ! The fool, bloody fool!"

His face is tightly drawn and it's clear he's extremely angry.

"What?" I ask.

"Did you hear him? Did you hear what he said!" he almost explodes." He's only bloody gone and told the world that we have DNA evidence!"

"Is that such a bad thing?" I ask.

He takes a breath and now quieter, shakes his head when he replies, "Don't you realise what he's done, Maggie? Think about where that DNA was found and it's not hard to work out, is it? He's letting that poor woman; the child's mother, the grandparents and the rest of the family know what happened to her. He's let them know that before she was murdered, that wee four-year-old was brutally sexually assaulted."

****

To be honest, after hearing that none of us really felt like eating and though I invited Alan to stay and share the supers, he declines, saying he'd had an early dinner. I think he was fibbing, but I don't press him. That said, he makes no immediate move to leave and anyway, the suppers have gone cold and end up in the bin.

Switching off the television, Liz says, "Mum, would you mind if Colin and me went for a drive? Not that I don't want to spend time with you," she hastily adds, "but I'd like to get out and even if it is raining, Colin says we can take a turn down to Helensburgh, maybe grab a takeaway and sit by the pier. You don't mind, do you?"

It was her first night home and I'd like to have spent it with her, but I could appreciate that after four months in hospital she was probably feeling a bit stir crazy.

Forcing a smile and a lot more brightly than I feel, I tell her, "Of course not, hen. Only make sure you take your raincoat and," I joke, "don't let Colin out of the car in those clothes or he'll get himself arrested"

They are away in less than five minutes, but not before Liz says, "It was nice meeting you, Mister, eh…"

He solves that one by replying, "Call me Alan and at some point we'll need to have a word, but only when you're ready."

"Yeah, of course," she nods to him. Then, with a hug for me from Liz and a subtle glance that she'll be fine with Colin, they are gone. There is an awkward silence with both of us on our feet before I ask, "Another cuppa?"

"Yes, if you're making one," he replies and I indicate he sit down. The minutes in the kitchen give me the opportunity to collect my thoughts and to be honest; I'm wondering why he's still here? I mean, he's handed in the lawyer's card, so why is he hanging about? It crosses my mind that…then I recall Sheila's comment but decide no, it can't be because he fancies me, can it? But I shake the very thought out of my head and blush at my vanity.

In the front room I hand him his mug and primly sit back down in the armchair, my knees tightly together and wait for him to open the conversation.

"I'm kind of glad your daughter and her friend left," he says and I feel myself tense, for if this is the start of some chat up line…

"I needed to speak to you about your neighbour, Peter McGregor."

I don't know whether to be pleased or disappointed but I'm thinking, that will teach me to be presumptuous.

"Yes?"

He stares for a few seconds as though collecting his thoughts then says, "You told me that he's a lecturer at Stow College and that the day he tried to, eh…"

"Make advances?" I helpfully suggest.

"Indeed, make an advance towards you. On that day he said he was taking a couple of days off?"

"That's correct," I sip at my tea. "Said something about charging his batteries."

"Well, as I told you I would, I did make a discreet inquiry with a retired colleague who works in the security industry and whose firm is contracted to provide security at the college. What I learned is in the strictest confidence; you understand that, Maggie?"

"Of course I do," though I'm a little peeved he'd think I was a gossip.

He seems satisfied I'll keep my mouth shut and says, "My mate has heard that Mister McGregor is currently suspended with pay from his employment and has been for the last two months pending a college investigation into what my mate heard is acting improperly towards a number of foreign students. How many, he doesn't know nor does he know what acting improperly entails, but what he heard is that as you'd maybe guessed, all the students are female."

I'm actually stunned, for I definitely did not expect to hear this. Then I ask, "This improper behaviour? You think it's sexual, don't you?"

"What I think isn't relevant, but my mate likely won't learn any more because apparently the whole episode is shrouded in secrecy, but he did hear there is a suggestion that if McGregor goes quietly and doesn't make a fuss, he can leave with his pension rights and some months salary."

"What?" I'm outraged. "You mean if he's guilty, he gets away with it?"

"It's the way of the world, Maggie," he shrugs. "Think about it. All colleges and universities survive on annual intakes of foreign students paying their tuition fees and let's not forget, most foreign students rely on their parents for the fees. If news of this got out, if there's any hint that a lecturer is a sexual predator, it might seriously affect next years' student applications for what parent would risk sending their daughter to a university with such a reputation? The subsequent lack of revenue would be wide reaching and the domino effect would come into play. Courses dropped, lecturer's salaries affected, maybe even staff layoffs. No organisation whether it's educational or otherwise can afford such a scandal these days. Besides and remember, it's also a possibility that he might be innocent of these allegations."

I'm recalling his less than subtle approach to me and what Moira his wife told me about him, and I snap back, "I don't think so!"

Then I find I'm sighing and shaking my head because I'm not mad at Alan, but angry at a rotten system.

"What about the students he's supposed to have acted improperly against?" I ask. "What do you think they would they say if they heard of such an offer?"

"Obviously I don't know what they'd say," he shrugs, "but if you think about it. Let's say hypothetically a young woman who is a victim in the issue is offered a discount on her fees or even the cost of her course wiped out if she keeps her mouth shut. Who's to say that wouldn't be an attractive proposal to a foreign student who might be struggling to pay her fees; annual fees that might be as much as fifteen or twenty thousand pounds or more. Particularly a woman who worries if she complains it will affect her results and once her course is finished, she can return home with no one the wiser as to what happened to her. And let's face it," he shrugs. "If what he has done is kept quiet by the Faculty, the student might believe that she is the only victim and likely she'll also consider that no one in the governing body will take her word over that of a member of the academic staff."

"And you think maybe that's why he's picked on foreign students? So they *wouldn't* complain?"

"I don't know if all the victims are foreign students, but it's a thought," he nods.

"My God!" I'm shocked. "Does that kind of sexual harassment still go on these days?"

He's smiling at my anger and that in turn causes me to smile, but then I ask, "You read his statement?"

"I did," he sighs, "and unfortunately there's nobody nor anything that can alibi him for the time that Beth went missing to the time when she was discovered."

"So," my eyes narrow, "he's a possible suspect for her murder?"

"Like so many others who are not alibied, yes," but raising a hand to stop me speaking, he continues in a firm voice, "that's not to say you've to go and kick his door down, Maggie! I mean it!"

Yeah, like I'm going along the road to pull Peter McGregor from his house? I can see *that* happening and then I wonder; what is it about me that makes people believe I'm some sort of avenging Amazonian woman?

When I don't immediately respond, he then continues, "Other than his alleged preference for young foreign female students and attractive neighbours," I see him redden slightly, "there's nothing to suggest Peter McGregor has any paedophile tendencies. He certainly isn't known to the police for anything like that."

But then I take in what he said about attractive neighbours and I find myself blushing.

However, I'm sharp enough to pick up on 'anything like that' and tongue in cheek ask him, "But he *is* known to the police?"

He sighs at his slip of the tongue and replies, "Let's just say Mister McGregor has had a couple of issues, but not for a very long time."

A thought strikes me and I slowly ask, "What if he's *not* alibied for the time the Murdoch girl was taken from the foyer?"

He takes a breath and lets it out slowly before he tells me, "He is alibied for the time the Murdoch girl was snatched. When I was doing a background check on him I decided to check that out and discovered he was at his college meeting the Principle. That's when it was put to him about the offer to resign."

"But how can you be certain he actually attended?"

"Because in the event McGregor kicked off and there was some kind of confrontation, my mate was the security officer who was on hand to prevent any trouble. You have to remember, I do this for a living," he reminded me with a smile, then added, "Sorry, Maggie, I know how much you want it to be him."

But, I think to myself, it still doesn't alibi him for Beth's murder though.

"It's not that, Alan," I frown, "I'm not particularly wishing Peter McGregor to be the murderer of Beth. I just want whoever it is to be caught," I miserably add.

I shake my head and ask, "How will you deal with him, then?"

He sighs and says, "McGregor, like everyone else on my list, will be interviewed again, but remember I'm a one-man team though I'll probably start with him."

Really, I can't ask for anymore than that, can I?

As the seconds tick by I'm suddenly aware of a tension…no, that's not the word, it's like he wants to say or ask something, but can't quite bring himself to do it, so at last he stands up and says, "Look, I'd better be hitting the road. If there's anything further, I'll be in touch, okay?"

"Okay," I nod and leave the room to fetch his coat and the still damp bunnet from upstairs.

When I return he's in the hallway by the front door and handing him his coat, he slips it on then says, "It was a pleasure meeting your daughter this evening. Colin seems like a nice young man. I hope it works out between them."

He pulls open the door as I reply, "So do I," then he stares curiously at me before asking, "You have some reservations?"

"Just a mother's worries," I smile as I shrug.

"Wish my lassie's had that problem," he sighs then with a wave he's walking down the driveway to his car parked in the street.

Now, I wonder, what did he mean by that?

CHAPTER ELEVEN

Saturday should be the first of my weekend lie-in mornings, but the council in their wisdom decided this is the morning that the bins are collected. Course to those of us with bedroom windows to the front of the house, it's a source of complaint and mostly by the neighbours who are up and out early during the working week. We're woken at just after eight when the bin lorry's diesel engine as well as the hoist that tips the bins into the rear of the lorry make such a racket it's nigh on impossible to get back to sleep. Petition followed petition but still our local councillors have failed to get the day exchanged for a weekday. However, that particular morning I'm already wide-awake before the bin lorry arrives.

Though I didn't actually fall over to sleep till some time after midnight, for I'd lain awake listening for Liz coming home, I'm not at all feeling tired.

It was just after eleven o'clock when I'd heard Colin's car draw up and another ten minutes before I heard the car door close, then him drive off.

I smiled to myself as I listened to her tiptoeing up the stairs, trying to avoid the two creaky ones at the top, then the gentle tap on my bedroom door.

"Are you awake, mum?" she had whispered, but knowing I would be.

I leaned across to switch on the bedside light as she slipped into the room carrying her boots in one hand.

"The rain's off," she grinned then dumping her boots on the floor at the door, slid onto the bed to lie alongside me.

"Well?"

"Well, what?" I replied.

"You do like him, don't you?"

"Who?"

"Colin, ya daftie," she jabs me gently with her elbow.

"Seems all right," I offhandedly replied, knowing it would irk her, then seconds later I added, "He seems a very nice young man."

"So, you do like him?"

"Why wouldn't I?"

That was enough sparring I'd decided as with a smile I continued, "If he makes you happy, then yes, I like him, but I just want you to be cautious, Liz. I don't want you getting into any kind of relationship with him without first thinking it through, okay?"

"Okay, mum," she'd replied and gave me a tight hug.

Almost a minute passed before the question I was waiting for was asked.

"Did the detective stay long after we'd left?"

"Just long enough to give me bit of an update on what's he's doing," I carefully replied. "Maybe ten or fifteen minutes."

It was actually nearer an hour, but for some reason even I couldn't explain, I didn't want to admit that.

"I think he likes you."

"Nonsense," I huffed, but don't get me wrong, I was beginning to wonder about that too.

She'd sat up and stared at me and said, "When was the last time you looked in a mirror, mum? Do you even realise how good looking and attractive you are? Even Colin said that you could pass as my older sister, not my mum."

That's all I needed; compliments from my daughter's boyfriend, so I sighed and deciding to change the subject, told her, "I want to spend some time with you tomorrow, lady, so enough with the chat. Get yourself to bed because we're getting up early and going into the town shopping and for lunch, okay?"

She'd happily grinned and was gone almost as quick as I could switch off the light.

Funny, but after that I had a really good and deep sleep.

So now I'm out of bed and seeing Liz's bedroom door tightly shut, after making my toilet and a quick shower, I'm quietly creeping downstairs to the kitchen to make breakfast. To my surprise, when I open the door the radio is on low.

"Morning," Liz loudly calls out and I can smell toast.

"My, but you're up early," I'm grinning at her and seeing the teapot already brewing on the cooker, give her a quick hug and a peck on the cheek.

You know, I'm still amazed at the change in my girl and I thank God every day that at last she seems to be getting over the dreadful event of four months ago.

Like me she's wearing a dressing robe as she stuffs toast into her mouth.

"I'd forgotten we didn't eat last night," she says. "We'd decided against a takeaway, so I'm ravenous."

"Well, don't stuff yourself because remember, we're going for lunch. My treat."

"On that point," her face turns serious, "I've no money mum, and until I get myself a job I can't pay you rent or anything."

"Rent?" I'm staring at her in amazement. "Liz, wherever did you get the idea you need to pay me rent? This is your home, sweetheart, for as long as you need it to be and as for money, you know you only need to ask."

The next thing I know she's crushing me to death and I have to tell her to let go so I can breathe.

Minutes later we're sat opposite each other and I just know she wants to tell me something, so I ask, "What?"

She shrugs and says, "Colin and me were talking last night. He said that if the worst came to the worst and you needed your own space, he'd look for something for the two of us."

"Liz!" I stare at her and I'm a little surprised how annoyed I am. I mean, as if I'd put my own daughter out onto the street.

"Oh, no," she's waving her hands and laughing, "He said there would be no…what was the word again?" her eyes narrow.

"Something like improperly or something like that."

"You mean impropriety?" I can't help keeping the sarcasm out of my voice.

"Aye, that was it." Her face is a little downcast at my disbelieving attitude and she softly says, "He means it too, mum."

"I'm sure he does," I mutter, but I'm not convinced. Nice enough young man that Colin is and while he might himself believe that he would keep his promise, even first thing in the morning with her hair in disarray my Liz is a lovely young woman and I find it hard that he or indeed any man could resist her. She's a real catch is my lassie.

"Right, enough of this," I pretend to be stern. "Finish your toast and tea and let's get our faces on and dolled up for our trip to the town. You nip up and have your shower and shout me when you're out." I

rise from my chair and cheerfully continue, "I'll clear these things away and then the Brogan girls are going shopping."
****

Liz is walking down the driveway as I'm locking the front door when I see my next door neighbour Willie McPherson on the pavement collecting his bin and notice that mine has been returned to the side of my house. I wave at him, but I don't think he sees me, so as Liz stares at me I walk past the car to catch him just as he's towing his bin behind him.

He hasn't seen me approach and I startle him. I'm about to say thanks for getting the bin, then as he lowers his head I see his left eyes is bruised and blackened.

"What happened to you?" I'm stunned because Willie is a slightly built man and the last person you would ever imagine who would get into any kind of a fistfight.

He's clearly embarrassed and replies, "I had an argument with the kitchen wall cupboard, Maggie. I opened the door and dropped a packet of biscuits then when I bent to pick them up forgot about the door and cracked me face against it when I stood up."

"You were lucky not to lose and eye," I cringe at what might have been a lot worse.

"Aye," he shrugs. "Moira says I'm a clumsy bugger at the best of times, but I've surpassed myself this time. Anyway, I'll get this bin round the back," and shyly smiles. He glances at the car and his eyes narrow as he peers and then asks, "Is that Liz home then?"

"Yes, she got home yesterday," I nod and turn to smile at her sitting in the passenger seat watching us and see her wave at Willie.

He solemnly nods in greeting and says, "You'll be pleased to have her home, eh?"

"Over the moon," I agree.

"Right, I'll be seeing you then," he starts to pull the bin towards his driveway.

I'm turning to get into the car when, what do you call it when something catches the side of your eye? Oh, the peripheral vision, I think it's called. Anyway, I see the slightest movement of the curtain at Willie's front bedroom window and I'm almost certain that Moira has been at the window, watching us.

Poor Moira, I'm thinking, but I suppose some people are just happy in their own company.

****

After doing the rounds, I manage to get parked in the open air car park at King Street to the east of the St. Enoch Shopping Centre that only a couple of hundred yards away is nice and handy for the Centre. The car park is mobbed, as you would expect on a bright and sunny Saturday, though there's definitely a chill in the air. I'd thought Liz might want to drive, but she'd declined and asked that I give her a few days to come to terms with being out of the hospital. I'm wearing a Dorothy Perkins rose coloured trench waterfall duster coat over my fawn coloured top, jeans and black ankle boots while Liz has borrowed my white coloured Evans blush stud longline jacket. With her red blouse, black coloured jeans and black, knee high boots, she looks like a young model. However, she really needs her own warm, winter jacket and some new underwear to, so Debenhams is our first port of call.

"Lingerie, mum," she grins at me when I mention bra's and knickers. "Get with the times," and snakes her arm into mine.

We're a good hour in Debenhams going through the sale items and finally leave with new bras, knickers and a beige coloured Lands End hooded coat. Liz insists I also try it on because believe it or not, we're the same size and makes me walk up and down while she inspects it from all angles. I'm happy with the purchase because it's a fine coat and at one hundred pounds, almost half the original price. We're at the till and with both of us having our hair pinned up, she stares at me with narrowed eyes and her finger to her chin, says,

"You know, Colin was right. You could pass for my older sister."

"So, apart from the hair colour, not twins, then?" I joke, but her expression says definitely not.

In The Body Shop I treat her to almost forty-pound worth of new make-up and she asks,

"Are you sure you can afford to keep treating me like this?"

"Let's just say I'm spending your inheritance," I grin at her. I know that she's a bit embarrassed that I'm paying for the clothing and even more so when I insist she stick two fifties into her purse, but if I can't treat my daughter, what's the point of having money?

Now, don't be thinking I'm made of money or anything like that. I've got a few quid in the savings account and I am not a spendthrift, so I'm fortunate that I've no real need to count the pennies.

By the time she's used the testers for the different shades of lipstick, eyeliner and whatever, it's almost twelve o'clock when we leave and we've only visited three or four shops.

"How about some lunch?" I ask her.

"Actually," she muses, "I'm not *really* that hungry, but I could probably suffer a coffee and cake?" she smiles.

That's fine by me so we agree on the Costa Coffee on the ground floor and though the place is quite literally jumping, we manage to squeeze into a tight wee table by the window that faces out onto St Enoch Square. While Liz guards the table I join the queue and am amazed that the young folk behind the counter can be so cheerful when they're so busy and honestly, not everybody waiting to be served is as patient and polite as me.

Back at the table we enjoy our cake and coffee and while we're sitting there I point to the building that now houses Café Nero in St Enoch Square and tell her that used to be the entrance to the underground station back when I was a younger woman.

"Aye, in the olden days," she laughs. "When I saw photos of you when you were wee I used to wonder if everything in those days was in black and white."

Cheeky besom.

We're finishing our coffee and honestly, there's folk actually standing watching us, almost hovering over us and waiting for us to leave so they can snatch the table.

Back in the hustle and bustle of the Centre, we're carrying the bags and wandering through the crowds when Liz laughingly pulls me into the Ann Summers store, a shop I've never visited. Wandering through the store I admit to being amazed at some of the things on sale. Liz gives me a bright red face lifting items and pretending to try them on or whatever, some of which I'm too embarrassed to mention. I'll tell you right now in case you're wondering; no, I did *not* buy anything.

Well, we're just leaving the shop and you'll have heard the saying that the world is a village? Glasgow is no different. It's always been my experience that whenever I shop in the city centre which to be honest, hasn't been often too often in the past few years, I inevitably bump into somebody I know or who knows me. If you're a Weegie or live in a town or a city or somewhere like Glasgow, you'll know what I mean.

Anyway, Liz and I are pushing through the door to leave Ann Summers when to my surprise, who's wheeling a buggy past the door, but Alan Reid.

He's wearing an old, green coloured anorak over an open necked shirt, brown corduroy trousers, brown brogue shoes and is unshaven. He's carrying a grey coloured baby changing bag over one shoulder and don't ask me why, but what continues to strike me most of all is he still needs a haircut.

To say I'm shocked to see him is an understatement and by his face, he's as shocked to see me too, but whether it's because it's me or the fact I'm coming out of an Ann Summers store, I can't quite tell.

My face is scarlet and I'm aware my mouth is hanging slackly open for it's almost on the tip of my tongue to blurt out, 'Honest, it was Liz who dragged me in there. I was only in looking,' but like I say, I'm absolutely gobsmacked.

It's Liz who recovers first and she greets him with, "Hello, Mister Reid," and then bending down to the wee boy in the buggy, smiles and asks, "Who's this wee guy?"

He's still staring at me and my red face when he begins to smile. You know, that kind of smile that says, 'Caught you.'

Then glancing down at Liz, he bends over the buggy and ruffling the wee lad's hair, replies, "This is Finn. He's just turned three. Finn, say hello to Liz and Maggie."

The boy stares inquisitively at Liz then up at me and shyly mutters, "Hello."

Still crouching down by the buggy, Liz offers her hand and the wee boy solemnly takes it then she turns her head to glance up at Alan, she asks, "Is he yours?"

"My grandson," he smiles with definite pride.

I finally find my voice and manage to squeak, "Doing some shopping?"

My God, I'm thinking. What a stupid question! Why else would he be in a shopping centre if he wasn't here to shop!

"Ah, no, I'm here with my daughter, Fiona. She's just nipped to the ladies. She's the shopper, not me."

"Oh," is all I can manage and an awkward silence falls, but broken when a smartly dressed young woman a few years older than Liz arrives and staring uncertainly from her father to me then Liz, breathlessly says, "Hi."

She's slim and as tall as me with short, curly brown hair and has her father's eyes and is wearing a bright yellow coloured slicker rain jacket, black skinny jeans with slashed knees that is so popular among young women these days and light brown leather hiking boots, though I'm imagining that the boots are more for comfort than hiking.

I can see the curiosity in her eyes as Alan introduces us.

"This is my oldest girl, Fiona. This is Missus Brogan…eh, Maggie, and her daughter Elizabeth."

"Just Liz," she stand up and greets his daughter with a wide smile.

I'm conscious of the young woman staring at me, then her eyes light up and she says, "Oh, *you're* Maggie," as though she knows of me and stares at me in such a bold manner I feel I'm being critically appraised.

Now it's Alan's turn to blush and I wonder what he's told her about me.

Before I can respond, she slips an arm through her fathers and smiles, "Dad was just about to buy me a coffee. Would you like to join us?"

Right away something tells me that coffee isn't actually his idea and I see his mouth open as though he's about to protest and realise he's uncomfortable. However, he nods and I continue to wonder what he's told his daughter. For that heartbeat, a black cloud descends on me and I'm thinking he's discussed with her meeting the grandmother of a murder victim and I'm about to reply that no thank you, we've just had coffee.

But to my surprise, Liz gets in first and says, "Yes, thanks, that would be lovely."

Honestly, I could kick her backside from one end of the Centre to the other, but before I can intervene she turns to me and says, "That would be lovely, eh mum?"

I can feel my face pale, and tight-lipped I smile and nod.

****

Five minutes later finds us crowded around a table, but on this occasion in Café Nero with Finn lifted from the buggy and placed into an Ikea high chair. His mum produces a carton of orange juice and a biscuit from the changing bag and while he's happily playing with two plastic dinosaurs, his grandfather leaves to fetch four coffees.

I decide to take the plunge while he's away from the table and force a smile when I ask, "So, I gather your dad's mentioned me?"

Fiona stares a little warily at me and nodding, replies, "He told me he's visited you while he was working and you fed him. Is that right?" she smiles.

"You fed him?" Liz interrupts and stares curiously at me.

"It was just a bowl of soup," I casually respond. "Besides, I was having my own lunch. It was only me being polite to feed your dad too."

"Well, he thinks you're very nice for doing that," she smiles at me, then as though surprised, adds, "Though I didn't think you were so young."

"See, told you that you look good for your age," Liz smirks.

"Your age?" Fiona's eyes widen as she stares from Liz to me.

I glare at Liz and softly reply to Fiona, "I'm forty-nine."

"Never," she says and I'm pleased that the genuine surprise in her voice is without any pretence at flattery.

I find I'm blushing and turn to glance at the counter where I catch Alan's eye and he gives me a nod, though I'm guessing he's desperately keen to know what's being discussed out of his earshot. In an attempt to change the subject, I politely ask, "Shopping for anything special, today, Fiona?"

"Well," she grimaces, "I brought dad in with me in the mistaken belief that I could get him to buy something new for himself. Maybe come into the twenty-first century one day," she sighs and rolls her eyes to heaven.

It occurs to me that surely that's a wife's job, to accompany her husband clothes shopping, but I keep my mouth shut.

"Forgive me for asking," Fiona slowly says to Liz, "but dad told me that when he was moved to Maryhill, he's been working on a recent murder case involving a child." Her face displays her horror and anxiety as she asks, "Was that your child?"

Nodding, Liz turns pale, but before she can reply, Fiona reaches out and takes hold of her hand and says, "Oh my God, I'm so sorry. I didn't realise," then glancing at me I see tears in her eyes.

To my astonishment it's Liz who comforts Fiona for she reaches her body across to hug her and quietly says, "Thank you. Thank you."

Finn stares at his mother and though there is a right hubbub going on from the rest of the customers round about us, he picks up on her emotion and his little lips begin to quiver. However, before he can burst into tears I lift a dinosaur and grinning at him like an idiot, I loudly growl.

He's that taken aback he just stares for a few seconds, then, grabbing at the other dinosaur, growls back at me. Within seconds, we're the best of pals and both dinosaurs are biting and grabbing at each other as they slide among the biscuit crumbs and spilled orange juice on the tray of the highchair.

At last Liz and Fiona separate and both reach into their handbags for handkerchiefs, then laugh at their mutual embarrassment.

"I'll just nip to the loo and wash my face," Fiona dabs at her eyes.

"I'll come too," Liz rises from her chair.

They've no sooner left than Alan arrives at the table with a tray of four coffees, four plates and yes, four large muffins.

"Queue there like an execution," he groans, then asks, "Where are the girls off too?" he nods at our departing daughters.

"Powdering their noses."

"Again? Oh, right. Anyway, I just got a selection," he shrugs, then with a wide grin adds, "The lassie assured me they're all low calorie."

Aye right, I'm thinking.

His forehead wrinkles. "Oh well, gives us time to chat," he smiles and reaches across to tickle at Finn.

"He's a lovely wee lad," I nod to him, but it's really just for something to say, though I have to admit with his thick blonde hair and piercing blue eyes Finn is a fine looking boy.

"Where's his father?" I ask.

"He's on shift today. Mike's a uniformed cop working out of the Helen Street office over in Govan."

"Keeping the job in the family, then?" I smile and stir at my latte.

"Something like that," he nods, then in a deliberate attempt to embarrass me, supresses a grin as he says, "So, Ann Summers?"

"Don't you start, Alan Reid," I pretend to scowl. "I'm a decent Catholic woman and I was dragged in there by my scoundrel of a daughter."

"Oh, so you didn't buy anything interesting?" he teases me.

I stare at him and decide to turn the tables by asking, "Why? Would you be interested to know if I did?"

His face turns bright red, but before he can reply the girls return to the table and Fiona says, "Oh good. Muffins. I'm starving." She helps herself to a blueberry one and breaks off a bit that she feeds to Finn.

I give the briefest of glances to Liz, but she ignores me and helps herself to a muffin.

"Fiona says that she's trying to persuade you to buy yourself some new clothes, Alan," I continue to tease him.

"Aye, she thinks I'm getting to look too raggedy these days," he frowns at her.

"Well, look at you," she counters. "The first thing you should do is get yourself a good haircut."

Exactly what I'm thinking and though I do agree with her, it's not my quarrel. Besides, he's a handsome man and would suit a trim I'm thinking, then I'm inwardly shocked at myself. I mean, why would I even think of him like that and him, a married man.

I'm suddenly aware that Liz is paying attention to Finn, leaning into him and winding a finger into the locks of his hair. I'm also aware that Fiona and Alan are keenly watching her too. Then as if realising she *is* being watched, she blushes and withdrawing her finger, says, "Sorry, it's just that this is the first time I've been around a child since…you know, since I lost my Beth."

In that instant I'm so proud of my daughter; so very, very proud, for I realise then that she is indeed facing up to the reality that Beth is gone, yet not forgotten, for now she can publicly talk about her daughter without breaking down.

"Well, anytime you feel the need to take this little rogue out for a stroll, just give me a call. Would the month of December suit you?" Fiona jokingly breaks the ice.

The tension is immediately gone and the atmosphere at the table lightens as we return to the issue of outfitting Alan. Minutes pass by then Fiona glances at her wristwatch and frowns as she says, "Oh, bugger. Dad, sorry, but I've the in-laws coming for dinner in a couple of hours and I haven't prepared anything." Then to Liz and I she says, "It was so nice to meet you both and especially, you, Maggie."

I smile at the comment, yet wonder at it as they both rise from their chairs with Alan lifting Finn out of the child seat.

Fiona reaches down to give us a both a hug, again saying sorry for leaving so quickly, but we wave off her apology.

We watch as they hurry from the café and I see Alan turn for a last look, but curiously he smiles at me.

It's on the walk back to the car that Liz says, "I'm stuffed after those two cakes. I won't be fit for dinner with…" then grimaces.

I pick up on her hesitation and say, "I'm guessing you're going out to dinner with Colin?"

"Is that okay, mum?" I see the doubt in her eyes.

What else can I do but smile and reply, "No problem, hen? Besides, I want to catch up on Casualty. I'm a couple of episodes behind, but I've got them taped."

"Taped?" she guffaws. "Recorded, mum, recorded. Tapes went out with the Ark."

"Aye, very good," I glower. "You know fine what I mean, my girl."

"She seems a nice young woman, Fiona," I open the conversation.

"Yes she does, and her wee boy is gorgeous. Did you see how blue his eyes are?"

I'm just about to remark they're just like his granddads, but catch myself and fortunately Liz doesn't see me blushing.

We begin to make our way through the car park and then, with some thought and though my hearts in my mouth, I gently ask her how she felt sitting beside the wee boy.

She stops and I do to as I turn back and see she's staring at me, then clearing her throat she says, "I'll always miss Beth, mum, and it will haunt me that nobody's been arrested for her murder. But Doctor Francis and Colin have helped me move on and I know while I'll still have moments of grief, maybe even cry a lot, but I won't let her death stop my life. I refuse to stand still and let the world pass me by."

I feel tears in my eyes, but force myself not to cry and can only nod. Then in the middle of that wasteland that's a car park, I hug my daughter. Course, we get a few strange glances from passers-by and I hear some idiot who sounds likes he's got a drink in him shouts out from across Stockwell Street, "Get a room, ya pair of lesbo's!"

But who bloody cares what other people think, I tell myself.

I stare into her eyes and I smile, inwardly thanking Doctor Francis and yes, young Colin too, for giving me back my daughter.

Then when we're in the car and I'm starting the engine, my nose gets the better of me when I ask, "So, did you and Fiona have a nice chat when you were at the loo?"

"Yes, we did. She's really nice, mum. She's married to a policeman."

She stops and like most mothers, I know when my daughter is holding back something, so I ask, "What?"

She takes a breath and says, "She told me that her dad is smitten with you."

"What!" I'm that surprised I nearly stall the car at the exit.

"That's what she said," Liz very matter-of-fact tells me. "Says when her dad arrived at her place this morning, he was only there ten minutes and started telling her about this really nice woman he's met called Maggie Brogan and that he's very impressed by her. She was a bit surprised when she saw you because when her dad was talking about you and described you she thought you were about his age, but when she saw you she thought you were a lot younger than him and right away she had misgivings about you, thinking you were maybe a bit too young for him." She smiles and adds, "But then you told her your age and that made her feel a bit better. And before you ask," she sniffs and pretends aloofness, "he's fifty-one."

"Whoa, hold on there a minute, Liz! Flattered as I am, none of this matters, hen, and I'm surprised at you too, talking like this!" I risk turning to glance angrily at her. "You know me, Elizabeth! I would never, ever, consider any kind of relationship with a man who is married! That is just not me!"

I'm a bit surprised that she isn't fazed at me being angry, but then she lays a comforting hand on my arm. I throw a questioning glance towards her, but she just smiles and says, "I know all that, mum, but you see, that's the thing. Alan Reid isn't married. At least, he's not married any more."

CHAPTER TWELVE

Well, that wee gem took the wind right out of my sails, I can tell you.

I don't immediately respond because to be honest, my heads in a bit of a whirl and I'm not really certain how I feel about that.

I'm driving on automatic, my head I mean, not the car and wondering why I'm so pleased at hearing Alan's not married. It's not as if there's anything between us, I tell myself and besides, I've only known the man for a few hours in total and that time only over a few days. Who in their right mind fancies somebody without really knowing them? Okay, we all fancy the film stars or the people on the television, but that's just pie in the sky stuff we don't just take a fancy to people that we've actually just recently met.

Do we?

Now look at me, Liz has got me so confused I'm questioning myself. This is silly. I give myself a mental shake, but then Liz's voice intrudes on my thoughts when she asks, "So, how do you feel about him fancying you, mum?"

"Can we please change the record, Liz? Alan Reid does not fancy me like you think. He's maybe…" I'm thinking on my feet here, "maybe he likes me because I've been nice to him."

Except perhaps when I threw him out of the house, but I don't bother mentioning that.

I'm making my way through the city traffic towards home while Liz prattles on and I'm nodding or shaking my head when she asks me something and pretend that I'm concentrating on my driving, but the truth is I'm thinking about Alan Reid.

No, not anything naughty or anything like that, but daydreaming what it might be like perhaps to be asked out to dinner by him, spend time with him, nonsense like that.

As if *that's* going to happen, I come down to earth with a crash. Then my thoughts turn to Alex and what my life was like with him. Don't misunderstand me when I tell you this because I loved Alex, but life with him, particularly after the first few years of marriage was, well, kind of routine I suppose is the word I would use. Yes, we had our tiffs like any other married couple, but always made up and usually with him bringing me flowers because like most women, I was rarely if ever in the wrong.

During our life together and even after Liz came along, we had our annual holiday that started in the early years with a local seaside resort that as time went by and the things got financially easier, became a week then a fortnight on the Costa Blanca. Funny, I find I'm inwardly smiling, I always fancied a cruise but that was just a little beyond us; well, it was until his life insurance money came in and I had money to spend, but what's the point in going on a cruise alone?

As for our married life and by that I mean the sex, I've nothing with which to judge it by for our wedding night was the first time for us both. I suppose we just kind of settled into a routine there too, until it became a weekly thing and usually at the weekend when neither of us had to get up early the next morning.

Now, here's a wee confession.

I was and sometimes still am partial to women's books and some of them can be a bit racy too. Often in some of the books the heroine would describe her different sexual adventures and I used to wonder what it would be like, you know, trying the different positions. God, I'm almost blushing and my hands are gripping the steering wheel so tightly my knuckles are showing white. I never did have the nerve to ask Alex if he might like to be that adventurous too and sometimes, particularly when I'm alone at night at home or lying in my bed, I feel that I've lost out on something.

My throats dry and I hear Liz thanking me again for subbing her for the coat and the underwear…lingerie, I mean and without thinking, I'm telling her it's fine.

I try not to smile and wonder if Alan's daughter Fiona did actually used the word smitten or that was Liz's interpretation of what Fiona told her, but I don't have the nerve to ask.

Now, don't get me wrong, I'm well aware that I'm probably considered attractive by men of a certain age group and let's face it, what woman wouldn't be flattered by the attention of a man? The difference with me is that I don't go out of my way to be attractive to men.

So why then, I ask myself, am I so pleased that Alan has apparently taken an interest in me?

My head's full of thoughts as I wonder why he's not still married and is it possible for somebody to be smitten after just a few hours over a few days?

"I said Colin's picking me up at seven. Are you listening, mum?"

"Sorry, hen," I apologise, "I was miles away."

"What," she grins, "thinking about Alan Reid?"

"Certainly not!" I snap back, but that doesn't stop my face reddening and I know I've been caught out in the lie. "Well, if Colin's picking you up at that time I'll maybe go to the Saturday Vigil Mass at seven. Where are you going to eat?"

"It's a surprise, but he said I've to wear something nice."

"Oh, well, you'd better have a bath when you get in and I'll help you with your hair," I risk a glance at her and smile.

****

While Liz has her bath I prepare a quick pasta dish, not a full meal, just enough to keep her going till she has her dinner later that evening.

After I help her set her hair and fortunately because we're the same size, she chooses a sleeveless, black knee length dress from my wardrobe. It's a dress she's always liked and though I think it's little snug on her, she just laughs and says it's shows off her curves that little bit better and believe me, Liz has some lovely curves.

She looks so lovely I fetch my mobile phone and though she half-heartedly protests, I take a couple of photographs while she comically postures.

I watch her pose in the wardrobe mirror and my heart beats a little faster. Now, the reason for that is that Liz has been detained within the hospital for over four months and I'm a little concerned that if things between her and Colin get a little heated…what I'm trying to say is if things get too intense and particularly if alcohol is consumed, I only hope that one of them has the sense to consider some form of protection for I don't think it's likely Liz will be up to date with her prescription.

I flush as the thought of what she might get up to passes quickly through my head and taking a breath I nervously ask, "Will you be coming home tonight, hen?"

She looks curiously at me then frowns and replies, "Why wouldn't I be, mum?"

I shrug and say, "It's just that I thought, well, I thought maybe Colin and you might have, eh, other arrangements. I mean," I raise my hands, "I don't want to interfere or anything…"

She grins at me then says, "Look, mum, Colin and me are only going out on a date. I know you worry about me and…" she stops and begins to laugh out loud. "Oh, my God!" she shrieks, her hands pressed against her cheeks. "You think we'll be having sex!"

"It did cross my mind," I dryly reply, but can't help myself and start to giggle like a teenage schoolgirl.

She wraps her arms around me and hugs me tightly, then says, "Mum, much as I like Colin, I would not do anything inappropriate and especially on a first date. Maybe on the second date," she coyly grins. "Besides, don't you remember? He told you he lives with his parents so where would we go? Some sleazy hotel room? Oh, what about the back of his wee car?" and again she bursts into uproarious laughter.

I know I'm being teased and playfully push her away before telling her, "Five minutes, young lady, then the pasta is on the table."

After showing her what I've photographed, I leave her in the bedroom and going downstairs I smile at the screensaver that is a photograph of Beth in her new school uniform, taken on the day she started primary one. It's a photograph that I'll keep and treasure; a bit like having the phone number of someone who has died. Deleting the number is almost like a betrayal, isn't it?

Downstairs I busy myself and switch on the television for the Saturday's six-thirty STV news, but the news is only for about fifteen minutes of which a good seven or eight minutes is taken up with football news. The wee Murdoch girls murder is the second item, but there's no update yet. Waste of time watching it, I'm thinking.

Liz comes downstairs for her pasta before she applies her make-up and teases me again about Alan Reid, suggesting I phone him to let him know I've an empty for the evening.

Cheeky besom that she is.

While she's eating and in such a good mood, I decide I'll tell her about Ian Chalmers visiting, but not the full story; only that he was here trying to scrounge some money from me. Her attitude changes for she's appalled and very angry, but as I correctly anticipated she's determined she won't let it ruin her evening out.

"But there's also a bit of good news that came out of it," I smile.

"Oh, and what could possibly be good news about him," she scowls.

"Well, Alan Reid turned up while Ian was at the door and gave him short shrift; quite literally chased him off the driveway," I grin at her and tell her the story.

"And that's the good news? That Alan gave him a fright?"

"No," I then tell her about her sister-in-law Linda disclosing that Ian's got a girlfriend and that Alan suggested Liz might be able to divorce him on the grounds of adultery.

"I'll need to get a lawyer, then."

"Well, when you caught Alan at the door yesterday, he was here to hand this in," and I gave her the business card.

She stares at the card and her mouth is tightly set and I can see she's pleased that she might have the opportunity to beat Ian at his own game.

"I'll give this guy a call on Monday," she nods, then her brow knits when she asks, "What did Linda say about this woman he's shacked up with?"

"Maybe you're better giving Linda a phone yourself," I suggest, then remind her Colin will be arriving within ten minutes so she'd better get a spurt on.

In fact, I'll need to watch my own time for the Vigil Mass starts sharply at seven, so as I'm going out the door I see Colin arriving and wave him away from the driveway so I can get out.

"Everything okay, Missus B?" he asks.

I've time to tell him everything's fine, but that I'm in a hurry to get to Mass and as I'm getting into my car, Liz is letting him in the front door. I give them both a wave cheerio and I'm off.

****

The Mass has already commenced by the time I arrive so I slip into a pew near the back and see there are no more than forty or so parishioners in attendance.

Father O'Brien whisks through the Mass so quickly I suspect there must be football on the telly that night. Taking communion, he gives me an audacious wink then leaning forward, whispers, "You'll be taking a cuppa later?"

I give him a wee nod then return to my pew.

When Mass is over I join maybe thirty or so of the parishioners, mostly pensioners, who make their way into the draughty Church Hall. It's the Saturday evening ritual of a cup of tea and digestive where discussions include church fundraising, who's getting married, who died, who's *likely* to die and a dozen other topics. I don't always attend, but Father's subtle invitation is more of an order than a request.

His housekeeper, Katie Doherty, is there at the table with the urn and plates of biscuits and ably helped by an elderly, widowed pass keeper who is a member of the St Vincent De Paul and is rumoured locally to be Katie's admirer, whatever that entails. Needless to say the pair are one of the topics discussed, though never to their face, of course.

I'm joined by two elderly ladies, Betty McFarlane and Isa Fullerton. Not because they like my company, but knowing sticking to me like a rash usually guarantees them a lift down the road. Both are widows and in their late seventies and live in the sheltered housing in Mill Road two and half miles away. Saying that, it sounds like I'm complaining, but their patter is good and they're like a double act the two of them and I can't help but compare them to Jack and Victor from 'Still Game,' though without the coarse language.

Stood there with our teacups and saucers and making polite conversation, I'm watching Father doing the rounds and having a laugh with his parishioners, when Betty takes a sly glance over to Katie Doherty and in a low voice, says, "See that, Isa? That's him sidling close to her again. Did you clock that?"

"Oh, aye," Isa sniffs, her arms folded across her massive bosom. "And in front of Father O'Brien too. Damn cheek of him, Betty, eh? Forgets where he is and him only widowed three years. Should be ashamed of himself, he should."

"Aye, Isa," Betty agrees. "Damn cheek, so he is."

I sneak a glance over to Katie and see her reach up to touch the pass keepers arm and I suppress a giggle for I'm almost certain the old bugger did it deliberately to provoke comment.

Betty leans towards me and says, "Do you think him that's arrested for the wee girl in Yoker, Maggie. Do you think he might be responsible for your Beth, God bless and keep her?"

I feel my blood run cold and as I slowly turn to her my face pales, for her eyes narrow and she says, "Did you not hear about it, hen? They've arrested somebody."

"So ladies how are you this evening?" Father O'Brien has come up behind me, but I ignore him and my voice almost a hiss, I ask her, "What did you hear, Betty? Who told you this?"

Her eyes widen and she's rapidly blinking as she takes a step back, for she must think I'm going to leap on her, but then she stutters, "It was Sammy, you know? You've heard us mention Sammy before. I'm sure you have, hen. Sammy, the duty caretaker at Mill Road. He told us while we were waiting for the bus tonight. Says he heard it from Bobby McLaren. That's right, isn't it, Isa?" she turns nervously towards her pal.

"Oh, aye, it was Bobby right enough that told Sammy," she vigorously nods. "That's what Sammy told us, wasn't it, Betty?"

Honestly, it's like drawing teeth, so I hiss, "And *how* did this guy Bobby find out someone's been arrested?"

"Someone's been arrested? Why? For Beth?" Father O'Brien chips in his tuppence worth, but by now the whole hall has stopped talking and they're all watching me, the mad woman with the raised voice interrogating the two defenceless old ladies.

I don't immediately realise it, but then see it in their faces that I'm scaring Betty and Isa and I force myself to be calm.

"Please, Father. It's not Beth, no," I raise a hand to quieten him and turning to the two women I ask in a slow and controlled voice, "Do you know how this man Bobby…"

"Bobby McLaren," Betty thinks she's being helpful.

I grit my teeth and repeat, "Okay, Bobby McLaren. Do you have any idea how he found out someone's been arrested for the wee girl's murder in Yoker?"

"There's been an arrest?" Father butts in.

"Eh, it was on Bobby's radio, I think Sammy said," Isa replies and looks at Betty for confirmation.

"Aye," her head's nodding so fast her necks squeaks like it needs oiling. "Bobby's wee private radio, you know? I'm sure we've mentioned Bobby before, hen," she stares curiously at me.

"Bobby McLaren? Auld Bobby that worked with the telephone people, the BT?" Father O'Brien interrupts.

I'm about to snap I don't give a damn where 'auld Bobby' worked, but Father turns to me and explains, "Bobby's a radio ham, Maggie. You know, one of that crowd who talk to each other across the world by radio."

I thought that was why we'd mobile phones and Skype these days, I feel like saying, but hold my tongue and let him continue.

"He's been playing about with radios since he retired from his job. He must be what, fifteen years retired now," he glances at Isa and Betty who shrug and nod in rhythm.

"If he's heard anything on the radio," Father continues, "then I'm guessing he must have intercepted a police radio band. Do you follow me?"

God give me strength, I silently pray. My heads in a whirl as I turn to the women and I tightly ask, "And Bobby lives near you in the sheltered housing?"

"Oh, aye," Isa nods. "He's two doors away from me. Well, there's the bin shelter between us too, but I don't really count that as a door, do you know what I mean?"

God, I'm inwardly praying again, give me patience!

"Right, ladies," I force a smile and lay my cup and saucer down onto a table, "this is important. Hurry up ands finish your tea and I'll take you up the road. I need to speak with your pal Bobby."

****

It's just over two miles from the church hall to the sheltered housing in Mill Road and I'm driving quickly with Isa in the front and Betty sitting silently in the back.

That's the longest I've ever heard they two go without saying anything and to ease the tension I say, "Sorry if I was a bit upset there back in the hall, ladies. You fairly took me by surprise telling me that somebody's been arrested, you know?"

I can feel two sets of eyes boring into the my head, then Betty sniffs and replies, "Aye, fair enough, hen, but we thought you were going to take the heads of the two of us, you were that snappy."

Minutes later I'm turning into the car park of the one storey flats and helping Betty, the more infirm of the two, out of the front seat.

"Easy there, Maggie, I'm no as agile as I once was," she groans.

"I don't hear you complaining when Archie White gets you up for the jigging at the Thursday afternoon tea dance," Isa huffs.

"Aye, well, see what a couple of nips of vodka do for your old bones," Betty cackles back at her.

I'm sighing and interrupt with, "Right, where does Bobby live?"

Isa stops and pointing her walking stick, replies, "See the path through the buildings there, hen. Bobby's in the first close on the right, one up on the left."

Assured that they'll find their own way from there, I hastily make my way to the close and find the main door is a button entry. There's no names so I guess at the flat number being 1/2 and an elderly man's tinny voice says through the speaker, "Hello, who is it?"

"Is that Bobby McLaren?"

"Aye, maybe. Who are you?"

"My name's Maggie Brogan. I'm a pal of Isa Fullerton and Betty McFarlane. Is it possible to come up and speak with you for a minute, please?"

"Isa who?"

Oh, this is going to be good, I tell myself and repeat the names.

"Oh, Isa, aye, I think know Isa. She's the wee woman who wears a green coat, is that right, hen?"

I sigh and agree she wears a green coat, to which he replies, "But she doesn't live here, hen. She's across the way in one of the wee bungalows. If it's the same woman, you understand?"

This is getting even better and I'm wondering what I've let myself in for.

I force my voice to remain calm and tell him, "No, Bobby, it's you I need to speak with. Can I come up?"

"Oh, why didn't you just say so," he grumpily moans, but presses the entry button anyway and half a minute later I'm at his door.

The door is open a crack and I can see a pale, unshaven face behind the safety chain. I spend the next minute at his door explaining that I just want a word with him about something he told Sammy the caretaker.

"Do you have a search warrant?" he asks me.

I'm surprised and tell him I'm not the police.

"You said your name is…?" he peers at me.

"Maggie Brogan, Bobby. Can I come in and speak with you?"

"It's a hell of a time of night, but I suppose so," he mutters.

He continues to stare suspiciously at me then with obvious reluctance, slides the chain from the door and lets me into a narrow hallway then I sense almost with reluctance, he opens the door into his front room.

Bobby McLaren is a tall but stooped, thin man in his early eighties with a shock of grey hair to his collar, a couple of days' stubble and wearing of all things, a navy blue boiler suit and black slippers.

I don't know what I was expecting, but the one-bedroom flat is scrupulously clean and there's a strong smell of coffee brewing. However, although the living room is not a big room, almost half of the back wall is taken up with a long and wide bench upon which sits…well, the only way I can describe it is it looks to me like a mass of electronics and radios and there's at least one large microphone sat beside a clipboard. I see a big white mug that's lost its handle and is filled with pens and pencils and a mass of wiring that looks like a multi-coloured spaghetti running from behind the bench to an array of sockets under the window. One thick, black coloured cable runs out through a hole in the wooden frame of the window and disappears out of sight. You'll have guessed that outside my mobile phone and my IPad, I'm a bit of a technophobe.

He doesn't offer me a seat and to be honest, I'm just as keen to be on my way after I hear what he has to say.

I begin, "I was at the church hall with Isa and Betty and they told me that you heard someone has been arrested for the murder of the wee girl in Yoker, Bobby. Is that right?"

"Who told you that?"

"Eh, Isa and Betty. You know, two of the women who live here in the sheltered housing."

"No," he frowns and he shakes his head, "that's not right, hen. I don't know anything about that. Isa and Betty you said?"

Right away my heart sinks. It's been a wild goose chase.

He stares suspiciously at me and asks, "*Are* you the polis, hen?"

"Me, no, not at all. I work as a cleaner in the town. Look, I'm sorry I bothered you, Bobby," and raise my hand in apology. "It's just that…you see, my granddaughter was murdered just over four months ago and well," I take a deep breath, "when I heard that you might have learned somebody was arrested…" I shrug and leave him to make his own mind up.

To my surprise, he grins widely and shaking his head, says, "You're not the polis right enough. Okay, sit down and I'll get us a coffee. Milk and sugar?"

I'm a bit taken aback at his sudden change of attitude and as I sink down into an armchair, I mumble, "Just milk, please."

A minute later he's back carrying two mugs of steaming coffee and hands me one.

"Sorry if I put you through the wringer, hen, but you kind of caught me on the hop there," he grins and his eyes twinkle, then he stops and staring at me asks, "Maggie, you said?"

"Maggie," I confirm and I'm beginning to understand that he's been conning me.

"You thought I might be a police officer?"

"Aye," he exhales. "Let's just say that the setup I've got here," he nods towards the bench, "isn't strictly legal or licensed, if you know what I mean," then taps the side of his nose with a bony forefinger.

I'm smiling and I ask, "So I'm guessing you're a lot sharper than the daft old man you pretend to be?"

"Something like that." He frowns and says, "I'm sorry to hear about your wee granddaughter, Maggie. I mind reading about the murder in the papers. Tragedy that a wean goes before the parent let alone the grandparent," he shakes his head and softly adds, "I was never blessed with children, but losing my wife was like losing half of me."

I'm keen to hear what he's learned and I ask, "So, have the police arrested somebody for the murder?"

He stares at me for a few seconds and replies, "Let me take a minute to tell you how I come to hear about it. If you don't mind, that is?" he smiles at me. "You see I seldom get visitors these days and particularly not a young, attractive woman."

There's that twinkle in his eyes again and besides, what's half an hour out of my life if I can learn what I hope he's going to tell me, so I nod and settling himself into his chair, he begins.

"I joined the Post Office almost seventy years ago as a telegraph boy. In time I managed to get a position in what was then the Telecommunications Department; everything from line work up the telegraph poles to working at the exchange in the city centre. Then in 1980, when British Telecom came into being, I was well established and working in Research and Development. You know what that is?"

"I'm guessing bringing in or trying out new equipment?"

"That's as good a description as any," he grins at me.

"Came the time fifteen years ago the buggers retired me, but I didn't leave empty handed," he smiles and again nods at the bench. "Took me several months to smuggle all that equipment out of the building. Anyway, I'm right into radios and frequencies and that sort of thing, but I'll not bore you with the technology of it all. Suffice to say I keep in touch with fellow radio hams all over the world. A kind of network if you will. However," he sneaks another grin at me, "I like to do a wee bit of cheeky interception; locally only though, like listening to the radio taxi networks, the Glasgow Airport control tower and the Airwave networks too. Those sorts of places. Really interesting it is and it sometimes earns me a few bob too," he smiles at me.

"You get paid for it?"

"Well, let's just say that on the odd occasion I hear something of interest to the newspapers and as long as they don't reveal their source, I kind of give them a heads up and get myself a wee backhander for it."

Intercepting the taxis and the airport I understand, but I have to ask him, "Airwave?"

"It's the network used by the emergency services, Maggie. The police, fire service and the ambulances service too. It's just a hobby, nothing sinister in it," he assures me.

"I'm surprised because I thought those kind of networks would be, I don't know," I shrug "protected somehow?"

"The word is encrypted and they are, but," he taps his nose again, "I've a lot of experience in this field so without going into too many details, let's just say I'm a dab hand at breaking into the networks, encrypted or not. That's why I got a wee bit panicky when you came to the door and I put on the old dementia routine," he widely grins.

"And you did have me fooled," I tell him and can see he's pleased that he conned me.

I'm keen to prompt him and ask, "And that's how you heard about an arrest? You listened into a police call?"

He nods.

"Was there any details, who it might be or anything at all?" I eagerly ask.

"I just happened to be scanning the airwaves when I heard the exchange between a man and a woman. It was a bit scratchy, hen, and all I could make out was that some officers who sounded like they might be detectives had lifted a man out of his flat," he rubbed at his stubbly chin. "I don't know where the flat is, but they said they were taking him to Maryhill police office and asked that the boss be informed immediately. The woman taking the information asked if the arrest was for wee Kylie…" he saw my eyes widen and nodding, continued. "Aye, the woman definitely mentioned wee Kylie and the man that answered confirmed it was. I'm sorry, Maggie. But that's really all there was to it. I just assumed that whoever they were taking to the police office was under arrest and it was something to do with the wee girl that got murdered, Kylie Murdoch. My mistake was mentioning it to that big mouthed git Sammy when he come up to deliver my evening 'Glasgow News," he snorts. "Man's got a mouth like the Clyde Tunnel; never bloody closes. Should have kept my own mouth shut."

Bobby's information doesn't really tell me anything about my Beth's death, but knowing that a man has been arrested for the Murdoch girls murder instils in me a faint hope that the same man might just be Beth's killer too.

****

Driving home after visiting Bobby McLaren, I switch on Smooth radio in the car, but just miss the hourly news. When I get into the house I sit with a cup of green tea (every now and then, I kid myself that I'm cleansing my body of caffeine) and turn on my iPad for the STV and BBC (Scotland) news websites, but while there is a sizeable article on the Murdoch child's murder, there's no updated news though the article includes a photo of the poor child and it makes me stop and wonder. I'm staring at the angelic face of the wee girl who is standing smiling at the person taking the photo, a large plastic dolls house behind her in what looks like a front room somewhere. Who is it that provides such photos to the media? Is it a family member at the request of the police or is it someone who has taken the photo, perhaps on a mobile phone and who believes they can make some money from selling it to the papers or the television reporters?

Anyway, it still remains is there is no update about any arrest.

I wasn't disappointed though, because I reasoned that it being late on a Saturday night it was unlikely the police would be contacting the newspapers or TV to inform them they had arrested someone as a suspect. I wonder if arrest is the right word to use? I'm not really sure what the difference is between arresting someone and detaining someone. I'll need to remember and ask my pal Sheila.

It's then I notice the wee red light flickering on the answer machine and rising from my chair, I press the play button.

After the tape rewinds, I hear the hesitant voice begin:

Eh, Maggie, it's Alan Reid. Eh, just to say…oh, it's just gone seven o'clock and I'm hoping I'm not disturbing you. Anyway, I'm just calling to say that it was very nice seeing you today, eh, and Elizabeth too. Eh, I'm actually off duty tomorrow as well. My once a month weekend off and was wondering if perhaps you weren't doing anything, eh, if you might like to meet for a coffee? Nothing serious…no, what I mean is, ah; well, if you're up for it. On my Sundays off I like to pop into the Botanic Gardens Tearooms round about eleven'ish, maybe get a spot of breakfast while I'm there. Only if you're doing nothing, that is. So, if you fancy a coffee or a tea, I'll see you there then, but no pressure, mind. Eh, it's me, Alan Reid. Oh, did I already say that? Bye.

I find I'm smiling and thinking if his voice is anything to go by that must have been absolute torture for him trying to ask me out for a coffee.

So, why am I smiling? Well, I can't remember the last time I was asked out on a date.

A date, I wonder? Is that what this is?

But then I find I'm not smiling anymore for remembering how I've come to know Alan Reid I remind myself he's the man who has been tasked with going over the statements and monitoring the investigation into my granddaughter's murder and suddenly, for no accountable reason, I feel dejected.

Yes, I know what Liz told me earlier today about how his daughter thinks he's smitten by me and yes, he is quite an attractive man, his uncut hair aside, but is it right seeing the man socially who is supposed to be overseeing Beth's death.

I'll give it tonight to think about whether to go or not. I mean, if I don't go and he ever asks I can just say that I didn't listen to the message when I get in. But that would be a lie, I'm thinking, and one thing I'm not good at is lying.

I'm glancing at the clock on the mantelpiece and I wonder how Liz's date with Colin is going.

I decide not to wait up. I mean, she's a grown woman and she's not daft; well, not as daft now as she was when she met Ian Chalmers, I correct myself.

Finishing my green tea, I carry the mug through to the kitchen and running it under the tap, suddenly stop at the sound of raised voices. In fairness, the voices are not that loud, kind of muted if you know what I mean, but my curiosity is piqued.

At first I'm a bit confused as to where the noise is coming from. I think I mentioned that sometimes and particularly in the summer, I can hear kids across in the park when they're carrying on, but usually I only hear them when I'm in the front room, not in the kitchen and besides, it's really a chilly night and threatening rain so I can't imagine the teenagers being out. No, the voices are certainly coming from out the back somewhere and at first I'm thinking maybe from the houses across to the rear of mine. I switch off the light and open the kitchen door then carefully step out into the darkness. Years ago Alex had fitted an outside light just above the door that was handy when putting out the bin in the dark, but the bulb died months ago and I keep forgetting to replace it.

It's a man and a woman's voices I hear, but it's the woman who's doing all the shouting.

But where is it coming from?

The voices sound, how can I explain this…muffled; is that the word? It's then I realise the shouting is coming from my neighbour's house through the wall, the McPherson's. They're in the back bedroom and the reason the noise sounds muffled is because the double-glazed windows are tightly shut and the curtains pulled closed, though I can see the light is on. I'm not usually one for being nosey, but it's so unusual to hear anything from them and so I stand and stare up at the window. I strain to hear what's being shouted and find I'm smiling, for though I can't make out what's being shouted it sounds as through Moira in her shrill voice is fairly ripping into Willie. Now, I wonder, what has he done that's made her so angry that's she's tearing a strip off him like that?

As suddenly as it seemed to begin, it stops. I see the light go out almost at the same time as there is a loud bang, like a door being slammed.

I'm smiling to myself and trying to make sense of what I heard. Moira and Willie have always been such a quiet couple and like I told you before, anytime I meet her in the passing I hardly get as much as a 'Hello' let alone a conversation. Even Willie, though he's a wee bit more communicative, tends to avoid any real conversation. But like my old dad used to say, better a noiseless neighbour than a noisy neighbour.

It's only when back in the kitchen and I'm locking the door behind me that my curiosity gets the better of me and then it strikes me and causes me to wonder; what were Moira and Willie doing arguing in the back bedroom of the house?

CHAPTER THIRTEEN

I'm awake just after seven and find my kindle lying under my hand on the quilt cover. I must have been really tired for I've slept so soundlessly I can't even recall opening the kindle nor do I recall hearing Liz come home.

My eyes are narrowing as I wonder, did she come home?

I slip from the bed and quietly opening my room door I glance down the stairs and see the porch light is off and know that she would not have left it on when she come home, so slightly relieved I realise she is in her bed.

Alone, I hope and smile as I give myself a mental kick for thinking so badly of my daughter.

Well, I sigh, I'm up now and fetching my dressing gown from the hook behind the door, slip on my slippers and as quiet as I can be and conscious of the top two creaking steps, make my way downstairs to the kitchen.

I'd left my iPad charging so after switching on the kettle I search for the STV news website and right away it's there; an arrest has been made in the Kylie Murdoch murder investigation, though it doesn't give any further details other than to say a twenty-three-year-old man is assisting the police with their enquiries.

My head's in a spin and I suddenly feel as though I'm drained and it's only the button on the kettle clicking off that startles me out of my trance.

Almost mechanically I rise from the chair and filling the teapot when the door is pushed open and Liz, yawning widely, then says, "Morning, mum. That the tea on?"

Rubbing at her eyes she slumps down into a chair and it's then I realise I've left the iPad on the STV news website. Pulling it to her, her eyes scan the page open wide and she stutters, "They've arrested somebody? Does that mean…?"

She doesn't finish before I interrupt, "I don't know, hen, but they're bound to ask him about Beth."

I turn away and taking a deep breath, busy myself filling the toaster then set out two plates and knives, milk the mugs and fetch the butter from the fridge.

Glancing at Liz I see she's scrolling down to read more, but the site hasn't been updated since just after five that morning so we won't learn anything else at the minute.

I'm keen to change the subject and I force myself to brightly ask, "How did your diner date go?"

"Oh," she glances at me and smiles, "great. We went to a small

Italian restaurant over in the south side, on Mosspark Boulevard. Bella Vita it's called. It was great. Colin had booked us a booth and it was just as well, because it was very busy."

"Food nice?"

"Delicious. He said maybe you'd like to come with us, sometime. Maybe invite his parents too," she stares expectantly at me.

"Oh, meet the parents is it? Sounds serious," I tease her with a grin.

"Mum," she pretends to frown, then breaks out into her own smile and adds, "Yeah, it could get serious I suppose."

I feel a lump form in my throat for I can't recall the last time I saw my wee girl so happy and instinctively move over to give her a hug. "I just hope things work out between you, then," I tell her.

We part and while I'm buttering the toast, she says, "What do you think about this man being arrested? Do you think he might have something to do with Beth?"

I'm relieved that Liz can discuss the arrest without breaking down and once more I'm reassured that if not already there, she is definitely on the last stretch of the road to recovery.

I pause before answering and then placing her plate and mug in front of her, reply, "Time will tell. I haven't mentioned it before but I'll share this with you. You already know I'm friendly with Sheila, the policewoman who was the liaison officer during the time…well, when it happened. Sheila knows someone who is on the inside of the investigation so as long as we keep it to ourselves, she'll let us know if the man that's been arrested knows anything about Beth."

She's gloomily quiet before she asks, "What about Alan Reid? Won't he be able to tell us?"

"Ah, well, don't mention to him that we know in case it gets Sheila into trouble, but it seems he's been cut out of the investigation. Something to do with an incident that happened, but I don't know the details," I fib and hope she doesn't pick up on the lie.

"So, Sheila might keep us informed?" she thoughtfully says and munches at her toast.

I nod then she asks, "What are your plans for today?"

I turn away to fetch my mug and plate off the worktop and take a few seconds to work out how I will tell her, and as I sit down, I slowly say, "Actually, I've been asked to meet Alan Reid for a coffee."

I bite at my lower lip and staring down at my plate, wait for the outburst.

"Mum! He's never gone and asked you out?" she's grinning widely.

"It's only for a coffee and I suppose he just wants to discuss how he's getting on working his way through the investigation statements," I offhandedly reply.

"*That* he could do here at the house," she splutters crumbs all over the table. "So, when and where are you meeting him and what are you going to wear?"

"Wear?" I stammer through a mouthful of toast because frankly, I hadn't given it any thought. I hadn't decided till a few seconds ago I *was* going to meet with Alan. "Oh, I suppose just my jeans and a top. It's Sunday coffee, Liz, not a date," I'm trying to sound cool about it, but failing miserably.

"Oh, no, my lady," she grins. "It's a bath for you and then we're going to impress!"

I admit to being a bit taken aback and ask, "You're not a little, I don't know, upset about me meeting a man for coffee?"

"Upset?" her face registers her confusion. "Why would I be upset?"

"Well, I mean, after your dad…"

"Mum!" she sharply interrupts. "I loved dad, but he's been gone a long time now. I think it's about time you got yourself back out there, meeting men and generally having a good time. You really need to get yourself back into the world, you know," she gleefully tells me.

Any further discussion about Alan Reid and me is halted when I hear my mobile phone beep in the front room as it receives a text message. I glance at the kitchen clock and see it's just gone twenty minutes past eight and I'm wondering, who the devil can it be at this time of the morning?

I fetch the phone from the coffee table and scrolling down, I read:

Maggie. My mary told me your lassie is looking for a job. Mary is on early shift and phoned to say asda is hiring part time staff and if liz pops up to the store the now mary will put in a good word for her with her boss in the department. Sorry to text so early but thought you might want to know right away. C u tomorrow. Jessie x

I read it twice then take it through to Liz and hand her the phone.

"Right now?" she stares at me.

"I'm a big girl, sweetheart. I can get myself dressed for meeting Alan and besides, you said you were looking for a job," I smile at her.

"But I've always been in sales. I've never worked in a food store," she's clearly bewildered.

"Isn't selling clothes just like selling food? It's all sales," I try to encourage her.

She takes a breath and nodding, replies, "You're right. This girl, Mary. What's her second name?"

"Mary Cochrane," and I describe her as best as I can.

"Okay, me first for the shower," she darts away, but stops at the door and coming back hugs me and gives me a quick peck on the cheek. She stares at me and says, "Thanks for being my mum and for all your support. Love you," then she's off before I can respond.

I'm sniffing away the happy tears and while I clear away the breakfast things I wonder, what *am* I going to wear for meeting Alan Reid.

****

In the short time since Jessie's message arrived Liz has showered and changed into a white blouse and grey pencil skirt, sensible black shoes and with her hair tied back into a tight ponytail and carrying her new coat and one of my black patent handbags, looks the picture of health and eagerness.

"Mind and tell Mary's boss that there will be no bother getting there for the different shifts," I remind her, "that you've got your own transport."

"But what if you need the car and I'm on the same shift?" her brow creased with worry.

"We'll sort something out," I usher her through the door. "First things first, just get the job and everything else will fall into place, okay?"

I know she is nervous, but I bet she isn't as nervous as I am.

I decide it's more important that Liz uses the car than me and wave her off just before nine o'clock.

Now that she's gone I decide on a relaxing bath and while the water's running I search through my wardrobe.

He's already seen me in the floral dress, I mumble to myself, then with a glance out of the window at the threatening clouds, decide it might be prudent to wear my black jeans and my black leather ankle boots. When I'd seen Liz off at the door it had been a bit chilly so I decide I'll wear my red coloured, long sleeved sweater and pleased with my choice, I head for my bath.

It's while I'm soaking I wonder again about the man who was arrested for the wee girls murder. Is he a suspect or someone that might have seen or might know something?

Tempted though I am, I wonder will it be appropriate to phone Sheila Gardener and ask if she can find out?

Too many questions are running through my mind and almost in frustration I pull the plug and stand upright in the bath drying myself as the water gurgles away.

The steam from the hot bath has clouded the mirror, but as it clears I catch sight of myself stood naked with my hair piled up into an untidy mop on top of my head.

Turning back and fro I critically examine my body and for no more than a heartbeat, I realise I miss the touch of a man.

I shake my head at my foolishness and stepping from the bath, make my way into my bedroom to get dressed.

The clock on the bedside table tells me it's five minutes to ten and I'm thinking I've plenty of time, but then remember that Liz has the car and if I'm to be at the Botanic Gardens for eleven then I'd probably need to phone for a taxi.

I smile and tell myself that though by nature I am a good timekeeper, perhaps on this occasion it might do no harm to be a few minutes late.

Keeping an eye on the clock I decide to give my pal Jessie a phone and thank her for the text.

"Hello, Maggie?"

"Jessie, just a wee call to thank you for that text. Liz left to go to Asda over an hour ago, but I've not heard anything yet so hopefully it will go okay. Will you tell Mary I'm awfully grateful that she let us know about the vacancy?"

"Oh, aye, no bother," Jessie replies in a low voice and I'm guessing she's not able to speak, particularly when she suddenly says, "I'll see you tomorrow, hen okay?"

"Right then, bye," but she's already hung up leaving me hoping that she's all right, that her husband isn't back to his shenanigans again.

It's gone ten now so I head back upstairs to apply my makeup and ten minutes later even I'm pleased with what I've done for let me tell you, there's no critic like a woman herself. Scrutinising myself in the mirror, I'm glad I decided to leave my hair down on my shoulders. That done I'm back downstairs and beginning to feel a little nervous about meeting Alan.

Like I've said before, you have to remember that I've now been out with anyone since Alex died and I'm half expecting what I told Liz about Alan just wanting to have a chat about the investigation might in fact be true.

I've just lifted the phone to dial a taxi when I hear the sound of the car being driven on the chips in the driveway. When I open the front door I see the rain is pelting down outside and with her coat over her head, Liz makes a run for it from the car to the house.

I stand to one side to avoid her splashing me and she greets me with, "Bloody weather. I only walked from the store to the car and got soaked," as she slips off her coat and shivers. "Cold too," she adds. "So, how did you get on?"

She shrugs and her voice is noncommittal when she replies, "I met Mary when I got there and her manager, Mark, was very nice and seems to think highly of her because he told me that if she's recommending me I must be okay. I filled in an application form and told him about my work experience, but then he asked me for the details of two referees," her face fell and she groaned.

"What did you say?"

She blows through pursed lips and tells me, "I couldn't think of anybody off the top of my head, so I gave him Ian's sister-in-law Linda's details, and Father O'Brien too. I also told him that I've just finished a lengthy spell in hospital," she screws her face and winces as though she's considered on hindsight, maybe that was not such a good idea.

"Did you say which hospital?"

"No," she shakes her head. "He never asked nor did he ask what was wrong with me."

I try not to show my disappointment that sometimes these details get out and the stigma of her being detained in Leverndale for all those months might somehow affect her employment chances. Smiling, I tell her, "Well, first thing you do is phone Linda and give her a heads up. I don't doubt that Father will give you a cracking reference, but likely he'll be at morning Mass so give it an hour or so then phone him as well."

"Okay, mum," she forces a smile and hands me the car keys.

I'm tempted to take the car, but then I'm worried that whether it's raining or not the area around the Botanic Gardens is always very busy with traffic and being so close to Byres Road means parking can be a hit or a miss. Maybe I will be better getting a taxi and decide that's what I'll do.

I shake my head and hang the keys on the hook behind the door and tell her of my decision.

"You look really nice," she says as I dial. "Hope he knows what a lucky man he is, getting a babe like you," she grins then brightly asks, "When will you be home?"

Her face is full of innocence and right away I know there's something behind her question.

"Why?" my eyes narrow.

"Oh, it's just that Colin finishes his shift at four and, well, he might be dropping in for something to eat. But I'll put him off if it's a problem?"

I don't expect to be any longer than an hour having coffee with Alan Reid, but she's so happy with this new romance that I don't have the heart to put her off, so I reply, "Well, I'll likely be there for quite a while and I might take a turn into the Buchanan Galleries. Remember, Debenhams's have a good sale on so maybe about five o'clock? But if you want me home sooner…" I tease her.

"No," she hastily replies. "Five is fine, mum. If you need a lift from the town, just give me a phone."

"Aye, I'll do that," but we both know fine well, that won't happen.

Phoning for a taxi, I'm wondering what I'm going to do with myself for four or five hours after my coffee meeting?

CHAPTER FOURTEEN

The taxi drops me at five to eleven at the entrance to the Botanic Gardens on Queen Margaret Drive and though the rain has lessened slightly, I'm glad I brought my pop-up brolly with me.

Needless to say, the large forecourt at the tearoom is empty other than the cast iron tables and chairs that sit forlornly in the rain.

At the door I shake my brolly free of the rain and hurry inside to find that there are just half a dozen hardy people who have braved the weather and my heart stops, for I can't see Alan.

Then I hear my name called.

"Maggie."

I turn and to my relief he's rising from a table by the window that looks out onto the forecourt, one hand raised in greeting and a smile on his face. As I approach the table I'm taking off my coat and to my surprise he gallantly steps behind to help me with it then hangs it across an empty chair upon which sits his own Australian oilskin coat and bunnet.

The first thing I notice about him is that I see he's had his hair cut. My surprise must have shown on my face for he grins and tells me, "After you left us yesterday, Fiona literally marched me to across to the St Enoch Barbers next to the Times Square pub and told me if I'm to make a good impression with you I've to tidy myself up."

He's wearing a light blue shirt with a navy blue tie, dark grey sports jacket and sharply creased black trousers with polished shoes. Spreading his arms wide he jokingly pirouettes, then says, "So, what do you think?"

I smile and nodding tell him, "I approve and I think you look very smart."

I'm not being polite. He *does* look smart and though he's not Richard Gere handsome, he is a fine looking man. It also occurs to me if his daughter did say that, she must approve of her dad seeing me.

"I wasn't sure if you'd make it," he clears his throat and pulls out a chair for me, then sits opposite. I try not to smile for I realise that he's nervous too.

"You mean with the bad weather?"

"No, what I mean is…" but stops and makes a face when he cottons on I'm teasing him.

He is about to speak, but a young waitress arrives to take our order and we both settle for a pot of tea for two with a cake each.

"Anyway, as I was about to say, when I phoned last night and didn't get you, I thought maybe you hadn't got the message. Did I sound like an idiot?" he grimaces.

"Just a wee bit," I assure him, then I grin.

I nod at the sodden bunnet and ask, "Have you come far? I mean do you live locally?"

"Not too far and yes, as a matter of fact, I do live locally. I have three-bedroom flat or more correctly, a duplex in Huntley Gardens. Do you know it?"

"Huntley Gardens?" I repeat and shake my head then show my ignorance by asking, "What's a duplex?"

He's beaming and replies, "It's a fancy word that simply means a house split into two different apartments. Don't worry about not knowing," he lowers his voice and as though about to impart a secret, leans forward and whispers, "I had to look it up in the dictionary."

"Anyway," he sits back, "I've had it for, ah, about twenty odd years now. Parking is a bit of a problem though. Moved in when house prices in the west end were a lot cheaper and there weren't so many cars about. Huntley Gardens wasn't my first choice, to be honest. Of course, now both the girls have moved out it's far too big for me to be living there alone, but I like the area and it's handy for Byres Road and the town and of course," he waves a hand around him and smiling, adds, "this place. I really like it here in the summer months."

As if reluctant to change the subject, he continues, "Yeah, when we moved there at first, the mortgage rates were sitting about fifteen per cent and the monthly payments nearly broke us because in those days every penny was a prisoner. It was spam and beans for the first few years," he smiles. "I shouldn't really complain because being the west end and through the years, the house has now appreciated greatly and is far more valuable than when I purchased it so in the long run it's worked in my favour."

I take the bull by the horn, as they say, and boldly ask, "When you say we, I assume you're talking about your ex-wife?"

His brow knits as he stares curiously at me and asks, "How did you know I was divorced and not widowed? Did Fiona mention anything to your daughter?"

"She might have, but all Liz told me is that you are no longer married and believe me, Alan, if I thought you *were* still married, we wouldn't be having coffee right now."

He's about to respond, but stops when the waitress returns and we wait till she's left before he replies, "But how do you know I'm divorced and not widowed?"

I show him my left hand and point to the wedding band on my third finger.

"I'm not a detective," I blush, "but in my experience people who are widowed seldom remove their wedding rings. It's different when you're divorced, is it not?"

"Very clever, Maggie," he grins and nods at me then continues, "Yes, I'm divorced. Twelve, no, thirteen years now."

"Am I being too impertinent to ask what happened?"

I'm pleased that he remembers I like my milk in first and watch as he pours a little into both cups before lifting the teapot. As he pours the tea he says, "Karen liked the finer things in life and was keen for me to progress in the police. Unfortunately, I'm not as ambitious as she wished me to be and just like any other job, promotion means a better salary. She worked part-time in an office in the city and it was there she met someone who *was* ambitious."

He smiles but behind the smile I sense a little sadness when he says, "The real ones who suffered from the breakup were our daughters."

I was surprised and blurted out, "But you kept the house?"

"Yes, and only because of the girls," he adds, then shaking his head, continues, "Don't let me kid you, Maggie, running the house while I worked full time and bringing up two teenage daughters was no easy task, I can tell you. If the house was so expensive, you're probably wondering, why did I keep it on? Well, the girls were at a local school and I didn't want to move them away from their friends and interrupt their education, so I took the hit and we stayed where we were. You're a mother, you know that when you have children they come first, right?"

"Right," I slowly nod as I agree and wonder for I can't imagine a mother giving up her children. I mean, I don't know the circumstances of this woman Karen leaving him, but surely a mother would give up her last breath before she would surrender her children, even to her husband?

My unasked question must have reflected in my face because he says, "Look, I don't want to paint Karen in a bad light, it's just that she was a very ambitious woman and very career minded. Our marriage had run its course and we realised we wanted different things in life."

It was as if he read my mind for then he said, " I can guess you're wondering why she didn't take the girls with her? Well, at first she did visit and see the girls every weekend, but as they got older," he shrugged. "Well, she'd formed another relationship and her new man wanted her to spend more time with him."

"You don't sound bitter."

He doesn't immediately respond, but then says, "I suppose in a way I was a bit relieved. Before she walked out the arguments had become very distressing for the girls and on one occasion," he wryly grins, "I had the polis at the door. A neighbour had heard us shouting at each other; well, to be more correct, Karen shouting at me and called the local station. Fortunately, the two cops were satisfied that as nobody was being murdered, no action needed to be taken."

I don't know what to say and a bit of an awkward silence falls between us, so to lighten the atmosphere, I tell him about the rammy I heard last night between the McPherson's next door.

He smiles and asks, "Is that a regular thing?"

"God, no," I hastily reply. "Moira's in the Salvation Army…" I stop. "No, she was in the Salvation Army, but I haven't seen her attending there for some time or what I should say is, I haven't seen her wearing her uniform for some time. But she's usually as quiet as a mouse and her husband Willie is nearly as quiet as she is."

When he replies, "Aye, some people surprise you because you never really know what goes on behind closed doors, do you?" it makes me suspect that he's maybe referring to his own failed marriage. However, my curiosity gets the better of me again and so I say, "I know it's not my place to ask, but does she still see the girls?"

"They're grown women now, so if they do see their mother they keep it to themselves and I never ask. I have a terrific relationship with them both, but don't let me kid you," his face contorts, "it was hard work raising them and we had more than our fair share of teenage angst and hysterics."

Then he laughs softly and said, "I can bet you've had your share of those with Liz."

"Oh, aye," I smilingly agree.

We sit in silence for several seconds before I ask, "Twelve years. Has there been anyone since?"

"Oh, dozens of women," he boastfully pouts.

I'm smiling as he shakes his head and goes on, "Well, maybe not dozens, but there have been a handful of which there were two who lasted for a little longer than the others. One a long time ago that fell through within a couple of months because my daughters didn't like her and made it very clear with their huffy attitude. As it turned out, they were correct. Female intuition, I suppose," though he doesn't explain further and I'm too reluctant to ask.

"Then just under five years ago I was seeing woman called Agata for, oh, almost a year. Turned out that she had baggage that she forgot to tell me about."

This does intrigue me so I ask, "What kind of baggage?"

He drolly replies, "A husband and two children back in her native Poland. I found out about them when early one morning the husband called at my door looking for her with photos of their kids clutched in his hand that he almost shoved in my face. I don't speak Polish, but there was no doubt what his opinion of me was. It was even more embarrassing when my girlfriend or I should say his estranged wife, pops out of my bedroom wearing my dressing gown over her nightie." He grimaces, then adds with a sigh, "Fortunately he was a good bit smaller and a lot skinnier than me otherwise there might have been a problem. Didn't make me feel any better when he started crying," he shrugs.

"How did you resolve that one?" I work hard at keeping my face straight.

"Actually, it was Fiona and Bryony, my youngest girl, who resolved it for me," he smiles. "I was trying to calm the husband and believe me, that's no easy task when his wife is screaming at him in Polish and he's screaming back at her, though God alone knew what they were saying. Anyway," he shrugs again, "while I'm at the door trying to keep them apart and don't forget, she's still in my dressing gown, Fiona appears behind us and literally threw her handbag and her clothes out onto the landing, grabs me by the back of my shirt and pulls me into the hallway as Bryony slams the door closed while the two of them continued to bawl and shout at each other out in the landing."

I can't help myself and start to laugh.

He stares at me with a rebuking scowl and nodding adds, "And yes, before you ask the downstairs neighbour *did* call the polis again.

Fortunately, by the time the cops arrive Agata and her husband had gone."

"Seems you don't have a lot of luck with women, Detective Sergeant Reid," I mock him.

"Not so far," he breezily replies, then stares at me till I blush and adds, "but maybe seeing you will change all that, Maggie."

I'm a little stunned at his words, and it's some seconds before I ask, "So, why exactly did you invite me here this morning?"

He doesn't immediately respond, but still staring at me at last says, "How do you explain attraction? You're a damned attractive woman, Maggie. Smart too and there's something about you that, oh, I don't know how to explain it; just tells me that I want to get to know you better."

"Oh," is all I can say and damn it, there's me blushing again.

"Can I get you anything else," says the young waitress.

Alan pretends to be startled and smiling tells her, "You came up on my blind side there, hen." He turns to me and asks, "Another pot of tea or something to eat?"

Please God I'm not going to regret this, I tell myself, and I can feel my heart thumping when I ask, "You said your house is what, less than a ten minute walk away?"

He's staring curiously at me and nods.

My mouth is suddenly dry and I can feel my body tensing when I slowly continue, "Then why don't we just go there and have a coffee, if you like?"

For that two seconds, I worry he'll say no, but then he turns to the waitress and with a smile, says, "We're fine thanks. Just the bill, please."

When she's out of earshot, my courage fails me and I stutter, "I'm just curious to see where you live, Alan. Nothing else. You *do* understand?"

He lifts a hand and replies, "You have my word, Maggie, there will be no impropriety by me. On the other hand," his eyes are almost twinkling, "I can't speak for you."

That's the second time I've heard that word impropriety used in as many days, I tell myself. First Colin to my Liz, now Alan to me.

What is it about us Brogan girls that attract courteous men?

Now on my feet I draw myself up to my full height and give him a look that quite clearly says try it on, pal, and you're in danger of losing more than your dignity.

He winces then grinning, pretends to be alarmed before he says, "I think for your first visit, we'll just have coffee."

****

He is right enough. The rain has almost stopped and within seven or eight minutes of leaving the tearoom we're walking in Huntley Gardens. He's offered me his arm and I decide it would be churlish to refuse and I'm so glad I didn't because I'd forgotten the nice feeling I get of walking arm in arm with a man.

In Huntley Gardens I'm immediately impressed by the lovely blonde sandstone terraced buildings while across the road there is a good-sized park with paths running through it and benches beside the paths.

"The park over there," he nods towards it, "is solely for the use of the residents. In the summer on my days off, I sometimes find myself sitting in there with my morning newspaper and a flask of coffee."

As we walk along Alan explains that most if not all the houses are now duplex and pointing to the basement and ground floor windows explains they belong to the bottom flat while the first and second level windows belong to the upper flat. Wrought iron railings protect the pedestrians from falling into the basement area and all the houses are reached via stone stairs to a communal door.

We stop outside a white painted door and he says, "I've the upper flat. I share the main door and hallway with Mister and Missus Morrison. They're a doddery old couple and been here longer than me, but for all their age they're as sharp as pins and particularly their hearing," he grins.

I don't know what I expected, maybe something like a Glasgow tenement 'Wally' close, but when Alan opens the door I see the original wide staircase has been retained from the time when the two flats were one house, though I suspect the hallway and stair carpets have often been replaced.

I see Alan smiling at my surprise and he tells me, "The Morrison's and me pay for the upkeep of the hallway and at the insistence of my daughters, I also have a woman who comes in Tuesdays and Fridays to clean the flat." He raises a forefinger and his face solemn adds "But I do my own cooking, washing and the occasional ironing."

"So domesticated," I pretend to mock him, but can't stop smiling. Almost without thinking, he takes my hand and leads me up the stairs to his flat.

Well, if I thought my two bedroomed semi was spacious for me alone, I could not have envisaged Alan's home without seeing it for myself.

"Look, I'll shove the kettle on," he takes my coat from me, "and you have a wee wander about the place. There's nowhere you can't go," he smiles.

Now, let's not forget I'm a woman and by nature all women want to know every little detail of a man who is interested in them, so why should I be any different?

When he disappears off through a door into what I'm guessing is the kitchen, the first door I open is a spacious cloakroom toilet while the door next to that opens out into a large dining room with a table that is surrounded by eight chairs. I've never been good at judging distances, so many yards by so many yards or that kind of thing, but let's just say the dining room is easily twice the size of my front room. Folding wooden doors that are open lead into an even larger room that Alan later mockingly calls the drawing room and is large enough to play football in. The room is light and airy with bay windows that overlook the park to the front of the building and I'm a bit overawed by the beauty of the polished wooden floor, the bright décor and old fashioned, but comfortable couches.

I take a deep breath and retrace my steps and back in the hallway I go up the staircase to the upper floor where I find two large bedrooms, one of which is almost the size of the drawing room and I guess is Alan's room because of the en-suite, but the real giveaway is the shirt hanging over the back of a chair and, I smile, the tartan slippers under the chair. There is also an enormous family bathroom and on the same floor, I'm surprised to find a large utility room too. I find myself smiling with pleasure and memories come flooding back from my childhood in the tenement flat I grew up in Drumchapel when in the utility room I see there is an old fashioned ceiling pulley that has shirts and towels drying as they hang from it.

Though both bedrooms have built in wardrobes, there are two spacious cupboards in the hallway. When I pull open a third door in the hallway, instead of a cupboard as I'd thought I find a further set up stairs going up into what I guess must be the attic area. At the top of the stairway I find a large bright and airy room with a single bed and Velux windows set into the roof that overlook the enclosed rear garden below. Posters on the wall indicate that the room must have been occupied by one of Alan's daughters and when I peer at a photograph on the dressing table, I assume the young girl must be Bryony, for it's definitely not Fiona.

I stare out of the window, stunned at the size and beauty of his home and for some curious reason, I feel a little guilty.

Making my way back down the stairs I smell something aromatic cooking and following my nose I enter his kitchen and find it to be a very wide, galley style room with modern appliances. Bright red coloured shiny cupboards occupy one wall and a kitchen table with four chairs is set along the opposite wall. A panoramic window faces out onto the rear garden.

I almost laugh when I see him wearing a black coloured apron as he says, "I thought as we hadn't eaten, I'd shove some food on, if that's okay with you?"

"Yes, fine," I stutter and slide down onto a kitchen chair.

"It's just peppers and chicken bits in a herb sauce with microwave rice. Nothing too fancy," he shrugs.

I smile for I don't recall the last time a man made me dinner.

I get to my feet to peer at a large cork noticeboard on the whitewashed wall above the table that is covered with postcards, some takeaway menus and lots of photographs pinned to it. Some of the photos feature groups of people and include Alan and Fiona, who I recognise and who in another photo is being cuddled in a park somewhere by a young man I assume to be her husband. There are photos of their son Finn at various stages of his three years and a number of photographs of the girl I recognise from the picture in the attic room and who I assume to be Bryony. In some of Bryony's photos it also features a dark-haired young man. Curiously I see that in the two or three photos he appears in, he isn't smiling in any of them.

Alan sees me looking at the photos and with his ladle, points and says, "Fiona and Finn you've met. That's her with her hubby Mike, who is a good guy and you might recall I said is a polis and Bryony with her current boyfriend, Alistair. He's the painter, by the way," and he sighs.

It was the way he said Alistair that made me wary and I cautiously ask, "You said before that you're not too keen on him?"

"Bit of a blowhard," he shakes his head, "but if I tell Bryony I don't approve of him, well, you've a daughter. You know how touchy they can be when they think you're interfering in their love life."

I think back to when Liz first met Ian and slowly nod in agreement when I reply, "When my daughter first brought Ian Chalmers to our home, Alex and I saw right away that he was a rotter, but Liz was too close and couldn't see beyond his veneer."

Alan shakes his head and with a sigh replies, "I just keep my fingers crossed that some day Bryony will see him for the egotistical prat he is and hopefully before they think of making their relationship legal."

As he opens the sauce and stirs it into the Wok, he reaches into a cupboard and fetches out two plates, then asks, "Still want that coffee or maybe a glass of wine?"

"Are you trying to get me drunk?" I joke.

"If I thought it might work, I would try," he grins.

"What about that promise of no impropriety?"

"Oh, aye, that," he pretends he's forgotten.

"Maybe just water then," I tell him.

"Then water it is," he nods and filling a glass jug, adds ice from his refrigerator and places it with two glasses on the table.

"Can I do anything to help?" I ask.

"Just sit there and continue to look pretty," he grins at me and I find I'm blushing again.

I hadn't realised how hungry I am and ten minutes later I'm wolfing down my meal. I stop and raising my head, see he's grinning again at me.

"Well, it's very good," I defend my gluttony, but with a mouthful of chicken and rice.

"Thank you," he nods and points with his fork to the dribble of sauce on my chin.

Using my paper napkin, I dab at the spill but some inner sense tells me that there's something on his mind.

I'm aware my eyes are narrowing when I ask, "Something you want to say, Alan?"

He's hesitant, but then replies, "It's the elephant in the room, Maggie, but I'm guessing that you've already heard the news about there being an arrest in the Murdoch girl's murder, yet you haven't mentioned it. To be honest," he draws a breath, "I didn't because frankly I don't want to spoil what has been a lovely day. Not that I'm dismissing Beth or Kylie's deaths or anything like that," he hastens to add, but I'm already holding my hand up to quieten him. I begin by smiling because I don't want him to think I'm not also having a good time, then, I tell him, "Yes, I know from the news there has been an arrest, but you told me that you weren't part of the investigation so I just assumed you wouldn't have any information about it. The one thing that obviously interests me is that if there is a connection with Beth's murder, will you be informed? I mean, you told me that you are my contact with Beth's investigation and promised if you learn anything you would tell me. Does that still stand?"

"It does," he confirms with a nod. "The problem I have is that I'm kind of locked out of the current investigation because…" I see him struggle whether or tell me or not, but then he continues, "The reason I was moved to Maryhill, Maggie, is that I lost my temper with a senior officer and punched him."

When I don't reply, his forehead creases and frowning, he stares suspiciously at me then says, "Ah, but you already know that, don't you?" He shakes his head and adds, "I'd forgotten. You have a friend in the Division, haven't you? The liaison lassie, Constable Gardener."

"Sheila, yes," I admit, "but for what it's worth she has nothing but good to say about you and after what she told me," I can't help my voice becoming brittle, when I add, "you should have hit him a lot harder than you did."

He softly smiles then says, "So, you're not upset that the man making inquiry into Beth's murder has been handed the case because he's a pariah?"

I take my time in replying and slowly using my fork to stir the pasta, inhale as I make my decision. I'm very conscious of what I'm doing and what I'm about to say for believe me, it *is* a big decision on my part. I reach across the table to gently place my hand on top of his and tell him, "If doing what's right and just makes you a pariah, Alan, then I do not want anyone else going after the man who killed my precious wee girl."

That kind of takes him aback, I think, or perhaps it's because my hand is still resting on his.

"I'll do my best," he replies and do you know what?

I believe him.

****

With unspoken agreement, we find we've changed the subject.

He asks me about my life with Alex and I find that I can talk freely and tell him that yes, we did love each other but through the years that love developed from a passion for each other into a deep friendship. Then to my utter amazement, it's like a dam has burst.

I find I'm sharing with this man that I've known for just a few days my inner secrets, that my married life though happy, was dull.

I can't believe it's me that's talking!

I mean, I've not had any alcohol; I'm not on medication, so why the *hell* am I running off at the mouth with all this? It's not as if I'm criticising or complaining about my life with Alex. I really *did* love the man, but as I go on I'm coming to realise that our married life had stalled and yes, I admit it; we had become stuck in a rut, a routine with both of us accepting that we did not need anything more from each other than simple companionship.

To my dismay, I listen to the sound of my own voice as I confess that sex with my husband was…predictable.

Yes, that's the actual word I use.

Predictable!

I stop and stare at Alan, aware that soft tears are running down my cheeks and horrified at what I'm saying, but he returns my stare with sympathy in his eyes and I see him nod before he says, "Let me get you a handkerchief."

He leaves the kitchen and returns a minute later with a neatly ironed cotton hankie that he hands to me before resuming his seat.

I feel such a fool and tell him so, but he slowly shakes his head and softly replies, "It's always been my experience that sometimes it's easier to reveal things to someone you don't know well than to someone who has been in your life for a long time, Maggie." He raises his hand and continues, "I feel privileged that you felt you could share this with me but I need to tell you this and don't ask me to explain it, but I'd like you to consider seeing me. Not as a man who's working on Beth's inquiry," he hastily added, "but as someone that wants to get to know you a lot better. Eh, you follow me?"

I try to smile, but it's not easy when tears are trickling down your cheeks and your lips are quivering. Not trusting myself to speak, I can only nod that yes, I do follow him.

He suddenly gets to his feet and says, "If you'd like to wash your face, the cloakroom is just out in the hallway and I'll clear the dishes away."

I take advantage of his suggestion and five minutes later when I leave the toilet I hear him call through from the front room or I should say, his drawing room, that he's in there.

When I join him I see he's brought through a tray with coffee and biscuits that sit on a table between the two large armchairs. Outside, the rain has come on full pelt and is lashing against the bay windows.

I'd practised in the toilet what I was going to tell him to explain my behaviour and taking a breath as I sit down, I begin, "Sorry..." but he waves away my apology and handing me a mug, says, "I was just trying to work something out there."

"Isn't that a prerequisite for being a detective?" I sip at the coffee and tease him.

"Aye, very good, Missus Brogan. Anyway, I was trying to work out something that you had told me, but whatever it is, it's slipped my mind."

"Is it important?"

He screws his face and replies, "I don't want to go on at length, but it's something that you said when we were talking earlier."

"Something I said when?"

"That's the thing," he sighs. "Not only can't I recall what you said, but I can't remember when you said it." He points to his head and grins, "I'll need to start writing things down more frequently."

"I'll get you a Dictaphone for Christmas," I joke.

"What, with all the fancy mobiles these days, do they still make they things?"

I'm smiling and when I sit back in the comfortable armchair with the rain beating a tattoo against the window, the warm atmosphere of the room and the meal I've just eaten all combine to cause my eyes to flutter and I can't stop myself from yawning.

"Am I boring you, Maggie?" he smiles at me.

I return his smile and tell him, "No, Alan. If anything, you make me feel very relaxed and comfortable. Thank you for a lovely day."

I know it, I can feel that he wants to come over to me, yet something stops him and I surprise myself because *I* want him to come over. I realise that if I don't make a move I'm in danger of inviting him to me and don't forget, it's been a very long time since I've had a man take such an interest in me or I in him. What surprises me is that I want him to come closer, to feel him near to me, his breath on my skin…

God, what's happening to me?

Almost in shock at what I'm thinking, I take a deep breath and sitting upright, I tell him, "Perhaps it's time I went home."

"In this rain? Are you sure you won't stay a little longer till it calms down a little?"

"I'm sure," I smile, then add, "But if you're serious about me, I could visit you again sometime?"

"I'd like that," he nods.

He phones me a taxi and now we're standing at the front door of the house with the rain lashing down outside. The taxi arrives within five minutes and he turns to glance at it before turning back to me and to my surprise, holds me tightly to embrace me then grins, "You've bewitched me, Maggie Brogan, but I really don't care. Call me and tell me you've arrived home safe."

"I will," but as I reach up to give him a peck on the cheek, he turns his face and our mouths clumsily collide. I gasp, then seizing his head in my hands, pull him down and kiss him fully on the lips.

In the taxi, I'm waving through the rear window and grinning at my audacity, but then I have a sudden thought.

On the journey home, I realise why earlier I felt a little guilty. Though I've known him for such a short time, I have an increasing affection for him and that's what worries me for Alan is an attractive and successful man with a large and beautiful home. Though obviously not wealthy on a police sergeant's salary, he is far more affluent than me, a woman who cleans offices for a living and who lives in an ex-authority semi.

I don't want to be a problem between him and his daughters, so will they see me as they probably they did the other two women he had affairs with?

Will they see me as a woman who simply wishes to improve my lifestyle?

CHAPTER FIFTEEN

The weather has taken a turn for the better and Monday morning arrives bright, though chilly.

I've had a good night's sleep having gone to bed just a couple of hours after I got home. Not my normal time to retire, but when I arrived home I found Liz and Colin curled up on the couch in front of the television so I decided an early night with my Kindle was preferable to watching some science fiction rubbish about dead people running around and chasing then eating the live ones.

Oh, and I didn't forget to phone Alan to tell him I was home safe and thank him for a really nice day. Took me twenty minutes to get him off the phone after that.

I woke when the toilet flushed just after midnight, so I'm guessing Liz had a late night and not wanting to disturb her, I shower quietly and with my clothes in my hand, creep downstairs to dress in the kitchen while the kettle boils.

Now, you'll be wondering if I gave Alan Reid any thought while I lay in my bed?

Course I did and I'm wondering, just how much *do* I like him?

Well, it seems I'm beginning to like him a lot, but the thought of his protective daughters still worries me a little.

The kettle boils and once I've had my toast and I'm ready, I leave the house, happy that Liz still hasn't stirred.

After parking and giving my wee pal a wave, I hotfoot it to the office and when I push through the door, who do I encounter but Jessie. She doesn't say anything, just gives me a quick hug and I see that her eye is almost healed, though she has applied a little foundation cream to cover the last of the yellow bruising.

"Aye, that'll be the gruesome twosome back on the prowl," I hear big Eileen call out, but she's grinning so I smile back at her and give her a polite nod.

Then she surprises me by sidling up and asking, "How's your lassie, Maggie?"

There's no deceit or nosiness in her voice, so I tell her, "She's doing really well, thanks Eileen. Better than I hoped for and even applied for a job yesterday up in the Maryhill Asda, thanks to Jessie's daughter."

"Good for her," she beams and with a grins, says, "Welcome back, Jessie. Any time you need that bastard of a man of yours sorted out, we'll do for him, eh girls?" she turns to the rest of the cleaners who give a wee cheer of support.

Embarrassed, Jessie doesn't know what to say other than mumbling, "Thanks, girls."

Seems then that my wee pal's domestic situation is no secret then.

The revelry is cut short when Tommy Burton enters the locker room and clapping his hands, calls out, "For Christ's sake, ladies, time to get your arses out onto your floors, eh?"

He sees Jessie and nodding at her, asks, "You up for this today, hen?"

"Course I am," she scoffs.

"Well, you're back on the fourth floor with Maggie," then turning away continues to cajole the cleaners to get out to their jobs.

The time fairly flies past and we're that busy that Jessie and I don't get much chance to talk.

Before I realise, it's almost nine and we pack away our cleaning equipment and head back down to the locker room.

On the way I ask her, "Are you straight off to you're cleaning job at Asda?"

"Not today," she shakes her head. "Mary got the keys of the flat on Friday and gave me a set, so I'm heading up there to give it a once over. It's not needing decorated right away, but it does need a good clean. Her pal's got a motor so she and Mary dropped off buckets and cleaning stuff there, yesterday evening after she'd finished her shift at Asda. Oh, and she's got some stuff from the second hand furniture store getting delivered after two this afternoon, so I'll need to be there for that."

I'm thinking, what am I planning to do but go home and tidy an already tidy house, so what's the harm in helping my wee pal out?

"Is there a kettle in the flat?"

"Eh?" Jessie is confused and staring curiously at me, replies, "A kettle? Eh, I'm not sure. No, I don't think so," she's shaking her head. "Why?"

"Right," I firmly tell her. "We'll go and fetch my car, I'll get the teabags, the milk and sugar and we'll see if we can pick up a kettle too and…" I almost forget. "Does she have mugs?"

"No," she firmly shakes her head. "She doesn't have anything like that yet, Maggie. She didn't want to buy anything and bring it home to the house in case, you know, in case Ernie and the boys got suspicious."

"Okay," I slowly drawl. "I'll buy us some mugs, we'll get the shopping and grab something from the Greggs in the Maryhill Shopping centre for lunch. Then, my lady," I stare firmly at her, "once we've eaten, you and me will clean the flat together. What do you say?"

I can see she's stunned, but I'm taken aback when tears form in her eyes and she bites at her lip to stop herself from crying.

Blinking heck, have we two not shed a lot of tears between us in the last couple of months?

I feel a little guilty that this woman who considers me to be her best friend hasn't had the friendship returned like it should have been and I vow from today that definitely is going to change.

I ignore the looks I'm getting from the arriving office staff and wrap my arm around her shoulder then giving her a squeeze, tell her, "Let's go."

****

On the way to the car I leave a voice message on Liz's phone telling her I might be out for most of the day and now I'm parked in the shopping centre's car park.

The first shop we visit is the Tesco where I buy the groceries. Carrying them between us, we visit the Marie Curie charity shop where we find a nearly new electric kettle and half dozen mugs still in their cardboard packaging that I tell Jessie, "These should do Mary till she gets what she wants."

Our last port of call is the Greggs bakery where I treat us to a couple of steak bakes and an icing bun each.

Jessie is overwhelmed at what she calls my generosity. I dismiss her thanks for to be honest, that only makes me feel worse that I've never fully acknowledged her friendship.

She directs me to Killearn Street and I park in a bay outside the modern three storey flats that are opposite a row of Victorian red sandstone tenements.

With the shopping bags in our hands, I can see that Jessie is nervous when she opens the close security door then tells me, "The flat's on the first floor."

When she opens the door to the flat there's an immediate smell of unwashed clothes and sure enough we find when the previous tenant has decanted from the flat, they've left a pile of dirty washing lying in the middle of the floor of the larger of the two bedrooms and plastic bins that needed emptied. Needless to say, the marigolds are on straight away, the rubbish into bin bags along with the pile of clothing and then it's all thrown out into the landing for the time being.

We glance at each other and wrinkling our noses, decide the food will need to wait for we don't want to eat in the smelly kitchen without at first giving the whole place a good clean.

The first thing we do is throw open all the windows to air the flat. Mary has left a good selection of cleaning materials so Jessie and I set to work. Now remember, we do this for a living so by twelve thirty the flat is looking and smelling a whole lot better; so much so that both Jessie and I take a wee bit of pride in what we've done. Ten minutes later we're stood in the kitchen at the worktop wolfing down the now cold steak bakes, savouring the sugary buns and sipping at our tea.

"When Mary told me about you moving in with her I hope she didn't break a confidence," I hesitantly ask.

She takes a deep breath and shaking her head, replies, "No, not at all, hen. I can't take any more of his nonsense, Maggie. It's not just the drinking and the attitude of him and the boys it's the random violence. Ernie slapping or punching me when he can't get his way or his constantly expecting me to work myself to death to keep him in the bevy and at the bookies. Won't get off his fat arse…sorry," she grimaces, "I know you don't like me swearing."

She pauses for breath before she continues, "He's bone idle, so he is and always has been. I'm fed up paying for everything. And as for my sons," she chokes back a sob, "never once have they ever stood up for their mother. Not once!" she spits out. "If it wasn't for Mary and my oldest boy Billy down south, I think I'd have done myself in years ago."

"Don't speak like that!" I tell her a little more harshly than I intend. "You've a daughter that loves you and needs you and from what you've told me, your Billy is making a good life for himself and his wife and kids in Bournemouth, so you've a lot to be proud of, Jessie."

Her heart's breaking and I instinctively move to give her a comforting hug as she cries into my shoulder.

At last I hear her take a deep breath and she gently pulls away from me and says, "Thanks for being my friend." She glances about her at the sparking clean kitchen then adds, "And for this."

"Nonsense," I force a grin. "You can pay for the foreign holiday."

"If I win the lottery," she guffaws, "you can be sure of it."

"When do you intend moving out?"

Her face darkens when she replies, "He doesn't know, but I've already packed a case and it's under my bed. Besides what's arriving today, there are two beds from the second hand store and brand new mattresses getting delivered tomorrow. Mary's used her store card to buy bedding that her pal's bringing over to the flat tonight." She takes a breath and her eyes narrow and I can see she's thinking about the enormity of her decision. "I'm bringing the suitcase with me tomorrow morning when I leave for work and I'll not be going back."

My throat is tightening because I'm imagining Jessie humping her suitcase down the stairs at that time of the morning then arriving to the curious glances from the rest of the cleaning staff, so I make my decision.

"I'll be outside your close in my car at six-thirty tomorrow morning. We can leave the case in the boot and then after our shift I'll bring you back up here so none of the women will know what you're up to, okay?"

The relief in her face brings on more tears and I reach behind me for a sheet from the roll of kitchen towel. When she's composed again, I'm glancing around the kitchen and I ask, "Has Mary got a wee table and chairs yet"

"Eh, no, I don't think so."

I'm smiling and tell her, "I want to give you both a wee moving in present. Nothing fancy, but if I go down to Dumbarton Road to the one of the second hand stores and find a kitchen table, you know," I glance again at the kitchen, "maybe one of the drop-leaf ones and a couple of chairs; will that do you in the meantime, do you think?"

"Oh, Maggie, you don't need to do that," she replies, but I can see she's pleased.

"I insist," I hold my hand up firmly to curtail any protest. "Besides, we're back at work for five so, as there's no point in going home a wee bit of retail therapy will make me feel better," I grin at her.

"Right," I'm sounding very business-like, "if you hang on here for the furniture that's coming today, I'll head down to Dumbarton Road. Now," I place a hand on her arm, "will you be okay, getting to work from here?"

"Maggie," she's smiling through fresh tears and shaking her head, softly adds, "It'll be no problem because I feel like I'm flying. Thank you."

****

Making my way down the road I switch on the radio in time for the three o'clock news and the first item is that the police are questioning an unnamed suspect about the murder of both Kylie Murdoch and Bethany Chalmers. I'm so shocked I almost stall the car and crunching the gears, pull into the side of the road, oblivious to the curious stares of the middle-aged woman pushing a buggy and the angry taxi driver who beeps at me.

There's no details given but I feel my chest tighten and my hands grip the steering wheel so tightly my fingers ache.

I take a minute to calm myself then fetch my mobile phone from my handbag and call Liz.

She answers within seconds causing me to think she's been waiting on my call and greets me with, "You've heard."

"Yes," I realise my breathing is rapid and my chest is still feeling tight.

Her voice sounds dull and distant.

"It was on the midday news. Where are you?"

"Eh, Jessie, my friend at work. She needed some help. That's where I've been."

"Are you coming home?"

"Do you need me to?"

There's pause then she says, "No, mum. I'm fine. Colin finishes again at four and he's going to pop in." There's another pause and she asks, "Are you okay? Mum?"

I swallow because my throat is suddenly dry then reply, "I'm okay, love. Really."

But I don't feel okay.

I feel…numb.

"Mum?"

"Yes?"

"You sound upset. Be careful when you're driving. Please. I can't lose you too."

It's role reversal again. Now my little girl is worrying herself sick about me.

"I will," I manage to stutter.

"Oh, mum?

"Yes?"

"I phoned that lawyer this morning, the guy on the card that Alan Reid left. I've an appointment at twelve o'clock tomorrow morning with him. Can you come with me?"

"Me? Why, is Colin on a shift?" I joke, but then realise that sounds sarcastic and immediately say, "Sorry, hen, you know I'm only kidding, don't you?"

"Yeah, well, leave the jokes to me in future," she replies.

"Of course I'll come with you," I smile, happy that it is me who will accompany her, but I'm annoyed that I'd forgotten all about it, particularly as it's important.

"Will you be home after work?"

"Yes."

"Love you, mum."

"Love you too, darling."

After the call ends I sit for a few minutes and wait for another moment or two. When I feel I'm ready, I start the engine and pull out into the traffic.

****

I'm now in the third charity shop in Dumbarton Road, the large Salvation Army shop just along the road from the Kelvinhall and still haven't found anything that might be suitable for Jessie and Mary. Their kitchen isn't too small, but I'm thinking if I find a table that is drop leaf it gives them that wee bit more space.

Wandering through the store I ignore most of the stuff that I wouldn't give houseroom too, but then I see it. A Formica topped table with white painted, solid wood legs and four sturdy white painted chairs with one of the chairs having a small paint chip out of the leg. On the plus side there isn't a mark on the table, but it isn't drop leaf. However, it has an extending section in the middle that would be useful if they cater for more than just the two of them. In fact, it's a really nice piece of furniture that I wouldn't turn my nose up at. The kitchen would probably only need the two chairs, but the other two might come in useful in the bedrooms. It's priced at seventy-five pounds, but I'm guessing it cost far more than that when it was bought new. Five minutes later I've paid the bill and an extra ten pounds to have it delivered at midday on Wednesday. Pleased with myself, I check my wristwatch and see it's just half past four. I'm due back at the work for five-thirty so decide to grab a coffee in the Big Mouth Coffee Co just along the road from the charity store.

I haven't been in the café before and settling myself down onto a comfortable armchair, I smile at the portraits on the wall, recognising David Bowie and a few faces that I can't put names to. While I'm sitting, I decide to phone Alan.

"Hello?" he answers the call and I realise he won't recognise my mobile number.

"It's me, Maggie," I'm suddenly wondering if this is a good idea, then taking a breath, ask, "Can you speak?"

"Maggie," much to my relief he sounds pleased to hear me then says, "Yes, of course. I'm still at the office. You okay?"

"I'm fine. Just calling from a café on Dumbarton Road before I start my shift at five-thirty. "Ah, how are you?" I'm wincing because honestly, I've not thought this through.

"Oh, so-so. Are you calling about the, eh, you know, the news?"

I hadn't even thought about it and hastily reply, "Actually, no. I was just phoning to speak to you about, well, nothing in particular."

I can't believe it. It's not as if he's standing there in front of me! I'm speaking to him on the phone and still I'm blushing!

"Well, I can truthfully say this is the best call I've had in a very long time," I hear his voice soften, "and it came at just the right time."

"Why's that?"

"Oh, I've had what is known in the trade as a right shitty day, pardon my French."

"Pardoned," but my curiosity is aroused.

I'm taken aback when he asks, "I recall that your shift finishes at seven. So, you doing anything after work?"

"I was intending going home for some dinner. Why," I can't believe

I'm being so forward, "do you have something in mind?"

There's a slight hesitation then he says in a more formal voice, "Well, Missus Brogan, I promised to keep you informed of any developments in the investigation, so if I bring chip suppers over to your place, will that be okay with you?"

"That will be fine, Mister Reid. I'll be home for about seven-thirty."

"Eh, what about Liz. Shall I bring something in for her too?"

"Let her and her young man feed themselves," I'm grinning. "See you at mine," and I end the call.

Sipping at my coffee, I can't help but wonder what he has to tell me?

****

"You're working like a woman possessed," Jessie had teased me, but I didn't want to disclose that I was keen to get home and not you might think for the fish supper, but because I wanted to see Alan again. Doesn't it strike you as a little strange that even though I questioned him liking me after just a few days, here I am walking to the car and looking forward to being near him again. Maybe it's the west of Scotland thing that we Weegies don't like to openly display our feelings for someone until we are absolutely, one hundred per cent certain that they are the one for you.

Reaching the almost deserted car park, I'm smiling when I recall telling Jessie about the kitchen table and chairs. I almost forgot that right now, with everything that is going on in her life, she's in a real emotional state. Anyway, it took her nearly five minutes to stop crying and fortunately before Tommy Burton come up to the fourth floor to check on us.

I'm turning into Clarion Crescent when I see a wee white car coming towards me and flashing its headlights. Pulling into the side of the road, I slow down then stop when I see it's Colin's Nissan Micra, but it's Liz who's driving and Colin in the passenger seat.

When she draws abreast with my car I lower my window and call out, "What's going on?"

"Colin's put me onto his insurance," she excitedly tells me, "so we're going for a drive."

"Oh, will you be long?"

"Quite a while," she replies then gives me a wide smile when she adds, "Besides, you've got a visitor."

"Well, be careful," I tell her and wind up my window before she can tease me.

I'm grinning when I arrive at my driveway and getting out of the car see a newish, light blue coloured Volvo saloon on the roadway outside the house.

I then realise each time Alan called at the house he was in a CID vehicle and guess the Volvo must be his own car.

Opening the door, there's the aromatic smell of fish and chips and my mouth begins to water.

"Hello," I loudly call out and hear Alan reply, "In here."

I slip my jacket off and make my way through to the kitchen where I see he's set the table and warming two plates in the oven while the teapot brews. An insulated food bag sits on the worktop.

Conscious that not only have I been out of the house since half past six this morning and completed two cleaning shifts at my work, but I've also helped Jessie clean out her new flat, I ask him, "Don't suppose I have to time for a shower?"

He leans across towards me and theatrically sniffing, shakes his head and replies, "No, you're a bit smelly, but you'll do for the minute."

"Cheeky bugger!" I slap at his arm then settle myself down at the table.

I watch as he serves the fish and chips and pours us each a mug of tea before settling himself down opposite me.

"So, dear," I stare innocently at him. " Tell me about your day."

He's grinning and I realise I'm feeling very comfortable with this man. In fact, I surprise myself by thinking I'm so comfortable I could get used to seeing him sitting opposite me every day.

We eat our meal with small talk, some of which is me telling him about Jessie Cochrane and her family and I blush when he tells me that I must be a good friend to do what I did to help with cleaning the flat.

When Alan rises and places the plates on the worktop, I watch him sit back down and from the expression on his face I guess that what he's about to tell me won't please me.

"The news reported that the man arrested is being interviewed for both the murders," he begins, "but that's not quite true."

I have to know and ask, "But is he a strong suspect?"

He nods and replies, "For Kylie Murdoch, yes. However," and I tense for just know this is the part I'm not going to like, "there's not a lot of evidence to suggest he's the man responsible for your granddaughter, Maggie."

I feel myself frown, but realise what he's said and so I ask, "When you say *not* a lot of evidence. Does that mean there might be some evidence that he *is* the man?"

"First of all and," he stares expressively at me, "I'm trusting you with this information. It's not even for Liz's ears, okay?"

"Okay," I nod.

He takes a sip of his tea and licks at his lips before he continues.

"The guy is called Graham Copeland and he's aged twenty-three. He lives on the fifth floor of the same flats where the Murdoch girl lived.

"So he knew the wee girl?"

"Yes, well, to see though I don't know if he'd ever spoken to her or her mother. My information about the investigation is sort of third hand, as you might have guessed."

I hadn't, but nodded anyway.

"Well, it seems that when they did background checks on all the male residents of the flats…" he stops and slowly shakes his head, "Copeland was already recorded on file as a sex offender. Kids. That's why they were able to quickly arrest him."

I feel my blood run cold and my face pale, then I ask, "When you say he was already recorded as a sex offender, surely there should have been some sort of warning system in place for the women with children who lived in the flats. Even those who lived nearby?"

He inhales and wraps his hand around the mug, but doesn't lift it.

"You're right, of course," his voice sounds bitter. "More than likely when that little gem hits the media it will cause a right stooshie, but my guess is," he makes quotation marks with his forefingers, "that old chestnut, you know the one; the 'lessons have been learned' statement will be rolled out again."

"My God," I'm thinking of wee Kylie's mother. "She'll be horrified at that news, that her wee girl might have been…what's the word, targeted by that, that…fiend."

I sit in silence for a few seconds, reflecting on what Alan has disclosed, then I ask, "But what about my Beth? Why do they suspect he's the man who killed her? What's the evidence they have? Do you know?"

He shrugs and replies, "The guy who gave me the information, a decent man that I've known for some time, says that when they checked Copeland's criminal record he has convictions for breaking into cars in Clarion Crescent. Apparently it happened about a year ago."

I think back and recall that a little over a year ago, Phil Cuthbertson, the local constable, chapped all the doors to tell us to watch out and not leave anything visible in our cars, that a couple had been broken into at the other end of the Crescent.

"That's right," I nod. "I remember."

"Well," his voice sounds to me to be full of doubt, "DCI Tarrant in his wisdom thinks because of that Copeland probably knows the area and might have seen Beth out playing when he was hanging about here."

"But what do you think, Alan?"

"I can't dismiss Tarrant's theory; however, it would take a lot more than that to convince me that after screwing two cars over a year ago, Copeland then decided…" he stops and adds, "assuming he did see Beth playing at that time, that if he returns to Clarion Crescent he's going to find her out playing alone. No," he shakes his head, "it's too coincidental for me and I do not believe in coincidences."

"Do you know if Copeland has confessed to killing the Murdoch girl or said anything about Beth?"

"All I know is that on the advice of his lawyer he's saying nothing, but the DNA result of the evidence found…" he hesitates, "I mean, discovered on Kylie Murdoch should be known within the next twelve hours."

"But you don't think Copeland killed my Beth?"

"I really don't know, Maggie, and to be frank, I don't think Tarrant knows either."

I'm a little confused and staring at him, I ask, "Then why did Tarrant leak to the media that this man Copeland is also being interviewed about Beth's murder?"

He doesn't immediately respond then softly says, "What I'm about to tell you is just my opinion, Maggie, nothing more, you understand?"

I know that again I'm not going to like what he tells me, so I simply nod that yes, I understand.

"Let me digress a little. The police like all professional organisations monitor their performance by statistics and of course the police performance is scrutinised by the media who are quick to point out their failings to the politicians and the public of whom many enjoy seeing the police taken to task. Do you follow me?"

"Yes, of course."

"Well, for many years it's been common practice for police forces throughout the UK to, how can I put this, contrive to present their statistics to reflect a better job than they're actually doing."

I'm anxious to know how this affects Beth's death, but rather than interrupt him, I nod that he continues.

"Let me give you an example. If a man is arrested for housebreaking and admits to, say, five break-ins in a local area, then often as not previous break-ins with the same or a similar MO…"

He pauses and asks, "You understand what I mean by MO, the *modus operandi*?"

"Yes, it means the method used, doesn't it?"

"That's correct, yes. Anyway, to continue. With no evidence of who perpetrated the *unsolved* break-ins, the man caught for the five break-ins will find the unsolved break-ins libelled against him too. When the report is compiled, the PF will be informed that there is no evidence for these added on break-ins and the trial will proceed with just the five that can be proven."

He sees that I'm a little puzzled then further explains, "Those break-ins that cannot be proven because there is no evidence against the culprit are written off as solved anyway and thus they become a *positive* statistic. Do you see?"

"So, what you're saying is that the police manipulate their figures to show their detection rate is higher than it actually is?"

He smiles and replies, "Exactly! See, Maggie Brogan, I *knew* you were a smart cookie the first time I laid eyes on you."

I feel my cheeks redden as he continues.

"Now, by intimating to the media that his team are questioning Copeland about Beth's murder, Tarrant is sowing the seed that Copeland is guilty of that too. However, there is absolutely no evidence yet or that we know of to suggest Copeland killed Beth."

He pauses and stares into my eyes and says, "I stress it's only my opinion, but I believe that when Tarrant reports Copeland to Crown Office for murdering Kylie Murdoch, he will include an additional charge of murder against Copeland for killing Beth, but in his summary will explain there is insufficient evidence to prove the charge."

He clears his throat and adds, "In essence, Copeland will forever be suspected of Beth's murder though of course without any evidence, he won't be convicted of it."

I stare at him, appalled by what he is suggesting.

"Then what you're saying is that Tarrant can claim he's solved my Beth's murder, but the man charged with it, whether there is evidence or not, will never be convicted?"

"I'm sorry, but yes. That's exactly what I'm saying."

I'm totally stunned then my voice barely audible, I ask, "The investigation into Beth's murder will cease, won't it? She'll become one of the police statistics," I hiss in anger. "A solved murder that isn't really solved!" I'm shouting at him now. "You'll be taken off the investigation and it will be closed down, filed away in some cupboard because Tarrant has made up his mind that guilty or not, Copeland will be recorded as the murderer!"

I shove back my chair and stand up, my body shaking with rage. I'm crying and shouting, though I don't know what I'm saying and I want to hit out at someone, anyone, break something…but suddenly Alan has his arms wrapped about me and is holding me, pinning my arms against his body so tightly I can hardly breath. I struggle to break free of him, but he is too strong for me and I weep into his shoulder, my body shuddering against his.

How long we are stood there I don't know, but at last I cry my final tears and shivering, I sigh.

Slowly he realises me and gently tells me, "Go and have your shower and I'll clear up here."

Wordlessly I turn and leave him standing in the kitchen staring after me.

****

I'm all cried out.

Now freshly showered I feel a little better, but still there remains a furious anger at Martin Tarrant for so easily dismissing my Beth's murder.

I tie back my damp hair into a tight ponytail and dress in a yellow coloured sweater blue jeans and my old slippers and then head back downstairs.

Alan has cleared away, washed up the dishes and has the tea brewing on the cooker. Pouring me a mug, he nods we go through to the front room for a more comfortable seat and we sit opposite each other in the armchairs.

"Sorry," I raise the mug in both my hands and bend my head to sip at my tea.

"For what? Being human? Being you," he gently smiles at me, then adds, "I'd have been surprised if you didn't react as you did."

The news that he disclosed has certainly killed the atmosphere of the evening.

We sit quietly sipping at our tea then glancing at the clock on the mantelpiece I see it's almost nine.

Alan catches me looking and rising from his chair, says, "I'd better be going. You've had a long day and you told me you're picking your pal up early, aren't you?"

"Yes, about half six."

"Well then," he leans down over me and as though it's the most natural thing in the world, kisses me.

I smile and ask, "When will I see you again?"

"Wasn't that a song by the 'Three Degrees' back in the seventies?" he grins at me.

"Before my time, then," I pretend to smirk.

"I knew that," he smiles then adds, "I'll give you a phone tomorrow, okay?"

"Okay," I nod and he kisses me one more time before he leaves.

I don't get up, just sit there and listen to the front door closing behind him.

I finish my tea then take the mug through to the kitchen sink, then glancing at the wall clock, I head upstairs to bed.

CHAPTER SIXTEEN

I'm ten minutes earlier than the six-thirty I'd agreed with Jessie and sitting in the car outside her close with the engine off. I can see her windows and an occasional glance catches the curtain being drawn back and a hand waving at me.

While I'm sat there I'm thinking of Liz's arrival home last night, sometime after ten.

Obviously unaware I'd gone to bed though I was still awake, I'd listened as she and Colin had laughed when they come in the door, then the realisation I must be in bed and the hurried cheerio before I heard his car driving off.

A minute later there was a light tap at my door and when I'd called out for her to come in, she literally bounced on the bed in her excitement to tell me that she'd had a text message calling her back to Asda the following day for a second interview.

"And don't forget, you'll come with me to the lawyer's tomorrow, won't you? The appointments at twelve o'clock," she'd reminded me.

After I'd agreed and told her I wasn't coming straight home after work, that I was first dropping off Jessie at her new flat, I decided that it was to late in the evening to disclose what Alan had told me and anyway, she was too happy with her news about the prospective job to deflate her.

No, that would be when we were alone and I could calmly and rationally explain to her that we were being let down badly by a police detective who was using a corrupt system to close her daughter's murder investigation.

Curiously and upset though I was, I'd slept soundly yet awoken with Martin Tarrant's decision still to the forefront of my mind.

My attention was taken by the close door opening and Jessie struggling with a large black coloured suitcase that she pulled behind her and at least four plastic shopping bags grasped in her other hand that were also were crammed with clothing.

Getting out of the car I rushed to help her and being the bigger woman of the two of us, took hold of the suitcase only to discover that it was very old and did not have trolley wheels. Let me tell you that at the back of six in the morning, I was sweating like an Irish navvy by the time I lugged the thing into the boot of my car.

I watched Jessie pack the plastic bags around the case as she whispered, "This is awfully good of you, hen," then we're in the car and off.

I couldn't help but notice that she didn't give the building a backward glance.

I glance at her and see her face is pale and quietly ask, "Are you sure about this, Jessie?"

"Oh aye, absolutely," she turns her head to firmly nod at me.

After parking the car, we make our way through softly falling rain to the office building and the hours pass quickly, but I can tell by her quietness during the shift that Jessie is tense and any time I try to make conversation I can see she's jumpy.

At five minutes after nine we're done for the morning and heading back to the car park when my mobile phone activates with an incoming text message, but it's still raining so I decide to read it when I'm in the car.

"Right, your new flat," I smile encouragingly at Jessie, "but give me a minute to read this text."

I open the phone and see it's from Liz and simply reads: *call me when you can. X*

It's not like her to phone me when she knows I'm at work.

"Hello, Liz, it's me. What's up?"

"Mum," I can hear the sobs in her voice, "it was on the news at nine. That man who was arrested is appearing at court today and he's been charged with Beth's murder too."

"What's wrong, hen? Is she okay?" Jessie has a hand on my arm and is asking me, but I raise my hand to quieten her and tell Liz, "Listen to me, sweetheart. There's nothing we can do at the minute about this. Look, I'll drop Jessie off…"

"I can get a taxi, Maggie," Jessie is interrupting me.

"…then when I get home…"

"Honestly, it's no bother, hen," Jessie thinks she's being helpful, but I wish she'd just shut up!

"…you and I will talk about this, okay?"

"I'm telling you Maggie…"

I turn to my wee pal and snap at her, "Give me a minute, Jessie!"

Her face falls and I can see she's miffed at my attitude, but I've other things on my mind and as calmly as I can, I ask Liz, "Did you hear me, sweetheart? Wait till I get home, okay?"

"Okay, mum," is the quiet response.

I end the call and turning to Jessie, take a deep breath and say, "Sorry, I didn't mean to snap at you there," and tell her about what Liz has heard on the news.

"Oh my God, they've got him then? Is that not good news, hen?"

I stare at her, but realise that as much as I'm becoming fonder of Jessie I know she's not the brightest bulb in the pack and decide I'll be wasting my breath trying to explain what Alan had told me last night about why Graham Copeland is being charged with Beth's murder.

Tightly smiling, I tell her, "Let's get you up the road to your new home, eh?"

****

After waving aside Jessie's protest and humping her overladen suitcase up the flight of stairs to the flat, I'm ready for a cuppa, but make my excuse to go and explain I'm anxious to get home. After a grateful hug from her, I tell her I'll see her at the evening shift and make my way back to the car.

It's fortunate I'm travelling against the traffic heading into the city so I'm home quickly and find Liz sitting in her dressing gown at the kitchen table, an empty mug in front of her, hair dishevelled and her eyes red from crying. Seeing me provokes another bout of tears as she gives me a tight hug.

"Is it really over?" she sobs. "Have they caught him at last?"

I want to tell her yes, it's over, yet some part of me hates the thought of lying to her and all I can think to say is, "Well, let's wait and find out, eh?"

I'm annoyed with myself for I can't help but think I'm deceiving her, but consider that a vague answer is far preferable to an outright lie.

I sit her down at the table and turn to fill the kettle while I argue with myself that she deserves the truth. Then I consider if I do tell her the truth, will she be able to handle it or will the walls that she built up to protect herself from the loss of Beth come tumbling down once again.

Then a thought occurs to me and when I send her to the toilet to wash her face and brush her hair, I phone Colin Paterson. To my relief he's off duty today and when I explain I need him right away he doesn't ask what the problem is, just says he's coming and will be here in twenty minutes.

If I had any reservations about that young man, then I'm beginning to regret them for he's gone up a few notches in my estimation.

Liz returns from washing her face and I see she's not only tied her hair back, but changed into jeans and a loose black coloured tee shirt too; however, I don't tell her I've phoned Colin.

I make her French toast and she smiles, for when she was a young girl whenever something bothered her, whether it be exams, boyfriends or whatever, she could always rely on her mum telling her that a couple of slices of French toast resolved all issues.

"Are you still up for going to the lawyer's?" I ask her.

She nods and wiping crumbs from her mouth, replies, "Yes. I've been practising what I should tell him and I'd like you to be there so you can relate what Linda told you about him having a girlfriend."

I've given it some thought while she was in the bathroom and tell her, "I don't think it's a good idea to follow the news stories about the man who has been arrested. They'll only upset you."

"Might be hard to avoid," she sighs then says, "We might have the reporters back at the door."

I hadn't given that any thought but I'm determined if the buggers do turn up they'd get short shrift from me. I'd had enough of them the last time.

I'm pouring myself a second cup of tea when the doorbell rings and Liz springs up from her chair and says, "I'll get it."

She comes back a minute later dragging Colin by the hand and wearing a wide smile.

"You know I love you," she grins at me, 'but you are a very sneaky mother."

"Thought you might need a bit of support," I pretend to be aloof.

"If that's a brew on, Missus B," Colin smiles at me, "I haven't had any breakfast yet."

"Well, you're in for a treat," Liz turns to him and adds, "My mother makes the best French toast in the world?"

"Really?"

So while they settle themselves at the table, I'm back at the cooker though it occurs to me I should remind them it was me who was up for work before six this morning.

****

While they occupy the front room, I take the time to have myself a shower and think about the visit to the lawyer's office. One thing I make my mind up about is I will ensure that both Liz and I dress appropriately and in my bedroom, I look out a white blouse and my tailored navy blue skirted suit that's usually reserved for the occasional formal function or funerals. I startle for I realise that the last time I wore it was for Beth's funeral.

Wearing my dressing gown, I go downstairs to remind Liz about the twelve o'clock appointment. When Colin begins to rise to his feet, I tell him, "There's no need for you to go, son. Stay and watch some television. We'll not be back for some time because Liz has her second interview with Asda, but if you want to stay you can have dinner with us when we get back.

"Thanks, Missus B," he grins at me then smiling at Liz, tells her, "You'd better go and get changed, love."

I don't know what it is. Maybe it's because he addresses her as 'love' or perhaps it's the light in his eyes when he looks at her, but just then, right at that minute, I realise Colin really does have feelings for my daughter. And you know what?

I'm happy for them both.

****

We don't have to wait any time at all for a minute or two after twelve we're shown in to meet Alan's lawyer friend, Nicholas McSweeney, whose office is located in Exchange Square in the city centre. I glance at Liz and see a young woman, her fair hair pinned up, wearing a charcoal pencil skirt, light grey blouse, black high heels, matching black shoulder bag with her new coat carried over her arm and an immense surge of pride sweeps through me.

"Come in, come in," he stands up from and waves us towards two chairs that are placed in front of his desk. I don't know what I was expecting, but I see he's a small man with a large stomach that spills out across the waistband of his trousers and his loud paisley pattern tie is undone over a white shirt whose sleeves are rolled up to the elbow.

He's going bald, but slicked his hair back and looks more like a bookie than a divorce lawyer.

Reaching across the desk, he smiles and staring at me, says, "So you're Maggie. My goodness, Alan was right. Aye," he nods as he grins, "you're a looker right enough."

Now that takes me by surprise, but I'm determined not to blush and reply, "Yes, I'm Maggie, but it's my daughter Elizabeth who needs your help, Mister McSweeney."

I'm aware that Liz is trying not to laugh and I feel like slapping her, but now he's grinning and jovially waving us down into our seats, says, "Don't mind me, Maggie. I'm a happily married man with two grown up sons and believe me, with this figure," he pats at his midriff, "I'm not a threat to women anymore, more's the pity," he adds and causes Liz to snigger, but I think it's more her nerves than his joke.

"Can I call you Maggie?" he asks, but as he already has I simply nod and reply, "Yes, of course."

"And I'm Nick. I'm pleased to meet you both. Now, to put you in the picture, Alan's a good friend of mine and frankly," he holds his hands up, "anything he needs from me, he gets. Did he tell you we went to school together?"

"Eh, no, he's not actually spoken about you. He delivered your business card to us, to Liz I mean, but he's not told us anything about you."

"Well," he sits back and folds his hands across his belly, "Alan and I started at primary school and went through high school together. Look at me, a wee fat guy and I wasn't much different then. It was a rough place out in Easterhouse where we were brought up, but the big man never let anybody lay a finger on his wee pal." His brow creases, as he seems to remember and continues, "He took a couple of sore faces protecting me back in the day, you know." He rubs at his nose with a stubby forefinger and leaning forward as though about to reveal a secret, sombrely adds, "And I don't forget that kind of friendship."

He stares at us in turn and eyes narrowing, says, "Now, what exactly can I do for you ladies?"

****

Over an hour passes before we leave the law office and Liz is much cheered by the help that he promises. When she passed him the letter she had received from Ian's lawyer, he'd grinned when he'd read it and shaking his head, almost under his breath had said, "Who the hell do they think they're kidding?"

Even though we were with him a little over an hour it went very quickly and to be honest, though I was a bit sceptical when I first met him, Nick impressed with his straightforward, no nonsense attitude and though his questions were probing, he was very professional. In short, he's told us that he has an arrangement with a fellow lawyer who contracts a private inquiry agent, a former police officer called Tom McEwan who Nick will employ to make inquiries to verify Linda's information that Ian is now living with a woman in Garscadden.

"If that is correct and we can verify it," Nick had told us, "then there is every likelihood that we will be able to demonstrate your husband's extramarital situation is absolute grounds for divorce. Now," he peered at her, "can you confirm that you yourself, Liz, are not in a similar situation?"

Almost guiltily she had glanced at me, her face reddening, but then replied, "I'm seeing someone, Nick, but I assure you there has been no, ah…"

"Coitus?" he'd smiled at her.

She'd turned to me as if for an explanation and I had softly teased her, "Nick is asking if you and Colin have had a sexual relationship?"

"No!" she'd snapped back and looked horrified at the very idea.

"I think that's very clear," he'd smiled at me then turning to Liz, added, "But can I ask for the duration of this process, Liz, that you and your young man…Colin?"

She'd nodded, still embarrassed by his question.

"That you and Colin abstain form any sexual activity or at the very least," he'd leaned forward and peered at her over the top of his glasses, then lowered his voice and gruffly said, "don't get caught."

"How long is the process?" I'd asked while I'd fought to stop laughing.

"Well," he'd sat back and brow knitting while he considered my question before he replied, "an irretrievable divorce can be obtained if one of four points are proved. In your case, Liz, if we can prove adultery and unreasonable behaviour that is corroborated by a third party, you will have proved two of these points and that, I believe will be sufficient for you to win your case. The law says that a simple undefended divorce can be settled in two to three months. Where property is concerned…" he'd shrugged and was about to continue, but was interrupted by Liz who firmly told him, "There is no property to contest. Ian sold all our furniture and skipped the rent on our flat while I was detained in hospital. He even got rid of my daughter's toys too," she quietly added and I had glanced sharply at her, for that was something I hadn't known.

She'd turned to me and said, "Linda told me a week after I lost Beth, he'd sold the dolls house and some other things to one of his pals," then explained to Nick who Linda was.

"Is that so," his eyes had widened and he quickly made a note on his legal pad then asked Liz for details of both their landlord and Linda. It didn't escape my attention that she referred to Beth as her daughter and not their daughter.

As for the cost of the divorce and his legal bill, Nick had waved a hand at us and said, "We'll deal with that when the time arises." Promising to keep us apprised of how things developed, he left his desk to show us to the door, but not before giving me another red face when with an outrageous wink, he said, "Oh, and if things don't work out with Alan, give me a bell and I'll ditch the wife."

Making our way out into Exchange Square and as Liz's recall to Asda for her second interview is not till two o'clock, we decide to have some lunch in the city. As the car is parked with my old friend in Carrick Street, we make our way to the Wetherspoons in Argyle Street near to the Hielanman's Umbrella.

"So, what do you make of Nick McSweeney?" she asks me when we're seated with our food.

"Definitely a charmer," I smile.

"Seems that Alan Reid must have told him all about you, how he really fancies you," she replies and I know it's me who is being teased now.

You might think that I've forgotten about what Alan told me last night, but you'll be wrong. I just don't know how I can break that sort of information to Liz and after much thought I have decided that I will let things play out, let the police pretend that they've caught Beth's killer.

Why, you might ask? Why let that pompous man Tarrant get away with it?

Well, the reason is simple.

Closure.

If the real killer is unlikely to be found and if Liz can believe, rightly or wrongly, that the man who killed her daughter has been locked up, albeit for another child's murder, then I cannot in good faith tell her otherwise because I worry that to do so might bring the return of the pain and agony she underwent that almost cost her own life.

I just cannot do that to my child.

"I said, what was his house like? Are you even listening to me, mum?"

"Sorry, I was miles away, thinking about your divorce," I smile as I glibly lie.

"His house?" she presses me.

"Unbelievable," I smile at her and as best I can recall, describe Alan's two story flat or his duplex, then pretend how knowledgeable I am by explaining what a duplex is.

We agree that as she is already dressed for it, I will drive Liz to Asda in Maryhill and do some shopping while she is being interviewed.

Our meal finished, I excuse myself and nip to the loo and when I return, I see Liz texting on her phone.

"Colin?" I ask as I sit back down.

"Ah, no. Fiona."

I think I know most of Liz's friends or at least the ones who have stuck by her, but the name Fiona doesn't ring a bell. She sees I'm puzzled and as though I'm expected to know, then adds, "Fiona Thornton, Alan's daughter."

Yes, I'm taken aback and she can see that, so she continues, "Fiona and I kind of bonded when we met them on Saturday in the town. We've been texting and that's us arranging to meet for coffee."

I'm not exactly speechless, but I'm a little suspicious for I remember Alan's story about the two women he went out with and his daughter's reaction to the women, their obvious protectiveness of their father and wonder if this is some sort of ploy by Fiona to check me out.

"What?" I hear Liz ask.

"Oh, nothing," I force a smile.

"You don't approve of me seeing your boyfriend's daughter?"

"First, he's not my boyfriend…" but before I can continue, she interrupts, "Oh, grow up, mum. Alan's keen on you, a blind man can see that so why can't you? I mean you've already been out on a date with him…"

"That was just coffee…"

"Just coffee? He invited you to his home, mum!"

Her eyes narrow as she stares suspiciously at me, then asks, "When you were there, you didn't…I mean…"

"No, I didn't!" I angrily burst out, but loud enough to attract attention from some of the people at nearby tables.

Embarrassed, I tell her, "We just had some food, that's all!"

She's grinning at me and I realise I'm being good-naturedly goaded, then leaning forward, softly asks, "And why didn't you? I mean, you're a very attractive lady and he's quite a good looking man, well now that he's had his hair cut," she covers her mouth with her hand as she sniggers.

I'm still too embarrassed to discuss this and particularly with my daughter, but then in a more serious voice, she says, "Look, mum. Dad's been gone for five years. It's about time you got yourself a life and though I obviously *don't* know Alan as well as you do…"

There's that innuendo again!

"…guys like him don't come along that often. Take a chance on some life. For my sake as well as your own," she reaches across the table to take my hand.

I find my voice that's almost a whisper and ask, "For your sake?"

She gazes at me, surprise on her face, then replies, "You don't think I don't worry about you?"

I take a breath and shaking my head tell her, "Yes, I like him, but I worry that maybe I'm not the type of woman that he's looking for."

"What do you mean?"

I tell her about the two women he had in his life after his divorce and how neither had the approval of his daughters.

She gapes at me like I'm mad and says, "You don't think you're good enough for him?"

I'm swallowing hard and unable to reply, but then she gets angry and with tears in her eyes, continues, "You are a bright and attractive woman who has endured the worst nightmare that a mother and grandmother can and while going through it all without any thought for yourself, you have supported me during the darkest period of my life. Not good enough? Nonsense! Alan Reid will be lucky to have you and as for his daughters, it was Fiona herself who told me that!"

I can't help but stare at her in surprise and though tears trickle down her cheeks, she sees how stunned I am and continues again, "Fiona isn't daft, she knows about what happened to Beth and what we've endured and told me that her father has never spoken about anyone the way he talks about you. So do me a favour, mum. Live your life for yourself for a change and *stop* bloody worrying about everyone else; me included."

I can't speak and frankly don't care what people round about us hear or think. I get up from my chair and move around the table to tightly hold my daughter.

At last both of us are calm and I send her to the loo to wash her face while I sit quietly and ignore the curious stares.

Minutes later I see her returning and lifting her coat from her chair, help her into it then taking her arm in mine, I tell her, "Let's go, sweetheart."

****

She's been gone over half an hour and I'm at the till paying for my groceries when I feel my arm touched and turning I see it's Jessie's daughter, Mary.

"I've only got a minute, Maggie," she glances around her, "but just want to tell you thanks for what you did at the flat. Me and my ma are dead grateful, so we are. And she says you've ordered us a table for the kitchen? You shouldn't have bothered, really," but her face is flushed with pleasure.

"It was no bother, hen," I smile and remind her it's only second hand, but that I think it will do in the meantime until she gets what she really wants.

I can see from her face that she's supposed to be somewhere else, so I quickly tell her that Liz is in for a second interview.

"That's great," she grins at me then giving me a thumbs up, walks off back into the store.

I carry my purchases out to the car and am just loading them into the boot when I hear Liz calling me. Turning, I see her hurrying across the car park and from the expression on her face I know it's good news.

"I've got the job," she tells me, and taking my hands in hers, dances me around until I'm laughing too.

"I start a weeks training next Monday and that will be four hours a day to Thursday, then it's a sixteen-hour week on shifts, but there will be more hours available if I'm willing to work at short notice. Isn't that great?"

I'm puffed out and gasp, "Brilliant, sweetheart. Before you know it you'll be running the place."

She stops and staring at me, simply replies, "Thanks, mum," but I know there's more to that thank you than she can say.

It's almost three o'clock so I've time to deliver Liz back home and while we drive I put to her something that has been running through my head for a couple of hours.

"If you're going to be working shifts, sweetheart, I think we should consider getting you a car."

She turns to face me and already I can hear the protest, so before she puts up a fight I quickly continue, "Look, I know you've no money right now and won't have till you're earning a wage, but here's what I'm thinking. Right," I take a breath, "proposal one."

"Go on," she slowly says.

"I've savings put by, money that came from the insurance when your dad died. Not a fortune, but enough to keep me comfortable. What I'm proposing is that we look for a wee runner for you that I'll buy and you can pay me back a small sum each month."

"Mum, on top of my keep, that won't leave me with much and besides, I don't want to be in debt to you either."

"Okay," I nod, "then here's proposal two. I buy you the car outright and it comes out of your inheritance."

There's a couple of seconds silence and she laughs before she replies, "Mum! I'm your only child! If there is any inheritance, I get the lot! You're conning me, aren't you? You thought I'd just agree to your second proposal without giving it any thought, didn't you?"

I'm laughing and nodding as I tell her, "Okay, you've found me out. I'll buy you the car but on the condition you find it yourself. I don't want to be the one who chooses the car only for you to later tell me it's a banger, okay?"

There's a couple of seconds silence then she says, "You know, Colin's dad's a manager now, but he was a motor mechanic and he works in a garage over in Finnieston somewhere. Maybe I should get him to look for one for me."

"So, you agree," I turn to briefly glance at her.

"Yes, mum, I agree," she smiles. "Thank you."

When we arrive at the house Liz rushes in to tell Colin the good news about the job.

While I'm hanging up my coat I hear him call out, "I've put the kettle on, Missus B. Coffee or tea?"

"Tea, please," I call back and make my way upstairs to change out of my suit. Minutes later I'm downstairs in my working clothes and Colin is agreeing that he'll get his dad to look for a car for Liz, but then asks me, "What sort of price range are we talking about, Missus B?"

"Oh, anything between a fiver and a tenner," I smile, then tell him, "If he can get a bargain for say between five and six thousand pounds..."

"Mum! Five or six thousand pounds! That's too much," she's shaking her head and crossing her hands in front of her.

I glance at Colin, but he's pokerfaced, so I ask him, "Is that a lot for a second hand car, Colin?"

He screws his face, but it's Liz he tells, "Look, love, your mum's right. If you want something reliable and in reasonably good condition, even a three-door motor, you're going to pay about that anyway. With that kind of cash in your hand you can be looking at getting a thirteen or fourteen plate. Maybe even a fifteen plate, depending on what make you go for."

"Then it's settled," I quickly interject and sniffing the air, I ask, "Is that the kettle boiling?"

He grins and taking the hint makes his way into the kitchen.

I realise that Liz is still uncertain and softly tell her, "Then if you have your own car, you can run Colin around for a change, eh?"

That brings a smile to her face.

The phone rings and she rises to answer it and I hear her say, "Oh, hello Alan. Yes, she's here."

Handing me the phone she smirks when she whispers, "It's your boyfriend."

I take the phone from her and pull a face before I say, "Hello?"

"The man I spoke about," he quietly begins and I realise he must be in his office. "Still nothing from him about that issue we discussed, though he's been charged. He's appeared at the two o'clock sitting of the court and been remanded as you'd expect. His name will be released on the news tonight if it's not already on the radio."

I glance at the clock and see I've missed the three o'clock broadcast.

"Have you spoken to Liz about what we discussed?"

I glance at her, but she's walking into the kitchen so I reply, "I've decided not to. I'll explain when I see you."

"Oh, so you do want to see me again?" he light-heartedly replies.

"Look, pal, I met your friend Nick today and he reckons I'm quite a catch, so consider yourself lucky," I tease him.

"How did that go?"

"Better than we expected, but…"

"You'll tell me when you see me," he interrupts.

I smile and ask, "When do you want that to be?"

"What time do you finish work tonight? Oh, wait. It's at nine, isn't it?"

"Yes."

"Then why don't I pick you up and we can have some supper at mine?"

I'm quickly thinking and decide Liz can drop me at work, so reply, "That will be fine," and give him the address of the building.

****

Liz drops me at work and I assure her that I won't need a lift later, that at worst I'll get a taxi home.

"Tell Alan I said hello," she calls out as she drives off.

I'm smiling because it seems that in a few short days, Alan has become part of our lives, so much so that I can't deny I'm eager to see him tonight.

Jessie is already changed into her tabard apron and I see right away that something's bothering her; however, I wait till we're on the fourth floor before I ask.

"It's Ernie," she sighs. "He's been phoning me all day, but I've been dizzying his calls. Then Mary phoned me from her work to let me know he turned up at Asda to speak to her. Demanded to know where I am and she says he's going off his nut, wondering why I didn't go straight home after work this morning to make his breakfast. Lazy bastard," she shakes her head. "He's probably looking for a hand out to go to the pub and the bookies. That will be the real reason he's been looking for me."

"You're not thinking about changing your mind, leaving him I mean?"

"No, not at all," she vigorously shakes her head and head bowed, stares at the floor. "It's just that, well, I can't really explain how I feel at the minute."

I'm desperately keen to tell her that she's doing the right thing, but I know it's a decision that Jessie will have to come to herself. All I can do is remind her of her husband's violence towards her and the fact that she's holding down two jobs to provide him with money for his bevy and the bookies.

"Aye, I know you're right," she sighs again, but before she can say anything further, Tommy Burton arrives on the lift so we pretend we're hard at it mopping the corridor floor.

"Eh, Maggie, can I have a wee word?" he beckons to me.

I follow him through an open door into an office and with a glance towards Jessie to ensure he can't be overheard, he says, "Jimmy McKinnon is chucking it at the end of the week. He's got himself a job as a janitor in a council primary school. Anyway, that leaves a vacant supervisory position in the janitorial team here in the building and I was thinking of putting your name forward, if you're interested. It would mean a wee bit more responsibility, checking the cleaners' hours and their work and of course it would mean a change in your own hours, but with a better rate of pay. What do you think?"

"Why me, Tommy?"

"Well," he shrugs, "you're a damn sight smarter than the rest of them and you're not afraid to stand up for yourself." He hesitates before he continues, "Sometimes working with a crowd of women can be a bit daunting for a man and to be honest, I don't think it would do much harm to have a woman on the team."

Typical me, though, because I'm a bit suspicious of his motives and so I say, "I'm grateful for the opportunity, but can you give me a day or two to think about it?"

"Eh? Oh, aye, of course," he nods and with a wave, he's gone.

"What was that all about," Jessie asks as she watches the lift descending to the next floor.

"I don't really know," I quietly reply, then add, "Tommy's looking for a woman to join the janitorial team and asked me, but I'm wondering if I'm the only one he's asked."

"He's a right sleekit git, is Tommy Burton. I'd be wondering too," Jessie sneers.

"Anyway, I haven't given him an answer, so keep it to yourself for now," I tell her.

"No problem, hen. My lips are tighter than an Aberdonian's wallet."

The rest of the shift rushes by during which I tell Jessie that I'm getting picked up from work and without me saying a word, the bugger cottons on to the fact it's a man.

She's grinning like the proverbial Cheshire cat and asks, "Anybody I know?"

"Just a friend," I start to say, then can't keep my mouth shut when I add, "He's a policeman. Someone who is working on Beth's investigation."

I don't give her any more information and to my surprise she doesn't ask any further.

In the locker room at a couple of minutes to nine, it's the usual chatter and cheerios' when Jessie and I are signing ourselves out of the building.

I don't know if I mentioned, but we enter and exit the building through a service door in a wee lane at the side of the building and it's very well lit at night. It wasn't always like that but we complained to our company that we weren't happy leaving in the dark and last year they got the situation sorted.

I push open the heavy fire door and Jessie is rambling on about looking forward to the delivery of the kitchen table tomorrow when she stops dead and I almost walk into her.

"Ernie," I hear her say and I can hear the fear in her voice.

Then I see him.

He's leaning with his back against a wall smoking a cigarette that he then throws to the ground and stamps on.

He takes a step towards us and don't ask me why, but I suddenly find I'm pulling at Jessie and pushing her behind me.

He stares at me then ignores me as he addresses Jessie and says, "You didn't come home after work today and you're not answering your mobile, hen. What the fuck's going on, eh?"

It's then I realise his voice is slurred and realise he's been drinking. My throat's dry and I'm about to tell Jessie to go back into the building, but I hear the door squeak open. I don't turn around, but I sense that someone else is coming out into the lane.

"I'm not coming home, Ernie," her voice is faltering. "I've found somewhere else to live. We're finished, you and me."

He steps to one side as though to get a better look at her and I turn slightly to face him using my body to shield Jessie.

Listen to me. Who the hell do I think I am? Wonder *bloody* Woman?

"What?" he snarls and his eyes narrow when pointing at me, he says, "You going to live with this fucking lesbian whore?"

I almost burst out laughing. I've been called a few names in my life, but that's definitely a first.

"It's none of your business where I'm living," I hear her voice become a little stronger as she shuffles behind me and I feel her hands clasping my waist.

"You're leaving me and the boys without any money? How the *fuck* are we supposed to get by?"

"Try finding a job, you lazy bastard!" she hisses over my shoulder at him.

His eyes widen and I can see saliva dribbling down his unshaven chin.

You might recall when I first met Ernie at their flat I mentioned he was fat and balding and when I saw him he was seated in his armchair, but now he's stood in front of me and I see he's nearly six feet tall.

"Bitch!" he suddenly screams and lunges at Jessie, but of course I am sheltering her so I'm in the way of his grasping hands.

Now, I've never in my life been in a fight other than playground school tussles when I was about five years old, but I realise in that split second that if I don't defend myself then Jessie or more likely me will get hurt, so I raise my hands to ward him off.

It's completely the wrong move.

He's swinging a punch at Jessie, but idiot that I am I try to grab at his arm and getting in the way I take the blow to my face.

I've never been punched before and believe me it really did hurt.

I know that I'm falling and that I'm being knocked to the ground and as I'm falling…no hang on. You know that old chestnut about seeing stars? Well, I didn't see any stars, but almost in slow motion, what I did see and am conscious of is the ground rushing up at me and I hear shouts and screams, but it's more than just Jessie. I hit the ground with such force I'm winded and gasping for breath, but then a heartbeat later my head hits the cobbled lane and as they say, the lights go out.

****

"Maggie! Maggie, can you hear me?"

It's a bit difficult opening my eyes and when I do I get the shock of my life at the brightness and squeeze my eyes tightly shut. It's only a few seconds later when I've adjusted to the light I realise I'm lying down in the back of an ambulance and that it's Alan who is seated on the opposite stretcher and who is holding my hand.

"Maggie," he bends towards me and asks again, "can you hear me?"

I try to smile but it feels as though my lower jaw isn't working and then the pain in my head hits me and I hear myself moan.

"Don't try to talk…" he begins, but then a green uniformed ambulance woman stares down at me over his shoulder and says, "Leave it the now, pal. We're taking her to the Royal if you want to come too."

"Aye, I do," I hear him say, but I can't keep my eyes open and think I'm about to fall asleep again.

****

I open my eyes again and this time the light is more subdued and staring at a white painted ceiling I realise I'm in a room.

"Thank God you're awake," I hear Alan say and turning my head, though it hurts, I see him sitting by my bed and he's still holding my hand.

"Eh, what happened?" I hear myself mumble.

"Doesn't matter at the minute," he quietly says and I see concern etched on his face. "What matters is that you're going to be okay, Maggie. The doctors have examined you and told me you have a bad concussion as a result of your head hitting the ground. Do you understand?"

I try to nod I do understand, my but my head hurts so much I just lie there and stare at him. I feel a trickle of tears running down my cheeks and watch as Alan uses a hanky or something to wipe at my face.

He's staring down at me and quietly says, "Lucky it was your head and nothing vital, eh?"

I don't bother trying to reply, just narrow my eyes at his poor joke. There's movement behind him and the next thing I see is Liz, leaning over the other side of the bed.

"Mum!" she's crying and grabbing at my free hand.

I try to tell her I'll be fine, but all that comes out is a rambling noise and then a male nurse behind Liz says, "Maybe we should give Missus Brogan another opportunity to get some rest, eh?"

Much as I'd really like to know what did happen, right now all I want to do is close my eyes.

CHAPTER SEVENTEEN

I've woken with a blinding headache and can see that I'm in a hospital room on my own. I've no idea what time it is but I know it's not daytime because there's no light filtering through from the badly fitting curtain on the window. The room door is tightly closed, but I can hear people speaking as they pass by in the corridor outside. Turning my head slowly I can see a water jug on the bedside cabinet and I'm really gasping for a drink, so push myself into a sitting position and believe me, the way my head feels, that's no easy feat I can tell you. That's when I realise I've a needle running from a cannula that is inserted into the back of my right hand that in turn is attached by a tube to a stand with a bag of clear fluid. My previous training tells me it's probably a saline drip. I'm also wearing a hospital gown and my eyes narrow for I can't remember being stripped.

In fact, I can hardly remember why I'm here in the first place.

Apart from when I had my tonsils removed as a wee girl and when I delivered Liz, I've had no other reason to be in hospital and to be honest, my head is that sore I'm a little worried that something might be seriously wrong with me.

At last I'm sitting upright and I sluggishly reach for the jug and conscious of the drip attached to me, very slowly pour myself a half glass of water.

I'm licking my lips as I drink and let me tell you, right at that time no wine could ever taste sweeter than that glass of tepid water.

I can feel the water dripping down onto my chin, but I really don't care and just as I'm about to refill the glass the door opens to admit a young blonde haired nurse about my Liz's age who says, "Ah, you're awake, Maggie. How you feeling? My name's Jenny."

I watch her as she flicks with a finger at the bag of fluid then stares down at me and smiles.

I try to smile back but even that's an effort and nodding my head and my voice a whisper, I tell her, "Like I've gone five rounds with Mike Tyson."

She's grinning as she pours me another glass of water and replies, "From what I hear, it sounds like you did. Are you up for some visitors?"

"Eh, yes. What time is it?"

She glances at the wee watch she has pinned to her tunic and tells me, "It's a little after seven in the evening."

Even in the dull state of my mind, I know it can't still be Tuesday because I finished work at nine in the evening and a little befuddled, I ask, "What day?"

"Wednesday," she grins at me and says, "You've had a right good sleep. Shall I send them in, then?"

"Eh, yes, please."

"Right, well, before we let them in, let's get you tidied up a bit, eh? You'll not want them seeing you with your hair like a burst mattress."

I don't see from where she produces it, but the next thing I know is she has a hair brush in her hand and is roughly combing my hair into some semblance of order, then I hear her mutter, "I'd better mind those stitches."

Before I can ask what stitches, she's standing back and grinning, says, "You'll do."

I watch her leave and seconds later the door is opened by Liz with Alan behind her.

She's fighting back the tears and rushes to hug me while Alan stands back, but is that relief I see on his face?

"Oh. Mum, you'll be the death of me, worrying about you," she gasps. "What the hell were you thinking, squaring up to that man?"

"What man? What happened?" but she sees through my pretence and gives me a grim scowl.

It's coming back to me now and I quickly ask, "Jessie! Is she all right?"

"She's fine, Maggie," it's Alan who replies. "She's worried about you and told me she's coming up to see you when she finishes her shift tonight."

"Tonight?" I duly repeat, then remember it's now Wednesday and foolishly ask, "What happened to the rest of Tuesday night and all day Wednesday?'

"You slept most of it," he grins at me.

"Do you remember anything at all?" Liz asks me and draws up a chair, but before I can reply, she says, "Is it okay if Colin comes in?"

"Eh, of course," I tell her, but it's Alan who goes to the door and beckons Colin into the room.

He gives me a shy wave and says, "Hi Missus B. Hear you've been in the wars, eh?"

The two men stand together while Liz returns to her chair and I tell them, "I remember Jessie's husband waiting for her outside the building and I remember he was going to hit her, but…" I stop and shudder. "I think I got in the way."

"That's not Jessie's version or what your pals who were leaving at the time told me," Alan says. "According to them you were protecting Jessie and lifting your hands as though you were going to get into a boxing match with Jessie's man."

"Oh," then my eyes narrow as I recall.

He punched me on the face!

My hand tentatively reaches for my left cheek.

Alan's smiling as he says, "Don't be looking in any mirrors for a while, Maggie. You've got a right shiner there, I can tell you, but fortunately, no real damage was done other than you'll be using blusher for a couple of weeks."

So that's why my eye and my cheek bloody hurts, I'm angrily thinking.

That bullying…*bastard*!

He punched me!

"Anyway," Alan continues, "it was your head hitting the ground that caused the doctor at the casualty the most concern. The Neuro Consultant who was called out has examined you and at first considered sending you over to the Neuro at the Queen Elizabeth Hospital, but once you'd been X-rayed, she changed her mind. Anyway, she's satisfied that apart from the concussion, there's no damage to your head. In fact, apparently the X-ray even indicated you had a brain there. However, they did have to sew up a gash in your scalp so you lost a patch of hair, but don't worry, they assure us it'll grow back," I can see the twinkle in his eyes as he tries not to laugh.

"Is he trying to be funny?" I turn to Liz, but wiping at her eyes with a handkerchief, she's grinning now so there's no support there.

I sigh at the idiocy of the two of them and turning, ask Colin, "Am I going to get any sense out of you or are you as daft as these two?"

He holds up his hands and grinning, replies, "I only know what I've been told, Missus B, but here's a suggestion."

He turns to Liz and nodding to the door, says, "Why don't we go and grab a cuppa if we can find a machine and let Alan tell your mum what happened, eh?"

With a worried glance at me, she nods and telling me they'll be back in ten minutes, I watch them leave.

Alan sits down in the only chair and drawing it close to the bed, gently takes a hold of my hand.

"First thing you should know is that you're in for one more night, but if the Neuro Consultant is happy with you in the morning, you'll be discharged. Now, last night. Well, to my embarrassment I was late coming for you and got to your building minutes after it happened to find you on the ground covered with a coat and your friend Jessie telling me the police and an ambulance had been called. Of course she didn't have a clue who I was, but she does now," he smiles at me. "Apparently she knew I was coming to pick you up and you'll be surprised to hear I'm now officially your boyfriend. Or at least, that's what she was telling the other women while I was there."

I'm smiling back at him and ask, "Is that okay with you?"

He clears his throat and replies, "I wouldn't have it any other way. Right, when he was arrested, Jessie's husband, Ernie Cochrane, was taken to the casualty here at the Royal by the first police car that attended."

"What, there was more than one police car?"

"Aye, three cars and a handful of beat officers," he smiles. "Whoever made the call said there was a riot going on and believe me, when I saw the women round about Cochrane, I thought so to. What a kicking he took from them. The women were literally pushing each other out of the way to have a go at him. Frightening, it was," he shudders.

I'm frowning when I ask what happened to him?

"It seems that the other women who were leaving the building and saw him punch you…" he stops and his eyes narrow when he asks, "I think one of them is called Eileen? Is that right?"

"Eileen McNulty. A big woman with dyed blonde hair?"

"That's her," he nods and slowly blows through pursed lips. "Anyway, the long and short of it is that Eileen and the other women set about Cochrane and gave him one hell of a hiding. Talk about handbags at dawn," he grimaces. "Anyway, as I said, when the uniformed cops arrived they had to take him to the casualty for treatment. If you think you look poorly, you should see the state of him," he wryly grins. "After the doctors patched him up he was charged with seriously assaulting you and a common law assault on his wife."

"What will happen to him?"

"Well, by the time he was patched up and discharged from the casualty and the arresting officers returned him to Stewart Street police office, it was after midnight. Because of the charge of domestic assault on his wife, he's been detained in custody as of today and due to appear on the next lawful day at the Sheriff Court and that means tomorrow. Don't worry, though," he grimly adds, "he won't be coming near you or if he knows what's good for him, his wife either."

Curiously, I'm not so much worried about myself as poor Jessie having to face Ernie again.

The door opens and the young blonde nurse Jenny pops her head in and grimacing, says, "Sorry, but that's visiting time finished. Maybe take a couple of minutes to say cheerio to your husband, Maggie, then I'll come back and change your drip," then she's gone and the door gently closes.

I'm taken aback, but not so much as Alan who stares at me then bursts out laughing. I find I'm laughing too and that's when I realise my headache is all but gone.

It seems that humour is a powerful remedy for stress.

Slightly embarrassed we wordlessly stare at each other then he rises from the chair to kiss me. He's standing upright and staring down at me when the room door is opened by Liz who hastens in to say goodbye, while Colin, holding a plastic cup in his hand, waves from the door.

It's only when Liz and Colin have left the room and before he goes through the door, Alan turns and quietly tells me, "I have some news about the arrest of Graham Copeland, but it's not good. I'll tell you about it when I see you tomorrow."

****

Well, talk about a cliff-hanger? As you'll guess I spent the rest of that night wondering what it was Alan had to tell me and a number of different things went through my head.

Just as she'd promised Alan, Jessie arrived at quarter past nine with her daughter Mary who carried a big bunch of flowers and a Get Well Soon card signed by all the cleaners. Though it was well past the visiting time, Mary persuaded Jenny the nurse to let them into the room for a couple of minutes.

Actually the visit was a washout in the real sense of the word for Jessie couldn't speak. All she did was hold my hand and weep for the five minutes she was in.

"We're so sorry," said Mary, who was close to tears herself and kept apologising.

I spent the short visit trying to convince Jessie that she was not to blame for her husband's behaviour and even made her tearfully smile when I said, "I might have been beaten up, but isn't that what best pals are for?"

When Jenny came to remind them the five minutes was up I didn't forget to ask Jessie to give my thanks to Eileen and the rest of the women.

Shortly after they'd gone and without explaining why, I managed to persuade my nurse Jenny to let me visit the ward's television room in time for the ten o'clock news bulletin and she only consented if I agreed to be wheeled there in a chair. To my disappointment there was nothing on the news about the murder of Kylie Murdoch or Beth.

It left me wondering that as I'd missed a day and Copeland's appearance at the court had been on Tuesday, it must now be old news.
****

When she'd wheeled me back to my room, Jenny found a couple of women's magazines for me to read, but the next thing I know I'm being woken by a cleaner coming into my room and pulling open the curtains and I see it's a bright day outside.

The early shift Staff Nurse, Carol, provides me with a towel, soap and a clean gown and I shower in the room's en-suite.

"Your daughter phoned earlier, Maggie," she tells me, "to let you know she'll bring a change of clothes and she'll be here to pick you up when you've been discharged."

In the en-suite I stare for some time into the mirror and I'm appalled at my face. Granted it's mostly bruising, but my left eye is bloodshot and I realise it will be at least a week before it's fully healed and what I'm thinking is that right now I could use some of Jessie's jar of Arnica.

It is a little after ten when the Neuro Consultant arrives in my room; a tall, statuesque African woman in her late thirties who examines me and makes me blush when she introduces me in a loud voice to her male colleague as, "Missus Brogan who was injured protecting her friend against a drunken madman."

God, I'm thinking, I've a reputation I don't deserve.

I try to explain that's not really what happened, but all I do is present myself as some kind of reluctant hero and to be honest, the whole thing embarrasses me.

Anyway, when she's finished examining me she pats me on the shoulder and tells me I'm fit to be discharged, but cautions me that if I feel faint or dizzy I'm to have someone bring me straight back to the ward and insists I take the next few days easy; no work and no strenuous activity.

The two of them have no sooner left the room than the door opens and it's my Liz who carries a bag with my clothes and thoughtfully, a large jar of coffee and packet of biscuits for the ward staff.

However, she doesn't exactly cheer me up when she greets me with, "God, mum, you look a right sight."

I spend five minutes changing and applying blusher and lipstick in the en-suite, but when I finish and stare at my image I frown for I've ended up looking like Frankenstein's monster.

Bugger it I decide and rub off all the make-up. I'll wear my wounds with pride, I tell myself, and just won't leave the house for a month.

When I come out of the en-suite Liz is grinning when she hands me a large pair of sunglasses and says, "Maybe you'll not look so gruesome with these on."

Much as I don't appreciate her wit, she's right. The glasses hide most of my sore face.

On the way home she chatters away like a budgie on speed and tells me that Alan's working today, but that he hopes to pop in at some point because he wants to speak with me.

"Do you think it's personal or is it to do with the man they've arrested?" she briefly glances at me.

I won't lie to her and tell her that before he'd left last night he'd said he'd some news about the man charged with Beth's murder, but it wasn't good.

She drives in silence for a while and then says, "Do you want me to be there when he arrives?"

"How do you feel about that if it's *not* good news?"

"It is what it is," she replies and again I realise how much she's come on since that horrible day.

When we arrive home I glance at the house and even though I was only in the hospital for such a short time, it's a real pleasure to be home. When she pushes open the door I see Liz stoop to pick up a card and turning, she says, "There's flowers for you been left next door with the McPherson's."

"Oh, right, you go and get them and I'll stick the kettle on," I tell her and taking my bag from her, make my way into the kitchen.

A couple of minutes later Liz arrives back with a bouquet of a dozen red roses that she hands me and reading the card, I smile when I see they're from Alan.

When Liz reads the card she grins and says, "You do know what a dozen red roses signifies, don't you?"

"No, but I'm certain you're about to enlighten me," I glower at her, expecting some witticism.

She sees my face and holding up her hands, says, "I'm not joking here, mum. A dozen red roses are the definitive symbol for true love. Honest," she laughs. "You seem to have Alan Reid well and truly hooked."

Not the expression I might have used, but I smile anyway and am glad to receive the flowers.

"Right, you get the tea on while I put these in a vase," I tell her. While she fills the kettle, she says, "That was odd."

"What?"

"Well, when I was walking up the McPherson's drive I could see her, Moira I mean, at the window behind the curtain watching me, but when she saw that I saw her she ducked out of sight."

"Maybe she was a bit embarrassed at getting caught watching you."

"Well, when I chapped their door…do you know they don't have a doorbell?"

"What's that got to do with anything?"

"Anyway," she tosses her hair, "it was Willie who came to the door and he'd the flowers in his hand, so Moira must have told him I was coming to the door."

"What did he say?"

"That's the odd thing. He didn't say anything and wouldn't even look at me. Never even spoke, just handed me the flowers and shut the door before I could thank him. Weird, eh?"

I think back to the night of the argument they had and tell her about what I heard.

"So you think they know you heard them and that's why they're embarrassed?"

"Possibly," I shrug. "You know how quiet a couple they are."

"Aye, but still weird," she grins, then adds, "Did you know they're moving?"

"Moving?"

"Aye, there's a 'For Sale' sign in their garden."

That causes me to walk to the front window where peering out across the high hedge that separates our gardens, I see right enough there's a pole with a sign planted in their grass at the end of their driveway.

"You know as well as I do, sweetheart," I turn away from the window and tell her, "they're not the chattiest of couples so no, I didn't know they were moving on."

"I'm going to check the iPad and see what they're asking for the house," she mischievously grins, "and maybe get a look to see if there's any pictures on the site of the inside."

I can't explain why or maybe it's because we're talking about the neighbours, but I then tell her of Peter McGregor's attempt to chat me up. Then his wife Wilma's rant at me when she accused me of approaching him.

Liz's eyes widen as I relate the story and her hand over her mouth, she rocks back and forth on her chair and giggling, cries out, "Never!"

"Oh aye," I nod, but decide not to tell her what Wilma said about Peter's fondness of young girls. No, that would have maybe set Liz's mind off wondering if he was somehow connected to Beth's murder.

"What's your Colin up to, today?" I ask her.

She smiles at me and lampoon's my voice when she replies, "Oooh, *your* Colin, is it? Coming around to him then are you?"

"I've never said anything bad about him," I huffily reply.

"Well, for your information, he's on shift…" she hesitates.

"What?"

"He's taking me for dinner to meet his mum and dad on Friday night. Says he wants his dad to discuss what kind of car I should go for. Is that okay, mum?"

"Oh," I'm stuck for something to say. It's a big move him taking Liz to met his parents and so I make light of it by smiling and reminding her that she can purchase as high as six thousand pounds.

She doesn't get the chance to respond for the doorbell rings and I tell her, "I'll get it."

When I open the door I'm surprised to see it's Alan, but there's a man stood slightly behind him, a sturdy looking man about fifty wearing a beige coloured raincoat and with a scar on his right cheek.

"Maggie," Alan says to me in a polite, but formal voice, "we need to speak. Can we come in?"

****

Once they're seated together on the couch and Liz and I settle down into the armchairs. I take a good look at the man and see he's well dressed in a good dark grey coloured suit, dark hair greying at the temples and there's something about him that makes me think he's trustworthy. Female intuition? I don't really know; it's just a feeling I get. The scar on his cheek that looks about two to three inches long, is faded and looks old.

"I'm sorry, what did you say your name is again?" I ask him.

"Charlie Miller, Missus Brogan, I'm a Detective Superintendent and on Monday I was appointed as the Head of the CID for the north of the city and the Argyle area. I'm Alan's new boss, as it were and if I can just explain…" he stops and peers at me and says, "Can I call you Maggie?"

"Eh, yes, please do and this is my daughter, Liz," I nod towards her.

"Well, if you call me Charlie it makes things a lot easier," he returns my nod. "Now, I've known Alan here for a number of years and at one time I used to be his Detective Inspector when he was a DC and we worked together at Maryhill. Before I begin I want you to know that I trust Alan and he tells me that he trusts you. Would that be correct, Maggie?"

"Yes," I slowly nod.

"Liz?" he turns to her.

"Yes, I suppose so," she dully replies, but I hear a wee bit of suspicion in her voice.

"Well, in that case I'd like to think I can trust you too, so if you bear with me, I'll explain why I'm here."

He takes a breath then says, "You are of course aware that a man called Graham Copeland has been arrested for the murder of the wee girl, Kylie Murdoch. Copeland was also charged by the SIO..." he paused and is about to explain when Liz interrupts with, "DCI Tarrant, the Senior Officer Investigating."

He tightly smiles and says, "Correct. However, what I'm about to tell you both I trust will remain confidential for reasons that I will explain later."

I don't miss the briefest of glances he gives Alan who at this point has said nothing.

Charlie continues but directs his attention to Liz.

"In his enthusiasm to solve your daughter's murder, DCI Tarrant has mistakenly taken what little evidence there is that he believes implicates Copeland in Bethany's murder..."

"Beth!" Liz angrily snaps. "We called her Beth."

I flinch at her harsh tone, but Charlie simply nods and says, "My apologies. Beth. Anyway, DCI Tarrant has taken what little evidence he believes implicates Copeland in Beth's murder and on the basis of that, he's charged him with her murder."

He glances again at Alan and says, "Unfortunately, what DCI Tarrant was unaware of but what Alan here discovered was that on the night Beth was killed, Copeland had earlier that afternoon been detained for shoplifting at the Marks and Spencer store at the Fort Shopping Centre out in Easterhouse, just off the M8. What Alan was able to prove is that from the material time Copeland was detained by the security staff then handed over to the local officers and up till his eventual release from custody, this lengthy period of detention and arrest provided him with a watertight alibi. In essence, what it means is that it was impossible for Copeland to be responsible for Beth's murder."

I'm shocked and snapping my head round to look at Liz, I see her pale.

"I'll stick the kettle on," Alan rises from his seat and makes his way into the kitchen.

"I'm sorry," I hear myself say, "but surely that would have been checked, his whereabouts on the night Beth died?"

Alan passes me and hands Liz a glass of water that she gulps down, then taking the glass from her returns to the kitchen and I hear him busy himself with the mugs.

I see Charlie's throat tighten and his eyes follow Alan through the door, then he replies, "You're correct of course, Maggie, but it seems that when he was interviewed Copeland couldn't recall where he was that many months back. The standing operational procedure in the circumstances is that a background check should have been completed, but for some reason that I can't explain, the inquiry team missed the fact that during the time of Beth's murder, he was first detained then under arrest."

"So my daughter's killer is still out there?" I hear Liz mutter and I'm now worried that she is so angry, she might kick off.

"Yes, Liz, I regret he is," he nods.

"And what about Tarrant?" I ask. "Will he get away with this…this…stupid *bloody* mistake?"

"For the sake of a conviction, I'm sorry but yes, he will," he nods then adds, "Let me explain."

I hear the kettle whistle and my hands clasped tightly on my knees, I suddenly realise my throat is parched.

He continues to address Liz when he says, "If it becomes public knowledge that DCI Tarrant has charged Copeland with your daughter's murder and that, ah…" he sighs, "let's be frank here, a stupid mistake was made, it will cast aspersions on Tarrant's competency in handling the Kylie Murdoch murder inquiry. Now," he raises a hand, "there is DNA evidence and, please keep this to yourselves," he glances at us both, "Forensic fibre evidence that unequivocally indicates Copeland murdered that wee lassie. However, in the hands of a capable defence counsel and believe me, ladies, there are many of them out there, if it's learned he's charged Copeland with Beth's murder *without* real evidence, Tarrant's competency as the SIO will be questioned. If such a mistake becomes an issue at court…

"You mean, if we kick up a fuss?" Liz hisses at him.

He stares at her and then quietly responds, "Yes, as you so succinctly put it, Liz; if you kick up a fuss…"

Alan brings the tray with four mugs into the room, but stands till Charlie finishes speaking.

"…then it will almost likely throw doubt on the DNA and Forensic evidence and quite possibly cause a jury to hand down a not proven or even a not guilty verdict in the case against Copeland for Kylie's murder."

"So," I hastily interrupt before Liz goes off on one, "correct me if I'm wrong, but what you're telling us is that your…the Crown Office is it?"

"Yes."

"Your Crown Office will simply drop the charge of murdering Beth and proceed with the other murder charge and you hope that nobody will be the wiser and realise Tarrant has made a huge mistake?"

"Yes and no," he's nodding. "His solicitor will of course realise that the charge of murdering Beth is no longer on the indictment but unless they learn otherwise, will probably assume that Crown Office has simply decided not to proceed with that charge. However, if his defence team at time of trial are aware of the circumstances of the charge being dropped because of a police foul-up, then they will concentrate their argument on the police incompetence and it is more than likely Copeland will get off and not be convicted."

More like Tarrant's incompetence, I'm thinking but I keep the thought to myself.

"I assume like me," he adds, "you will not want the wee girl's mother to go through the same heartache you are currently experiencing."

"Nothing to do with the police's reputation for solving crime, then?" Liz snaps at him.

"Oh, don't get me wrong," he wryly shakes his head. "There's that too, because if Copeland gets off with this, the knock-on effect it will have will be…." he pauses and shakes his head, "frankly it will be calamitous, for every case where Tarrant has obtained a conviction will come under the microscope and the appeals will flood Crown Office. I can only imagine the man hours and resources as well as the years that will be spent reinvestigating those cases and in the long run, it will be the public who suffer."

"Even though the convictions are probably genuine?" I ask.

He nods and quietly replies, "Martin Tarrant isn't a *bad* detective though he has his…how can I put this? His unique way of doing things."

Alan lays the tray down onto the small coffee table and starts handing out the mugs.

"Yes, we've experienced his *unique* way, as you put it," I bitterly tell him.

As Charlie accepts his mug, he nods his thanks and turning to me, continues, "I wasn't in charge when the decision was made to downsize Beth's murder investigation, Maggie. However, I am in charge now."

"So, what does that mean?" I ask.

With both his hands wrapped round the mug, he gives Alan a quick glance and says, "The polis, like any other professional organisation…"

I ignore Liz's derisory snort.

"…have their internal strife and politics, so, while I cannot be seen to publicly countermand a decision that was made by my predecessor, I have instructed Alan here to assemble a small team and reinvestigate your granddaughter's murder; a case review of the evidence as it were. For the duration of that investigation, he will assume the rank of acting Detective Inspector and will report directly to me. In essence, DCI Tarrant will no longer be involved."

I feel my chest tighten as I look at Alan who gives me a small but encouraging smile.

Liz remains sullenly silent and I can only imagine the rollercoaster of emotion that she is experiencing.

Charlie continues, "The only thing I must stress is that I don't want to give you false hope." He nods to him and says, "Alan is a good and competent detective, but so are many of the detectives who worked on the inquiry from the outset and unfortunately as you are aware, they were unable to find a suspect."

"How many of your detectives will be working on the new investigation?" I ask.

"I can give Alan a team of five and that will include the police officer who served as the liaison officer during the first days of the investigation. A constable…" his eyes narrow questioningly as he glances at Alan who speaks for the first time when he says, "Sheila Gardner, boss."

"Five, is that all?" Liz scowls at him.

"You have to remember, Liz," he patiently tells her, "that most of the legwork and door knocking has been done. The team will be going over all the statements and what little evidence there is with a fine tooth comb to ensure nothing has been missed."

"But isn't that what Alan was already doing?"

"Yes, it is, but there is far too much for one officer to deal with on his own and besides," he smiles, "even for a detective as competent as Alan is, it's good practise to have other officers to double check his work and share the burden of such a major investigation."

"Now," he sips at his coffee for the first time, "do you have any questions for me?"

She glances at me before she asks, "What will happen to him, DCI Tarrant?"

I'm a little tense for her voice is calm and uncannily controlled. Charlie's expression remains the same, but it's the way he replies when he says, "Martin Tarrant will for the meantime and until the Kylie Murdoch trial is concluded, continue in the role of DCI; however, I expect that in due course he will seek promotion and the police are always looking for capable administrators."

"So, he gets a promotion even though he's fucked up!" she snarls.

"Liz!" I'm livid by her language.

"Sorry, mum" I can see she's close to tears and without warning, she suddenly gets to her feet and leaves the room, then I hear her rushing upstairs.

"I'm sorry, she's not usually so rude."

"No worries, Maggie," he grimly smiles at me. "I believe she has every right to be rude. The police haven't served her very well. In fact," he smiles humourlessly, "she's absolutely correct. We have fucked up, pardon me, but believe me when I tell you that I know that Alan and his team will do everything they can to resolve this situation. On that you have my word. Now," he nods at my face, "let me digress because I've been hearing you've had a wee issue yourself the other night?"

Alan's grinning and I find myself blushing when I reply, "As you see, I forgot to duck and came second, but the man that did it was arrested."

"Aye, Alan told me the story. Says that you stood up for your pal and when you're up against a man bigger than you it takes some guts, so well done to you. Now," he turns to Alan, "your man here has been upfront with me and tells me that you two have developed a close friendship. Much as I'm pleased for you both and let me tell you," he winks at me, "this guy deserves a break, can you assure me there won't be a conflict of interest in the investigation?"

"No, not at all," I hurriedly assure him, but he's smiling and I can see I'm being teased. "Oh, very good," I frown at him, but I'm also a little pleased.

"Right then," he slaps his hands onto his legs and suddenly getting to his feet, says to Alan, "I'm heading back to Maryhill to sort out your team, but as of now and as it's your rest day anyway, I suggest you stay here and liaise with Missus Brogan, okay?"

"Fine by me, boss," Alan replies.

"Maggie," he turns to me and shakes my hand, "I know I've upset your Liz, but there was no easy way to break this to you both and for that I truly am sorry. I only hope that Alan and the team can deliver some good news in the near future. Remember, if there's anything that you need answered or anything my guys can do for you, if Alan's not immediately available I've no objection to you or Liz giving me a call on my direct line, okay? Alan will provide you with my mobile number."

I see him to the door while Alan returns the mugs to the kitchen.

A minute later Liz comes down the stairs and I can see she's been crying and seems surprised that Alan is still here.

"Oh," she starts, "I thought you'd gone. Sorry," she shakes her head, "what I mean is…"

"No need to apologise, Liz," he kindly says, "and my boss said to tell you he's sorry for upsetting you. It's been distressing for you hearing about this. Look, I assure you, me and the team I'm getting will do our very best."

"I know you will," she nods, then takes a breath and a little brighter, continues, "Did you hear I got the job at Asda?"

"Good for you," he grins. "When do you start?"

I leave them chatting in the front room and go to refill the kettle for I'm still parched and could murder…oh, oh, bad choice of words; I should say I fancy another coffee so shout through to the front room and both tell me they'll have one too.

My mobile phone rings and when I answer, it's Jessie asking how I'm doing.

I spend the next couple of minutes assuring her I'm fine and she tells me the kitchen table and the chairs had arrived and how pleased she and Mary is with it.

"Ernie's appearing at two o'clock at the Sheriff Court today, Maggie," she says and I can hear a hesitation in her voice. "I was thinking of going along to see how he gets on."

I rub wearily at my forehead and reply, "That's your decision, Jessie, but remember what you promised yourself, that you were done with him."

"I know, but he's still my man, isn't her?"

I suppose I could try to dissuade her, but really, she's a grown woman and she knows that if she does go to the court and sees him it will be the start of the return to the Craigbo Place flat and the life that she thought she could escape from; the life of drudgery and abuse. I suspect she doesn't really want things to go back to the way they were, but much as I hate admitting it, it's like her comfort zone; what she knows. Like it or not I suppose I just have to accept that Jessie is a professional victim and always will be. However, there is *one* chance and I seize it when I ask, "Have you told Mary?"

"Oh no," he hastily replies. "She'd go off her nut if she thought I was going back to him."

"And do you think that's because she loves you and doesn't want you to be a punch bag all your life?"

There's a few seconds silence and yes, I know I'm being hard on her, but in my heart I know that aside from asking how I am, Jessie has phoned me to tell me about going to court in the hope that I will change her mind.

At last she says, "I'm being really stupid so I am, aren't I, Maggie?"

"In my opinion as your friend," I smile then add, "as your *best* friend. Yes, Jessie, you're right enough. You *are* being really stupid. The next time he hits you might end up in the hospital like I did when he hit me."

I know that's a low blow, but I'm pulling no punches here, if you pardon the puns.

I hear her sigh and take a deep breath then almost happily she says, "Thanks, Maggie. I think I really needed convincing. Sod him! The bugger can go to jail for all I care!"

I know it's a small victory in what is likely to be a long running war, but at least the first battle has been won.

When we end the call I turn to see Alan stood in the doorway smiling at me and he says, "I could only hear your side of the call, but well done you." He strides towards me and gives me a hug and I feel…well, I feel protected, but then I tease him when I point to my cheek and say, "And where were you when I was getting this?"

"Oh," he grimaces and shakes his head, "don't rub it in. I feel bad enough as it is."

"Well, you made up for it with the roses. They're lovely. And they're red, I noticed," I grin at him.

He stares curiously at me, then says, "You think there's some kind of significance in the colour?"

I'm swallowing hard for I really don't know how to answer that and instead ask, "Where's Liz?"

"Eh, she's gone outside to make a phone call. Colin, I think."

"Oh, is that right," I'm smiling now, then wrapping my arms around his neck, I tell him, "if you really want to make amends, *acting* Detective Inspector Reid, why don't you invite me to your place this evening for a bit of hanky-panky?"

I can't believe I'm saying this and I start to blush, but you know what?

Right now I really don't care.

CHAPTER EIGHTEEN

Ten minutes later the three of us are in the front room finishing our coffee and Liz is discussing with Alan the merits of a diesel car against a petrol car when the phone rings.

Liz grabs the phone and answers and I hear her say, "Yes, she's right here," and handing me the phone says, "It's a detective from Stewart Street police office. About you being assaulted."

The detective, DC Shona McClure, tells me she is the reporting officer for the case against Ernest Cochrane and needs a statement from me and wants my injuries to be photographed.

Alan is listening as I'm speaking and waving a hand, whispers, "I can take you to Stewart Street this afternoon and get it over with."

"Eh, will this afternoon be okay with you?"

DC McClure agrees and we set the time for three o'clock.

I excuse myself telling them I want to shower and change and when I'm dried, I dress in the navy blue suited skirt and a clean sky blue blouse, my leather, black knee high boots and a matching black leather handbag. I tie my hair back into a ponytail, but other than a spray of perfume, don't apply makeup. However, I decide that perhaps the sunglasses might be a good idea and shove them into my handbag.

Downstairs I see Alan has slipped on his jacket on and is waiting in the hallway and when I put on the sunglasses, his eyes widen and he says, "My God, you're like a young Audrey Hepburn."

"Aye, but with wrinkles," I smile.

"Not that I'd notice," he pulls open the door as we both call out cheerio to Liz.

In the car I ask him about his boss, Charlie Miller.

"A good guy and smart too," he nods as he concentrates on his driving.

"That's some scar on his face," I add.

"Yeah, he got it a few years back. I don't know the full story other than when he was a DS he was injured when a car blew up somewhere over in the east end of the city, but the rumour is that he was on some sort of antiterrorist job at the time."

"Married?"

"Aye. His wife's a cop too. A uniformed sergeant over in, eh, I think it's the Baird Street office."

"Kids?"

"What's this," he glances at me with a grin. "The third degree? It's me who's supposed to be the detective here, Missus Brogan. And yes," he sighs, "as far as I recall, he's got two wee girls."

"He seems a nice man."

"Well, in my dealings with him, to use the old Glasgow saying, he would do you a good turn before he'd do you a bad turn."

I'm silent for a moment then I ask, "What do you think, strictly between you and me," I hastily add, "will happen to Martin Tarrant?"

He takes a few seconds to think about it then he replies, "Charlie's not daft and he'll realise that Tarrant's messed up big time and obviously this is just conjecture on my part, but I think he will arrange for Tarrant to be quietly removed from investigative duties. If it means getting the bugger promoted to get rid of him to an administrative post, then so be it, but he won't do it without telling Tarrant why it's been done. He's not backhanded like that," he's shaking his head. "No, he'll confront Tarrant and tell him exactly why he's being taken out of the CID."

A thought occurs to me and I ask, "What about you? Will Tarrant try to get even with you for finding out about Copeland being arrested at the time of Beth's murder?"

"Getting even with me?" he shakes his head as though my question is crazy. "The bugger should thank me for saving his career! Can you imagine if that information had came out during a trial, if the defence had brought that up? He'd have been the laughing stock of the CID and the police service as a whole and would not have survived the aftermath because it would have embarrassed the Chief Constable and in this job, Maggie, embarrassing the Chief is the one thing that is *real* career killer."

We sit in silence for a few minutes then he asks me, "Do you think Liz will be all right? I mean she's had quite a shock learning that Copeland didn't kill Beth."

I hesitate before answering as I think of Liz as she was and as she is now, then reply, "Liz is emotionally a lot stronger now than she was four and a half months ago, Alan. During that period, she was in a very bad place and her life was quite frankly terrible. She was going through the stress of having a husband who is a lazy good for nothing and was thinking of leaving him and worried about the impact that would have on Beth. Then losing Beth, it was just too much for her. But now," I find I'm smiling, "she's found herself a nice young man and is about to start a new job too. Yes, I agree it was distressing knowing that the man who killed Beth is still out there, for both of us actually, but Liz has come through the worst of it and I believe that the support she now has will be enough for her to continue to get on with her life."

"I like Colin," he's smiling. "He strikes me as a good guy and there's no doubt in my mind he's very fond of her."

And long may it continue again runs through my mind.
****

Alan finds an empty parking bay in the street round the corner from Stewart Street and walking round to the office insists on taking my arm in his.

Pushing through the front doors he walks to a reception window on the left and a young woman, not a policewoman, a civilian I think, approaches the desk from the other side and greets him. Alan shows her his warrant card and says, "DI Reid with Missus Brogan to see DC McClure."

"Do you know where you're going, sir?" she asks and I see her glance at my face and likely is wondering why the big sunglasses.

"I take it she's in the general office?"

"Yes, sir," the woman reaches for a phone. "I'll just let her know you're on your way through."

He leads me to a corridor on the opposite side of the foyer and I follow him into a large office with about a dozen desks and I see three people sitting at the desk, one of who is a young dark haired woman wearing a black coloured business suit who I guess is in her late twenties. Though I never said to Alan, I'm a little nervous and stand at the door as he calls out, "DC McClure?"

"That's me, boss," the woman rises and walking towards him, they shake hands.

"Is there somewhere a little more private we can talk?" I hear him say, and with a smile at me, she leads us back into the corridor and turns into a smaller room with two desks.

"The DS's are both out," she explains and when we're seated, she behind the desk with Alan and I facing her, her brow creases as she says, "Can I ask why you're here too, boss?"

"Hands up," he smiles. "Missus Brogan is my girlfriend."

"Oh, fine," she replies, but I can see she's a bit taken aback. To be honest, so am I for that's the first time I've heard myself being called his girlfriend and I know behind my sunglasses, I'm blushing.

The detective shuffles some papers and says to me, "I have most of the story about what happened, Missus Brogan…"

I can only guess Alan thinks his presence is making the lassie uncomfortable, for he interrupts and says, "I'll leave you to it, Shona, and grab myself a coffee, okay?"

She smiles and I can almost see her relax as he leaves the room and she continues. "I have statements from the friends you work with Missus Brogan…"

"Please," I raise my hand. "Maggie."

"Then I'm Shona. Now, Maggie, all I need from you is your version of events that night and I'll take some photographs of your injuries if that's okay with you?"

Alan had told me what to expect, so I nod and remove my sunglasses.

"My God," she's clearly startled. "He's gave you some face, didn't he?"

"It probably looks worse than it is," I tell her for by now even though I can see the bruising has spread to most of my left cheek and the eye is still bloodshot, it's a little tender to the touch but the pain is not so bad.

"I've a statement from the attending doctor at the casualty and the consultant who told me that once the bruising goes there will be no lasting effect. However, the consultant also told me that you're fortunate for it could have been a lot worse," she tells me.

She gets down to it and I relate what I can recall of that night which to be honest, isn't much, then I ask, "What do you think will happen to him?"

"Well," she sits back and lays down her pen and notebook, "he's appearing at the Sheriff Court today, though I've no information yet as to how he pled, guilty or not guilty. If he has pled guilty, he'll either be sentenced today, but more than likely be remanded in custody or released, to be sentenced at a later date. If he pleads not guilty, there will be a court date set and likely you might have to give evidence. However, I have numerous statements from witnesses who saw him punch you and are you aware, Maggie, he tried to stamp on your head? It was his wife that pushed him away before his foot connected with you. If he had succeeded, you might not be sitting here the now because he was wearing heavy boots and that's the reason he was charged with serious assault. Oh," she grins, "I've taken his boots from him as productions in the case."

I'm shocked because I did *not* know this and can only imagine what it took for the slightly built Jessie to tackle a man his size, then I shiver when I think of the injury I might have suffered.

I feel my face pale and she asks, "Do you want a glass of water or something?"

"No," I wave a hand, "I'm okay. Honest. Please, go on."

"Right, I've got what I need so there's only the photographs now." She reaches into a pocket of her jacket and fetches out a mobile phone and laying it down onto the desk, explains, "What I need for evidential purpose is you to attend and have your injuries photographed by our Identification Bureau, but here's what I'm proposing. I'll make a phone call in the morning to the Fiscal's office and find out if Cochrane has pled guilty. If he has, there will be no need for you to be photographed. If he has pled not guilty, I'll contact you and make the arrangements for the photos to be taken. In the meantime, though, I'd like to photograph you with my mobile phone and maybe I can persuade the Fiscal depute in the case to accept those photos rather than have you take time out to attend the IB. How does that sound?"

"Yes, okay," I nod. "No problem."

"Right then," she points to a blank wall that is painted a dull green colour, "if you stand there against the wall I'll get the photos."

She snaps about half a dozen headshots and close-ups of me from various angles then satisfied the photos are what she needs, we sit back down.

She's smiling when she says, "I see you live in Clarion Crescent. I was brought up in Gask Place, not far from where you live. Do you know it? It's off Yoker Mill Road."

"I know Yoker Mill Road," I tell her, but admit I'm not familiar with Gask Place.

"Aye, I lived there with my folks till we moved over to the south side when I was sixteen. In fact, I went to school with a boy who lived in Clarion Crescent, Craig McGregor. Do you know him? His mother is a hairdresser or she was. A good-looking, blonde haired woman. I haven't seen him in years."

You might recall me saying that Glasgow is a village that there is always someone you meet who knows somebody that you do and this again seems to be borne out by this young woman.

I reply, "I know Craig and his parents. They live along the road from me. He's got a brother, Ian."

"Aye, that's right," she smiles. "Craig was a *right* good looker," she grins at me. "All the girls in my year fancied him rotten. I remember when I was," her eyes narrow and she nods as she recollects, "Aye, I must have been about fifteen or turning sixteen because we were all in third year and he invited a crowd of us to his birthday party at his house. His dad was there too," and her face clouds over. "I didn't like him. He was a handsome guy, but I thought he was a bit sleazy, you know? Eyes everywhere and kind of stood right close to you when he was talking to you as it he was trying to see down the front of your dress. I mean, you know that feeling you get when you think a mans looking through you, through what you're wearing and believe me, back in the day we girls weren't wearing that much," she half laughs as she shakes her head at the memory.

She can't possibly realise that when she describes Peter McGregor, I know exactly what she means.

"One of the lassies at the party, Margo something; I can't remember her second name, but I do remember that she was quite busty and wearing a black dress. One of those short, halter neck dresses and hanging out of the top of it and getting a lot of attention from the boys at the party. She'd brought two half bottles of vodka with her and was well pissed within an hour. Mister McGregor decided that she needed some air and was," she makes quotation marks with her forefingers, "helping her out of the back door in case she was sick, but his hands were everywhere, or so Margo said. I didn't see it, but drunk as she was I didn't doubt Margo either. Anyway, whatever happened the music was turned off because Craig's mother came home and went ballistic at her husband for something and we were all turfed out of the house. I think he'd tried it on with Margo and that's what upset his wife. Funny that," she smiles, "I'd forgotten all about that until we started talking."

I have a strange feeling running through me that this is important and licking at my lips, I say, "Shona, would you mind very much repeating to Alan what you told me? I don't know if what you remember is important, but I think it's something he might want to hear."

She stares at me and I can see the confusion in her face, but she nods and replies, "Of course. No problem."

****

We're back in Alan's car and driving away from Stewart Street before I ask, "So, what do you think?"

He purses his lips and replies, "I've met with McGregor and went over his statement with him, but there's nothing I can find to implicate him or cause him to be a real suspect. At least not at the minute. However, I'm still looking at him, but we already know he has a predilection for young women. Whether or not that includes children," he turns to me and grimaces, "that's something I intend finding out. Leave it with me for now, Maggie, because believe me, it won't go unattended to."

"Now," his voice is a little brighter, "I was thinking of feeding you myself, but on second thought I've decided to take you for dinner. How does that sound?"

"What," I'm aghast, "with my face looking like this?"

"Ah, I hadn't thought about that," he sheepishly admits.

Typical man, I'm thinking, so I suggest, "We could get a carryout, if that's okay with you? Would save you cooking."

"Good idea," he grins and we head for his place.

Twenty-five minutes later and after purchasing a Chinese takeaway, Alan manages to squeeze his Volvo in between two parked cars thirty yards from his front door. The rain is pattering against the car windscreen, so he hands me his house keys and tells me, "I'll grab the grub while you make a run for it and open the door."

A minute later we're both safely inside the beautiful hallway and giggling like children.

Upstairs in his flat and while he warms a couple of plates and sets the table, I use his bathroom and take the opportunity to brush my hair and apply some lipstick.

When I get back to the kitchen I can smell the food, but he gently takes me by the arm and leads me through to the dining room where I find he's set the table and besides the food, there's a bottle of white wine opened with two glasses already poured.

"Thought we'd have a wee celebratory drink," he grins at me.

"And what exactly are we celebrating?" I ask as I slide into a chair that he gallantly pulls out for me.

"Oh," he pretends to be thoughtful as he sits opposite, "how about we celebrate that in the direst of circumstances, something good has come out of it."

He can see I'm puzzled and softly explains, "I found you, Maggie."

I can almost feel my heart quicken for after all, how can I possibly respond to that?

CHAPTER NINETEEN

I can't use the wine as an excuse.

In fact, I have no excuse and no explanation other than the truth is, what happened between us is what I wanted to happen; what I'm certain Alan wanted too.

And so early the next morning I waken and for the first time in five years, I am with a man.

I don't move for fear of waking him, but as my eyes roam across the ceiling I blush for I remember that beneath the quilt cover, I am naked.

He's lying on his back, breathing softly and when in his sleep his arm brushes against my skin, I shiver with the memory of the night before. It's not that the lovemaking with Alex had been…I suppose pleasant is the word, but if I'm honest, if I'm really honest, it had always been what my mother had told me on the eve of my wedding night is the missionary position and until tonight, I had known no different.

But last night with Alan changed all that and I smile at the memory of his gentle touch, his hands upon me and of how he pleased me in ways I had never before known or imagined.

I take a few minutes and indulge in the fantasy that this is how I want my life to be, to lie here with this lovely man and share his home with him.

As slowly as I dare, I slide my legs from under the cover and finally after several heart stopping seconds, I'm out of the bed. In the dim light that peeks through a crack in the curtain I see clothes scattered across the carpet; among them my underwear, skirt and blouse lie abandoned on the floor. Conscious of my nakedness, I know I have to pee and quietly make my way to the en-suite where I find his dressing gown hung on a hook on the wall. I decide that I won't get dressed right away, that I will first have a shower, but have no wish to disturb him at this early hour of the morning. Opening the en-suite door as slowly as I dare, I collect my clothes from the floor and make my way out of the room into the dimly lit hallway. Downstairs I pull the dressing gown tightly about me, dumping my clothes onto a chair I shiver in the cold of the kitchen. Curiously though, my feet are not as cold as they might have been then I recall Alan telling me that some years ago he had under floor heating installed beneath the tiles.

I raise the window blind and see that it's another wet Glasgow day, but the view from panoramic window across the rear gardens makes me smile and I realise it's not the view, it's the way I'm feeling. Though I find it difficult to explain, I feel happy, really happy.

The kettle boiling causes me to turn and finding two mugs in a cupboard, I spoon coffee and pour milk into them both.

"Hope one of them is for me," I hear the voice behind me and turning, see Alan wearing boxer short and his now rumpled, but unbuttoned shirt from the previous evening.

"Morning," I greet him and can't believe how shy I feel.

"Look," his face is serious, "I'd give you a big, sloppy kiss but I've got morning breath and I don't won't to ruin what to me was one of the best evenings of my life."

I don't think I knew what to expect from him, what he'd say, but suddenly I feel…relieved, I think is the best way to describe my feelings.

He holds out his arms and asks, "Would a morning hug be in order, do you think?"

I walk into his arms he gives me a crushing hug that almost takes the breath from me.

"I don't think I want to let you go," he whispers in my ear and like a fool, I feel tears trickling down my cheeks. No, not sadness, but tears of happiness.

When I'd stared out of the kitchen window, I'd thought there might have been some embarrassment, certainly from me and perhaps from Alan. But now stood here with his arms wrapped about me, our night together, our lovemaking, now seems to have been the most natural thing in the world.

"It's just gone seven and I've work to go to," he releases his tight hold and stares down at me. "There's no need for you to rush away, Maggie. I want you to treat this place," he glances about him, "like it's yours too."

"That's quite a commitment you're making, Mister Reid. Asking me to treat your home like it's my own," I try to smile but end up sniffing though fortunately the tears have stopped.

God, I think, I've been weeping buckets in the past week, haven't I?

"Well," he drawls and gently stroking some hair from my bruised cheek, says with a wide grin, "I hope that you'll be here a lot more often spending time with me, now that I'm officially your boyfriend."

"Oh, that," I pretend surprise. "What if Fiona and Bryony don't approve of their father having a girlfriend?"

"You've already won over Fiona and believe me, she's the Doubting Thomas of the two, so don't worry about Bryony. Now, if I grab my coffee and head upstairs for a shower and change, what's the chance of some toast before I head out? I'm meeting my new team this morning and I'd like to be early."

"Toast and scrambled eggs?"

"Even better," he grins and kisses me on the forehead before he leaves.

I stand for a moment taking in my surroundings and typically cynical me, I wonder again if things with Alan are moving too quickly and with that thought on my mind, I start to prepare his breakfast.

****

I've taken Alan at his word and now that he's left for work, I'm lazily relaxing in the old fashioned, freestanding bathtub with the claw feet and can't help but smile. I've brought my clothes and mobile phone into the bathroom with me and though I'd sent Liz a text the previous evening saying I might not be home, I wanted to speak to her and called her number.

"Mum? You okay?" I could hear the anxiety in her voice.

"Absolutely fine, sweetheart," I reply.

"Did you…where did you spend the night? At Alan's house?"

"Eh, yes, I'm still here, hen. Are you okay?"

"Yes, I'm fine," she snaps back and I wonder what I've done to cause her to be angry.

"I did send you a text," I remind her.

"Yes, you did and it arrived at almost half two in the morning, Mum! Up till that time you weren't answering your phone! Do you know how many times I tried to call you? And Alan as well?"

"Hold on," I tell her. My hands are slippery with soapy water but at last I manage to check my calling list and see I've missed half a dozen calls from her.

"Sorry, the phone was downstairs," I say then tightly shut my eyes at my slip of the tongue, but she catches on and sarcastically replies, "And why were you *upstairs*?"

Talk about role reversal! Here's me trying to excuse myself to my daughter that her forty-nine-year-old mother was incommunicado because she was in bed having sex!

So, I did what any honest and caring parent would do in the circumstances and holding my head in shame, I meekly apologise with, "Sorry, Liz."

But she's not finished because she spends the next minute telling me how worried she was and how she almost contemplated phoning around the casualty wards to ensure I wasn't a patient.

"I even phoned Mary Cochrane to ask her mother Jessie if she might know where you were," she continues her rant. "Needless to say because Jessie's husband had been bailed from the court yesterday, they worried that he might have come after you, so I suggest as a matter of urgency, *mother*, you phone your wee pal and tell her you are fine because she is as worried as me!"

"I will, Liz, I promise I'll phone Jessie. Now, did you say her husband was bailed yesterday?"

"Yes, apparently it was the duty of the police to inform Jessie that her man was at liberty or something like that, so she is to contact them if he tries to approach her."

"So he pled not guilty?" I ask.

"I don't know about that. Maybe Jessie will know. Right, when are you coming home?"

"Eh, I'm just having a wash," I do not tempt fate by mentioning the luxurious bath, "then when I get dressed I'll phone for a taxi.

"Okay, I'll see you when you get home and you can tell Alan Reid I'll be having words with him too. Pair of thoughtless buggers that you are. You should know better at your ages," she finishes.

I know I should be sorry, but when I lay the phone down onto the stool by the bath, I burst into laughter and am still laughing when to my surprise, I hear a door downstairs being banged closed.
****

I hold my breath and listen; I hear the sound of a radio being played. Dripping wet, I climb out of the bath and wrap myself in Alan's dressing gown then tiptoe to the bathroom door and pulling it open, listen intently.

Yes, there's definitely someone moving about downstairs, but then I hear the sound of a hoover and with a smile, I remember.

When I first visited the flat, Alan told me he had a cleaner call in Tuesday and Friday's so I reason it must be her.

I quickly get dried, dressed and pat my hair into some semblance of order, then taking a deep breath, make my way downstairs. I don't want to startle the lady and several times loudly call out, "Hello?"

She doesn't hear me because of the noise the hoover is making and when I move into her vision, I end up giving her a fright.

"Jesus Christ!" she jumps back, her eyes wide and staring. "Who the *fuck* are you! Sorry! I mean, you gave me one hell of a scare there, missus, pardon my language."

"I'm so sorry," I hold out my hands defensively. "My name's Maggie. I'm a friend of Alan's and I'd stayed overnight," though why I had to tell her that, I can't think.

I see her to be in her late fifties to early sixties, stout build and wearing a bright floral wraparound overall over baggy black coloured trousers and a V neck blue coloured polo shirt with training shoes on her feet. Her salt and pepper hair is swept up into a tight bun.

"Eh, I'm Ann. Annie," she corrects herself as she switches off the hoover. "I'm Alan's cleaner. God, hen, you gave me such a fright," holding one hand over her chest, she shakes her head.

"Well," I smile apologetically at her, "if I make you a cuppa, do you think you'll feel a bit better?"

"I think so, aye," she nods and when she smiles the laughter lines round her eyes crease and it's like her whole face lights up. I can't explain why, but Annie seems to me to be one of those people who seem to radiate cheerfulness.

Or maybe it's just the way I'm feeling.

Five minutes later I'm calling Annie through to the kitchen where I've laid the table with two mugs, milk and sugar and a plate of toast and chocolate biscuits.

"My, this is grand, Maggie," she sits down. "I'll not bother with the biscuits because I'm at the Slimming World in the afternoon," then she proceeds to scoff two slice of heavily buttered toast and takes her tea with three spoonfuls of sugar.

"Look at me," she jokes. "And me getting weighed later. What am I like," then bursts into high-pitched laughter.

Her mirth is so infectious I find I'm laughing along with her.

"So, are you Alan's girlfriend then?"

No beating about the bush with this lady, I gather.

"Eh, yes," I find I'm blushing. "He and I are seeing each other."

"About time that man got himself a woman," she sniffs. "Waste of a good man, so it is. He'll be good to you, hen, mark my word," she solemnly nods. "If I was ten years younger and six stone lighter, I'd be chasing him myself," then starts laughing again.

I grin then over the course of the next twenty minutes, I learn Annie has been cleaning house for Alan for nearly ten years, that he's one of nine clients she has but he's definitely the best and tapping a stubby finger against her nose, adds, "…the cleanest of the lot and him a man too! Who'd have thought?"

She smiles when she tells me she is married to Donald who is retired from the painting and decorating after having suffered a stroke, but keeps busy tending the garden and his vegetable plot; that she and Donald have four children, three of whom are married with their own kids and the youngest one serving in the Merchant Navy.

"I think he's gay," she confides in a whisper though there's only the two of us there, "but he'll not come out and admit it. Thinks his Da and me would disapprove. Would I?" her lip curls. "I really don't care what he is," she answers her own question with a shake of her head. "As long as he's happy, safe and content. I mean, that's all you want for your children, isn't it?"

I don't set out intending to disclose my own family details to Annie, but find myself telling her about Liz and the loss we suffered and as I do, she reaches across the table to tightly hold my hand.

When I finish, she just shakes her head and sniffing to hold back her tears, says, "My God, you and your daughter have been through it, haven't you, hen? Heavens, look at the time, Maggie. You've kept me back from my work, here. Mind you," she winks, "Alan's such a clean bugger there's hardly anything to dust or polish in this house." She stares keenly at me and adds, "I hope I'm going to be seeing a lot more of you, Maggie. I think you and me can be friends, eh?"

I find myself smiling when I reply, "I think so."

I clear away the dishes and after they're washed and dried, I phone for a taxi and bid Annie cheerio before I leave.

****

I'm in the private hire taxi on the way home when my mobile activates and I see the caller is Jessie.

"Thank heavens you're okay," she gasps and I feel a little guilty that I didn't contact her earlier when Liz told me how worried Jessie had been.

I'm aware the taxi driver sitting up front might be listening so I tell Jessie that I'll call her later and let her know where I'd been.

"Was you with him?" she asks and I hear a trace of excitement in her voice.

"Yes," I slowly drawl, then move the phone from my ear when she squeals so loudly I think she'll deafen me.

"Great! You can tell me all about it when you phone me," she says.

"Indeed I will not," I huffily sniff, but not so much to upset her then I add, "I'll just say this and no more. He's a lovely man and I had a nice time so use your imagination."

I think the part about me phoning her later seemed to have passed her by for then she says, "Did your Liz tell you that Ernie got bail?"

"She did. Does that mean he pled not guilty?"

"No, hen. He pled guilty right enough, but the Sheriff let him out for what they call background reports to be compiled or something like that. But he's been told to expect what they call a custodial sentence. The jail, you know? And he's not to approach me or Mary and he's to stay away from you as well. Anyway, he's not got our new address and he doesn't know where you live."

But he knows where you and I work, I think to myself.

There's a pause and she continues, "He's got an awful face on him, Maggie. The lassies fairly set about him."

I flinch and the ask, "You must have seen him then, Jessie, so you went to the court after all?"

I can almost hear her grimacing at getting caught out and after telling me that she wouldn't go to the court.

"Listen," I patiently begin, "you've been married to Ernie for a very long time, Jessie, so it's understandable that you might retain some affection for him, even after what he's done to you. It's not for someone like me to tell you not to go and see him, but all I'll ask is that if you do intend seeing him again, you make sure you have Mary with you and that's it's in a public place, somewhere that he won't kick-off and try to hurt you, okay?"

"Okay, Maggie," her voice is low and subdued.

"Now," I force myself to sound a bit cheerier, "tell me what's happening at the new flat?"

By the time Jessie is finished the taxi is drawing near to my house and I tell her, "That's me almost home now, hen, so tell you what. When you finish work tonight, why don't I meet you in the Wetherspoons for a quick drink and," I'm thinking on my feet here, "bring some of the girls along too. Tell them I want to thank them for coming to my rescue and I'll stand them all a drink."

You'd think I'd told Jessie she'd won the lottery, she's that pleased and says she'll see me there just after nine.

I'm paying off the driver and I see the front door opening and Liz is stood there, her arms crossed, her foot tapping and a scowl on her face.

As I walk towards her, she calls out loud enough to alert the neighbours ten doors up, "So, the scarlet woman returns, eh?"

"Liz!"

That's when she breaks out into a shrill laugh and jumping down the stairs wraps her arms around me squealing, "My mother! The dirty stop out!"

Well, I'm fair embarrassed and hustling her indoors she turns and wagging a finger at me, continues, "Now I want you to be cautious, mother because I don't want you getting into any kind of relationship without thinking it through, okay?"

My face tightens and I try to look grim, but Liz's grin wins the day and I know she's parodying me because that's almost exactly what I told her when she went on the date with Colin.

I admit defeat and end up smiling.

"The kettle's on so come through to the kitchen and tell me all about it," she starts, but then stops and shaking her head, frowns and adds, "I mean, just the romantic bit. None of that yucky sex stuff. After all, you *are* my mother," her face contorts and she pretends to shudder.

I'm old enough to know when the mickey is being taken and friskily push her ahead of me into the kitchen.

Five minutes later having our coffee she tells me that she received a letter in the morning mail from the lawyer, Nick McSweeney, and handing me the letter goes on to relate its content.

"Nick says in the letter he's engaged the guy he told us about, Tom McEwan, who has already identified the address that Ian is living at. The letter said Ian's living with a woman called Paula McGuigan and asked me to phone Nick if I know her. I phoned anyway and told him I'd never heard of her. He said this woman McGuigan's introduced Ian to her neighbours in the close as her fiancé and the guy McEwan has statements from the neighbours saying that they are cohabiting. Nick says McEwan did a check with the Housing Association in Garscadden and the woman has not listed Ian as a resident in her flat and McEwan thinks if she did in might affect her housing benefits. He's also found out she works as a barmaid in a pub in the Saracen area, but she's drawing unemployment benefit too and that Ian hangs about the pub. Nick also said that this guy McEwan is going to put it to her if she gives a statement about them, you know, being together he'll not inform the DSS about her working and drawing unemployment benefit."

"Is that not a wee bit like blackmail?" I frown.

"I thought that, but Nick said, and get this," she grins. "All's fair in love and war and this is war. And get this too," her eyes flare with excitement, "McEwan has photos of them together, kissing and…well, stuff like that."

"So," I glance through the letter, "Nick thinks you have a case against Ian for divorce?"

"Well," she's grinning now from ear to ear, "he thinks…no, what he *said* is it's rock solid though he did remind me on the phone, no hanky-panky on my part because if Ian's lawyer got a sniff of impro…improper…"

"Impropriety?"

"I keep forgetting how to pronounce that word," she shakes her head and sighs and suddenly in my minds eye, she's a little girl again.

"So I take it you and Colin will be keeping your hands off each other for now?"

"Mum!" stares at mockingly me. "Who do you think I am? You?"
****

I get a text from Alan later that morning telling me that if I'm not doing anything, he'll pop by the house and let me know how his investigation is going. However, I text him back to let him know that just after nine I'll be meeting the girls from work at the Argyle Street Wetherspoons and almost immediately get a reply from him that reads: *Fair enough. If you want a lift after your boozy night call me and I'll be outside like the White Knight in my trusty steed, a well polished Volvo. PS. On this occasion I promise I'll be on time! X*
Boozy night indeed! However, I can't deny I'm pleased at his offer and besides, trying to get a taxi at that time of the night in the city is murder so I text him back that it would be grand to get a lift.

The rest of the day passes by without any drama and though I'm embarrassed to admit this and will *never* dare tell anyone, I'm tired out after my late night activity with Alan and at midday I decide if I'm off out tonight, I'd better have a nap.

Liz wakes me from a dreamless sleep just after three o'clock with a cup of tea and her eyes wide, says, "My God, mum, you were certainly out for the count! I've run a bath for you, so take a couple of minutes to come to and then come down when you're ready. I've made beef lasagne for your dinner if that's alright with you?"

"Sounds lovely," I tell her, before asking, "But just for me? What about you? Are you not eating too?"

Making her way out of the door, she calls back, "Yes, just for you because Colin's coming round and we're…" she stops and turning, stares at me and sighs. "You've forgotten I'm meeting his parents tonight?"

I close my eyes tightly and grit my teeth in shame.

"Sorry, sweetheart, hands up," I tell her. "Yes, with everything else that's been going on it clean slipped my mind.

"No worries," she sharply replies and brightly smiles, but the smile does not reach her eyes and I know from her expression she's thinking by forgetting such an important night that I've let her down. I quickly make amends by telling her, "Look, you don't want to go empty handed and we both know you've not started earning yet so here's what I'm thinking. Nip downstairs and take my bankcard from my purse, then head up to the florist's shop, the one in Lauderdale Drive, and get a nice bouquet for Missus Paterson. Something in the region of twenty pounds. I can't remember the shop's name but…"

"I know the one. Flowers and Design. It's a really popular shop," she interrupts and nods before asking, "Would I not be quicker if I just nip along to Asda or Tesco's or somewhere?"

"Definitely not," I vigorously shake my head. "The woman will recognise the flowers you bring her are from a florists and she'll realise you've made an effort to impress her rather than having just nipped into a local store."

"Right," she slowly nods, then her eyes narrow when she asks, "What about Mister Paterson?"

I smile and reply as though I'm a worldly-wise woman, "Listen to me, sweetheart, it's the mother you have to win over. Colin's father will take one look at you and be dead chuffed his son has a good-looking girlfriend like you. That and he'll be pleased that you're coming to him for advice and help in buying a car."

"You think so?"

"I *know* so. Now, you've got my PIN number?"

"I'm your daughter, mum. It's tattooed on my wrist."

"Aye, very good," I grin. "Lock the front door behind you," I tell her and begin to rise from the bed, "because I'm going for a nice, hot bath."

****

I'm still in my dressing gown when Colin arrives to pick up Liz then before she leaves, she waits till Colin is in the car and turning back towards me at the doorway, hurriedly whispers, "Will you be home tonight?"

I admit to being kind of taken aback because the last thing I expect is my daughter inferring that I might again be spending the night with a man who is not my husband.

"Who are you, my keeper?" I give her a sly look, then smile and add, "Yes, I'll be home but probably late, though."

She seems assured and give me a hurried kiss on the cheek before she races off through the falling rain to the passenger door, but I'm inwardly thinking that if Alan Reid asks otherwise, there could be a change of plan.

I watch them drive off and mentally cross my fingers and toes that the night goes well for them both. I can't imagine what Colin's parent's must think, him bringing home a former patient of his who was admitted because of her depression and attempted suicide, but if they've any heart at all and particularly the mother, they'll give Liz the benefit of the doubt till they get to know her.

Or so I hope and pray.

I glance up at the sky and though it's dark with clouds, the rain had finally stopped. Then I remember that if I intend drinking tonight I should take my pop-up umbrella with me and grabbing the car keys from the hook on the wall behind the door, go to fetch the brolly from the boot.

I'm just about to close the boot when I'm startled by a flash of lightening that completely lights up the whole world. Just a flash that lasts for, oh, what? A millisecond?

Now, lightening itself doesn't frighten me and truth be told, I rather like watching it as long as I feel safe indoors. However, standing outside next to a metal car with my hand on the metal of the boot that's something else.

But it's what happens during that flash of lightening that astonishes me.

I'm going to find this hard to describe, but believe me it's happened and it's really freaky; like something out of a Hitchcock movie.

In that millisecond, that space of time that was faster than a heartbeat and quicker than I can blink, my head's already tilted back with my eyes drawn up and I see my neighbour, Moira McPherson, silhouetted in the upstairs bedroom window of her house and she's leaning against the window with her hands flat against the glass while she stares down at me.

The whole thing is…what's the word; surreal?

God, I can tell you it sends a shiver down my back.

As quick as it arrived the flash is gone and the darkness envelops me. The only light now is the street lighting behind me, the light from my open front door and the chink of light escaping the closed curtain of my front room for curiously, the front of the McPherson's house is in total darkness.

I lock the car and make my way back inside just as a roll of thunder arrives. For some inane reason I'm grinning like an idiot as I'm wondering what the hell is she doing?

The only thing that comes to mind is that Moira heard Liz and Colin leaving the house and decided to have a wee peek outside and not wanting to get caught being nosey, switched off the room light. Just her bad luck that the lightening arrived at the wrong time.

Aye, that must be it, I convince myself then dismiss it from my mind.

****

I decide to dress casually for my boozy night, as Alan described it in his text and slip on a pair of black jeans, but unlike the young women of the day mine don't have tears in the knees. I remove the price tag from the dark green floral print jersey top that I bought in the Debenhams sale and pull it on. Stood in front of the wardrobe mirror I tie my hair back into a ponytail and I'm pleased with the effect; or as pleased as I can be with one side of my face looking like a rainbow.

The use of the Arnica gel has helped a lot, but the next ten minutes is spent in front of the bathroom mirror daubing my cheek with a translucent blusher that tones down the faded colours of the bruise and at last, I'm as satisfied as I can be, though there's nothing I can do about the bloodshot eye. Maybe after a few drinks, I jauntily think, the other eye will go the same colour.

I pull on my faithful black leather boots and I'm ready, though a glance out of the window reveals the rain is still pouring down and in the distance I can hear more thunder. That seems to indicate the bad weather is moving away to the east.

Seems then it's a night for wearing my raincoat and not the snazzy new black bolero jacket I was hoping to show off. But that's me all over, practical as hell.

The taxi arrives fifteen minutes after my call and after my first stop at an ATM, the driver deposits me right outside the Wetherspoons pub, the Sir John Moore in Argyle Street, so I've only a few yards to race through the rain to the door.

As you can imagine, it's Friday night in Glasgow city centre so the place is absolutely mobbed inside and I give thanks that the smoking ban was introduced all those years ago for if the number of people inside were having fags it would have made it impossible to breathe. There are no free tables to find but I can see that a lot of the groups seem to be office workers having their Friday night drinks before they go home so as I'm about five minutes too early, I take off my raincoat and with my handbag on my shoulder, I stand by the door and watch for a table being vacated.

"Want a drink, darling?" says a slurred voice beside me and I turn to see a balding, fat middle-aged lothario, his tie undone and food stains on his pale blue shirt and likely who has a wife and a brood of weans at home while he's here in the pub giving me the glad eye.

"Oh, yes please," I gush like a schoolgirl and give him a big smile. "That's awfully nice of you. A double vodka and coke for me and a pint of heavy for my boyfriend over there," I give a nod in the general direction of a group of workmen who look like they've just come off a building site.

If I had told the drunken sod I was a man in drag, he couldn't have shuffled off any faster and almost had his nose punched when he bumped into a group of big, rugby type lads and spilt his beer on one of them.

Minutes later I hear my name being called and the crowd of punters standing by the door part when like a noisy tidal wave, in they come, shaking umbrellas and peeling off their coats. I'm really taken aback because it seems that all the cleaners have turned up and right behind them is Tommy Burton and two of the male janitors.

The charge to the bar is led by big Eileen, with Jessie beside her and Eileen's pal, wee toothless Janey acting like a shepherd as she ushers everybody towards me. Grinning like an idiot at all the handshakes, kisses on the cheek and pats on the back, I'm swept along by the tsunami of women and I have to admit I'm a little overwhelmed and very touched that the lassies and the three men have turned up to see me, though on hindsight maybe it was the promise of a free drink.

I'd drawn eighty quid from the ATM thinking it would do me for the night, but when I see the crowd who has turned up, I shove the money into Tommy's hand and tell him, "That's for the bevy and if it's any more than that, give me a shout and I'll use my card."

"No sweat," he manages to tell me, then proceeds to order a round of drink.

There's a dozen questions thrown at me from all sides, from "How are you, hen?" to "When are you coming back?" and even one of the lassies asking me, "Heard you've got yourself a new man? Are you shagging him yet?"

I glance at Jessie and she's got the good grace to blush and avoid my eyes.

Try as I might I can't answer everybody and just on cue a drink is shoved into my hand by Tommy, who mutters, "Rum and coke do you? It's on special tonight."

Now, I definitely do *not* drink rum and coke, but what the hell and throw it back then almost immediately gag and start coughing.

Big Eileen sidles up to me and slapping me on the back, grins and says, "Heard that Jessie's man is going to get the jail. Good enough for him, the bastard," she shakes her head. "Hitting women is just not on and maybe now the wee yin will get some peace."

On that we agree and as another drink, again a rum and coke, is slapped into my hand, we toast each other.

And that's how the night goes on. One thing that I like about the Wetherspoons is that there is no loud music banging on so aside from the noisy chatter, you can actually hear yourself in their pubs and we end up pushing three or four tables together and hogging a corner near to the bar.

Well, don't ask me how many rum and cokes I had but what I do know is that I had no need to pass Tommy my bankcard as I'd thought for the lassies were very generous.

And who knew that big Eileen had such an amazing voice and her rendition of Adele's 'Hello' accompanied by some of the 'Cleaners Choir' had Jessie, me and a couple of others all sobbing and singing along with her.

But then again, maybe it was the rum and coke.

The next thing I know is the women, Tommy and the other two guys are all saying their farewells and Jessie is telling me it was time I was going up the road.

I must have told her about phoning Alan because she has my phone in her hand and scrolling down till she finds his number and I hear her telling him, "Aye, she's had a wee bit too much to drink. Fifteen minutes? Right, Alan, we'll be outside."

And that's how I end up disgracing myself for when he arrives Jessie is holding my hair back and I'm being sick on the road.

The thing is I knew exactly what was happening to me, but the world is going back and forward and when I close my eyes, it starts going from side to side.

Rum and coke? Never, ever again!

I'm vaguely aware of apologising to Alan as he helps me into the front seat of his car and him repeatedly telling me, "It's okay, Maggie. Let's just get you home."

He's leaning across me to belt me into the seat and I reach up to stroke his cheek, but only succeed in poking him in the eye.

"Sorry," I mumble as he squeals, "Ouch!"

The wind is blowing in my face and I'm dimly aware he's wound down my window.

From the back seat I hear Jessie rambling on and realise he must be giving her a lift home too.

I don't remember her getting dropped off and the rest of the journey is lost to me as well for the next thing I'm aware of is Liz is there at the door and helping me out of the car.

I hear her telling Alan, "I've never seen her like this. What happened?"

Is that him sniggering, I wonder? If it is…

"Her wee pal Jessie told me that the rest of her mates got her pissed," he's smiling at me. "She said that they fed her with rum and coke."

"Rum and coke!" I hear Liz angrily reply as she and Alan are helping me up the steps and into the house. "Mum doesn't drink rum and coke! She doesn't drink spirits at all! She's lucky if she can finish two glasses of white wine! Why the hell did they buy her rum and coke?"

"I don't think it's so much the drink," he's closing the front door behind us, "as the fact that it seems it was a party atmosphere and she's got caught up in it."

"Stupid buggers," Liz grunts, her voice sounding harsh in my ears because all I want to do is sleep. "Help me get her upstairs to bed, if you don't mind."

"No problem," I hear him say and, well, that's really all I can recall.

CHAPTER TWENTY

As soon as I open my eyes I know it's a mistake. A huge, head splitting, mouth as barren as a desert, mistake.

You have to understand the last time I was drunk was when I was fifteen and Josephine McBride and me shared bottle of her mothers Advocaat, so this is *not* a usual occurrence. I'm lying face down on the bed with the quilt cover over me, but still wearing my underwear. No, wait. My bra's been taken off.

Dear God, please, *please* promise me it was not Alan who removed my clothes!

I sigh almost with relief when I remember that Liz helped me up the stairs and reason it must have been her who undressed me.

I try to turn my head towards the digital clock, but a low moan involuntarily escapes me and I feel the bile well up in my throat. It doesn't help any that I'm literally bursting to pee.

I slowly take a breath and I see the note lying propped up against the clock, obscuring the digital time and there's a mug there too. Oh, I realise it's light enough to read the note so I'm guessing it's definitely the morning. Ignoring the pain, I narrow my eyes and read:

Mum, bucket on the floor beside you and a mug of water on bedside table.

Right now I'd kill for two or maybe a dozen Paracetamol.

Slowly, very slowly because every movement provokes the drummer in my temple to bang away, I reach for the mug and turn so that I can take a swallow.

Another mistake.

The bile threatens to explode from me and regardless of my aching head and without any thought to the fact I'm wearing nothing but a pair of black, lacy knickers, I jump from the bed with one hand over my mouth and run for the toilet.

I slump down onto my knees in just the nick of time for a stream of projectile vomit hits the pan, some of which splashes back up into my face and hair.

If you've ever been in that position, you'll know that by now I'm past caring.

I've now got both hands on the pan as my body shakes, I retch and my stomach continues to heave the contents.

"Mum?" I hear Liz behind me then in seconds, she's holding back my hair and dabbing a cold, wet flannel onto my forehead.

"There, there, there," she says as though I'm a baby she's soothing, then to my everlasting shame I feel a dampness and know I've peed myself.

I sense rather than see Liz rise to her feet and hear the shower running.

"Here, let me help you," she's got her hands under my arms and is half lifting me and helps me step over the rim and into the bath.

My arms are wrapped around my breasts and the lukewarm water hitting me comes as a shock, but is almost a relief too.

Hard to explain, but standing there I can almost feel the headache ease. I realise I'm still wearing my now sodden underwear and one hand on the wall to support myself, carefully bend to strip off my knickers.

Liz is gone, but reappears minutes later with the mop and a bucket that smells strongly of pine disinfectant and mops cleans the floor. She catches my eye and I shamefully mutter, "Sorry."

She stops and reaching into the bath, turns off the shower tap and staring at me, calmly says, "Don't be sorry, mum. Don't ever be sorry. You've needed something like this for a very long time and

I'm only glad that for once in my life I am able to be there for you, just as you are always there for me."

Stupid, I know, and maybe's it's because I'm embarrassed and a little ashamed of my behaviour, but I start to cry.

I'm naked, I'm feeling miserable, I'm soaking wet and I'm standing in the bath, but my daughter reaches for me and wrapping her arms tightly round my waist, gives me the biggest hug.

I feel her take a deep breath and letting me go, she then says, "Get yourself dry and dressed and come downstairs and," then almost with a twinkle in her eye, humorously adds, "I'll tell you all about what you did last night."

****

God, if this is what a hangover feels like, I'm never going to touch alcohol again, I tell myself.

Ten minutes and two Paracetamol later the pain of my headache has dulled to a slow throb and even that lessens by the time I go downstairs to the kitchen. I'm braless and dressed in an old grey coloured sweater that is threadbare at the elbows and cuffs, black jogging pants that have seen better days, my pink fluffy slippers are on my feet and my towel dried hair is still damp, but tied fiercely back into a ponytail.

What does surprise me is that the kitchen clock reads it's almost ten o'clock in the morning.

I didn't think I would feel hungry, but there's something about the smell of toast. I mean, if you're anything like me and I don't profess to be a big eater, but if I have a full meal and then smell toast I can always manage at least one slice.

"Thought something light for now," Liz tells me as I slide onto a chair. She sets a plate of heavily buttered toast and a mug of tea in front of me and I watch as she refills the kettle then lifts two more mugs out of the cupboard.

"Eh, who are they for?"

"Oh," she turns and places the mugs onto the table. "Alan said he'll be by about tennish with a colleague to update us on how his investigation is going. He was going to give you an update last night, but thought you might appreciate a good nights sleep first."

"You're kidding!" I hiss because I'm suddenly aware of how I'm dressed. "You are kidding, aren't you?"

"No," she grins.

And that's when the doorbell rings.

I've no time to tidy myself up or get changed out of the old clothes I'm wearing and can only sit there and glare at Liz as she leads Alan through to the kitchen. He of course is looking his handsome self and is dressed in a smart suit, shirt and tie and the only relief I get is that his colleague turns out to Sheila Gardener, who is smartly dressed in a bottle green skirted suit with her auburn hair tied up in a bob and looking a damn sight fresher than I feel and who grins knowingly at me.

Alan greets me with, "Thought you might appreciate a visit from a friend," and nods at Sheila.

"Tea or coffee?" Liz asks.

They both opt for coffee and sitting staring at Sheila, I feel like a bag of rubbish tied in the middle that has been dragged backwards through a spiky hedge.

"How you feeling?" he asks me and I can see he's trying not to smile.

"Humble," I reply and quietly add, "Sorry."

"For what? Liz and I had a great laugh, didn't we?" he glances at her then he does smile as she grins down at me.

I realise now I'm having the pee taken out of me, but I feel humiliated and I'm about to get to my feet to go and change out of the old clothes I'm wearing when he says, "Yes."

Hands on the table, I stare at him because frankly, I'm puzzled and slowly resume my seat.

"Yes?" I repeat.

"She doesn't remember," he says and turning almost sorrowfully pouts at Liz.

I know there's something going on now and likely Sheila is part of the joke too, so I sigh and ask, "Okay, you're telling me yes. What exactly *don't* I remember?"

"Oh," his eyes open wide and his face is the picture of innocence when he tells me, "you said last night that I should consider asking you to come and live with me, so I thought about it and I'm saying, yes. That would be very nice, thank you."

I've heard of people's mouths falling open, but I always considered that to be some sort of made up expression. However, believe me, it's not. My mouth literally hangs open like the mouth of the Clyde Tunnel and I begin to stutter, "Eh…I mean…I can't have said…"

"Oh, you did," Liz interrupts and is grinning at me. "You were all slobbery when you got home last night. Oh, *Alan* is this and *Alan* is that and *please, Alan*. Very embarrassing, mum," she pretends to frown.

My face is beetroot and I'm speechless.

"Sounds like you had a really good night, Maggie," I hear Sheila say and in fairness, she's being light-hearted.

However, enough of the mickey taking I decide because not only am I totally mortified, I feel my nerves shredding and a sudden anger overtakes me. I suddenly rise from my chair and snap at them, "Excuse me! I'm going upstairs to change!"

I push past Alan as Sheila behind him quickly steps out of my way. In my bedroom I slump down onto the bed as tears bite at my eyes and I wonder, just how much of a fool did I make of myself?

If you ever *have* been drunk, you'll know that skin crawling feeling when wee bits and pieces and stupid things you did or said do come back to haunt you over the next day or two and that's what is happening to me right now.

I've only been sitting for a few minutes when the door is lightly knocked and Liz's voice says, "Can I come in, mum?"

I'm too upset to reply, but she pushes open the door anyway and comes to sit beside me on the bed.

"You know we are only joking, don't you?"

I nod and sniff.

"The thing is that it's so out of character for you to be like you were that it was…" she pauses, then shrugs and continues, "it was really funny."

Calmer now, I take a deep breath and slowly let it out.

She reaches for my hand and squeezing it, says, "Alan's putting the kettle on and he says to tell you he does want to speak to you and me. Why don't you wash your face and come down when you're ready, eh?"

She's about to leave when I say, "I'm sorry, I'd forgotten. How did last night go with Colin's parents?"

"Great," she smiles. "I'll tell you all about it when they're away. Oh, and I found out something really interesting too," she says, but she's away before telling me what it is.

I change out of the old sweater and shrug on a bra and a bright yellow coloured polo shirt, but decide to keep the jogging pants and my slippers on. After all, it *is* my house I tell myself, so I'll dress how I please.

Before I push open the front room door, I force myself to relax then entering the room I see Alan is sitting in an armchair while Liz and Sheila occupy the settee.

"Ah, at last," he rises from the chair and making his way into the kitchen, returns with a mug of coffee that he hands to me.

I sit down in the other armchair as he glances at both Liz and I, then he begins.

"As you will have guessed Sheila is part of my team and while I regret that at this time we haven't made significant progress, I can tell you that we're wading our way through all the witness statements and choosing those that we deem to consider worthy of re-interviewing. In short Liz, Maggie," he stares at us in turn, "you'll get the best service that the team and I can provide."

"We really can't ask for anymore than that, can we mum?' she turns to me.

"No, thank you. Thank you both," I force a smile.

"And one more thing," he stares at me. "I'm sorry for earlier. You know, when you weren't feeling yourself. How are you feeling now?"

"Better," I nod and toast him with my coffee.

A few seconds of silence falls between us before Liz jumps to her feet and brightly says, "Sheila. Come into the kitchen and I'll tell you about my new friend, Colin."

I'm not daft and I see what she's doing, but Sheila dutifully gets to her feet and follows Liz into the kitchen where she shrewdly closes the door behind her.

"How are you really feeling?" Alan softly asks me when we're alone.

I smile at him and reply, "Foolish. Very foolish."

He doesn't immediately respond then says, "I know that earlier I said it jokingly about you coming to live with me and yes," he holds a hand up, "you were really drunk, but if you want to consider moving some of your clothes over to mine…" He pauses then continues, "Just to let you get the feel of the place, if you like. In fact, I couldn't be more pleased."

I don't know how I feel for all I can think, is this too soon? This man, lovely man that he is, is offering to share his home, maybe even his life with me, but I've known him for just over a week. Am I ready for such a commitment?

Call me cynical, call me hesitant, but I think it's what is more commonly known as Catholic guilt.

Then again, he *is* suggesting I move some clothes over to his place, but not to move in for good, so perhaps like me he wants some time to get to know me better.

Yes that must be it, so I reply, "Can I think about it?"

I see it in his eyes. It's not quite disappointment, but I don't think it's the response he was anticipating.

He tightly smiles and nodding, says, "Yes, of course. Look," he sighs, "things between us are maybe moving a little too quick for you and maybe I'm coming on too strong. I'll understand if you want me to back off a little. Give you time to come to terms with all that's been happening over the last week; first the news that Beth's killer is arrested, then learning it's not him. It must be a hell of a wave of emotion for you and Liz."

"Thank you," is all I can think to say.

"Well," he suddenly stands up, "I think Sheila and I should be getting along."

Before I can reply, he's knocking on the kitchen door and calling out, "Time to go, Constable Gardener. Things to do and people to see."

Sheila walks through and following Alan to the door, glances back at me and says, "I'll give you a call."

I'm still seated when I hear the front door close and a little stunned that he's gone so quickly for I have a sinking feeling that where he and I are concerned, it might be for good.
****

"Are you okay, mum?"

I'm startled out of my self-pity trance by Liz who is standing in front of me, then handing me a fresh mug of coffee sits down opposite.

"Eh, yes, fine," I manage a tight smile, but it's as false as the hope that has now deserted me.

"Yes, well, you don't look fine. Things between you and Alan not go well?"

"No, not too well. In fact, I don't think there is a *thing* anymore," I admit with a shrug.

She's shaking her head when she replies, "I don't know, mum. I think you're misjudging him. One wee argument doesn't mean a breakup and let's not forget you're not exactly in peak condition at the minute."

"Breakup?" I seize upon the word and wryly smile. "We never got properly started to have a breakup, sweetheart."

"Look, I think you underestimate what a catch you are, mum," she leans forward to stare at me. "Alan's not daft, he knows you're a bit under the weather and no," she holds up her hand. "I'm not talking about the alcohol. You…both of us. We've been under a great deal of strain since we lost Beth. Besides, a couple of minutes' disagreement doesn't always need to lead to a lifetime of of regret, does it?"

When did my daughter become so wise, I wonder then I think, funny; I've come to notice that in the recent past Liz doesn't talk about her daughter being murdered. It's always been since she was lost. Is that some kind of denial, I wonder?

"Maybe so," I finally reply, but I'm keen to get off the issue of Alan and I and say, "Tell me about your visit to Colin's parents."

It was the right think to ask for her face brightens and she smiles. The first thing she says is, "You were right about the flowers. Missus Paterson noticed straight away they were from a florists and commented on it then gave me a hug. Anyway, from there things just got better."

She tells me about the detached house they live in, the welcoming reception she received and the lovely meal Missus Paterson prepared. "Her first name's Grace and his dad's called Neil, but I decided I'd call them mister and missus."

"Quite correct until they tell you otherwise," I agree then ask, "And did Mister Paterson discuss you buying a car?"

"Well, he works in a garage in Finnieston and now that he knows what my budget is, said he'll keep an eye open for a good one coming in as a part exchange. Apparently if it's family he'll get a good deal too."

"So, you are family are you?" I smile at her.

She blushes and is clearly happy that they seem to have accepted her and continues when they asked about her being still being married, though she was nervous, she'd been upfront with them and disclosed she was in the process of divorcing her husband.

"Did they ask about Beth?"

Her brow knits when she replies, "Missus Paterson said they knew about Beth, that Colin had told them and it was because of Beth's loss…"

There it is again; loss not murder.

"…they were aware that I had been admitted to hospital, where I had met Colin. They didn't ask about my time in Leverndale and Colin said later that he had confided in them and told them that my treatment had been successful."

"So, all in all it was a good night?"

"Yes, mum," she happily smiles. "It was a good night."

I'm glad that at last things seem to be going Liz's way and it's when she's about to rise from her chair I ask, "You said in the bedroom about finding out something really interesting. What is it?"

She sits back down and her eyes open in glee as though she is about to divulge something really important.

"Well," she begins, "you know I said Mister Paterson works in the garage in Finnieston, that he's a manager there?"

I nod.

"When Missus Paterson asked me where I lived and I said Clarion Crescent, he said he worked in a bus garage a couple of years ago with a man who he thought lived here too, in Clarion Crescent."

I'm about to ask who it is when she adds, "Through the wall. Willie McPherson. Now, isn't that a right coincidence?"

It comes sharply to mind Alan telling me there is no such thing as coincidence, yet here's a second one within two days. First the young woman detective at Stewart Street knowing Peter McGregor, now Colin's father knowing Willie McPherson and I think, I'll need to tell…but then I stop, for I remember that I might no longer be on sociable speaking terms with Alan.

"Yes, that's pretty strange," I nod. "Does he keep in touch with Willie?"

She frowns and shaking her head, replies, "No, I don't think they were friends or anything. Mister Paterson is a manager in the Finnieston garage in the repair side of the business and I think from the way he described it when he worked with Willie in the bus garage, he was Willie's supervisor or something. I told him that

Willie's a quiet man and we don't really know him that well and then he said something funny."

"Funny?" I stare at her. "You mean funny in a ha-ha way or funny as in odd?"

"Odd, I suppose," she shrugs. "He said that Willie had to be let go because he was always coming into work with a sore face and said it was from falling over and that Willie eventually admitted it was to do with his drinking."

"Drinking? He said Willie was a drinker?"

"Aye, that's what he told me. Does Willie drink?"

I shake my head and reply, "I don't know, sweetheart. I've never seen him drinking or should I say, I've never known him to be drunk, but who knows what goes on behind closed doors."

I have a flashback to Moira's night-time rant and then add, "He might be a secret tippler."

"The McPherson's could be thinking that of you if they'd seen you getting hauled out of Alan's car last night," she teases me, then seeing my face fall, says, "Sorry mum. You okay?"

"Just tired," I smile at her, but the truth is I want to go back to bed and draw the cover over my head then go to sleep and forget what a mess I've made of what might have been a good relationship with Alan Reid.

****

The rest of the day is a blur. At Liz's suggestion, I return to bed just after midday for a nap that lasts right through to almost six o'clock when she wakens me with a cup of tea. Going back to bed was the right thing to do for I feel much better, if a little depressed about Alan.

She plumps up the pillows behind my head and when I sit up with my back to them, she squats on the edge of the bed and says, "It's been raining, but it's stopped now. Look, Colin's on a late shift and I've told him to go straight home and get a good nights' sleep. I was thinking, you know that I've not had much time for the church these past few years, but why don't you and I go to the Vigil Mass tonight? Maybe get a something from the Saffron Indian takeaway on the way home."

Frankly, I'm taken aback and it crosses my mind that I'm being humoured, that Liz is trying to make up for her earlier teasing.

But seeing her eager face I smile and nod before replying, "That will be lovely."

"Right then, finish your tea and get dressed and I'll see you downstairs."

With that she's gone and for the first time that day, I feel a little happier.

****

The rain stays off and by six-thirty I'm dressed and downstairs and we're both ready to leave. It's Liz's suggestion the fresh air will do me good so with my trusty popup brolly in my hand, we decide to walk to the church.

Arm in arm we begin to make our way along Clarion Crescent and then walking in Clarion Road we're at the junction with Archerhill Road when we see a couple walking towards us. Unlike us they are not arm in arm, but walking quickly with a few feet between them. They're on the same side of the road as us and it's when they get closer and though the man is wearing bunnet and the woman has a headscarf on, I see it's my neighbours, Moira and Willie McPherson. It's then that the most curious thing happens.

They can't be any further than twenty-five or thirty yards from us when Moira, who is walking on the road side of the pavement, apparently sees us and to our surprise, reaches across and literally pulls Willie's arm before both cross the road towards the row of shops.

What makes it even more unusual is that they have to dodge traffic as they hurry across Archerhill Road and one motorist even sounds his horn at their stupidity.

Gobsmacked doesn't do justice to what I think, but I'm conscious of both Liz and I slowing then stopping to watch them cross the road, but neither look back and they disappear into the Archerhill Licensed Grocers.

"What was *that* all about?" Liz turns to stare at me.

"I have no idea," I honestly answer, but a curious niggle starts at the pit of my stomach and though I can't describe it, I know something is definitely off.

****

It's the usual thirty or forty parishioners who are present when Liz and I arrive at St Ninian's and I supress a giggle when Liz nods at the pews occupants, and whispers, "It's like God's waiting room in here."

During the service, Father O'Brien catches sight of Liz and I and when I attend to take communion, he leans over and whispers, "I'll be seeing you both for a cuppa in the hall."

No pressure then, I'm thinking and when the service concludes we make our way to the church hall for the tea and biscuit.

In the hall I see the two old cronies, Betty McFarlane and Isa Fullerton and when I catch their eyes they smile and nod but make no attempt to come over to speak with us.

I assume they're worried about me the mad woman hijacking them again.

Father O'Brien arrives in the hall minutes later and after a few cursory smiles and backslaps to his parishioners, makes his way toward Liz and I.

"Ah, ladies, nice to see you both and particularly you, young Elizabeth, after so many years."

There it is, the implied 'Why have you stayed away from church for so long?' but to her credit Liz simply smiles, then replies, "Thank you for the reference, Father. I got the job."

"Didn't doubt for a minute you would, lass. Congratulations. Now, how are you holding up?"

"As fine as can be expected," she diplomatically answers and I realise she doesn't want to mention her pending divorce or new relationship; at least, not right away.

"And you, Maggie?" he turns to me. "The last time you were in here I saw you haring out the door dragging poor old Betty and Isa with you. Fair shaken to, they told me later," he chuckles at the memory. "Thought they were being kidnapped, they said."

"It all ended up as a big mistake, Father, and as for how I'm doing? I'm doing well," I grace him with a smile, but it's not how I'm feeling.

"Still no man in your life yet?"

I'm taken aback by his question, but it's Liz who rescues me when she replies, "Don't you think she's got enough to do with me back in the house, Father?"

He catches on right away and I sense she's kicking herself for opening her mouth when his eyes narrow and he asks, "And you're not back with your man then, Liz?"

I see her hesitate and I abruptly take over to tell him, "You'll recall me telling you, Father, that Ian Chalmers turned out to be less of a man than we thought. He abandoned my daughter at the time she needed him most so no, Liz is most definitely not going back with that excuse for a husband."

Then he takes us both by surprise when he gently smiles and nodding, replies, "I'm glad to hear that. I never liked that man. Thought him to be a bit of a chancer, so I did and he kind of put me in mind of my younger brother Seamus, God protect him and keep him safe in his arms. For all Seamus was thought to be a happy go lucky sort of man, he hurt a lot of people on the way and mostly because of his addiction to the Porter and the horses. Good for you, Liz," he clasps his hand on her arm and adds, "My advice is to follow your mother's guidance, for she is the one person in this world who has your best interest at heart."

Winking at me, he smiles and makes his way across the hall to speak with his housekeeper Katie Doherty who is stood beside the pass keeper, Patrick Reilly, the widowed St Vincent De Paul member who is rumoured to be her fancy man.

"Well," Liz quietly exhales, "I didn't expect that. I thought I was in for a lecture about not attending Mass or that he would tell me to try and fix my marriage."

"That's Father O'Brien," I sigh and think he's full of surprises and a lot shrewder and supportive than anybody might suspect.

The small number of parishioners begin to fade from the room so Liz and I take our leave of Father O'Brien with a wave and making our way into the night find it's again begun to rain.

"Wish I'd brought the car," I wryly comment as we huddle together under my brolly, but Liz laughs and replies, "Skin's waterproof, mum. That's what you always told me when I was wee. It'll not do us any harm getting wet."

On the way home we grab our takeaway from Saffron's and hurry up the road.

CHAPTER TWENTY-ONE

By attending Saturday evening Mass, it removes my Catholic guilt of lying in on a Sunday morning and let me tell you, I usually do enjoy my Sunday morning lie-ins.

But not this Sunday morning.

No, the headache if not the embarrassment of my boozy Friday night is gone, but already I miss Alan and can't get it out of my head that if only I had been a little less sensitive…

Anyway, I've never been one to cry over spilt milk and lying in my bed, my hands ball into fists and I fight against the melancholy that threatens to overtake me while I wonder what he thinks of me now. I *need* to get over this, I savagely tell myself and use the back of my hand to wipe at my eyes then turning I see it's a few minutes after nine.

I hear Liz in the bathroom showering and remember that though Colin is again working a late shift, he has arranged to pick her up and take her for breakfast before starting his shift.

I burp and taste again the Indian food I had for dinner and decide to get up and before I bathe, I'll give the bathroom a good seeing too, my face reddening as I recall my performance yesterday morning in there.

Opening my bedroom door, I see Liz leaving the bathroom and she cheerfully calls out, "Morning, mum. I thought I'd let you lie on and bring you a cuppa, but you're up now, are you?"

I know she's being polite and willing, but I nod and reply, "You get yourself dressed, sweetheart and I'll stick the kettle on and make you some toast."

"No, tea will be fine. I'm going for…"

"Breakfast with Colin, you said last night," I remind her. "Tea it is, then."

More than a couple of hours have now passed and Liz is long gone with Colin. I'm bathed, dressed in jeans and a favourite clean cream coloured blouse and because it's a dry and windy day, I've stripped both beds of their sheets and quilt covers and the washing machine is going at full pelt. The ironing board is set up, the television is showing a repeat of 'Call the Midwife' and I'm on automatic pilot and halfway through the clothes in the ironing basket when the doorbell goes.

I'm frowning as I glance at the clock on the mantelpiece and seeing it's not yet midday, I switch off the iron and wonder who's calling at this time of the morning on a Sunday.

Fortunately, I'm dressed in a clean blouse and a pair of jeans so patting at my hair that's hanging loose on my shoulders, I pull the door open to find it's Alan Reid who is holding a bunch of flowers in his hand.

To be honest, he is the last person I expect to find at my door and though I knew that at some point he'd be calling again with news about the investigation, I had supposed he'd phone first.

Before I can open my mouth, he warily looks at me and says, "I'll give you these flowers, Maggie, but only if you promise not to hit me with them or throw them back in my face."

I feel my face flush, but whether it's from embarrassment or just pleasure at seeing him, I'm not quite sure; however, I reach out and taking the flowers from him, I reply, "Come in. Please."

He nods and wordlessly stepping by me, I close the door and follow him into the front room.

"I was just catching up with some ironing," I begin then inwardly reproach myself for stating the obvious.

"I'm a detective. I guessed that," he grins at me.

"Coffee?"

"Please."

"Thanks for these, they're lovely," I smile at the flowers and head into the kitchen.

Filling the kettle gives me a moment to catch my breath and work out how again I can apologise for my behaviour the previous day. But then it occurs to me perhaps he's not here to renew what had been the start of our relationship. Perhaps he's just here to give some kind of update on the investigation.

But the flowers puzzle me.

I carry the two mugs through and handing him one I nod that he sits down.

It doesn't escape me that he chooses to sit on the couch rather than his usual armchair opposite me.

"I owe you an apology," he says and I stare at him for surely it should be me that's apologising, I'm thinking.

"We…I mean me; I teased you and went too far yesterday morning. I'm sorry."

"You've nothing to be sorry for, it was me who acted like a bitch," I reply and surprise myself. Bitch is a word I seldom if ever use, then guiltily recall the last time I said that word was to big Eileen at work. "No, no," he waves away my protests, then softly smiles and asks, "Can we start again? I mean, you and me?"

I suddenly feel as though a great weight has lifted from my chest and not trusting myself to speak, I bite at my lip and nod.

"Right, now that our first tiff has been settled," he squints at me and I find myself laughing, "a wee thing to mention about the investigation. I've made some discreet inquiry into your neighbour, Peter McGregor and while he's not completely out of the frame…" he stops and begins to explain, "By out of the frame I mean…"

I raise my hand and interrupt with, "Don't forget I read crime fiction."

"Oh, right then of course. Well, while he's not completely out of the frame, I'm more inclined to believe that even if he is a philandering threat to young women, in my own opinion I don't figure him for murdering Beth. Yes," he holds up a hand to stem my protest, "I could be wrong, but I have another idea about her killer. Something I'm currently working on. Background information that I'm trying to access."

"And what's that?" I lean forward with keen interest.

"Look, Maggie, I need you to trust me here, because I might be totally on the wrong track and I don't want to give you and Liz any false hope. Can you do that? Can you bear with me for now?"

I'm keenly staring at him and realise yes, I do trust him. Completely.

"But you'll let me know when or if you find out something?"

"Of course," he nods. "I won't hold anything back from you. I swear it."

Needless to say I'm intrigued but in the short time I've come to know Alan I realise that no matter what I say or try to cajole him, he won't be swayed and will tell me in his own good time. Now, I wonder, how weird is that? Here's me already defining my relationship with him and like I say, it's been such a short time too.

"Liz due back?" he asks,

"Eh?" his question brings me back down to earth and I reply, "Oh, they're out for breakfast. Have you had yours?"

"Coffee and toast," he glances at his wristwatch, "five hours ago."

"Well," I smile and rise to me feet, "let me see what I've got in the fridge."
****

He tells me he's on duty till about five o'clock, and minutes after I've fed him a ham omelette he tells me he has to leave. I walk him to the door where he wraps his arms about me and kisses me passionately before telling me he'll phone when he finishes work and if I'm up for it, take me for a late night supper to the Café Gandolfi in the Merchant City.

I wave him cheerio and I'm literally dancing on air that things between us are sorted out. God, I was so worried that he'd dump me before he really got to know me and I can't help smiling as I unload the washing machine and carry the basket out to the rotary dryer on the back green.

The wind is fairly billowing about as I try to hang the sheets and covers on the line and then I hear what sound like a bang or more properly, something like glass breaking from over the fence.

Let me explain. The dividing fence between my garden and the McPherson's is about eight feet high and was built by my Alex, oh, must be nearly fifteen years ago now. It is a vertical fence with the slats about an inch apart and when Alex built it we could see through the gap into our then neighbour's garden. However, when the McPhersons moved in almost right away, Jimmy added vertical slats to his side of the fence that covered the gaps and I assumed it was because he and Moira wanted privacy. I mean, what other reason would there be?

Hearing the bang piques my curiosity and I call out, "Hello? Jimmy? Moira? You all right there?"

Obviously because of the height of the fence I can't see over it and I don't get a response. I'm about to ignore what I've heard when I think…I say think, because I'm not really sure; I think I hear a whimper.

Now, I'm not a nosey neighbour, but if I have heard correctly then one of them might be hurt. I haven't finished hanging out the wash, but my conscience gets the better of me and I decide to run round and check that nobody has been hurt.

It's quicker if rather than going through the house I make my way along my driveway to the road and I race round to their semi and run up the driveway at the side of their house. Willie's car is in the driveway and is backed up against the fence that encloses their back garden, but the gate is unlocked and opens when I push at it.

"Hello?" I loudly call out as I walk into their rear garden.

To my surprise I see Moira at the back of the house wearing a pink coloured dressing gown and is barefooted. Her hair's in disarray, her face streaked with mascara and she's sitting huddled on a dwarf brick wall at their back door that is lying ajar. Her arms are tightly wrapped about her as she sways back and forth and she's weeping. An empty vodka bottle is lying at her feet and a broken glass beside it.

That's when I notice the blood. Not a lot of blood, but enough for me to see she's cut her foot badly.

My eyes open wide and I'm guessing she has stood on the shattered glass.

"Moira," I approach her with my arms out. "You've cut yourself, hen," I tell her then as I bend over her I realise and I startle! She can't be!

But she is!

She's drunk!

Not falling about, incoherently, out of her face, incapable drunk, but what we Weegies refer to in Glasgow parlance as steaming drunk.

I see her eyes are glazed and she's muttering to herself.

"What is it, Moira? What have you done?" I fetch my hankie from the pocket of my jeans and reach down to grasp her foot.

I can't know it, but while I am referring to her foot, she seems to think I mean something else for it's as if she's suddenly realised I'm there. Her eyes open wide and she stares at me in…in terror? In fear? I'm not quite certain, but she's definitely not pleased to see me and pulling her foot away causes her to overbalance on the small wall and she falls backwards onto her side and to my surprise, tries to crawl away from me.

She begins to wail and through her tears and blubbering, she repeatedly says, "I'm sorry, I'm sorry, I'm sorry."

"It's okay, hen," I try to comfort her, but it's not easy when she's trying to crawl away from me and I don't want to try and restrain her in case I make her panic or something.

Kneeling beside her I decide to throw my arm about her shoulder and attempt to calm her before I try again to examine her bleeding foot.

You might think I wonder where Jimmy, her husband is while I'm trying to assist her. Stupidly, I'm not giving him any thought. I suppose it is because I am so preoccupied by Moira.

"I'm sorry," she says again and she's crying loudly and I mean real heartache tears as though her very world is ending. Her body is shaking too, as she sobs.

"It's okay, Moira," I tell her again. "We'll get you inside and see that your foot is fixed up, eh?" I try to encourage her.

She stares at me as though I'm daft then and I'm taken aback when she scowls and her whole demeanour changes and believe it or not, I begin to wonder if she's going to attack me for little globules of spittle appear at the side of her mouth and she growls; yes, literally growls, "You had it all, but you didn't care, did you? It's your fault because you didn't *fucking* care and sent her out *alone*!"

I admit to being confused, but persuade myself it's the drink talking and raising my knees off the ground I'm still bending down over her when she hisses, "All I wanted was a fucking *cuddle*!"

Call me dim-witted for I don't immediately understand then think that she and Jimmy have had another fallout, that because of the state she is in he's refused to cuddle her.

But then my blood turns to ice when she slurs, "But she wouldn't let me, would she?"

Suddenly my throat tightens, my mouth is dry and my body begin to shake, but I clench my hands into fists so tightly the nails dig painfully into my palms.

My voice almost a croak, I force myself to be calm and in a voice as even as I can muster, I ask her, "Who wouldn't let you cuddle her, Moira?"

When she stares at me I see her eyes are bloodshot and again it's as though she's seeing me for the first time. Her face contorts and though it's not a word I would normally use I can only describe the way she looks at me as…malevolent.

Now our faces are so close I feel my stomach heave at the rancid smell of her breath and then, even though she is drunk, she finds her voice that is almost a whisper and snarls, "You and your *precious* daughter and your *precious* granddaughter. Why do you think you should have it all? What makes you so fucking *special!"*

Her eyes bore into mine, but I'm determined to get an answer. My whole being wants to take her by the throat and squeeze the life from her for I know what she did.

I know now who killed my Beth!

But I need her to tell me so I swallow with difficulty and ask again, "Who wouldn't let you cuddle her, Moira?"

She stares at me for what seems to be an eternity, yet it is no more than a few seconds.

Then she smiles.

She *smiles*!

"I only wanted a cuddle, was that too much to ask," she drops her voice and whimpers like a child before she adds with a sneer, "Bethany. Little…blonde… *precious*…Bethany. Wouldn't cuddle me! I would have loved her! I would have loved her a fucking sight better than you would! Said my breath was smelly," she drunkenly sniggers, but there's no humour in it.

My heart is racing and I hear the blood pressure drumming in my ears.

That's when I hit her.

With all the force and rage I can muster, I punch her to the face and yes, I want to kill her, but as she falls back I am hit on the back of the head and my knees buckle and I find myself falling over onto the ground.

This time though it's not like when Jessie's husband punched me. I'm dazed yes, but I still understand what's happening to me. Then I'm hit again and the pain is…excruciating is the only word I can find to describe it and for some unknown reason I think, he's going to burst the stitches in my head.

I say he because I knew it had to be him, her husband Jimmy.

He's come out of the house and hit me with something, then I hear him hiss, "What have you done, Moira? What did you tell her? Jesus Christ, *Moira*! What have you *done*!"

I'm aware of lying on the ground and I can taste blood. I know it's mine that is running down from my head to my face and I taste the salty blood that seeps into my mouth. But crazily, all I can think about is if the blood gets onto my cream blouse it's going to be the very devil to get out. I try to speak, but nothing comes out other than a cough.

Jimmy is shouting at Moira and all I want to do is stand up, but I can't because my legs won't work, then I'm grabbed by my wrists and pulled on my back into the house and I'm vaguely aware my slippers have come off.

"Jimmy," I hear myself gasp, but he ignores me and leaves me lying on the kitchen floor.

I'm lying on my side on the tiled floor and I see his legs and I see he's wearing brown corduroy slippers and…what the hell does that matter, I wonder? Then he's dragging Moira into the house by her arms.

"Fuck! Fuck Fuck!" I hear him repeat over and over and over.

I don't know how long I lie there, but when I use my arms to try and raise myself from the floor, I can't and I flop back down into my own pool of blood and I feel my head bounce on the tiled floor.

I see Jimmy's legs again and now he's bending over me and telling me, "I'm sorry! I didn't want any of this! Jesus, Maggie, I'm sorry!" Then he's gone again and he's back seconds or is it minutes later? I really don't know and now I'm beginning not to care.

But I know I have to stay awake and I fight the drowsiness.

He's pulling at my hands and turning me onto my front, forces them together at my back and confused though I am, I know that he's using something to tie or bind my wrists together. Then he places something across my mouth, something sticky and I realise it's a sticky tape.

He's left me on the floor and he's gone again, but comes back and I see his legs go out of the door.

I'm finding it difficult to breathe because the tape is so tight and I'm starting to panic and I'm gagging and forced to swallow a mouthful of my blood and I'm blinking because some of the blood has run into my left eye.

He's back again and he's lifting me to a sitting position and says, "I need to put you in the shed for now," or something like that.

His hands is under my armpits and he's pulling me backwards out of the door and my heels are dragging and they hurt when he bumps me down the back stairs to the slab path then drags me along the gravel path to the shed at the bottom of the garden. Both my heels are really hurting and I realise that with my slippers off, my heels must have scraped on the slabs.

But my eyes remain open and I'm still conscious and I *refuse* to fall asleep.

Not while that murdering *bitch* is in her house.

Jimmy pulls me into the shed and it stinks of paint and turpentine and God knows what.

He doesn't drop me, but gently lays me down onto my side and before he leaves I hear him mutter, "I'm sorry," and I hear a padlock being snapped closed.

I know it's still the middle of the day, but the shed is dark because there is a piece of old carpet across the only window, but a small shaft of light shines in one corner.

It's when I try to move my legs I realise he's put tape around my ankles too.

I don't know how long I lie there but try as I might to resist, I finally give in to both the pain in my head and the darkness and I fall asleep.

CHAPTER TWENTY-TWO

"Maggie! Maggie!"

I recoil when the torch is shone into my eyes and then I flinch when the tape is torn from my mouth.

Is it? Yes, it's Alan and here I go again, because I start to cry.

"Get me an ambulance, now!" I hear him shout and realise he's sitting beside me on the wooden floor of the shed and got me propped up against him, his arm about my shoulders then I hear him loudly call out, "A knife! Get me a knife! Quickly! She's got tape on her hands and feet!"

"Mum!" I hear Liz's voice call out, but it's as though she's some distance away then suddenly my hands are free and the pain is awful as the blood flows back into them.

My eyes hurt and glancing through the shed door I see it's now dark and there are torches being shone everywhere.

"Maggie Brogan," he says to me in a soft voice, a voice that is breaking with emotion. "Can I not leave you for a couple of hours but you're getting yourself into bother?"

"Ambulance is on its way, boss," a male voice calls out.

"Soon as they arrive have them up here with a stretcher," he replies.

"I can walk," I try to stand, but he firmly holds me and says, "No you won't, love. You've a head wound and you're in shock, so like it or not, you're going by stretcher."

Frankly, I'm glad he's insisted because to be honest, I'm really not sure if I can walk.

What seems like minutes pass then I'm carefully loaded onto a stretcher and carried along the garden path and see a dozen faces peering down at me, some of whom gently pat me on the shoulder, but it's Liz who walks beside me, her pale, tearstained face staring down at me as she clutches my hand.

I'm being passed into the back of the brightly lit ambulance and the dark sky seems to be filled with blue lights that flash all around.

Then I hear one of the ambulance people who is dabbing at the blood on my face with some sort of tissue, tell someone who I think is Alan that I'm going straight to the Neuro at the Queen Elizabeth.

I'm conscious of being laid down onto a kind of bed in the back of the ambulance and of Liz sitting opposite me when I hear Alan call out, "Wait a minute."

He's climbed into the back of the ambulance and leaning over me says, "I'll be over soon. Liz will look after you for the minute."

He stares down at me then gently brushing hair from my eyes, leans down and kisses me on the forehead before he gets out of the back.

Liz has stopped crying and still holding my hand, stares at me as though she expects me to disappear. I know I want to ask her what happened and how did they find me, but right now I think I'll just go back to sleep.

****

I think I did fall asleep in the ambulance, but I'm wide awake when I get to the hospital casualty department because this young doctor keeps shining a light into my eyes and I try to tell her it's blinding me, but the words just don't come out right.

The next…oh, I don't know…hour or so maybe? Anyway, it's a blur as I'm whisked from one room to another, poked and prodded and no bugger will let me go back to sleep.

Badly concussed is one phrase that I hear is bandied about though I do hear a grinning Jamaican nurse telling Liz I've a head like a bowling ball and that's what really saved me from real damage. Bowling ball indeed!

The long and short of it is that I end up in another brightly lit sterile looking room and get that *déjà vu* feeling.

"Certainly getting your money's worth out of the NHS, mum," Liz grins at me from a chair beside my bed, but her bottom lip is trembling and I can see she's close to tears.

And before you ask, yes, I've yet another painful headache though this one can't be attributed to alcohol.

"So, what happened?" at last I manage to ask her.

"Well," her slowly exhales as her face clouds over, "Alan says to tell you that the short version is the McPhersons have been arrested. However, he had to stay behind because he needs to interview them and will get here as soon as he can."

Then I remember.

I try to grab at Liz's arm and I struggle to get the words out, but at last I tell her, "It was Moira. It was her who killed Beth."

"I know, I mean, the police know it was, mum," she replies through her falling tears, then shaking her head, dabs at her eyes with a tissue and continues, "I don't know how he found out, but Alan knew it was her and that's why she was arrested. Jimmy," she spat his name out, "has been arrested too, for what he did to you."

I feel drained and my head feels tight too, but when I reach up to touch my head, Liz grimaces and raising her hand to stop me, sharply tells me, "Don't. Your head's bandaged mum and they had to shave off your hair."

"My hair?"

"The doctor told me you had a very bad wound to the back of your head and they had to shave off most of your hair to get it stitched. He said when you were hit it opened the other wound too and they had to re-stitch that as well. I don't know how many stitches you have but," she shrugs, "you can maybe wear a wig in the meantime, eh?"

With all that has happened in the last day and perhaps it's a vanity thing, but the news that my hair has been cut off is suddenly the worst and I begin to sob.

"Please, mum, don't," Liz rises from her chair to cuddle me.

"God, with my black eye and my hair shaved I must look like a monster," I wail, but she shakes her head and quickly replies, "Don't be silly. Yes, you've lost some hair but at least it will grow back and your eye is healing too. Mum, you're alive and you'll get better, so stop feeling sorry for yourself. There are people a whole lot worse off than you, you know."

If she thinks that is going to make me feel better, she's completely wrong because right now, I believe I have every right to feel sorry for myself.

It takes me a couple of minutes to compose myself and after she hands me a drink of water, Liz tells me, "Colin is coming over when he finishes his shift, sometime within the next half hour. I don't know when Alan will get here, but the nurse told me that you really need to rest and get some sleep."

She's right, for I feel very drowsy and nodding, I remember mumbling I need to shut my eyes or something like that.

****

Opening my eyes I squint for the room is very bright, but it's not the room light, it's the brightness shining through the opened curtains on the windows and I see it's a different room from the one I fell asleep in.

I'm aching all over then remember that I had been tied up for a time in the one position and reason that is why my body feels so stiff.

The door is pushed open and a young, fair haired Staff Nurse barges in pushing a trolley with a basin on top and says, "Morning, Maggie. How are you feeling?"

"Awful," I truthfully tell her.

She smiles and says, "Maybe you'll feel a lot better with a bed bath, eh?"

I stop her there and ask, "If you don't mind, I'd prefer a shower, even if you need to help me. Will that be okay?"

She screws her eyes and her face contorts with indecision, then she says, "Hang on, I'll check with Sister."

She's back in a couple of minutes and tells me, "Aye, that's fine, but I'll stay in the room while you make your toilet and shower and only if you keep the door open."

Evelyn, she tells me is her name, helps me out of the bed and then taking my arm accompanies me into the en-suite where she places a polythene hair net over my bandaged head.

"Mind," she wags a finger as she leaves, "I'm right here so don't overdo it and shout me if you need a hand."

I nod and remember I'm a woman, so I make straight for the mirror on the wall and gasp at the sight of myself.

I think haggard is the word I'll use to describe me.

After making my toilet I carefully I strip off the hospital gown and my knickers and step under the wet room shower. The hot water playing on my body feels wonderful and eases the ache in my shoulders and my legs. When I glance at my wrists and ankles the skin is a reddish colour where the sticky tape has marked my skin. It's what, ten minutes later I think when I dry myself during which time from the other room Evelyn has chattered away like a budgie, asking me all sorts of questions then I realise what she's really doing is looking for my responses to ensure I haven't collapsed unconscious onto the floor.

When I call out I'm done, she comes into the en-suite with a small travel bag that I recognise as mine.

"The nightshift said…your husband is it?" she stares curiously at me.

"Eh, no, my boyfriend," I smile and think of Alan.

"Anyway, he was here during the night sitting by your bed and brought this change of clothes with him."

From the bag she brings out clean underwear and a nightie that I assume Liz has given him.

"There was a note too on your file saying that he'll pop in later when he's free," she adds.

****

I learn from Evelyn I'm actually in the Neuro Ward and the rest of the morning is busy with several doctors calling in to check my wound and explain that due to the injury I received they wish me to remain for at least another forty-eight hours and tell me that is the critical time for head wounds such as mine, that if there was any delayed reaction to the concussion, it would likely occur during that period and I've also had my head X-rayed.

Of course I've no option but to agree and resign myself that I'm going nowhere for a couple of days.

Liz arrives for the afternoon visit and to my surprise brings two young women and a child with her.

Right away I recognise Alan's daughter Fiona and her son Finn, but the other girl isn't immediately obvious till I remember the photographs and greet her with, "You must be Bryony."

Fortunately, Staff Nurse Evelyn relaxes the 'two to a bed' rule and fetches a third chair.

"I hope you don't mind," Fiona sits the wee guy on her knee and nodding to Bryony, continues, "but when we heard what had happened we phoned Liz and she agreed we could come and visit."
"Besides," Bryony cut in, but with bright smile that reminds me of her father, "I was curious to meet the woman who's got our dad in such a fluster."
I feel myself blush and ask if he's okay?
I'm aware of both his daughters staring curiously at me, but it's Fiona who replies, "You've been through all this trauma, someone has attempted to kill you and you're lying here in hospital with a serious head injury and you're worrying about dad being okay? My God, Maggie, where *did* he find you? If he ever thinks about letting you go he's off his head and he'll have us to deal with!"
I'm that taken aback and as tears sting at my eyes I feel a great weight has lifted from me and I know this sounds really daft, but I'm too happy to even reply.
Anyway, the rest of the visit goes really well and then towards the end of the visiting time Fiona and Bryony leave to allow Liz the last five minutes alone with me.
"I met the girls downstairs," she begins. "Fiona phoned me this morning to ask how you were and when I said I was coming here she asked if they could come with me."
That's when I remember and I say, "But were you not due to start your training this morning at Asda, hen?"
"Mum," she wryly smiles. "you're the talk of the steamie. All the headlines in the papers are about you and the arrest of the McPhersons and the house phone has been ringing off the hook. When I phoned Mark, the manager at Asda, and told him you're my mother and I needed to be with you he said straight away it was no problem, that I'd to phone him when I was ready to start, so we agreed I'd commence my training next Monday."
"Thank heavens, I didn't want you to lose this opportunity, sweetheart. But," I'm curious, "how did you get here today if the girls didn't bring you?"
"Oh, I've Colin's car. Remember, I'm on his insurance?"
"Oh, aye," I nod.
"I dropped him at work and I'll pick him up when he finishes. He says to tell you it's his day off tomorrow so he's planning to pop

over to see you."

"God, all these visitors. I've never been so popular," I smile at her. And just then the door is pushed open and who should walk in, but Father O'Brien.

"Maggie, my dear. I hear you've been in the wars again," he grins at me.

"Right," Liz bends over the bed to kiss my forehead, "I'll leave you with Father and I'll be back tonight, Mum."

****

Father's gone, having visited for just twenty minutes during which time he prayed with me and thanked God for my deliverance from a near death experience.

Jokingly, he told me that he'd almost run out of candles in the church because of the number of parishioners who were also praying for my recovery.

I told him too I hadn't realised how popular I am.

Staff Nurse Evelyn has just popped in with my medication and I'm looking forward to a nap, but it's not to be. I'm about to sigh in frustration when I hear the door being knocked, but to my delight it's Alan and right behind him, I see a smiling Sheila Gardener.

"You do realise it's not visiting time," I pretend to scowl.

"This is police business, Missus Brogan, so I'll have none of your nonsense," he scolds me, then bursts into a wide grin and adds, "I'm glad to see you are your old self, Maggie."

"What, you mean bad tempered," Sheila interrupts as she drags a chair across to the bed.

I'm taken by surprise when he leans across the bed and kisses me.

"Oh, don't mind me," Sheila grunts. "I'd tell you two to get a room, but it seems you're already past that stage," she shakes her head.

He sits down and takes my hand before asking me, "How are you really feeling?"

"Still a bit confused about everything that happened, but I'm really keen to know the story. The staff here gave me a couple of newspapers to read, but other than telling me that the McPherson's have been arrested and an unnamed woman…me, I presume… has been seriously injured, there are no real details."

"And that's why Sheila and I are here," he replies.

"We've just come from the Sheriff Court," he begins, "and you'll be pleased to know that the McPhersons have been remanded in custody."

"The Sheriff Court? But if she killed Beth shouldn't she go to the High Court…"

He holds up his hand to stop me and says, "Let me tell you the story first and then if you have any questions, wait till I finish."

"Sorry," I meekly reply, but he squeezes my hand to let me know it's okay.

"When Beth's body was discovered it was assumed that she had been murdered by a male person who likely had sexual intent. However, as you are aware there were no witnesses and no indication her clothing had been disturbed, yet the supposition continued that the killer, again presumed to be a male, had been disturbed. The forensic examination of Beth's clothing and we only discovered this when we reviewed the statements…"

"*You* discovered it, Alan," Sheila abruptly interrupted. "Don't downplay all you achieved."

I didn't remark on it, but noticed her use of his forename and realising the formality of rank had been dropped, they must have become friends.

"Yes, well," he continued, "when I read a statement that said a couple of pink threads were discovered on Beth's jacket, I realised the threads had been dismissed because the investigation had centred on the killer being a man and it was wrongly accepted Beth being a wee girl, the threads must have adhered from an item of her own clothing. I then discovered that nobody had tried to match the threads to any item of clothing owned by Beth."

"An oversight?" I ask.

"No, Maggie," his voice is cold, "a damn neglect of duty is what it was. Anyway, that set me thinking and I remembered something you had said to me a while back."

"Something I said? What?"

His brow furrows and he says, "When you told me about the first time Liz brought Ian Chalmers to your house, that you and your husband saw through him right away and you said something like, 'Liz was too close and couldn't see beyond his veneer.' Do you recall telling me that?"

"Eh, yes, I think so."

"Well, because of the pink threads and no apparent attempt at, well, interfering with Beth, I was already considering that perhaps the killer was not male, but possibly female and if that was the case, then it was more than likely the female might live a lot closer to where you reside than you might have thought. That's when what you said came back to me and I wondered if maybe it was someone too close to where you lived, someone with a veneer of respectability and I recalled you telling me Moira McPherson was a member, or had been a member, of the Salvation Army."

"And," my eyes widen, "that's why you all but dismissed Peter McGregor as a suspect, because you then believed it might have been a woman who killed Beth?"

"Yes," he vigorously nods, "but I have to admit I was taking a leap of faith with that belief. Then when you told me about the strange occurrences at the McPherson house, I decided to do a little digging into them and found that prior to moving in next door to you, they'd lived in a place called Pollard Street in Rotherham."

"Rotherham?"

"It's in South Yorkshire. Apparently James McPherson met his wife down in England when he served in the army at Catterick. When I contacted the local police I discovered that they moved from Rotherham to Glasgow about five years ago?"

He looks at me for confirmation and I nod and reply, "That's about the time they moved in next door, yes."

"Well, just about the time they moved house from down there, a little girl called Emily Churchill, aged four, went missing from a street near to Pollard Street. Her body has never been found."

He turns to glance at Sheila. "As we speak the police in Yorkshire are digging up the garden of their former house."

I suddenly feel a chill and instinctively pull the cover up a little closer and I mumble, "She told me she'd killed Beth."

There's a few seconds of silence and nodding, Alan says, "She's admitted that, but said it was an accident, that she hugged Beth too tightly, that Beth had refused to give her a cuddle and when she tried to kiss her, Beth complained about her bad breath. Her husband confirms that's what she told him. It seems she suffers badly from halitosis and her husband also told us that his wife having suffered a number of miscarriages in her earlier years was unable to have children, but is obsessed with having a child of her own. She also said that she didn't mean to kill Beth," his voice grows soft, "that she panicked and she put her hand over Beth's mouth to stop her screaming."

I can imagine Beth, like any other child of that age and being the honest wee girl she was probably making that comment about Moira's bad breath then I shudder when I think of Moira holding her so tightly she can't breathe.

I suppose I should be tearful being told all of this, but I'm cried out and just sit numbly in the bed with Alan continuing to hold my hand.

"When we searched her house we discovered a pink coloured mohair cardigan and I'm confident that the threads found on Beth's jacket will match the cardigan."

"What will happen to her? Them, I mean."

"Well, in answer to your earlier question, they appeared this afternoon at the Sheriff Court where they are both remanded in custody. I will submit my report to Crown Office and they will both appear for trial at a later date at the High Court. Moira McPherson has been charged with the murder of Beth and if I'm correct, it's likely the South Yorkshire Police will want to interview them both regarding the disappearance of the wee girl down there." He pauses and taking a breath, slowly exhales and says, "As for her husband James McPherson. It seems that he was both dominated and intimidated by her and she wasn't beyond laying into him with her fists."

And like a jigsaw, the pieces start to fit together.

The halitosis likely explains when I tried to speak to her, why she always turned her head away or stared at her feet and when he tells me about the domestic abuse and I remembered then her breath when I tried to help her in the back garden. I recall Liz telling me that Colin's father related the story of Jimmy arriving at work with injuries to his face and I even recall seeing her wearing that pink cardigan Alan described

It had been there all the time, staring me in the face yet I hadn't seen it and I'm angry that I was so blind.

"Maggie, are you okay?"

I blink and stare at Sheila's concerned face and I nod that Alan continue.

"The husband James McPherson has been charged with attempting to murder you and abduction."

"Abduction?"

He smiles and replies, "We don't have kidnapping in Scotland, but by tying you up and hiding you in the shed he's abducted you, Maggie." His face pales when he adds, "If my suspicion is correct, what he intended for you might have been a whole lot worse."

His words cause me to shiver and I take a breath before replying, "Thank God you got there in time."

Then I ask, "What did he hit me with?"

"A frying pan. Fortunately for you, it wasn't one of those cast iron ones, but a lightweight, Teflon frying pan."

"It didn't feel very lightweight," I groan and that provokes them both to grin.

My eyes narrow when I ask, "But how did you know where I'd be?"

"I didn't, but when I arrived at the house with one of my guys to speak to you about the McPhersons we found your car in the driveway, the back door lying ajar, the washing you'd been hanging out was blowing all over the garden and being a detective," he grins, "I knew something as amiss."

"But how did you know where I was, that I was locked up in the McPhersons shed?"

He stares for me for a few seconds, then replies, "Sometimes you just have to go on instinct. While my guy called for reinforcements, I went to their door like a raging bull and bluffed my way into their house. When I got to the kitchen and I saw the trail of blood where he'd dragged you in the door, I kind of guessed you'd be nearby."

"Don't forget to tell her how you broke McPherson's nose," Sheila interjects.

"You what!"

He looks a little sheepish and letting go my hand, raises both his as though in apology and says, "You have to understand, Maggie, when I found your house deserted and then when I'm in the McPhersons I find her steaming drunk and in their kitchen I saw all that blood; that and the suspicion I had about them, well, I just kind of lost it…"

"And that's when James McPherson attacked you, isn't that correct Detective Inspector Reid and you were obliged to defend yourself," Sheila is slowly nodding her head at him as though to prompt him.

"Eh, yes, that's exactly what happened," his face reddens when he agrees.

"You seem to have a habit of breaking noses," I swallow my laughter, yet I'm secretly delighted that Alan was angry enough to punch Jimmy McPherson when he thought the bugger had hurt me. "Fortunately, my guy ran into the McPhersons a minute behind me and cuffed them together and then we started the search for you and, well," he inhales, "that's when I found you in the locked shed."

This time it's me reaching for his hand and my voice is a little squeaky when I mumble, "Thank, you."

Sheila gets to her feet and says, "Maggie, officially I'm here to get a statement from you, but I'll head off for a wee while so you and Alan can have a bit of time together."

I nod as she leaves the room, then ask, "You're not taking my statement?"

"I'm the SIO," he shakes his head, "and I'm too close to the witness, hence the reason I've instructed Sheila to do that."

"And how close to the witness are you?" I smile at him.

"When I get you back to my house, I'll be a lot closer than I am the now and that's a promise," he smiles back at me.

EPILOGUE

Over nine months has passed since I was first discharged from the Neuro Ward and there's a lot happened in that time.

Following my discharge, I experienced headaches for several weeks that were initially treated with medication; however, as the headaches increased the Neuro consultant ordered an MRI and the result disclosed a previously undiagnosed pressure on my brain and yes, it seems I do have a brain after all.

Was I frightened? Of course I was.

I was admitted to the Queen Elizabeth University Hospital in Govan for two weeks and following a seven-hour operation, it seems to have been a success, though I will continue to receive medication for a while and also attend for regular check-ups.

The downside is that because of the injury to my head and the necessity of the operation, I not only had to have all my hair shaved off, but had to pack in my cleaning job and for the time being I am no longer permitted to drive. However, the ban on driving will conclude in a little over three months and I can hardly wait to have the use of my wee car again.

Before you ask, I refused to wear a wig, but I do have a number of nice headscarves that I keep to remind me of how lucky I am.

Though I gave up the cleaning job and though the loss of the income will not cause me any hardship, I do stay in touch with my wee pal Jessie who several months ago disappointedly returned to live with her husband Ernie and who when we occasionally meet for coffee, repeatedly tells me he has changed.

Aye, right, but so far she's had no further black eyes though I keep thinking, watch this space.

You might recall me telling you that even though my wee Beth had been killed in the park across the road it wouldn't cause me to leave my house? Well, after the attempted murder of me by Jimmy McPherson, that changed my mind. A few weeks following my discharge from hospital I put the house on the market with Nick McSweeney's firm, Alan's lawyer friend, who handled the sale. Within a month I received a very good offer and on the completion date a little over two months after that, Liz and I moved out.

Where did we go to, you ask?

Well, when the sale of the house was concluded my furniture went into temporary storage and Alan kindly offered us accommodation in his home at Huntley Gardens, but with the proviso I stayed on and lived permanently with him and yes, I've been here ever since.

As for Liz, she remained with us for the six weeks after we'd left Clarion Crescent during which time her divorce from Ian Chalmers was finalised with Nick's private investigator providing sufficient evidence to the divorce court to prove that Ian was the guilty party. I take great pleasure in recalling that the court awarded costs against him, though they will be doing well to recover any money because likely he's still a shiftless, lazy git.

Moving on.

With the money I made from the sale of the house and remember, I owned the property outright and again with Nick's assistance, I was able to purchase a two-bedroom flat over in Middlesex Gardens in Kinning Park that was available as an immediate move-in yet still left me with a tidy sum in my account. As you might guess the flat is for Liz, her inheritance if you will, and it's a great start for both her and her new fiancé, Colin, and particularly as at no cost they completely furnished the flat from the furniture in the storage unit. While Alan's offer to accommodate us during the sale of the house was very generous and though I did not mind Liz sharing his house with us, to be very honest I was pleased when she and Colin moved into their new flat, selfishly because it gave Alan and me the opportunity to really get to know each other and I'm pleased to admit I grow happier as the days, weeks and months go by.

You'll be wondering about the McPhersons; well, there's a bit of a story there.

Sadly, Alan's suspicion proved to be correct. The Yorkshire Police discovered little Emily Churchill's body buried in a vegetable patch in the McPhersons former home in Rotherham and are in the process of compiling a case against them both. Even sadder is that two other English police forces investigating missing children are currently conducting inquiries at former addresses occupied by the McPhersons.

As for their involvement in Beth's murder, it turned out there was no need for a trial.

James McPherson pled guilty to attempting to murder me, Abduction and Perverting the Course of Justice by giving succour to his wife whom he knew to have murdered my Beth. Of course his defence team made a great play about how he was totally under Moira's bullying control, that she made him sleep in the back bedroom and treated him like a slave, beating him at her whim.

However, that didn't wash with the judge who sentenced him to life imprisonment. In addition, the judge issued a recommendation that Jimmy serve no less that eighteen years before he be considered for parole. However, and extremely disappointingly, Alan tells me Jimmy's defence team is trying to work a deal with the Crown Office that if Jimmy agrees to provide information to the English police forces about the whereabouts of the missing children, his sentence might be reviewed and for his own safety, he also wants to be imprisoned in a special segregation unit.

Alan later told Liz and I that anything to do with children, whether it is sexual molestation or murder is unacceptable even to the prison population.

You'll have guessed that if he agrees to provide the information and the Crown Office accept the deal, it must also include him implicating Moira and her part in the English children's disappearance. However, as yet no decision has been made, but it's my fervent hope the bugger is never released.

As for Moira, well, it seems that a battery of psychiatrists and psychologists examined her over a lengthy period of time and their overall conclusion was, though I forget the medical terms, that the bitch is really off her head.

The sum of it all is that she was unfit to plead to murdering my Beth. Alan told Liz and I it's something called a plea in bar of trial because of insanity. In short she was confined to the State Hospital at Carstairs. It used to be called the State Mental Hospital, but someone in authority got all politically correct. No matter what it's called, it's where the courts send all the violent and dangerous prisoners with extreme mental disorders and she'll be in there for an unlimited period, though how long that will be is anyone's guess.

I wasn't certain if they could detain her without a trial, but Alan explained the threads weren't the only evidence against her, that there was other evidence that was later overwhelmingly accepted by her defence counsel and reminded Liz and I that the pathologist at the PM concluded Beth had been smothered. He then told us that during their search of the McPherson's house and besides the pink coloured mohair cardigan she'd worn, police recovered a pair of lady's leather gloves and a short, wax jacket she'd worn over the cardigan. The Forensic people concluded when Moira clutched Beth to her, the jacket must have been unbuttoned for the threads from the cardigan to attach themselves to Beth. Anyway, a Forensic examination for the gloves and jackets proved they were contaminated with mucous that contained Beth's DNA and that she must have spluttered onto the gloves and jacket when Moira smothered her.

Of course it was hard hearing all this, but we had insisted he told us everything and to his credit he did it calmly and professionally and I have to admit Liz and I cried when Alan disclosed all that.

As you will guess, Liz and I have done a lot of crying over the last thirteen and a half months.

Maybe I sound bitter, but whether or not Moira intended to kill Beth or in her madness thought it was the only way to prevent her screaming, we'll never really know. Frankly I don't care and God forgive me for my unkind thoughts, but I hope she rots and dies in that hospital.

Anyway and again moving on.

Due to his diligence and arrest of the McPhersons, Alan was recommended by his boss, Mister Miller, for promotion and is now the Detective Inspector in charge of the Shettleston CID.

I'm very proud of him. We all are.

As the months passed, my anger towards DCI Martin Tarrant and his dismissal of the pink threads discovered on Beth's jacket and his single-minded assertion her killer was a man has somewhat faded, particularly when Alan was told by Mister Miller, in the strictest confidence of course, that Tarrant was required to resign from the police rather than risk the public outrage at his incompetence.

Fortunately, because his incompetence was never publicly disclosed, the trial against Graham Copeland, the killer of little Kylie Murdoch, went ahead without any fuss and it seems no one in the media is apparently the wiser about how close Tarrant came to losing the case.

Faced with the overwhelming forensic evidence against him, Copeland changed his plea during the trial to guilty of her murder and was duly sentenced to life imprisonment.

At one time I thought that Liz and I might meet wee Kylie's mother, perhaps help her through the pain of losing a child, but Alan didn't think that was such a good idea and that it was best left to her family to support her through such a difficult time.

So, where does that leave me today?

Well, let's get the priority out of the way.

My hair's grown back and is now just curling round my ears, though I was surprised that it returned a little greyer than before it was shaved. However, I'm a woman so now and again I'm entitled to some quality help from a professional stylist and it's now as jet black as the day I was born.

As for Alan and me? Well, I'm now living with a man I love and who loves me in a home I could only dream of.

My daughter has set up her own home with a lovely young man of her own, is happy and doing well at her job and currently caught up in her wedding plans and like the cleaning woman Annie said, that's all you really want for your children, isn't it?

As for Alan's two daughters. Well, I'm pleased to say they have not only accepted me as their dad's permanent girlfriend, but Fiona's wee boy has taken to calling me Granny Maggie. That and the girls have brought Liz and Colin into their circle, so I feel that I have a full family surrounding Alan and I, though of course Beth will always have a special place in my heart.

And right now?

Well, right now I'm just out of the shower and after I get dressed, I'm popping downstairs to boil the kettle and as it's a warm, sunny Sunday morning, I think I'll take a fresh flask of coffee over to the gardens across the road and join my lovely man who's relaxing there reading his morning newspaper.

****

Thank you for your support in reading this book.

Needless to say, this story is a work of fiction and none of the characters represent any living or deceased individual.

As readers of my previous books may already know, I am an amateur writer and self-publish on Amazon as well as also self-editing, therefore I apologise and accept that all grammar and punctuation errors are mine alone.

I hope that any such errors do not detract from the story.

If you have enjoyed the story, you may wish to visit my website at:

www.glasgowcrimefiction.co.uk

I also welcome feedback and can be contacted at:

george.donald.books@hotmail.co.uk

Kind regards,

George Donald

Printed in Great Britain
by Amazon

46339512R00165